needles

needles

a novel by jeremiah treacy

Registered Writers Guild of America
1976642

Cover design by Tim Paschke
Interior design by Liz Schreiter

Paperback ISBN: 979-8-218-05948-4
ebook ISBN: 979-8-218-05949-1

To my wife Rebecca. My first reader and the only woman I know who still carries a library card.

CHAPTER 1

THE BRIDGE

There are no words, so I don't know how they found their way *onto* this page. There are no words for this, so I don't know how they ended up in your hands.

There are no words for this.

I found him on the thick, pitted, and aged concrete of sixth-street bridge near Boyle Heights. This bridge had once been friendlier, a gentle beige or maybe a cream. Now, it's only a dirtier yellow, tinted by a deep, carbonized grime thickened through a century of Los Angeles exhaust. This is a bridge, steady and honest, the rebar and cement rising up hundreds of feet. At one time it did a good job of taking you from here to there. But it didn't do that for him. This was a bridge with other ideas.

It just took him away.

This is not what a father should see. This is not what a bridge is for. This is not what the architect, welders, engineers, and masons wanted when they rolled out the furled plans registering blue important dots stenciled to yards of drafting paper. This not a bridge built by men so a fourteen-year-old son can step over the rail and fall headlong into a death. Somehow, the words landed on the page.

The rail on the bridge was supposed to be there so he wouldn't be there.

But he is.

And he was.

I will not tell you what he looked liked. I will tell you that he played little league baseball and he was funny, and girls seemed to like him, and maybe he was just finding the power he had in that smile.

It was lovely. It is lovely. The universe now has all of him and will not give him up. Never. It is done.

I look up at the desert night sky and sometimes I think I can see so far beyond the blackness and the stars that I am almost sure I can see where he is. But this is just me putting all the pain into a deep laundry hamper that I keep in what feels like the pit of my stomach. It is my soul. I am sure of that. I remember picking up his dirty clothes and tossing them into that gray, soft rubber plastic hamper. The day he left me, the day he walked out the door. I threw in his socks, t-shirts, jeans and boxers, and two blue towels littering the floor, and I cursed under my breath that he really needed to start taking responsibility for his goddamn room.

I had no idea that his laundry would collect all of me. His dirty clothes would wear me. I would love that smell. It would kill me if I ever lost this fourteen-year-old boy of mine.

Kill me.

The phone rang and the planet continued to spin. It had no time for us. It had no use for our place in the orbit. The planet spun. No matter what I wanted. No matter what I thought I could do. It just did. It just was. The phone rang. Cellular airwaves popped through molecules and banged hard off the metallic silver towers stringing words together into our thin atmosphere where we lived as a father and a son.

"It's me." He was distant.

"Where the hell are you? You've been gone all day."

"LA."

"Of course you're in LA…where?"

"I don't want to say."

"You need to tell me."

"I don't want to hurt you."

"I'll come and get you. Where are you?"

"It's not important."

"It's all important, you're important."

"You always say that…"

"Because it's always true, you know that."

"I have to go."

"Where?"

"Away."

"I'll come get you." Silence. Pause. Breathing.

"I can't do this anymore."

The call got dropped. I dialed him back and my tremble went straight to voicemail. The automatic one that comes with the phone, or the service, or fuck, I don't know or care, but it was the automatic one that gave me his number and told me to leave a message. That one.

He had told a friend where he was. A girl called and said she had talked with him. The universe was playing with me. Here you go, dad: 6th Street Bridge, not a lot of traffic from the Hollywood Hills. You have about thirty minutes. Go. I went.

He was standing there. In the middle of this old bridge over a concrete viaduct wide and high enough to carry water. I wished there had been deep water down there. A running river of foaming water right down below. I wanted a dangerously high rise of water that would be cool, and blue and deep. and please send me some water.

Now, a few hundred feet below it was only dry concrete hardened with high slanted sides that guided the water when it poured through, irrigating the orange and lemon groves, and maybe the iconic palms people believed could only grow only in dreamy Los Angeles.

I stood. He stood. I walked toward him. He asked me to stop. It sounded more like a command. I stopped. I could only see all of his life in his one body. He was only sixty feet away. I had this memory of our days playing baseball when he pitched. The mound to the plate was sixty feet. I used to give him the thumbs up when he was close to striking out the batter.

Thumbs up meant go get 'em. Thumbs up meant you got him. Thumbs up meant everything. It carried us off the mound into days that would get tougher. Thumbs up was our language. It was how we talked. He stood there moving closer to the side of this concrete bridge. I took small steps hoping to get near him, maybe next to him. Put my arm around him. Pull him into my chest. Just a few more short steps. I inched. A silver plane left a thin, white vapor trail as it moved across the sky taking somebody away from here. A car drove by with a small, shaggy dog hanging out the rear passenger window, his tongue out. The wind of the car blew against the dog's dense coat, ruffling his thick, gray and black fur. The dog looked at me and yipped, panting as if smiling. And as the car passed, he turned back to watch the two of us. I thought the dog looked at him. I hoped maybe the look would mean something. I was hoping that dog was a talisman that saved us both and we would talk about it later when I was old and dying, and we would talk about our life when the wooly coated dog looked at him and he decided that the dog had it right—just put your head out the window and feel the wind, dude.

The silver plane caught the sun. Its metal tube flashed a blink. It was smaller now against the big sky. The car was smaller against the road. The blue-black sky fell around us. The earth rotated. The axis held. He moved along the rail. He looked at me. And then he put both feet over and he sat. He sat on the wide rail. Then, he slowly leaned forward. He was looking at me. I gave him our thumbs up hoping our code would break through. He stood up. I ran to him. He left. I ran to the place where he stood. And I wanted to jump, too. To rocket straight down through the air, flying straight to him before he hit the concrete that used to carry water to the groves. I was on another planet waiting for him to come home and pick up his room. I had folded his dirty clothes and wrapped them in a heavy, light brown butcher-block paper. I folded the paper sharply with hard, tight creases, precisely and exactly like points on an honored flag. I had taped the seams, stacking the paper packages and placing the bundles in the plastic rubber hamper that sits just over there, in the corner of the house. His room is clean. Forever.

The warming chill of the vodka rinsed and bleached and cut into my bones.

I wept.

CHAPTER 2

IDENTITY

He's dead.

And so was I. But I was lucky. I had my own bridge in that beastly medicine chest stocked with ready ampules of liquid cocaine along with the entire library of the mind-numbing FDA alphabet. Not quite Wikipedia; slightly smaller than the Library of Congress. My own bridge nudged me over the side. And my spiral of year-long binging catapulted my Gehry-inspired manse into a ground zero for the glitterati who were spectacular at fawning over a surgeon with a notoriously generous script pad signing off Demerol, Oxycontin, Morphine, Methadone, and Percocet. If you liked dropping into the deadening, syrupy, and sexy warming of the Quaalude, I wrote for Methaqualone. The young, slouched, A-Listers, finding their artistic romance in chipping horse, graded my compound as the righteous heroin substitute. No reason to cop your cartel tar over on Melrose; I was the man with the medical degree. I was legal. I was a physician. Everybody loved me until the volume of pharmaceuticals flagged the attentive DEA agents who decided that I had become a very bad man. They didn't care where it all went wrong. They weren't interested in the details of my life. They weren't interested in my reasons. Why would they be? They had a job to do. They had a bona fide Hollywood Hills plastic surgeon who would owe them. And so, they came up with what they considered a tremendously brilliant idea: recruit me as their own personal plastic surgeon—although I thought they all looked pretty damn good already.

The prescription pads that had rocketed my own celebrity quotient were now safely jacketed in their evidence room—they showed me the videos and the photos. I saw the close-ups. I watched the time-lapse footage. Sometimes, I even recognized a face or two. I remember thinking that the picture was pretty sharp for surveillance. I was impressed. I sat and talked. I sat and smoked. I sat and listened. I sat and knew I was fucked.

Two young, clipped agents in crisp, dark suits with glossy, plastic badges clasped to their breast pockets sat across from me at the dull grey laminate table in a small room spiked by not so flattering lighting. Their bleached white shirts and serious ties, knotted tightly into starched collars said that these spit-polished young agents had all the time in the world; nobody was going anywhere. They were both pretty fit and I guessed they did a lot of cross training. Or, like a few of my clients, were busy chipping HGH. I would have to remember to ask.

The shorter agent, who I'll call Robert McKinney because his plastic laminate said so, pushed over a thick, beige folder secured by bright, metal clasps. "Here you go, doctor. Take your time."

The fat folder sat in front of me looking every inch the government-issue dossier on somebody. And because my name was spelled correctly on the black and white label I didn't need to open it. I also passed on listening to the recorded phone calls. These guys spent a lot of time watching me; now, I was going to spend more time with them. I was flattered that they liked my work. No, not really.

"I think I pretty much know what's in there," I said.

The other crisply laundered agent, Tim Marshall, nodded to the folder. "We got you all over this deal." Agent Marshall was proud.

"I can see that. Sometimes I need things spelled out for me," I said.

"Just so you know, we don't do the good cop–bad cop thing," McKinney said.

"Way over the top. We're more, uh, what's the word? Subtle?" Marshall's question carried a proud smirk. I disliked the smirk in general, and even more so when sitting directly across from one.

"Subtle works." McKinney flipped a pen then clicked the button, an irritating habit. "But like life, you got choices. Yessir, life is rich with options." McKinney just smiled. Considering my current station, I could sense he was being sarcastic.

Neither of the young, fit, starched agents loosened their ties.

Marshall got up from the table, walked over to the small, white water cooler. The front was tagged with a DEA sticker just so we all knew who it belonged to. He pressed the blue button filling his Dixie cup. "Can I get you anything?" Marshall asked, looking back at me. For a moment, I pondered what DEA water tasted like. Was it filtered? If so, for what?

"Water's good," I said, thinking now might be a good time to turn over a new leaf. Generally, when sitting in a small room accented with government lighting and a folder with your name on it, it's a very good time to start thinking about your future because it's probably way too late to reconsider your past.

Marshall looked at me blankly, then tilted the cup back, draining the tiny, paper reservoir. "I was just kidding about the 'get you any-thing' part of the morning." Marshall toughened. "We got work to do." He poured himself a second cup, sat back at our table and put the Dixie in front of Agent McKinney. McKinney swallowed his, crushed the cup, pinched it into a beady paper ball, and flicked it across the table, delighted as the ball skidded over the top and into the metal wastebasket next to me. He was probably pretty good at foosball, too. Marshall high-fived him.

McKinney beamed. "Hey Tim, on second thought, maybe we should do the good-cop-bad-cop deal?"

"Jesus, you think? Maybe, long as we know who's who." Marshall shrugged his shoulders, raised his eyebrows, while looking at me.

"Give us a minute, will ya, Doc?" Marshall winked at me. They stepped away from the table; regrouped in the far corner.

There it was again, the nice cop. I wasn't sure who was what, but maybe that was their game plan. I was new at this. Evidently, they had enough training to make the one-two agent action plan work in their favor. They leaned into each other, speaking in hushed tones. Agent Marshall nearly turned his entire back away from me. McKinney occasionally peered over his shoulder at me. They bobbed their heads in conspiratorial agreement. For a minute the room was quiet. Their low voices a murmur only slightly louder than the sound of their starched, white shirts brushing against the slim-cut, cotton-Poly-blend suits. My mouth was dry. The lighting was drier. This room felt cramped. The room could use a window. I could use a glass of water. The cooler sat in the corner. That DEA logo looked larger. McKinney spoke into Marshall's ear while staring at me, expressionless. Only his mouth seemed to move.

I looked down at the metal wastebasket and wondered if I had become McKinney's other beady, paper ball. Something he could control with the flick of his finger.

After a few minutes of serious agent huddling, Marshall and McKinney stepped back to the table and sat for a quiet moment with their arms crossing their chests. Just looking at me. This was a good move because the silence and their body language made me jumpy. If that's what they wanted, they were pros. The damn lighting wasn't helping. This was not how I saw my Saturday going. Usually I was up in the hills, poolside with a cocktail.

"I get a lawyer, right?" I asked.

"This is the fucking U. S. of A—course you do." McKinney looked at me, then over at Marshall.

"Everyone gets counsel," Marshall said.

"Except for maybe right now," McKinney said.

"Yeah, this is our 'get to you know' time—you're special," Marshall said.

"*Very.*" McKinney emphasized.

"The kind of guy we don't run into all that often," Marshall said.

"My lucky day," I said. "But I will be talking to my attorney." I could give as good as I got when sitting in a room with two federal agents and a manila folder.

"Maybe, maybe not. Depends," McKinney said.

"If I play ball?" I offered.

"See that? Already a team player," Marshall said. "I got a good feeling about you Doctor Martinez."

"Ditto," McKinney said. "I'm feeling all warm and fuzzy, too." Good cop.

"You're smart, rich, but look, you did fuck up." Marshall tempered his reprimand with a hard glare. Bad cop.

"Big," McKinney said with emphasis, tapping on the fat, beige dossier radiating bad juju.

"Major of the fucking up," Marshall snickered, glib was a signature bad cop move.

"You got problems, we got problems." McKinney's attempt at simpatico.

"So, maybe we help each other out here." Marshall leaned in hoping to connect with a surgeon who probably fucked some of the girls he spent quality time with in last month's *Maxim* magazine.

"Let's start with some water," I said. I could see the agents were as surprised as I was at the strength of my request; sounded more like a demand. They looked at each other.

"Can we do that, Agent McKinney?"

"I believe we can Agent Marshall."

"Could be a gateway gimme, though," Marshall said. "Next thing you know," he tilted his head toward me, "Doc probably wants a smoke, too." Marshall took off his jacket. I could see the sweat stain from the compact firearm holstered up high on his side.

"Got a lighter?" I asked, hoping to mine a vein with whomever was now the good cop. "Hell yes, doctor. This is the goddamn American government at your service. We got everything," Marshall said, "Problem is, you gotta earn it."

"Even a lousy smoke?"

Marshall walked around behind me, put his hands on my shoulders. "Fucking lousy *everything*, especially a lousy smoke," he whispered into my ear.

Now, it was McKinney's turn. He got up and slowly paced the room. "So, here we go, Doc. And I—excuse me, *we*—are going to keep this simple. Like we said, you got choices. Either you can go away for a seriously long time or scrub up and punch a time card." McKinney's voice and tenor was even, almost sincere, as if he were sharing the company manual at a human resources workshop.

Marshall chimed in. "By us, Agent McKinney means the DEA. Apparently you know all about drugs, not a whole lot about how much we dislike pharmaceuticals dispensed like candy."

"Fact is, the general public should know about our august government branch—we're here to educate you," McKinney said. He would do well selling timeshares in Maui.

"At the risk of sounding obtuse, you fellows want me to work for the federal witness protection—what is it, a division or department?"

"A program, *the* program." Marshall said sharply. "And by the way, tell McKinney what 'obtuse' means," he added.

Marshall flipped him off. "This is what it means."

McKinney continued his ramble. "You're on the outside looking in, Doc."

"You want me working for the, yeah, the program, but I'm not in it. See what I'm getting at?"

"You work for us, we don't necessarily work for you…you need to do what we tell you to do. So, think of the federal government as your boss." Marshall said.

"Your supervisor," said McKinney. "You go where we want, when we want."

"What else?" I asked.

"Nothing much, you won't even have to change your name." McKinney said as he scribbled something in the folder, or maybe he was just playing hangman.

The agents repeated that mantra for the next four hours as they laid out the rest of my life as chief surgical counsel for select Russian mobsters currently squirreled away in witness protection. I would handle facial reconstructs. Russians got new identities. New attitudes would require another skill set.

"These are the kind of creatures that want it all," Marshall said.

"They like their lifestyle." McKinney continued my education. His jacket was now off, too.

"Kinda like you, Doc," Marshall said glibly.

McKinney continued his thought. "These assholes, they don't give a fuck what's going to happen."

Marshall hopped on McKinney's point. "Not until one of them has their head separated from their unusually large, Piroshki-stuffed torsos."

"Now that gets our phone ringing. Lotta texting after one of 'em goes buh-bye," McKinney added.

"We've had a few go out on their own, and next thing you know, they're safely belted into rich, French-stitched, leather seats of a late-model Mercedes."

"Except they're dead." McKinney smiled at me.

"Very dead," Marshall emphasized with an equally saccharine grin.

McKinney looked at his phone. He started texting while talking. "Usually drenched in high octane gas and left to burn outside the family home, but you'll be ok, we got your back."

McKinney showed his phone to Marshall and said, "Murphey's on his way."

Marshall nodded to McKinney, then looked back at me. "We do this for a living."

"Not much of a choice, really," I said to my new co-workers as I mindlessly thumbed the manila folder.

"Better than most," Marshall said.

"Worse than others," McKinney partnered.

"Three squares and a cot," Marshall volleyed.

"No more star fucking," McKinney said, making a sad face. He was good at glib.

"We'll be moving you soon to another pad. Something less, uh, showy."

"But hey, not Watts either," McKinney said. "Someplace nice."

"No pool though." McKinney wagged his finger.

"Gotta close your practice down, too, right Agent McKinney?" Marshall asked.

"We'll work out the details. New beginnings, Doc."

I felt the room shrink. "And the good news?" I asked, hoping for a silver lining, maybe a generous per diem?

"A different agent is assigned to you." McKinney said.

Both agents laughed.

"Not us." Marshall played to his partner.

"No, we got other fish to fry."

"Bigger fish."

"Piranhas." McKinney held up both hands, palms out, fingers assuming jaws and clamped them closed. "Snap."

"Crackle, pop…like the cereal," Marshall said, unaware of his obvious and lame non-sequitur.

McKinney caught it, slowly adding "But with guns and bad guys." Just then his phone vibrated in his pocket. He pulled it out, looked at it, and nodded over to Marshall, who paused, put his jacket on, slipped over to the door and leaned out into the hallway. "Agent Murphey, you're up."

McKinney was putting his jacket on too when Marshall stepped back into the room, holding the door open.

Murphey was older, medium build, still fit, a strong jaw with a sandy-colored moustache that could use a trim. Slightly thinning hair in a crew cut. His tan, cotton suit was a cut above theirs and I could see there was less starch in a more expensive brand of white shirt. His cuffs were monogramed. The dark brown wingtip Oxfords gleamed a high polish.

McKinney made the introduction. "Agent Jack Murphey, your new plastic surgeon, Doctor Dominic Martinez, formerly of the Hollywood Hills. Now a resident of wherever the DEA wants him to be."

Agent Murphey walked over. I glanced at the slight limp in his left leg. He caught my look. Murphey nodded down at his leg, then his green eyes locked into me. "Bullets have a way of fucking with your life—or dance moves."

"I hardly noticed."

"Don't be polite," Jack smiled, and thumbed toward Marshall and McKinney, "these assholes aren't." He paused. "Somebody get the doctor a soft drink and an ashtray."

"Sugar free if you got it," I said.

"Sugar free, diet; whatever. I even think we got an old case of Jolt Cola stashed around here somewhere," Jack said. "Supply side from the Reagan era."

Agents Marshall and McKinney offered tight, young Republican smiles.

Jack put out his hand. I shook it. "Nice to meet you, Doctor Martinez. Sorry to hear about your boy. I got three sons of my own." Agent Murphey looked me straight in the eye and firmed the steady force in his hand.

"You fellows can *vamanos*. Me and Doc got this now, my watch, as it were, right Doc?" Agent Jack Murphey smiled at me like we were in it together.

I didn't say anything. I was surprised to be enlisted immediately into the comforting bosom of this new agent. I nodded in a kind of impromptu affirmation that we did in fact, have this—whatever 'this' meant. Marshall and McKinney shot each other a glance. Their slimming suits looked cheaper. I hoped their collars felt tighter.

Jack had taken charge of my life and had bartered my deal. He saw something in me. Maybe it was my son. Maybe it was a life that could have been. Maybe it was Jack just being a genuinely nice fellow who wanted me to get another shot. I got the sense that this guy, Jack Murphey, could be a good or a bad cop.

Time would tell.

CHAPTER 3

JACK

After our introduction, Jack and I met nearly every day for that first week at the Denny's on La Cienega; same table if we could get it. I drank coffee. He ordered poached eggs, hash browns, cup of fruit. We were regulars. One of the waitresses almost remembered us. This was Jack's tab, but I added to his measly 10% tip, so she got better than most. Jack and I covered areas of interest regarding my new employment and Jack's role as my personal charge d'affaires. After a week of bad coffee served with indifference from the wait staff, I suggested we change it up a bit and rendezvous in the less real LA—Santa Monica. So, on a particularly sunny, southern California day we took a table on the deck of a busy, beachside tourist trap. The Santa Ana winds were kicking up, cleaning out the layers of smog. September days like this could be crystal clear, a nearly unrecognizable postcard sent from California's past life.

It was the late afternoon, almost happy hour, I sat across from agent Jack Murphey as he studied the menu. I chewed a politically correct orange Nicorette and watched a young family pack up their beach chairs, pails, and coolers. The toddlers, sandy from a day of bliss were trying to help mom out, but it was now all turning into "dad's job." Mom picked up both the kids and left him with the umbrella, backpacks, and boogie boards. It was definitely going to be at least three trips to the car. It could have been me, but it wasn't. I watched.

My life felt empty. One of the sandy boys reminded me of Quentin when he was five. The sun bounced off the Pacific. I think I could see

Catalina out on the horizon. It wasn't hard to imagine a time when orange groves outnumbered people. It was hard to imagine my life without him. I closed my eyes just to feel the warm sun, and then, just to feel.

"Hi guys, what can I get you?" Her voice snapped me back to the moment. The young, waitress did her best to seem interested in our table, but this was LA and everyone's an actor, or an actor writing or a writer who wants to direct. She forced a smile. It was almost believable. I appreciated the effort. I knew it well. She didn't want to be here, neither did I, but she was going to bring me a drink so I did my level best to smile back. I could play the part, too.

"Double Stoli, over, slice of lemon. Ice the glass." Jack looked over at me on my order. "Really, a double?"

"Yeah, really," I said.

The waitress caught Jack's parental guidance. Jack and I both appeared to be adults.

"Cool, if that's how we're going today." Jack was being a player. He flashed her a smile. "Same as the good doctor," he said, holding her gaze.

Jesus, my federal agent was flirting. I could only stare at him.

Young blondie with the killer body was evidently an Oscar-winning actress. She winked at him then whispered, "fab," while jotting down our order. And then she left her smile a little longer with Jack just to see if the man had any game. He blushed.

"Be right back gentlemen." She turned smartly and we watched her, wondering how those tan legs made a pair of tight, black shorts move like that. I'm pretty sure those hips were involved at the scene of the crime.

Jack turned to me, motioning his head toward her exit across the deck. "Must be a dime a dozen with you, right Doc?"

"Kinda like the Russians with you, right Agent Murphey?"

"Jack. Please, just Jack. We got a long way to go with this thing. I'm starving. Damn, we should have ordered appetizers," Jack said absently while glancing at the menu.

"McKinney, Marshall and you are talking Russians, but I'm a bit unclear on when and where, and maybe, who?" I said in my new hushed voice I had come to learn is an important part of my new government job.

"Maxim Gorikav is a guy you'll meet."

"Okay, that's 'who.' What about 'when' and 'where'?" I asked, popping a Nicorette. "And should I be concerned?"

"Look, we don't just saunter over and make the intros. Trust me, I set this up; you'll know, and then we go."

"Go?" I asked.

"Operate."

"Like that?"

"Like that." Jack was matter of fact. I looked out at the beach again. Dad and kids and family were gone. A seagull floated by and landed on a sign bolted to one of the pilings near our table.

"See that?" I asked, pointing to the words: *Please don't feed the birds.*

"Only one who doesn't know what it means?"

"Our waitress?"

"The fucking seagulls."

"Meaning?"

"Guess who's the damn bird? You know what you want; McKinney and Marshall know the score. But I'm the one doing the operating and I know nada, just a name. What's next? Secret handshake and a code?"

"Look," Jack lowered his voice. "Maxim is a bigger piece of a puzzle we have to protect, some things you don't need to know."

"Problem is, I'm working *for* the witness protection; I'm not *in* the program. At least not yet, knock wood."

Our drinks arrived courtesy of Jack's hot, new friend. My federal agent pointed to the menu. He paused while he scanned the menu. He ran his finger running down the specials.

"Calamari, olives, and," Jack turned to look up at our waitress, "you like the Bruschetta?"

"Love it." She winked at me. I thought I could do something with her nose. I didn't say anything, opting for professional neutrality.

"Then so do we," Jack said.

"And if you could be so kind," I said, hoisting my empty glass.

"What kind of doctor are you?" she asked.

"He's a plastic surgeon, Bel Air," Jack said.

I smiled at Jack, my new pimp.

"Love to get some work done. Nothing huge," she said, turning her head to the side. "See that little bump?" She touched her nose. "I'd like the Jennifer Aniston, but maybe, um, maybe more Jennifer Lawrence. I dunno, I'm conflicted."

"Aren't we all," I said, but saw that she didn't connect the dots. "Call me." I fished a card out of my wallet and handed it to her. She took it and gave me her patented killer smile.

"Not if you call me first." She wrote her number down on an old receipt and handed it to me. "I'll get the appetizers going." She turned and looked back at me to see if I was watching her walk away. I was.

"Maxim Gorikav is a bad mother," Jack warned trying to bring me back to the job at hand. I sensed he was jealous that I was stealing his girl. "And that Russian is going to need more than Jennifer's nose." He pulled out his phone, leaned in on the table and had to shield the screen glare from the afternoon sun. He flicked through photos of Maxim. Heavyset, pockmarked, early 50's, dark hair, balding. Maxim was right out of central casting—the Urals office.

"Gives me enough to work with," I said.

"Maxim is old school, straight out of Moscow with enough baggage to fill a freighter, which coincidentally he did on a regular basis with everything from munitions to Afghani smack—"

"Poppy's the state flower."

"It was good for Maxim. He comes with the usual that comes with guns, dope, and guys who have mother issues."

"Charming."

"They all are. We got a flotilla of Russians. Like a murmuration of starlings, these guys are constantly morphing and shifting into some new *Bratva*."

"So, Maxim will by my first."

"Gotta start somewhere. He's got a few assholes, Mikel and Anton, who are still out there but knocking on our door. The new blood coming into the southland. Seems nobody likes the idea of dying."

"So, if Maxim likes my work, I can expect a referral."

"Careful what you wish for."

"Speaking of wishes," I said, "Here comes my newest patient, Jennifer."

"Hungry and thirsty?" Jennifer Aniston-slash-Lawrence chirped, expertly serving the plates and our drinks, bending closer to me, working her newest cosmetic surgeon.

"You're an actress, right?" It was LA so my question was nearly rhetorical.

"Oh my God, yes." She liked the notoriety. Again LA.

"I think I saw you in something recently, too," Jack said, raising his sunglasses.

"Not a feature, but it was a national spot, for Big O Tires," our Jennifer said.

"Loved you in that." I swallowed my Stoli. "Seriously, give me a call, let's talk Rhinoplasty," I said, and immediately caught her hesitation and blink. "Your nose."

"Doctor Martinez lives up in the hills. Perhaps he'll invite you to one of his parties," Jack said, then turned his head, looking at me. "Oh right, that's not gonna happen. *C'est la vie.*" Jack raised his glass and popped a small green roasted olive into his mouth.

Our young, hot, nose-bump-Jennifer-waitress had other tables. Three hours later I got a text from her. Next thing I knew she was up at my place. Five hours later Jack called me. He was giving me a heads up that he and a few agents would be coming by in the morning.

"Nine's a little early for me," I said, looking over at the half covered bottom of my Oscar winner lying next to me. "It's a federal thing, you'll see."

"Jesus, my tax dollars at work."

"Gotta give the public their money's worth, we got Russians who need to stay alive."

"Thank God they have us on the job."

"Time to scrub up," Jack said.

"Time to say goodnight, Jack." I hung up. Jennifer moaned and moved her tan, young ass. I ran my hand over it. I went into the bathroom, crushed up a 20mg Cialis, snorted it, wincing at the powdery sting searing my nasal passages. I shook my head, pinched my nose, then went back to bed with my actress who was ok with sleeping her way to the bottom.

The next morning, like clockwork, Jack and three young, eager agents showed up at my front door. I would have appreciated something less formal than the dark blue, nylon windbreakers with large, yellow "DEA" initials on the back and the two, black, unmarked rollers sitting in my driveway. The agents lined up behind him.

"I know, I know, not what you were expecting, but we'll be outta your hair in no time," Jack explained.

"This was a visit, right?" I took a sip of my coffee while eyeing my neighborhood to see who was up and about.

"Well, yes." He handed me a thick sheaf of stapled papers. "With a little something extra. Didn't I mention we have to search the place?"

A producer slowly drove by in her three-year-old, silver Maserati. She paused behind her oversized Cartier sunglasses, then drove on. She hadn't had a hit in a while. That made two of us.

"I was thinking this would be more like coffee and croissants," I said, still foggy from last night's Stoli tasting and acting lesson. I stepped aside, gesturing for the government to be my guest. The nylon, logoed agents filed past, one even said good morning to me.

"Gotta be a 'by-the-book' toss," Jack said, as he directed agents, one toting a black utility box that made him look more like he'd come by to unclog my sink trap.

Jack saw me check out the bag. "Our lab. Personally, I couldn't give a shit, but some of this stuff—well you know, my hands are tied."

"Says here," I squinted at the warrant. "Class II controlled narcotics. That's pretty much everything but the sofa. Let me help you out—end of the hall, all the way down and to the left, my bathroom. Anything else you find, it's yours. Let's go poolside while these guys continue their Easter egg hunt...coffee?"

"Black, sugar."

"Maria, *dos cafés por favor para mi amigo senior Murphey. Negro y el azuca,*" I called out to my housekeeper as we walked to the deck.

"*Si senor, uno momento,*" Maria's voice from the kitchen trailed after us.

We sat out on the slate deck, the black-bottomed infinity pool mirrored the clear Los Angeles morning. Jack Murphey was going to change my life. I knew this because he said as much while informing me that McKinney and Marshall were clueless. Jack said he would make sure I could stay in my current Hollywood Hills' residence, and keep my Bel Air practice. He sat back and took in the view of the city.

Maria came out with a tray.

"*Gracias,* Maria," I said.

"*Gracias,*" Jack said.

She smiled at Jack as she poured his cup and refreshed mine.

"Nice view," he said, looking out. His two-way crackled. He turned it off. He sipped his coffee. "Santa Ana winds clear everything out. Almost can see what life used to be like."

"Back in the day," I said, the coffee cutting through. I lit a smoke. There it was—the nicotine and caffeine trying mightily to shake off the alcohol and cocaine still bumping around my synapses.

"Back in the day," Jack murmured in agreement. "May I?" He motioned toward my pack. I nodded. He shook a smoke out of the pack. I lit his cigarette. He exhaled. "You've done well for yourself, Doc."

"Like I said, back in the day. Now, I'm gainfully employed by the federal government, but without that pension."

"Still," Jack said, motioning to the view, "it could be worse."

"I bet you say that to all your surgeons."

"Truth be told, there are ways to put a little something away for the future," Jack said, measuring me for a reaction.

I was drinking coffee, smoking, and my head was hurting behind my sunglasses. There wasn't going to be a lot for Jack to work with. I managed a two-word sentence in the form of a question: "Excuse me?"

Jack went on to walk me through how his wife, Holly, and their sons, Conner, Colter, and Brendan were enjoying the house in La Canada, a pricey burb in LA. Holly's parents had gifted them the house. Holly had insisted on private schools for the boys, and the extra-curricular activities that went with it. Jack wasn't keeping up with the Joneses, he was slowly being buried by them.

"Sounds like trouble in paradise."

"Doesn't have to be."

I looked at Jack, not sure what that meant. He then cleared it up for me, so I wouldn't have to think.

"There are ways around things," Jack said, sipping his coffee. "Look, I got at least twenty guys lined up in witness—they're all loaded. They want favors, I want favors. They have cash, and I want cash, so technically this is all going to work out."

"So, why do you need me for fuck's sake? I mean, technically."

"We run it through your practice."

"What makes me believe that you can make this work?"

Before Jack could answer, I looked at my watch and realized it was nearing a brunch hour somewhere. "Maria," I turned and called out toward the kitchen. "Bloody Mary, *por favor.*"

"*Si senor Martinez.*"

"You?"

Jack shook his head. "I'm good."

"Before we start hiding cash, maybe you should tell me about that leg," I said. I popped a Nicorette. Jack looked at my cigarettes and the pack of Nicorettes on the table. Maria came by with my Bloody.

"In my line of work, people get shot."

"Good to know."

"Sometimes the wrong people."

"That's concerning."

"Somebody pushed the barrel of a gun into my thigh and somebody happened to pull the trigger. Nearly caught the—"

I finished Jack's sentence. "Femoral artery."

Jack was impressed. "I owed some guys a favor," he said hesitantly. Jack, I would later come to find out didn't like losing. Jack had his pride as an agent and a father, maybe, sure, even as a husband to Holly. So getting shot because he lost control of a situation was an ugly reality for him. I could see that in his face.

I tried to offer a shoulder, figuratively. "Sounds like quite a debt."

"The kind that can get you shot." His tone was matter of fact. He was trying to man up and put some skin in the game.

"Seems excessive, but what do I know." I left Jack the opening to fill in the blanks. He didn't disappoint.

"I failed to deliver on some paperwork. Visas, passports. Handy travel necessities one might need on a trip, say, if you're Russian and the Viking Riverboats cruises are all booked and you need to get out of the country without a travel agent."

"What kind of money is paperwork like that worth?" I asked, assuming my poker face and trying to only sound mildly interested. "It's all cash." Jack said flatly assuming I would do the math. "Put me in a ballpark, just so I can see where we're playing."

"Hundred thou." He lit another one of my smokes.

"That's nice paper." I said hoping my emphasis on the word 'paper" would make Jack feel I was part of his world.

"A hundred thousand…tax free. That's major upside," Jack said.

"Well, sure last I checked money and guns don't have a tax code… the shooting part is a little disturbing."

"Nobody to blame but me," Jack said. "I got it squared it away. Nobody died."

"Does Holly know?" I asked.

"Yeah, she picks up the bags of dough—for God's sake, of course she doesn't."

"The Russians are like a short term annuity," I said.

"See, already you're thinking investor relations."

"So, you want my practice to be the shell."

"You're working with us, it looks like fed, but priced like private sector," Jack said.

He looked around and leaned forward. He took a smoke out of my pack on the table. "I'm the agent in charge, the fucking force majeure, as it were." He grabbed my lighter and lit it. I did the same. We exhaled together.

"What I say goes. And that's a good thing. For you and me." Jack got up and walked over to the edge of the pool, turned on his two-way, the static popped.

"Rossi, we good?"

"Good to go, sir."

"Doc, you're gonna be just fine."

"And hey, if you ever get shot again, at least you have a surgeon," I said.

"I don't plan on that happening."

"Nobody ever does," I said.

"I have us lined up with Maxim Gorikav and his wife at your office, tomorrow."

"His wife?"

"What can I say, they're close."

"Lovely." I turned in the direction of the kitchen. "Maria, *uno mas bebidas, por favor.*"

"*Si senor!*"

"Get some sleep, Doc." Jack drained his coffee.

"Next time buy your own smokes."

"I'm trying to quit."

"Tell me about it." I popped a Nicorette and bit down hard, snapping the nicotine into service.

Jack slipped me a phone. "Use this from here on out. Your connection to the golden ticket."

I took it. "Do I get a code name?"

He paused. "How 'bout, oh, I dunno, let's call you 'Doc' and you call me Jack."

The agents gathered in the foyer, the one with the black lab bag motioned for Jack. The group met briefly to murmur about their pharmacological dig. Jack returned.

"Looks like everything squares with what you said is here. Pfizer would be proud."

"So, am I grounded, officer?"

"Fuck Doc, try to keep it clean, we got work to do. Your ass is on the line."

"Yeah, I got that, and then there's the cash part."

Jack reached out and shook my hand. "Sometimes the way we thought it was supposed to work doesn't. You gotta improvise." He put on his sunglasses.

"I was hoping the federal government had a better plan of action than improv."

Jack just smiled. "C'mon Doc, it's LA…everything's an act."

I walked him to the door. He and his pod of DEA upstarts piled into the black rollers, and left me to the day ahead. Or behind. I went back out to the pool. Maria had my Bloody waiting for me. I sat back in the lounger and watched the hot wind whip the city into shape, the way it used to be. When you could see for miles.

Maria sang in the kitchen. Her soft lyrical pitch carried through the house and out to the deck. Sweet, loving Maria. The same woman who scattered across the desert scrub following the coyotes who pushed her hard, relentlessly and across the fingers of dirt tracks that traveled into a brown, patchwork of the deadly Sonoran desert. The coyote led the tired and broken Mexicans to the narrow channel and across the border where an older US border patrol officer had been paid to usher the band of illegals into a van, slammed the doors shut, and sent the vehicle onto the lost highways of Arizona. It was north, always north, far from the southland. She was only seventeen then. Maria was the hope for her family. Her mother, father, siblings, aunts and uncles sent her north. They packed her things and wadded the money into a leather belt and watched her take the blue and pink painted bus down the dirt road, kicking up dust as they waved goodbye from the hopelessly adobe caked village in the state of Jalisco. Maria carried their hopes, and the belt of money that paid the two coyotes who beat the younger ones to keep up, and gathered the canteens of water to hold as ransom, measured out at the end of a day when blistered lips and the body begged for water. Maria Suarez made it to America, married and had three children, all girls, who had folded quietly into the Los Angeles fabric never to return to the Jalisco country or the other side of the border. Maria sang softly, with joy and sadness and with a way of keeping her present in the casa, the *cucina*—the one place where she felt safe. Maria Suarez sang with joy.

I liked to tease her. "Maria, you are my very own Lola Beltran." She would only laugh and call me *senor loco*. I sent money every month to the family of Maria forever locked into their life in Jalisco. Maria sang for her family still deep in Mexico, still proud of their daughter who walked through the desert and now works for a doctor in America.

CHAPTER 4

MAXIM GETS SOME WORK

Seventy-two hours after our beachside happy hour, Jack and I were sitting in my Bel Air clinic with the big fish, Maxim, and his wife, Darya. The Gorikavs seemed like a nice couple, particularly because Maxim had parked a slim, silver aluminum Halliburton by his side. He was beefy, pushing maybe 5'10", packing dense, stocky poundage that was broad in his belly and chest and up along his shoulders. One could still make out the profile of a younger, stronger man who had at one time offered a commanding presence. Now, he only looked stressed and the pounds and years had pushed him over to the typical aging Russian mobster side of his life. He wore a shiny, silk black shirt under a charcoal and black suit—a size 52 by my eye. Pricey, maybe even bespoke. His black, supple, cross-weave Magli slip-ons were a smart wardrobe choice for Maxim and his expanding girth. He could avoid the struggle of bending over and tying his shoes. The soft leather slip-ons were easy in, easy out.

Maxim's skin was worse than the phone pixels Jack showed me at our last Santa Monica beachside meet. Maxim's face was cratered, the effect of a deep and exaggerated case of acne. His dark, thinning, wavy hair was a flat black, a bad color job. He kept it on the longish side hoping that it covered his growing bald spot. Maxim was missing the pinky finger on his left hand, at the first knuckle. It was now only a nubbed, boney bulge; useless. His other good pinky had a thick, gold band set with a round, deep, blood red ruby. Maxim played with the ring, twisting it as we talked. Darya sat next to him. Mrs. Maxim Gorikav wore her hair short, colored in a shade of auburn tinged with lighter, blonde highlights. Her large, dark brown eyes sat under darker, pencil-thin and severely waxed eyebrows. Like her husband, she had her day and may have even been considered pretty by those in her immediate family. Time had not been kind. Her black denim was worn too tightly. The selvedge jeans slimmed to meet the strap on her more expensive, glossy six-inch pumps. Darya could have done herself a favor and gone up a size in her smooth leather, plum-colored jacket.

Evidently, Maxim was a generous man. His love could indeed be measured. There was no shortage of gold around her neck. The strands of necklaces competed with a matching set of diamond, sapphire, and ruby bracelets. There was a lot of metal on the woman. The bracelets jangled with her slightest move. The gold ring on her wedding finger held a square, seven-carat Asscher-cut diamond bordered by two, dark, pinkish red rubies. She had all of her fingers. And I would presume, her toes, as well.

When Maxim wasn't habitually turning his pinky ring, he held her hand. His tenderness surprised me. Actually, I was relieved to see the affection. It made me feel like maybe Maxim Gorikav was just a bad guy sitting the middle of a bad situation, or that the wife was softening his edges. Then again, maybe I had the deal wrong and Darya was a woman who knew her way around a razor sharp, medium-gauge wire garrote. I could see she was equally impressed with the dark, hand-rubbed Brazilian Ipe floors as she was by my hand-selected, grey Hestra deerskin suede office walls. She had discreetly touched a wall. It was hard not to. The office mirrors, metal and stonework, and back-lighting played well with the gentle sway of world fusion samba against the percussive click of Manolo heels on the dark, gleaming Ipe.

Clients felt good coming and going, and my practice rocketed with referrals from an A-List calendar that only took time out for the week in Cannes. I made sure everyone looked fabulous and wrapped my cli-ents in a softness that felt every bit as good as a cashmere blanket spun from the underbelly of the scarce, now even scarcer, Mongolian goat as they recovered with the slow, cozy nod of a morphine drip.

"Jack Murphey says you are good." Maxim looked around, obviously impressed with the office. And I don't think he had even felt the suede walls, yet.

He twisted his ring and continued. "Mr. Jack Murphey has me between rocking hard place."

"Rock and a hard place…" I joined in.

Jack shifted uncomfortably in his chair. He shrugged. I got the sense he, Maxim and Darya have covered this subject before.

"Or between DEA and ATF," Darya said, pulling out a gold lighter and cigarette case, and indicating—so thoughtful of her—if it would be ok to smoke. I offered her a thick, crystal ashtray.

"Swarovski?" she asked, taking it from me and placing it on her black leather padded end table.

I only gave her a discreet, affirmative nod. I didn't like to brag.

"I have two," she purred as she lit her cigarette and blew a smoke ring in my direction.

Maxim crossed his legs; he moved well for a big man. "Same thing, DEA, ATF," he said, dismissing Darya. Maxim was in charge, or at the very least was hoping to be. The wife might have other ideas. I got the sense that darling Darya could play anyone, especially her husband.

"That was a messy business, no doubt about it, but let's not get sidetracked," Jack said.

Maxim nodded toward me and said to Jack. "You tell him."

Darya picked up her husband's beat. "My husband did what he was told to do. My husband is good at his job, like you doctor."

"Not sure I follow here. Jack care to weigh in?" I asked.

"I don't want to get too deep into the weeds, here, but I believe the Gorkav's are touching on a little incident with two of our departments."

"Only two?"

Darya filled in my blank stare. "Now, my husband is paying him— Agent Jack Murphey—to get rid of ATF."

"Not exactly. I mean yes, we can cover the ATF issue, but there's more to it. Another Russian set would like to get their hands on Maxim," Jack said.

I looked at Jack, then Maxim, then Darya. Not sure where this was going. The three of them sat there—obviously we were breaking new ground and clearing the air, although I was lost in translation and not sure where I fit into the family bickering. I felt it best to shut up and let Jack, Maxim, and his lovely bride work out the kinks. Jack was going to now referee the government's role in a Maxim Gorikav deal. This was going to be fun to watch. I sat back in my black leather Eames, chased my menthol with a Nicorette; the rush of nicotine punched through.

Jack looked over at me. "Little problem a while back ago. Some ATF agents were running a gang sting ..."

"Getting guns off street," Maxim interjected.

"ATF is assholes," Darya feigned spitting into the gleaming hardwood floor. The Ipe was designed to withstand almost everything but venom.

Jack rolled his eyes. Apparently this was ground they had covered before. "We had a few agents set up a front—a warehouse as a distribution business. Boys set it up off La Brea with the intention of doing a gun buy-back deal..."

"The agents, they screw it up," Darya snarled.

"Fucked up," Maxim said looking at Darya who was now looking at me while I looked at Jack. I could see Jack was tired of this subject, but then there was money on the table, or near it, so he had to cowboy up and take a breath and manage his clients—our clients.

"Yeah, we stepped in it," Jack said. "Nobody's perfect."

"Now, they are having us pay for fuck up." Maxim said.

"Welcome to America," I said.

"Everybody is paying, jend for what? For living new life in witness protection...ATF was his problem," Darya said, lighting another cigarette and waving her lighter toward Jack.

"A comedy of errors, if you want to know the truth," Jack said. "Young guys, fresh out of the academy charged with setting up a business, a front specifically for buying guns, which they did. But turns out these cowboys didn't have a clue on how to make this deal work. Word got out, people saw what our agents were paying. They got religion and started buying guns at retail and selling them to our agents at something ridiculous like 200% over retail. The ATF sting was burning through cash. Next thing you know, the hood is flooded with weapons."

"What division of the government does 'clusterfuck' fall under?" I asked.

"Tell me about it. Now we got Crips and Bloods, hell, even the Mexicans…ATF had a waiting list of gang bangers trying to sell them guns. It was like a fucking Black Friday out there."

"This causing problem with crime. More guns on street." Maxim said.

"Cash is king," Darya said.

"Everyone wants to sell guns," Maxim said.

"Guns is big business for ATF," Darya said. "Now, he," she said looking at Maxim, "is only one on run."

"Now, am working with DEA but hiding from ATF." Maxim twisted his ring. The bad pinky looked bonier. His face was flush. I flashed on trying to remember where Sheila, my front office receptionist, mentioned she put our De-fib machine.

Jack continued to walk us through the new, modern way to not to handle sting operations. "It was a scene. La Brea became a freaking arms race, a neighborhood armory. The east side was moving more pistols and shotguns than the Iran-Contra deal."

"Time to call in Russians," Maxim looked over at his wife.

"Russians to solve everything," Darya added.

"We don't like to admit it, but sometimes we go outside the department to handle, uh, more sensitive issues." Jack almost sounded apologetic.

"Gangs?" I asked.

"When called for. We had to get 'street' on these guys, so we called in Maxim and asked him to do us a solid."

"Cleaning up ATF mess," Darya hissed. This time I think she did spit on my Ipe.

"So, they call Maxim," Maxim said, feeling a little puffed up. "We had to get a moving pretty quickly so we…"

"To rescue ATF fuck up," Darya interrupted.

"Jesus, can I finish my thought people? Thank you…yeah we had to call in Maxim and a few of his associates to rob the ATF warehouse, make it look like a gang rip, and torch it…only problem was two of the agents were still in the warehouse and got shot. Died right there, and the next thing you know everyone's lined up to point fingers, trying to make a career on bringing down whoever did this."

"Fucking DEA." Darya hissed. "ATF, too."

"Burned bodies tend to get people talking," I said.

"Yeah, especially considering it's on us," Jack said.

"Considering." I said.

Jack leaned back, rubbed his hands through his hair. "So, now the ATF wants Maxim gone, too—for all the obvious reasons."

"Obviously," I said.

"They have no idea he's working with DEA."

"At least that is what you telling us." Darya's vitriol was again pointed at Jack.

"I try to do favor for American government, I get this." Maxim was more than a little red in the face. Nobody likes the ATF getting busy with your day, or worse trying to end it.

"This what he gets," Darya said softly, looking at her husband.

"Hiding from ATF," Maxim said.

"Hiding from all of government," Darya said.

"Life's a bitch," I said. "Ever been in the States around April 15th?"

"We're doing the best we can," Jack said.

"A new you can help." I sounded like I was actually speaking with a real client trying to extend her career into a three-picture deal with points on the backend. "Anybody else we need to be concerned with?"

"Other Russians," Maxim said.

"Oh, right, those guys." I looked at Jack.

"Maxim is referring to a past life with black market rubies and Afghani poppies."

"Payment on the ATF deal or Russians?" I asked, mentally noting my scorecard for the Gorikavs.

"I got the ATF once we get the cash. Feds are piece of cake. Maxim's more concerned with the Russians," Jack said, "and I have to agree. Maxim needs to disappear."

"No more ATF?" Maxim asked.

"Not a trace. You're clean…the investigation goes bye-bye," Jack assured our clients.

Darya patted her husband's hand and nodded down to their silver, aluminum *get out jail free card*. "In case," she said to Maxim. "Show we know how to pay."

Maxim reached down and slid the metal Halliburton across the waxed Ipe over to Jack, who pulled it under his chair, tucking it between his legs.

"Now, we only deal with Russians," Darya said. Maxim shot her a look.

"See, already there's a bright side," I said as I flipped through my iPad, and proceeded to walk our new Russian client through his options to see how much better he'd look—different, too. But that was beside the point. I wanted to give Darya a handsome fellow she would be glad to be on the run with. A new Maxim she would be proud to show off in the old country. No sense being chased by ugly Russians and being married to one, too.

"We could put Maxim in a line up, even his brothers from the motherland couldn't pick him out." I said proudly. "Afghani smack and gem kings would mistake him for their new best friend. Gives you a little breathing room, Maxim."

"I will kill first," Maxim said. Darya patted his thigh. Like any Russian mob wife on the run from the feds and questionable, former business partners, she was comfortable with her husband's to-do list.

My new favorite federal agent, Jack, had negotiated his side deal of taking the ATF heat off Maxim and netting us $500,000 from Maxim's pocket. He sold Maxim on a few amenities that would come with the post-op recovery in the locale of Maxim's choosing with round the clock protection and, of course, anything extra his wife wanted—lipo, chin, a lift, or what the hell, a smaller butt, bigger tits, and a whole new lease on her past life. Darya could almost look hot…at least that's what he told Maxim. Everybody was coming in on the federal dime. As for making Mrs. Gorikav look 'hot,' I wasn't so sure of that, and I was the doctor in this deal.

"Dr. Martinez, how much to change?" Maxim struggled with his English. "New face is good, but wife would like to know what new husband will look like."

"Smaller nose, more chin, and we can," I pointed to the large, flat screen monitor feeding off the ipad, "reduce the ears, and bring up your cheekbones." I politely pointed to each area of focus on Maxim's photograph. "Think George Clooney but with a Putin swag." Darya smiled; she liked the Clooney reference.

"What about these?" Darya asked motioning to her face, clearly asking about Maxim's deeply cratered scars.

"Laser, good as gone." I leaned back in my leather Eames and lit a Menthol.

Maxim was a more stoic patient. He turned his ruby pinky ring. He tried to smile, but I could see he was nervous about surgeries sponsored by the federal government. The man was breathing hard. And he was only sitting. Probably better that his career as a killer was coming to a close.

"Piece of cake, Maxim, you're in good hands, Doc does all the stars." Jack said.

Darya tapped her lighter on her cigarette case. "How long is recovery?"

"Doc, if I may," Jack raised his hand, "let's talk before and after. That's kind of where we're all headed here."

"Post-op given chin, cheekbones, and we have to do something with the acne. Maybe thirty days to fully recover."

Maxim looked at Darya, nodded to her that this was acceptable, as if the decision was his.

"We can decide on where you'll be staying after surgery," Jack said to both Maxim and Darya. "Anywhere you want, provided Doc can check in on your progress."

"Laguna," Maxim said.

Darya countered, "Ritz Carlton."

"Let me check with my partner… Jack you ok with Laguna?"

"Is what it is. This is off the books, so whatever the Gorikavs want," Jack smiled at the Gorikavs as if he had just closed the deal on getting the couple into a new Mercedes.

'We've had clients down there," I said then ticked off a few names they would recognize. I was a team player. It was true. I could work with the Russian baddies. I was happy with the way our meeting was going. Maxim and Darya seemed satisfied with the pre-and post-op walk-through.

Jack chimed in, "Darya, remember, anything you want, Doctor Martinez can handle."

"Anything," I said, with a reassuring smile and that wonderfully practiced bedside manner my clients loved.

Maxim and Darya sat in my office and looked like a happy couple with their future ahead of them. Not exactly newlyweds, but still, at their age and with getting work done in Bel Air, things could be worse. Other than the ATF looking for his ass and his Russian associates who wanted their piece of Maxim, or hell, maybe even Darya, the Gorikav family could take umbrage knowing that they had highly intelligent, educated and professional men with desired skill sets in their corner.

That would be Jack and I.

We shook hands, Maxim and Darya left. Shortly after our meeting, I went to work on the new and improved Gorikav. Maxim looked damn good. Most importantly he looked nothing like his former self and did recoup nicely down in Laguna at the Ritz. Little did we know, but soon after, a series of events would turn out worse than anyone in the witness protection program could recall.

Jack did as he said he would. He came over to my place and put $200,000 in tidy, crisp bricks on a table. Right then and there I fell in love with the black bag.

We stood on the hand-quarried grey slate decking, sunset cocktails in hand.

"To Maxim," Jack raised his glass.

"To Darya," I toasted with my chilled Stoli. I had hit the drink with my private stash of liquid coke and didn't share with Jack. He would only get upset with me, and why ruin a perfectly good post-op bag of money that we could enjoy as fellow government employees. He had his, I got mine.

The distant city lights of the Los Angeles evening twinkled at our good fortune.

"Sometimes things just go right." Jack swallowed the chilled vodka.

"Here's to living right," I said, happy to drain my signature cocktail.

Two months later, the Gorikav deal went to shit when we put Darya on the table. She slurred as she went under, saying that she wanted to look like Basia, the polish singer who had a hit with *Time and Tide*—and I lost her. Died. Dead. On my table, at my clinic, right the fuck in Bel Air. Soon after, Maxim made it known that he wanted to be an important part of my life by abruptly ending it. Whatever was left of my practice, and me, was very much over. Done. Damn. Just when Jack and I were just getting started. Well, so much for the annuity part of our deal. The gravy train had officially jumped the track.

CHAPTER 5

THE FERRET THING

Only a few months earlier, the local news had reported on the magic of Maxim and his propensity for making his associates dead. They were dressed in matching blue and white, shiny Adidas leisure apparel. The bodies were discovered in a shallow tureen of water runoff spitting through a decaying viaduct in a forgotten patch of LA. The efficient use of wire ties strung their hands and feet together. When discovered, the skin was just beginning to behave like low-and-slow pulled pork falling off the bone. Their soggy bodies pressed into the slimy, slick film of green algae. The stench of the off-gassing Russians had wafted down the wide viaduct and into the world of a young, homeless couple encamped on the side of the viaduct's embankment.

Donny, the skinny homeless young man, and his waifish girlfriend, Marie, had set up house hidden up off the side of the viaduct, tucked away. Their own sweet little piece of heaven, until the bodies arrived. Or maybe the couple had been there first. Forensics would have to sort the logistics. The stinky, pungent air floated down, cutting through the sooty inversion layer that sat over the central basin, rusting the land-scape with a blanket of fossil fueled particulates. The smell got so bad it made Marie nauseous. The couple followed their noses and discovered the source. They reported the sketchy waste management problem to local authorities, figuring there might be some money in the deal, being good citizens and all. At least, that was Donny's thinking. Marie agreed with him. Donny was smart like that.

Officers Jake Reilly and Francis Rosen responded to the call. Reilly was young and new, Rosen, the veteran was already cranky and ready for a nap. Reilly parked the squad car on the narrow frontage road next to the loosely arranged camp nudged into the soft patch of dirt shrined in weeds and protected by a thick, brackish brown hedging. The heavy brush had been oxidized by the daily dose of smog. The isolated camp was maybe a mile off the busy freeway corridor channeling a constant buzz of white noise occasionally interrupted by a blaring horn, the high pitched panicked grab of rubber from a hard braking vehicle, or the shattering impact of the collision itself.

The day was pushing into the late afternoon. Reilly and Rosen were saddled with the mindless protocol of taking names and running background checks on the homeless crime stoppers. Reilly and Rosen were polite enough, dutifully filling out the report and checking their stories. They separated the couple and inquired about who they were, any arrests or warrants—the general milieu of good and attentive police protocol. The cops asked if there were any drugs or paraphernalia at the campsite, in the tent, on their persons. "Best to tell us now. If we find it, it'll only be tougher on you." The couple was familiar with this by-the-book roust.

"No sir, not me" Donny said, and then took a beat, and looked over at his girlfriend, adding, "neither of us." Marie's innocent, crooked smile backed up Donny's claim. Marie liked that Donny was speaking for her.

"Jug of wine, sixer of Shlitz, and a little pot, Mexican, but that's it," Marie offered. She was just over five feet, impish, and weighed next to nothing, with an oval face and deep brown eyes. You could see that underneath her misfortune she had a pretty face.

Young officer Reilly looked down at his paperwork, and nodded. "Uh, huh, well last time I checked, that Mexican shitty pot or whatever is still illegal." He then looked over at his partner, Jake Reilly, who winked, adding, "Unless you got a medical card."

Officer Jack Reilly lowered his voice as if in league with Marie. "But what the hell, you all reported a goddamn crime, so we can look the other way on that issue."

Donny and Marie relaxed on the news that they wouldn't be going to jail on some bogus Mexican weed charge, especially since they were the ones who actually called the police.

"What about our ferret?" Donny asked, nervously pulling on his braided, dirty blond ponytail.

"What ferret?" Reilly asked, turning to Donny.

"The dude we actually found with the freaking dead guys." Both officers weren't at all sure what Donny had just said.

"He's in there." Donny pointed over to the worn, blue and red nylon tent proudly displaying the North Face logo.

Rosen bent down, peering from a safe distance.

Marie sat crossed legged in front of the tent nervously chipping away her worn pink, fingernail polish.

"Baby, show him Oscar." Donny flicked his head toward their mobile home.

Marie reached back behind her and gently pulled on a loose piece of rope.

"C'mon baby, c'mon Osky…" Marie cooed softly. "Be a good boy…" Marie coaxed her newfound cuddle. Marie wanted to show the officers what a tender, responsible ferret mom she could be.

The officers looked at each other, then back at Marie who was now feeling a slight tension on the thin rope. She knew Oscar could be a handful. She tightened her grip. Marie gingerly pulled. The fidgety, smoky grey and black-masked, furry animal suddenly appeared, emitting high-pitched squeals and screams. The officers instinctively jumped back. The chattering, angry ferret didn't want to go anywhere, at least not with them, and not with the homemade leash. The gnashing ferret pulled hard on the rope and bucked, and jumped, and finally scampered back into the tent, racing from side to side, madly scratching and digging its sharp, ferret claws into the tenting. Oscar was desperate to break through the expedition-tested nylon and escape to freedom.

"Dispatch, advise on animal control. We have a wild varmint of some kind, ferret or something," Reilly barked into his two-way.

"*Ferret* or *feral?*" Dispatch crackled.

Reilly clicked his two-way. "Ferret…Fer-*rat*," he annunciated slowly.

"Roger. Rabid?" The dispatcher questioned, just to be certain.

"Unknown," Officer Jake Reilly said, shrugging, looking over to his partner for a more professional, department-approved answer.

"Tell 'em we're checking it out," Rosen said, shrugging back at his partner. "At least it's not foaming." Officer Francis Rosen steadied his hand on his Taser, not quite sure what to do with the sharp-clawed, hissing varmint.

"That thing have a freaking rabies shot?" Officer Jake Reilly shouted out at Donny and Marie, not sure what else to say about what he just witnessed or the situation at hand, but pretty sure the question regarding rabies was an important fact he needed to establish before considering the police officers' next move.

"Rabies? Don't know, never thought of that!" Marie shouted back at the officers.

Donny ran over to Marie, grabbed the rope and jerked it hard, yanking the stubborn ferret. The ferret flew out of the tent opening, rolling and clawing at the leash, and somehow wrangled its neck free of the noose, and raced away down the viaduct.

Marie called after her furtive ferret, "Osky! Oh my God…he's loose…Oscar! Donny go get him, please… Osky…Osky!" She was now in quite a state hoping that Oscar would somehow get turned around and stop or head back to the camp, or maybe the officers could do something—anything. But it was no use. Her homeless ferret was a ghost, now long gone, and soon would get back to his true ferret-ness, relieved that there would no panhandling in his immediate future.

Reilly could see that Marie was shaken with this turn of escalating events and the thought of losing her Oscar to the wild.

"What's the story with the varmint?" Reilly asked in his very finest LAPD bedside manner. Reilly dug deep and tried his best to put himself in Marie's shoes. "He was a pretty furry fellow…sorry to see him go…kinda."

Marie sighed, resigned to never seeing her cute little Osky again. "We found him next to one of the dead guys. He was just being an animal. He didn't know any better," she said, wanting to protect her Oscar.

"Next to?" Reilly asked, his antenna up. He was surprised at the girl's revelation.

"Well, maybe more like tied to," Marie said. "When we saw the two bodies, we couldn't quite make out what that thing was As we got closer Donny started freaking out."

"Who the hell wouldn't? I mean that ferret was tied to the dude's leg," Donny said defensively, looking at the love of his life, hoping to salvage some of his young pride.

"The ferret was tied…to a leg?" Reilly looked over at Rosen.

"So, you untied the damn ferret from the body?" Francis Rosen asked, looking up from his notebook while turning down the chirping police static on his two-way.

Donny and Marie had no idea where this line of questioning was going, and weren't so sure they would be heading to the shelter for a shower and a meal. The two looked at each other, feeling less confident about being crime stoppers.

Donny spoke up. "Looked like that ferret there was tied up pretty good and was doing everything it could to get free. Can't say I blame him…"

"Donny said the ferret was eating the dude, and we should… what'd I say baby?"

"You said, something like, 'Take the ferret into custody…' I think."

Marie put her arm around Donny's thin waist. "Yeah, that's right, *custody* is what I said." The petite Marie, just out of her teens into her first breakout year of being twenty, was satisfied with her word choice. *'Custody'* is a word she knew had a legal pop to it. Considering her current living situation in a camp with a wild ferret, two dead bodies, and two Los Angeles police officers holstering weapons, Tasers, and handcuffs, Marie was street wise enough to at least try to sound responsible. "Wish you hadn't told me that." Rosen sighed tightly, glancing over at Reilly.

Jake Reilly only shook his head. "Yep, now we got ourselves a situation."

Rosen stepped forward. "Ok, see, what we got is a crime scene, and you all can't mess with a crime scene. Which means now we got to take you downtown, take a statement, and do a bunch of crap nobody wanted to do today."

"We under arrest?" Marie asked. Her query made Donny nervous. He shook his head discreetly at Marie. Donny was of the mind that it's bad luck to even introduce the slightest thought of them in handcuffs. No reason to poke the bear, so to speak.

"Not unless you want to be," the older cop, Rosen, warned in a huff. His low blood sugar now made even worse by the ream of reports to be filed on bodies, the homeless couple, a ferret, and whatever else was going to come down. The officer looked at his watch—three in the afternoon, four more hours of his shift. He was lusting after a Lucky Boy's burrito over in Pasadena but—he checked his watch again.

"What about our stuff?" Donny looked over their pitiful camp, taking inventory of their possessions.

"Pack it up. We don't have all day," the veteran officer said impatiently.

Marie slipped on a pair of worn espadrille wedge sandals. "Osky was the coolest…we loved the little guy. He was sweet," she said softly to no one. She then turned and looked at Officer Reilly and presented her defense of Oscar. "He was in the wrong place at the wrong time, is all. You know, I read somewhere that ferrets are as smart as dogs. So yeah, Oscar was like the dog I never had."

"Good news is that he knows his way around this place," Reilly said, trying to sound like he knew something about ferrets. "So, pretty sure he'll be ok. The little guy will be just fine out there." He nodded out toward the viaduct's overgrowth and snapped his notebook closed. He walked over to his car and leaned against it while clicking his two-way, calling in cryptic police codes and requesting backup.

"Who were the dead guys?" Donny asked while stuffing a Desert Storm camouflaged-patterned Army-Navy surplus duffel bag with leftover remnants of packaged Raman, assorted food, clothes, a Sobakawa bean pillow, tattered comic books and a weathered paperback that caught the eye of the older cop, Officer Francis Rosen.

"You read that?"

"Naw, it's hers," he flipped his head toward Marie, "she even did almost a year over at community." Donny smiled at his fellow camper and love interest. Marie smiled back at Donny, happy for the compliment. Donny zipped up his sleeping bag. "I like the Marvel stuff," he said, tightening the roll of the tubular pop up tent, and sliding the cylinder into a silver compact bag. He was good at it. The officer tossed their two small aluminum beach chairs with checkered webbing into the open trunk of his car. Donny mimed if it was ok for him to throw his brown, canvas Army-Navy surplus duffel and the tent in there, too.

"Just as long as there's no lice," Rosen said.

"Dude, we may be homeless, don't mean we live like animals."

Marie walked over to the older cop. She pulled a faded, blue Dodgers cap out of her pack, put it on. With most of her brown hair now tucked under the cap, her face looked even younger. "So, who were those guys?" she asked, picking up Donny's question.

"From the looks of it," Rosen pointed his pen up toward the crime scene now busy with the arrival of assorted LAPD vehicles, "I'd say they were unlucky."

The backup officers got busy rolling out official yellow crime scene tape while mapping the area with small, orange plastic flags that dotted the camp, the embankment, and down into the viaduct.

Rosen turned his attention to Marie and offered up a paternal reprimand. "Good thing you weren't around when that shit went down, missy. Could be you with that ferret tied around a body part." He could see that his comment scared the girl. But maybe, he thought, that's what she just might need to get her life together, maybe even leave the homeless boyfriend. She was somebody's daughter. He had a little one at home. "I don't want to find the both you back down here, smoking crack and you pimping her out. Know what I mean?" He eyed Donny. "It's a hard life out here. You look like a smart girl. Get a shower, a meal, and call somebody, maybe welfare services or something. But get off the street. Who knows, maybe if you get place of your own you can head down to the pet store and find yourself another little Osky?"

"I'd like that." Marie brightened at the idea of her very own pet ferret at home on the couch, just the two of them watching a movie and wondered if she would still name her new pet, Oscar. Marie slipped into an oversized beige cable knit sweater that looked almost clean.

Saddened at Osky's great escape, she turned to Donny. "Donny, the furry little dude…he's gonna be like me, or us, just wandering around hanging…"

"Babe, maybe he can forage…" Donny said, hoping to add a brave hint of optimism as he pinched loose tobacco out of a Bugler pouch and rolled a tight cigarette. Donny struck a match, exhaling the smoke out the side of his mouth and through his nose. The hand-rolled cigarette dangled precariously from his lips; he tightened his ponytail. His dry, cracked fingernails were black with the city's sooty freeway exhaust. He took a deep drag and plucked a loose strand of the cheap tobacco off the tip of his tongue. The tobacco tasted good.

"I don't want our little guy to have to *forage*, Donny," Marie said protectively as she rolled out a tube of lipstick, leaned down, and using the car's side mirror, applied the light pink color, smacking her lips lightly. She looked better already. She thought about what Officer Reilly said. She did love reading; she even liked Hemingway. And she liked watching birds, which most girls her age didn't care about. She looked at herself again in the mirror. The warm LA sun had moved lower into the late afternoon and now sat directly behind her casting a halo around her small head. Marie looked at herself in the car mirror. She liked the glossy shine of the pink lipstick. Donny stared at her. He knew she was too good for him. She knew it, too.

The couple packed up their homeless camp and dipped into the back of squad car. Reilly rolled his window down to help with the sorry odor of the two unfortunates as the car headed downtown to take their statement about finding the bodies and the whole ferret deal.

"Animal control has to be brought in," Office Reilly was behind the wheel, and glanced back at the two. "We need a positive ID on the ferret, and since you kids had the damn thing on a rope for awhile… well, remember details are important in recalling a crime scene."

"Even with Oscar?" Marie asked.

"*Even*," Rosen pronounced.

"How long we down there?" Donny asked.

"Long as it takes. Like I said, in case you weren't listening, this is a—""I know, I know," Marie interrupted. "It's a crime scene," Marie finished, rolling her eyes over at Donny.

"There you go, Missy." Rosen said, almost sounding chatty.

Officer Francis Rosen glanced at his watch. The odds of him snagging a Lucky Boy burrito in Pasadena were quickly dimming.

The squad car pulled into the station. The young crime stoppers were ushered into a stale station room. Reilly pulled out a chair, offering it to Marie. Rosen signaled for Danny to take a seat as well.

They were offered water or coffee. The couple thought it was a nice gesture.

"Coffee, thanks," said Donny. "Whitener if you got it. Sugar?"

"Sweetener is all," Rosen said. Donny nodded that sweetener would be fine.

"Water, please…I mean if it's no problem." Marie politely added.

"Animal control will be here shortly," Francis Rosen said.

Jake Reilly pulled up chairs to the table. He and Rosen sat. Officer Rosen opened a notepad and clicked his pen and wrote something. It was only a short minute before a heavy-set, strong-jawed woman with kind blue eyes and wearing freshly pressed Khakis walked into the cramped conference room. Marie noticed two bright patches on the woman's light brown short sleeve shirt. One patch declared the county of her employ, and the other patch, her years of service. Her extra-wide braided black leather belt held a black and red 8-ounce can of Mace, a mobile phone holstered in place with Easy-Open-Easy-Close Velcro, monogramed leather lanyard clutching a hefty collection of keys, and a matt-black walkie-talkie with yellow tape banded around a slightly bent, stubby rubber antenna. The yellow tape was scribed with black marker that read "Channels." Aviator Ray-Ban sunglasses hung snugly from brown, nylon Croakies looped around her neck. Evidently, there was a lot to the animal control job.

Marie also noticed the woman wore brown leather ankle boots with thick rubber soles that looked amazingly comfortable, although the spongy soles squeaked as she moved across the polished linoleum floor.

The Animal Control Officer (ACO) had introduced herself as Debra. She pulled out a metal seat across from her witnesses. ACO Debra placed a large book in front the couple and even slanted the tome at a courteous angle so the policemen could get a good look, as well.

"I know this isn't easy," Debra said, tapping the cover of the bound catalogue, "so do your best. Believe me, the varmint family has a lot of lookalikes…a lot." She opened the large book so Donny and Marie could patiently flip through the colorful pages protected by glossy plastic lamination.

"Take your time. It's important that you get this right," Debra schooled as she glanced at her watch.

Donnie and Marie nodded together in an unspoken confederacy that they understood the import of ACO Debra's instructions. Donny and Marie leaned in closer to inspect the catalogue. Given this grave task, they wanted to show that they could be attentive, even helpful in solving the case.

The couple stared down at pictures of a dusky-colored, spindly-legged female coyote. Donny thought the coyote looked kind of scrawny, but said nothing fearing reprisal from ACO Debra. Donny was sure she didn't want to hear his lay opinion of LA wildlife. *Silver Lake, pack, June 2012* was neatly noted in the margin of the photo.

"Move to the section titled, 'Weasels'—right there." Debra reached over and expertly thumbed through a sheaf of vinyl pages until a section, tabbed 'Weasels' flopped open. She knew this book by heart.

Marie looked at Debra. "Weasels?" Marie didn't understand. "Pretty sure our cutie, Oscar is a ferret."

"Sounds like you know your *Mustelids*." ACO Debra offered a patronizing smile. "See anything?" Her lanyard of important keys jangled against the metal table leg.

Marie concentrated. Donny did, too. Officers Reilly and Rosen looked at the photographs with their practiced, professional policeman's eye.

"Take a real good lookie, real good…those weasels can be wily," Debra schooled.

The group concentrated on each colorful page, scanning the beady-eyed varmints, hoping to spot viaduct Oscar. After a few minutes, by page six, the couple identified their furry varmint.

"That's him." Donny said confidently. "Bigger than that there," Donny pointed to a weasel, "but that's gotta be him."

"You sure, baby?" Marie leaned closer to study the photograph. She bit her nails, anxious about the duty at hand in correctly identifying her favorite pet in the weasel lineup.

"Smaller eyes, but yeah, that's the little dude." Donny said proudly, particularly pleased to be the first of the seated group to spot Oscar.

"Damn, I think you're right," said the younger officer, Reilly.

"Bingo, looks like the very same," said the older officer, Rosen, squinting closely at the page.

"I guess it is, yeah, uh, sure…" Marie hated to admit it but her loveable Oscar, the ferret in question, was now positively tagged in the lineup.

ACO Debra turned the book around to see what the group had fingered as their culprit. "Yeppers, *Mustela Putorius*. Russian. This little bad boy is known for its fur," she said, running her fingers across the photo, perfectly pleased to have contributed to the growing evidence docket on this gruesome body count. She made a mental note to craft a carefully worded report that would help her move up to the supervisory rank and surely jump the basic merit raise.

Very few officers in her division had ever lucked into the professional bump that came from the notoriety of handling a varmint involved in a homicide case. *Homicide!* The bully breeds get a lot of press, but a wild ferret gnawing on a human leg in the middle of LA is just about as good as she could ever hope; this was sweet manna. She wasn't going to let the opportunity of a lifetime slide. That little Russian ferret was her ticket to the show.

"Mustela Putorius" Debra repeated slowly, locking eyes with the couple. Her rubbery soles squeaked against the flooring.

"Dangerous?" Marie cocked her head to look at the picture of the furry ferret again. Marie compared the photo to her Oscar, who, by comparison, looked super sweet and cuddly.

Debra looked at Marie. "Dangerous? Not if you don't consider crippling its prey by piercing the brain with its teeth, then storing the still living carcass in its burrow for future consumption dangerous… always has a meal ready to go."

"That's using your head." Donny grinned at his pun.

Marie recoiled at the thought and grabbed Donny's arm.

Debra looked at him flatly. "Wouldn't be so funny if it got its claws into one of you, now would it?" she said while patting her tabulated, color-coded catalogue closed. She jotted the catalogue number on a piece of yellow paper titled: Animal Control Report. Debra slid the official paper across the table to veteran Officer Rosen, who then slipped it into his report book for future reference. He glanced up at the room's wall clock. Rosen would not be lunching at Lucky Boy burrito today. Officer Rosen hated that ferret even more.

ACO Debra pushed her chair away from the table, got up and straightened her thick black belt. "I know this is an ongoing investigation, so whatever you need," she said, shaking hands with the policemen. She thanked Donny and Marie for their service to the case, tucked her glossy, vinyl-protected, picture book securely under her arm, and left. Donny and Marie, and officers Reilly and Rosen could hear ACO Debra's polyester-blend khakis brushing in concert with her noisy extra-thick rubber-soled shoes as she faded off down the hall to her next report, happy to have met the ferret, Oscar. She was going to ride that bad boy straight to the top.

The policeman escorted Donny and Marie out to the hallway, showed them a metal bench that sat off to the side of the green and gray linoleum hallway.

"Let's get you signed out of here. Give us a minute," Officer Reilly repeatedly clicked his ballpoint pen as he walked over to the day desk and organized his folder of papers for the Officer of the Day.

Donny sat leaning forward with his elbows on his knees, his dirty hands clasped together. He stared at the shiny speckled floor not sure what was going to happen next. The hallway was now scattered with a few patrol officers coming and going as their shifts changed.

"Goddamn ferret, we'd still be at our camp if it weren't for that little—" Donny caught himself.

"He's free now." Marie put her arm around Donny hoping to soften his critical feelings.

"I'd have some of them Vienna sausages, toke up that Mexican and fall asleep to the sound of that freeway, be nice and warm out there tonight."

"I know, baby...I know..." Marie's comforting voice trailed off. She pulled the used paperback out of her wheat-colored canvas purse. Donny was scavenging through a pile of cast-offs at the Salvation Army when he found the worn book of short stories. He had tied a pink bow on it for her twentieth birthday,

"Last time I ever try to do something good," Donny said to no one. Donny looked up at the overhead fluorescent lighting. The chatter of police officers floated through the station.

Being at a police station made Donny nervous. "Fucking Oscar... I'm going out for a smoke." And he did.

Marie turned the page of her book. She chewed on the quick of her nail, wondering what Oscar was up to and what Donny would do if she and Donny did get their own place and she brought another Oscar home.

Investigators determined that if the couple had not discovered the bodies, it would be safe to assume that the ferret, tied to one of the legs, could have eaten for weeks, devouring the evidence, and in turn, becoming one fat dude and eventually gnawing through his roped tether. Then, it would be time to find a lusty mate. Yes indeed, it was good to be Oscar the Russian wrapped in fur, bathed in the warm, California sun and now happy to have a den he could call home.

DARYA DID IT

Maxim Gorikv had removed their teeth and fingers, so it was going to take a while for homicide to figure out who was who. The insatiably hungry ferret and the viaduct's dank, watery slime made any kind of positive identification nearly impossible. A few days later, two more bodies, stripped of their clothes, turned up in one of LA's oldest Coptic parishes. Although fingerprints and teeth were removed as well, homicide caught a break. One of the bodies carried a rich and storied past as told by hard, etched Russian prison ink. Maxim was eventually pegged as a possible suspect. In fact, he was the only suspect. Maxim sat in a small holding room. He knew his rights and offered nothing. His lawyer showed up; Maxim walked. Homicide started a file on him. Then the heaven's parted—Maxim Gorikav's file was neatly buried. Deep. Like into the universal chasm of nothing deep. Compliments of my agent, my business partner, and keeper of the black bags, Agent Jack Murphey.

We were sitting at a Santa Monica sports bar. Jack was staring up at the monster screen TV showing file footage of dead Russian guys.

"Nobody gives a flying fuck about four dead Russians littering our city, unless they're union grips killed on a movie set," Jack said. He had already flagged the bartender for the 18-year old Macallan. Two fingers.

I sat next to Jack, ordered my usual double, two olives, rocks. I swirled the vodka and cubes into a perfect pirouette, chilling the libation. I drank it, polished off the olives, and held up a finger motioning that we should do this again.

"Ever have the Stoli Elit?" The young model-slash-actor-slash-bartender-slash-enabler asked.

"I've lived a sheltered life."

"Double, right?"

"Triple, if it saves you a trip."

Jack looked at me, bemused by my newfound friendship with a guy who could see I was most definitely good for more than a miserly 20% gratuity. I was ok with the buy in; some marriages are built on less.

My handsome new best friend returned with a ridiculously generous pour. We were getting along just fine.

"The Elit," he said, slowly pushing the clear, chilled glass over to me. "Let me know what you think."

I took a proper sip, then finished the Elit. I smiled and slid the glass across the shiny, copper- topped bar. "Let's fall in love."

My bartender could see I was passionate about my hobby.

He looked at Jack. "You?"

Jack nodded that, yes, another would be a perfectly fine idea.

"You see this?" Jack said, looking up at the giant plasma screen.

"The ferret thing?"

"Yeah, the weasel." Jack tipped his scotch back. "And let's not forget Donny and Marie…"

"They found the body, right?"

"Bodies, plural," Jack corrected.

"So, these kids are homeless and camped down there, what—off the 5?" I asked.

"There goes the neighborhood." Jack said.

Our drinks arrived on cue.

"Anyway, Donny and Marie called it in. Apparently even the unfortunates have cell phones." Jack is buzzed. He smiles a lot when over-served.

"Apparently there's a plan for everyone," I said.

"These two kids call it in and the next thing you know, bodies are linked to our favorite Russian."

"Gorikav?" I asked.

Jack put his patronizing arm around my shoulder. "Doc, you're well on you way to earning a gold shield, and you don't even have a year in. Way to go, doctor," Jack clinked his glass to mine.

"And the ferret?"

"Ferret's a mother effing Russian, too." Jack motioned for more salty snacks.

"A Russian ferret?"

"Go figure. Ask animal control, they got a bead on weasels from all over the world."

"So, why the ferret?" I asked. My chilled pour of the pricey Elit was starting to hit its intended mark.

"Ferrets love meat, sure-fire way to get rid of the evidence. Tie one up to a few dead guys, leave 'em for a while and voila, nada, nothing, zero…murder needs a body." Jack could see I was impressed with the ferret thing. "Smart, right?"

"Brilliant, actually."

Thanks to the easy pouring of our bartender, Jack and I were well into our cups while we discussed Maxim Gorikav, our share of the black bag, and the managerial responsibilities of keeping Maxim safely out of the reach of the ATF, and, of course, keeping the Gorikavs forever lost from Russians who were still mildly upset about that missing three million in counterfeit bills. Three million, even if it is bad paper, can do a respectable impression of real money.

Jack leaned closer in to me. "Maxim's got his hands full, deep into the Eastern heroin trade. Major screw up with the ATF deal and he needs to disappear…Mr. Fuck-My-Life-Gorikav is going to lead me, and selected parties such as yourself, down a shiny path littered with rose petals and warrants, arrests and the capture of a big *Bratva Pakhan*."

"*Pakhan?*"

"Boss," Jack said.

"Maxim could pull a trigger with a phone call, a smile and a nod," I said in a hushed tone that seemed to add even more weight to my new, federally funded promotion.

Jack spoke into his drink. "Maxim? Hey little buddy, let you in on a little something—it's the wife, Darya. She could take out Maxim if she wanted to…Showed up on our radar when we were working Maxim on the ATF deal."

"Darya?"

"Word came down that she showed up at the warehouse, not Maxim. Apparently, Mrs. Gorikav is pretty good with a Russian military knife, you know, the one she used on the two agents. After they were shot, she severed their tongues. Then, the warehouse was torched."

"Sweet. No wonder ATF has a hard on," I said.

"Maxim and Darya…power couple," Jack added.

"I'm already so over Brad and Angela…I did kinda like that Mr. and Mrs. Smith, though," I said, hoping to lighten our discussion.

"Plus, they adopted all those kids," Jack said, agreeing with my film notes.

"Here's to family life," I said.

We finished our drinks with details on how Jack was going to run the Maxim ATF federal witness protection program and how he would make sure the dead Russians' investigation would steer clear of Maxim.

"Doc, you're in charge of making Darya *vamanos.*"

"I can't wait." I said inhaling the last of my vodka, and popping two mint-flavored Nicorettes.

Jack called the bartender over, cleared the tab, counted out a raft of crisp bills, turned his glass upside down and tucked a fifty under it. "Leave another tip," he said.

"Thought this was on you."

"I can only expense so much. By the way you were just promoted, so yeah, congratulations."

Darya Gorikav was now on me—thank you Jack—and by the sound of it, she could easily out-Maxim, Maxim.

I knew this Darya deal was going to cost me. I just didn't know it was going to be right this minute. I threw a C-note on the shiny copper-topped bar. And yeah, I do recommend the chilled Stoli Elit, even if you can't expense it.

THE EXIT ROW

Two days after my gold shield promotion and Agent Jack Murphey's revelation about killer Darya, I called Jack. He was in the middle of shuttling his boys to a lacrosse camp and mentioned that Holly wanted to go car shopping. Evidently, Holly didn't ask too many questions and assumed the government was paying private sector money. She had come from upper middle class parentage and considered their life in burbs of La Canada just the way things were and always would be. She was comfortable with her life behind the wheel of her white, Mercedes wagon, getting the kids off to school, turning up Whitney Houston on her Bluetooth and spending quality time getting her nails done. Jack was out in the field somewhere and would come home to a clean house, dinner, and the boys doing their homework. If he had to cut a few deals to keep the home fires burning, he did. Part of his job, the way he saw it. Everybody had a hand out and the government made sure they got theirs. Jack's Russian mob side deals paid him well—his lockbox was evidence of the goodness of cash and his ability to provide for his family. Agent Jack Murphey considered the tight stacks of money as his payment-in-kind for the gun barrel that put that slug an inch away from ending his life with Holly and the boys. Maxim Gorikav was just one more asshole Jack could make a nickel off of. Private schools were expensive, too. And Holly wanted the new, E63 AMG wagon in her new favorite pretention, Glacier White.

Jack and I had become close. He liked my tales recounting the excesses of Hollywood. I liked his tales of being a kick-ass fed. He liked to knock down doors. I liked to make women look beautiful. It was perfect. Jack and I were real life action heroes thrown together in service to beefy, Euro-trash Russian hard-ons who loved our lifestyle of gorgeous women, guns, and the ever-popular witness protection program, compliments of America the beautiful and home of the brave. Land of the free? Sure, how much you got.

Russians on the run loved the idea of doing time in this country. Get a new face, profile, address, set up new connections for them and their family and everyday is the Fourth of Effing July. Jack was cleared to even throw in a car, like say, a late model Ford Taurus. But still, if you lived by the book and kept your Slavic nose clean, witness protection was a sweet way of cheating death. Sometimes. Most times. Ok, every so often one of them would step out and lose sight of the concept of living on the down low, and naturally someone gets sloppy and then the wife wakes up one morning and finds a serrated knife stuck in the jugular of her spouse still sitting upright in the Taurus parked in the driveway, blood everywhere. Jack will tell you. The Feds can only do so much. Leaks can get nasty. Accidents happen. That carotid artery can be a mutha.

Jack's phone rang. He picked up. I needed to walk him through one of my recent brainstorms on how I was going to deal with Maxim and Darya Gorikav and the other Russian immigrants who are in the business of killing people like me.

"Time to seek other career options." I said into my mobile as I eased onto one of the lounge chairs dotting my deck.

Maria had placed a Monkey Pod tray of cheeses with my favorite black Aragon olives next to my personal two-glass carafe of Stoli on ice and made sure the two large chocolate beige patio umbrellas were angled to handle a three-hour window of high sun. I poured three fingers of the hair of the big dog and sat back to suss out my current situation with the United States federal government and avenging Russians who were lucky to call LA home. Apparently, Maxim was still madly in love with his cherished spouse. And according to my federal sources, he took Darya's death hard. Clearly, we were remiss in anticipating his reaction and woefully underestimated Maxim's desire for killing the guy who killed his Darya. He was coming for me.

Maria turned up the *Vargas Mariachi* band and hummed along with the south of the border hit, *Mi Ciudad*; she knew the Vargas songs by heart. I should probably treat her and her family to the Vargas concert when the famed mariachis were playing the Bowl. She was a dear and had taken care of Quentin during some of his darker days. I was going to miss her.

"Don't sweat it, we got you," Jack said.

"Hmmm, not so sure about that. Maxim's not going to wait for his HMO case report on his dead Darya. Pretty sure she's met her deductible."

"Doc, trust me, my boys have been through this kind of thing before." Jack's reassuring voice was nice, but I wasn't buying.

"Really? The dead Russian wife married to the Russian mobbie who now wants his surgeon-dead kind of thing…really?"

"I talked to guys over at ATF. They know where Maxim is. We can yank his chain anytime,"

"Now would be good," I said, between my teeth.

"I knew you'd go there." Jack said, and I could pick up the sound of his brain turning like tumblers falling into place on a combination lock. He was stalling.

"Gee, really, look at you, a regular Edgar Cayce. Next thing you know you're mapping Atlantis."

"Give me a few days to wind up the ATF and handle Maxim."

"A few days like in, uh, forty eight hours, or a few days like in, oh I don't know, *a few days*?"

"Hang tight, and I'll get back to you," Jack paused, "don't do anything stupid." He warned, almost sounding like he cared.

"Stupid, me? I thought that was your job."

"I gotta go get Holly."

"I gotta pour one…could be my last," I said. "Believe me this is a small town, and I'm not that hard to find. Just ask my ex."

"Maxim doesn't know shit, but just in case, make sure you don't get close to the clinic."

"Just in case? Maybe you can crack the federally approved guidelines on getting the hell out of town because a civilian—that would be me—is gonna get dead by a Russian dude in our chain of command—that would be Maxim."

"Sit tight, Doc, we'll get you outta there."

"Hmmm, no, I think I'll get *me* outta here. I gotta go," I said.

"Go?" he asked.

"Yeah, the verb."

"You can't just 'go'," Jack was being bossy. It came with the paycheck.

"Watch me," I said. "Maxim wants his wife back. And last I checked, he didn't buy the platinum cryo plan…you want to break the news to him?"

"Maxim won't even remember her when I get though with him," Jack said.

"I can't take this shit anymore." I swallowed my pour.

"You have a choice?" Jack was pushing me.

"You can give me one."

"I like you Doc, but I'm only a freakin' G5."

"You got pull," I said.

"Let's say you do go—where?"

"I'll call you when I get there."

"Doc, you're a good surgeon, not a very good outlaw…this is no Sundance and Butch."

"The Fugitive," I said, lighting up another cigarette.

"Chrissakes…give me some time on this." I think Jack was trying to be helpful. Really.

"Gotta go, Jack, gotta go. Tomorrow's too late…I can feel it."

"I'm surprised you can feel anything."

"Let's talk intervention after I buy the next round."

"Sure you're not just hiding out at that Promises Place?"

"Pretty damn sure."

"Call me when you get there, and don't say I didn't warn you,"

"You didn't."

"I just did, goddamn it."

"Fuck you, too."

"I'll see what I can do." Jack was already thinking options and I liked that about him.

"You're sweet."

"I bet you say that to all your federal agents."

"Just the ones who love me. Gotta run."

"Wherever you go, it's not gonna be far enough."

"We'll see."

We hung up. I wasn't going to hang around.

CHAPTER 8

MEET HELENA, SHE'S RUSSIAN

Truth be told, I had squirreled away some secrets from Jack Murphey.

Secrets that were still only mine. I had been smart enough to hide Helena. When I cut my deal to handle Russian identities for the government and fell into favor with my new partner, the Fed All-Star Jack Murphey, keeper of Russian names and those hefty black leather bags of cash, I had another identity that Jack and his boys didn't know about. Perhaps they didn't even care. After all, I was channeling cash straight out of my Bel Air ATM and directly into their wallets. They liked having a doctor on call.

"You know, Doc," Jack had once told me, "we get you busy enough and pretty soon you'll be boating off the Bay Of Naples."

"I always did like to summer in Capri, but tough to get a table with any kind of water view in September."

Agent Jack Murphey had assured me on numerous occasions that managing the Russian clientele would have me tacking off the Amalfi coastline, a course correction that was most definitely in my future. I almost believed him.

Helena had walked into my office, pulled out an Afghani woven and beaded bag packed with cash and asked me to make her look like anybody—anybody but her. After our introductions, she sat down, crossed her legs, and simply said, "Make me disappear."

I don't get a lot of twenty-six-year old Russians seeking my work. Actually that would be none. But I do happen to have a weakness for Osetra caviar, long legs, blue eyes, platinum blonde bangs, and a girl on a mission. Oh, and killer eyebrows arched in attitude. But mostly, I just liked her. She had a soul. Which is tough to find in the Hollywood Hills, and even tougher to detect since I was losing mine. I remember thinking that this was a girl who was still young enough to do something with her life. After screwing up mine, I wanted to help her have the one she wanted. Needless to say I was intrigued. Plus, we had chemistry. I could smell Kahlua on her breath, mixed with a hint of strong tobacco. She tossed her beaded bag of cash on my desk and the woven bag landed with a promising, silky beady sound that carried the unmistakable thud of cash.

I was all in.

"Found you through internet," she said.

I quietly thanked that person who invented the internet of things.

She continued. "Lookink for new face…"

I did a quick study of her profile and concluded that I wouldn't want to do a thing to hers.

Helena could see I was trying to figure her out. Maybe it was the quizzical expression on my face. I was easy to read, or so I've been told.

"People vhant me dead," she said. I watched her eyebrows. Her bangs were crushing it, too.

"Some might consider that kind of move a little extreme. Most of my clients are primping for awards show season," I paused, "actually, to be fair, you came to the right plastic surgeon because certain people want me dead, too. So, good news, I know what you're going through." I could see I had Helena's attention.

I did my professional best to continue with a practiced decorum to provide sound medical advice. I offered her a Menthol. She cocked her head in a kind of shorthand charm that telegraphed *How nice of you* as she expertly plucked a cigarette out of my pack. I liked the way she smoothly handled the mechanics of her gold Hermes cigarette lighter as she lit mine then hers. We inhaled and exhaled on the same meter, and I passed her one of my Swarovsky cut crystal ashtrays.

"Vodka?" I suggested, ever the host.

"*Da*."

I opened a chilled bottle of the Stoli Elit. She smiled and blew a thin, perfect smoke ring that traveled toward me then faded into nothing. It was a nice touch. She could see I liked the move. She winked. Helena's baby blues would look stunning behind dark, thick-rimmed sunglasses on a sleek white boat cutting through the light blue foam of the Tyrrhenian Sea in a sun-drenched Italian September. Helena's Capri biscuit-toned tan would set off her creamy linen blouse. The warm and tender sea breeze opening a fluttering tease of buttons. The tight snap of the nylon sail would send the boat's rail slicing into the blue salt water, tossing a light spray into the air and beading up on the varnished teak deck. I could see Helena lazily stretched out, looking up at the full mainsail and feeling the rush and tug of the boat against the incoming tide and her gaze hypnotized by a single, feathering cloud that seemed to follow the tip of our mast.

I poured two large vodkas over ice. The conversation paired well with the frosty Elit as Helena explained her current state of affairs that involved her family in Moscow and a few suspect relatives in Los Angeles. I think I got most of the family tree without even doing a search on Ancestry.com. Somebody's running girls; somebody else was charged with questionable freight and shipping ledgers and manifests. Then another uncle decided to handle the guns and bad paper in the counterfeit division. Helena's family was an industrious lot prone to palettes of cash that were eventually laundered into real estate. Empire building can keep you busy.

And unless there's total buy-in on the family org chart, somebody's bound to get hurt.

"Seems you've run into the right person at exactly the right time." I turned up the in-office sound system. Getz and Gilberto.

Helena liked my selection. She gently swayed with the vodka and Menthol in hand. "You have *Bratva* lookink?"

"I got a guy who kills entire *Bratvas* for a living." I followed suit with a breezy sway of my own as I told her about Maxim Gorikav, who by now was supposed to have disappeared along with a lot of cash, courtesy of the Federal government, in exchange for information about some Afghani munitions-for-heroin-trade. I was part of the deal. The Feds gave me the nod and told me to get to work. I explained how the Russian was in my office, on my operating table, facing a heavy mask of anesthesia and the countdown had started to a new identity, and a new face. *"Nostrovia"* was the last thing this bad ass heard before he woke up with a whole new him.

"Deese eese good, no?"

"Problem was, I not only gave him a new identity, which is what I was supposed to do, but he also asked me to do a little work on his wife, also Russian. She wanted work on her chin, cheeks and while she was under, why not some decent sized implants? A few complications later and I was looking at one pesky problem: she was dead."

"Ok, now I am seeingk deese problem."

"So is everyone else. Maxim is the kind of married guy with a dead wife who wanted answers and nobody was doing a lot of talking. Not the Feds, and certainly not me. And of course, Maxim had unlimited amounts of cash, a bunch of other bad-ass guys he enjoys hanging with, and a brand-spanking new hobby of spending nothing but time trying to track me down.

"Retribution is killingk you." Helena demonstrated an uncanny knack for spelling out my obvious predicament in getting killed. And that could be soon.

"Yes, that's big on Maxim Gorikav's to-do list. And I'm at the top of it. Working with the Feds suddenly became very uncomfortable because now I'm the one who's running."

"You are vhitness who eese needink protection." Helena again, eloquently summed up my life.

"Protection would be a good thing, but so far I don't see anyone sporting a US Calvary uniform."

Although she didn't understand my Calvary reference, she recognized a doctor with a patient retention problem. She swallowed the last of her Elit, and motioned for a repeat on the pour.

"I have vhat you callingk predicament, too, of my own eese bad."

"Predicaments by their very nature are rarely something you run to."

Helena almost understood what I was talking about, and rather than explain myself, I wanted to hear about her Russians, all of whom seemed to have failed every Myers-Briggs marker.

Her mother Alena was only eighteen when she had her. Helena walked me through her life and the consequences of the family DNA with her father Kirill and his brother, Pavel. Oh, and I particularly liked the part about how the brothers Kirill and Pavel were trying to make a go of it with ambitious enterprises that ultimately ended with Kirill's murder. You know, the typical family business issues that seem to surface when one of the siblings decides to keep all the money. Helena was only five when Pavel called the hit on Kirill that left her mother, Alena, a widow without a ruble, penny, or dime to help the young mother make life in Moscow. The short fuse on Helena's future was sparked by brotherly greed that made the Murdoch dynasty look nearly neighborly. Months after landing in LA, Helena got the news that her mother died, an apparent suicide. Alena was found sitting in a bright orange Russian-made Lada Kalina parked in her apartment's underground garage with the exhaust pipe pumping. Helena didn't buy the official story. She knew Uncle Pavel was sending her a message.

"My mother is smart, so she eese fast learner. She is killed by Pavel, to be sure, 100%. I can tell you dat," Helena said, lighting another of my Menthols. "She is saved by own brother Nikolas who eese connective…"

"Connected, I think you want to say."

"Connected yes. Deese is Nikolas and he is showingk my mother how to make more money in black market currency."

"That's a good thing. And, if I may, isn't it great to have family helping out mom navigate the currency exchange. Back in the day I could have helped her work a studio deal seeking cash outside the usual channels."

"Even better when she pays money to officials in Moscow to ruin Pavel and destroy heem."

"I think I have most of this between Alena, Kirill, his brother Pavel and your mother's brother Nikolas, and now you." I said, happy to have followed Helena's family tree. I thought of the popular, hand-painted wooden Russian nesting dolls.

"And now?" I was bent on connecting the last of the Russian dots.

"Pavel vhants me dead. He is thinkingk my money eese his."

"So, kind of the trifecta of bad guy stuff with that scary Russian gangster retribution back end. Yeah, I think I kind of know what you're talking about. It's not his money, though, right…is it?" I wanted to by crystal clear that I understood just how Uncle Pavel was working the family. Just in case I had to bring Agent Jack Murphey into our Bratva committee of two and one of us had to know what we were talking about.

"He vishes…now Pavel has other Russians lookingk for me."

"They want you dead and they want to take your money because they think it's theirs. You'll find similar family dynamics on most day time reality shows. I get it."

"You are fast learned, too, doctor."

"Fast learner," I said.

Helena just looked at me.

"Forget it, yes, I am a fast learned." I said, thinking that I was starting to sound like her.

Helena walked over to the expansive Nanawall floor-to-ceiling window and looked out at the Los Angeles nightscape. "Maybe we are disappearing to somewhere vhit you?"

"Maybe." I said, and filed her suggestion, instantly liking it. Not a bad way to go. I did the math and it didn't look all that terrible. Hell, I was an adult. I didn't have to ask permission. I had already said goodbye to Jack. I had cash stowed in nice tidy bricks. So, yeah, my spring break was looking awesome.

My Bel Air office in this summer's evening could have passed for any doctor-patient consult, but tonight it was just two people who seemed to have it all. Helena was toting a beaded Afghani bag with a little over $900,000 in small bills. I was a bona fide plastic surgeon backed by our federal government and lined up to work with Agent Jack Murphey. Of course, there was this nasty bit with Maxim and now Darya, but right now, in this moment, I had Getz and Gilberto playing, my suede walls the perfect acoustic for Astrud Gilberto's liquid vocals. And well, we had access to my pharmaceutical cocaine droppers and other medical accessories, should the need arise. Over the next few days, Helena and I mapped our options and came up with a pretty good plan that Agent Jack Murphey wouldn't need to know about, at least not yet. People had to get out of town. And those people were us. We would be moving to another planet. And it wasn't anywhere near a brilliant white ketch slipping through the crystal Tyrrhenian Sea.

CHAPTER 9

DESERT AIR

We had been tucked away in the desert for over a year now. Safely nestled in the flatness of rock and cactus, sheltered in the middle of the red planet. Our welcome mat is The VistaVue trailer park, a sliver of forgotten divots that cost nearly nothing to place a trailer on a cement stamp. Park, close the door, turn out the lights and disappear. VistaVue was off the main highway out at the furthest end of a crisscrossed bramble of one-lane desert roads. You had to know it to find it. Otherwise it didn't exist. And that's how we liked it. We were good at blending into the collapsing desert ecosystem. We'd carved our life out of the barren rock and scree, and on occasion, we'd drive out to the river where we discovered a hidden inlet of a cove and a curtain of waterfalls that cooled the sting of the desert burn. If you closed your eyes the cooling water made you believe you were anywhere but here. The cascade of the Mighty Colorado felt like salvation.

The gorgeous and seductively dangerous Helena lit a cigarette and fed it to my lips. I rolled over and ticked the thermostat, generating the soothing sounds of the Airstream's AC to combat the morning heat already baking the desert pan.

"Your startingk coffee." Then handed me a tall coffee, iced, sugar. She dipped into the kitchen and quickly assembled a protein smoothie just to give my body a shot at normal. She's considerate like that. The first few hours of a morning appeared to be that time when iced coffee, a Menthol, and a newspaper still made sense. Who knows? We might even have breakfast. I could use a Denny's-sized Slam of some sort right about now.

Helena asked me if I could turn up the AC a bit more. Before I could answer, she took two steps toward the fridge, grabbed some ice, put the cubes in a kitchen towel, pulled the hammer out of my neatly lined, immaculately organized, surgically-dialed and hospital-approved utensil drawer, and with a few quick concussive strikes, smashed the cubes into fine, icy pieces of cold. Helena is very efficient. It was only ice, but her rapid, successive crushes did grab my attention—I winced, "Take it easy…Jesus. You do have countertops in Russia, right?"

Helena shot me a look, wrapped the crushed and wet bundle along the back of her sweaty, and I might add, long, beautiful Russian neck. I can only admire how this desert heat can make you impressively inventive about assembling cooling things. It's an art, really. A hammer, some ice, a towel and liquid *cocaina* and, *voila,* problem solved. I did like to watch the way she moved when wet. I felt a rush kick in. I loved her power. The day is settling into another version of Mojave hot. Our life here had taken on a serviceable routine that rotated around the daily dose of sun, our sequence of tumblers, and liquid droppers of the *pharma*. Helena liked my stories of my Russian gangsters, Federal agents and the rest of my world up in the Hollywood Hills. My life appealed to her sense of cinema. She told me I reminded her of James Bond. The Sean Connery one. Not the George Lazenby guy. I was at least hoping for Pierce. Her dark, arched, and spectacular eyebrows are mesmerizing, adding to the exaggerated drama of her every expression during our early morning states of euphoria where conversations got thick with repetition about my general theories of planetary truths and conspiracies. She talked and I watched her eyebrows dance. It's the Helena Show and I liked it. Helena, much like flight-risk plastic surgeon with an evergreen cache of narcotics, doesn't need to be reminded that there are still people out there who would like to get their hands on the people in here.

"Russian men like Maxim Gorikav are cowards," She said, out of the blue. Pouring another iced coffee with her signature Russian counter crushed ice. She eyed the thermostat. It almost moved on her stare. The girl was good.

"Really? Then you can deal with him. And them." I expertly squeezed the dropper, dosing my midday tumbler. The benefits of my practice, at least this one, had traveled with me, and served as a cozy memory of days and nights in the Hollywood Hills connected to a life of privilege and promise. Helena looked at me, gave me the hard stare, picked up the dropper and hit the tip of her tongue. Helena liked the numbing way it slides smoothly into her bloodstream. Liquid cocaine is like that. It's a heady little tonic that's a nice topper to your iced-vodka. It was a favorite pastime at my place up in the Hills— around dusk in the summer, with my infinity pool throwing off watery lights. The orange, pink, and red sunsets showed us all just how polluted the place had become. Still, life looked good. From up there. It was just all getting a little hazier. But fuck, those sunsets were golden. Already Needles was showing us how the desert could stand resolutely still and build to a searing 112 degrees in a heat so dry you would swear you could hear the desert air crackle. The temperature has pushed life underground, or under, a rock, or a under a piece of loose bark, or under anything that gives you a hope of shade or moisture—a particle of hydration and a way out of the solar system. Underneath and in the dark is where life is lived. You lay perfectly still, saving your energy, quietly, expertly, and you wait for night. You find a way to live underneath this desert or you die. Helena handed me my 16oz lime green plastic tumbler, iced up and good to go.

She added a slice of lemon to make it feel like we were expecting company, or relatives, or something, or somebody. She pulled her long legs into her body, and sat there with her magical blue eyes framed by that face and those eyebrows and she watched me. I looked over at the laundry hamper. My memory went back to Los Angeles for a visit with my son when he was younger, happier, and when I had no idea there was a Sixth street bridge. The carousel in my memory went around for a while until it stopped and I got off.

Helena and I had talked about Quentin when she and I first met in my office. She had picked up a picture fame sitting on my desk.

"Who eese deese? Your boy?"

"Yeah, my son, Quentin. He's no longer with me."

"Vhit mother?" Helena asked and then caught herself, as if she already knew the answer.

"Quentin when he was six and a million years ago."

"He eese lookingk like you."

"I wish he was here for you to meet him," I said.

"Me, too."

I went on to tell Helena about The Day and my past life. Helena saw and felt the depth of my loss and my pain and the way time was now only a marker of what was and what could have been. Today, in Needles in a July, it's good to have the aluminum capsule from Ohio as your home in a border town, and even nicer to know where to find your own cooling cove of Colorado water.

CHAPTER 10

DANIEL

She had recently moved her trailer right next to ours, so when she knocked on the door and introduced herself. I did the polite thing and invited her in for a drink. She was blonde, petite, early forties.

She pulled out a Pall Mall, "Mind?"

"Not at all," I said, Helena nodded in courteous agreement. We opened a few windows and cranked up the AC.

Our new neighbor, Mary, pulled out a tarnished metal Zippo lighter, and we all agreed that the cooling evening desert air was always good for a smoke.

"You look familiar," I said.

"You telling me you know me?" she asked. Her face felt sad, but she bravely tried to sound like she was up for a neighborly drink.

"I'm good with faces—just part of my trade. A while back you lost a boy, a son. I don't mean to pry, but that was you, wasn't it?" I saw Mary's eyes fall to the floor. I could see that maybe I hit a nerve. I thought I was being delicate. At least it felt that way. I knew about losing a child.

"Saw something on the news, maybe…read about you, right?"

"Yes, I am thinkingk same, too. Sorry to hear about, " Helena offered a note of shared solace.

She stared at us. She wasn't sure where she wanted to go with our query, and obviously our read on her past. She exhaled a thin, even channel of smoke out of her sunburned nose. She tightened her jaw.

I didn't mean to step on her toes, but it was her. I was pretty sure of that.

"Six months ago, half a year, but it seems to have filled a lifetime. Yeah, that's me…that was us," she said, picking slowly on a loose thread hanging from the hem of her jeans. She twisted on the thread, half afraid to look up, her drinking hand trembled slightly. She lit another smoke and finished her vodka. I courteously pushed a glass across the smooth, blond birch laminate tabletop, asking if she would like another. See? Civil, mannered, and what you might not expect from a physician on the run living in an Airstream in July in Needles.

"Sorry to hear that. I kinda wasn't going to ask but, yeah, maybe I shouldn't have."

"Forget it. Actually, sometimes it's better when I talk about it. Sometimes. It's just that I think he's still here." She tipped the glass back.

I offered a small plate with iridescent lines shimmering in four neat rows. She took the tightly rolled twenty, fiercely inhaled the white flake, shaking Machu Picchu.

"I know that one." I hit my iced vodka with my dropper, and Helena lit two Menthols and passed me one. She snapped her gold Hermes lighter tightly with a pricey closing click.

Mary Wysocki had lost her ten-year-old son, Danny, to the perfect pitch of an accident that happens in places like this. Danny and his friend, both newly uniformed scouts, rode their bikes into the Mojave to test their scouting handbook, trying to score a merit badge in this hard land of pit vipers, scorpions, and things that can go from very bad to very fucking wrong, very fucking fast.

"Your son and his friend, just the two of them, if I remember…"

"Yeah," she took a long, slow sip, "took off with a box of crackers, handfuls of hard candy, flashlights, a canteen, and off they went on their bikes. Oh yeah, Danny also loved his new, scout-approved, flint fire-starter kit—made him feel like that guy who has that television show about survival. Anyway, Danny left a note for me…said he was going camping just down the street in a neighbor's yard." She shook her head at the memory of Danny coming up with such a stupid white lie, and if she had only taken the time to check on it. But then, Danny wasn't like that, she said. He was a good boy, and other than the ridiculous stuff ten-year-old boys do, never gave her a reason not to trust him.

"And then they went missing?" I could be a rock star at stating the obvious—it's a gift.

She looked at me. Then Helena. Mary was being brave as she took a breath. Her mouth swallowed hard. Another cigarette. She crossed her legs, played with her glass of vodka. She took a strong drag on the nicotine and exhaled just as deeply. I reached behind me to turn down Cash. His vocals lost with the low chill of the Airstream's air conditioner as I listened to her heart. It was, just like the news reports said, a freak accident. Sitting across from Mary it seemed we were watching her boy leave her lips as she exhaled and told us about what had happened with Danny and his friend.

The two had started out early in the day riding through a mix of dirt trails and forgotten back roads. The thrill of the camp and the lure of adventure that could test their scouting mettle pulled them further out into the lonely Mojave. They rode for a few hours, rested, sharing their crackers and candy. The temperate, clear afternoon was perfect and the blue sky went on forever, and the day must have felt wide open and harmless to the fifth graders who liked their merit badges and scout jamborees. Scouting made the boys feel bigger, tougher, and part of something wild.

They rode harder and faster, thinking that as long as they stayed on the rutted, tire tracks, they could get home. But, after looking around and pecking at one dirt trail and then another, it seemed that every marker, every road, every brush or broken, rotted fence just blended together until nothing made sense. The boys were lost and alone, riding across one, vast, directionless piece of clay. The sky was still blue. And it still went on forever. Only it was later.

Now, it was just two, frightened, nervous kids on dirt bikes with packs that felt useless. Out here, when the late afternoon leads to early evening and the air cuts thinner and turns crisp, the boys would feel this change in the desert.

They zipped up their hoodies against the late afternoon chill, wishing that they really were camping in a neighbor's backyard, minutes from video games and pizza.

The big canopy of night would soon settle deep into their early lives.

The boys hunkered down together and built a scrub brush lean-to, stayed close for warmth and suffered through a sleepless blackness that brought them to tears. The boys were thirsty and they were now out of water.

The next morning the two would find the well.

"Danny had to be a hero; he had to try to rescue them. He was small for his age, but he was fearless and figured he could just go down, get some water, and they'd be all right. He climbed down into an old, forgotten reservation well that was dry, empty; nothing there. No water in the old well, but hell, how could he know that? The boys were desperate, and that's when he fell straight down."

Mary told us that the other boy didn't know what to do. He heard a muffled thud and for a quick minute thought it was Danny jumping down and landing on the bottom. He heard Danny's sharp cry and the boy kept thinking that Danny was alive, but soon it was clear that Danny was not coming back. Ever. Danny's friend and fellow scout was now very much alone in the desert. Danny's friend remembered the way the body was covered and wrapped in a tight, colorless, grey-zippered piece of vinyl, strapped with thick, orange webbing and big aluminum buckles that was a kind of seat belt for Danny. He remembered the click of the gurney wheels as the stretcher slid into the back of the emergency vehicle, the wheels locked. The metal doors shut tightly, and this desert was again quiet. The vehicle drove off as if ten-year-old Danny Wysocki was just catching a ride home.

Reports came back that the boys were found an hour or so after Danny snapped his neck. Search and Rescue said the boys were only about ten miles from home, but in the Mojave, it may as well have been a hundred. Sixty minutes sooner and Danny and his pal could have been safely at home sitting across from two disappointed, yet relieved mothers reprimanding them about the mindless stupidity of it all, and what were they thinking? If the boys had survived they would have enjoyed a free trip home in a chopper or an EMT vehicle, and maybe, like most ten-year olds with a spotlight of celebrity, they'd hang and laugh with the cool kids. Maybe later in the week the troop scout-masters would use the boys' lack of judgment as a fine example of why Danny and his friend were very lucky and why you should, indeed, always be prepared.

Mary beat herself up going over the timeline in excruciating detail, pouring over each minute hoping to find a sliver of reason, a sign or something, anything, on why Danny had to die.

"I feel like maybe God took him aways cuz of me…he was only ten," she said softly. I tried to comfort her, and reached over to hold her hand, but was vibrating on the last hit of my *pura*.

"These things happen," I said through dilated pupils. "Mine was fourteen. Those are his clothes," I pointed to the laundry hamper in the corner.

"He's still with you?" Mary seemed confused.

"He is, but he isn't. He left me two years ago."

"Danny's with me, too." Mary dipped her head down.

"They always are—will be." I said, exhaling, and then swallowed my drink.

"Maybe we should be better people…I mean for them, you know, better people while we're still here?"

"Maybe, I think Quentin, my son, knows this life, the one he left me with, isn't all it's meant to be…that's how I feel. He'd understand why I am. He was a smart kid."

"I don't know what I could have done…should have done. I wasn't there for him." Mary's repeated and exhausting exercise only made her boy's death another reason for her to drink. Rather than live with the ghosts of the family home, Mary packed it all up, put everything in storage, moved further out into the desert and closer to a place where lost souls might find a new way to live tucked away into the VistaVue landscape scattered with scree and brush and where a frozen quart of chilled vodka is served daily. Mary had found a new place to live without her other life. A place where she could sit quietly and go back in time, periodically looking at her watch, and account for the minutes of her life, recalling exactly what her day was like while Danny, lost in the Mojave, searched for his water. By now she could expertly relive the moments like well-worn flashcards she would reshuffle, hoping to remix the memory and find a prayer of grace and forgiveness. Mary would break down in tears or pass out and then promise penance by volunteering at the local shelter or doing something 'In Danny's name.' Right now she was over at our place and divine forgiveness would have to wait. Right now, with my vodka and my *pura*, it was about absolution and abandoning the terrible guilt every mother would carry. The kind of guilt a quart can't quite get its arms around. That guilt had big, sharp teeth that can tear into you. I knew it well.

Needles Water + Wells, had leased the land for their working wells and the company was found negligent for not closing up and sealing the well—their leased land, their liability. They were ordered to pay Mary Wysocki. Then, her ex surfaced and made her life even more tragic and miserable by dragging her though the insipid version of family court justice and grabbing a share of the settlement. Danny was gone, the ex shows up, and now everyone's living in the dark, lost in the desert without her Danny.

"His dad was long gone by the time Daniel was two. His father never knew him, never wanted to know him. Fuck him. But I tell you that boy was special. Danny could see things. Like when he listened to music, he could see the notes in color. Just floating out there in front of him. At first, I thought he was full of shit. Then I got scared, worried there was something seriously wrong with him. His visions scared the crap out of him, too, but after we went to the doctors, had tests done and they explained what was going on, he sorta liked it when it happened.

"The day Danny died the other boy said Danny told him he could swear he saw water down in that well. Danny used to tell me he was always smelling hot buttered toast, or burned waffles or something.

Weird shit at the oddest hours and it didn't matter where he was.

Goddamit, this time it was water in a well."

"Synethesia," I said.

Mary looked at me, surprised. "Yeah, that's what his doctors told us. How'd you know?"

"Med school," I pointed to neatly stacked back issues of the Journal of the American Medical Association. "Sensory neurological pathways that send up colors, letters, numbers, or even smells. We used to think they were just figments of imagination, drug induced or simply behavioral consequences. I'm sure Danny had a history of seizures." I liked my voice of authority. I was pleasantly surprised at how I could still sound like a bona-fide, card-carrying physician. Who knows? Maybe I had a future in medicine.

"Seizures? Yeah, he had more than a few. The doctors told us that's to be expected with Synethesia...that boy was close to mystical. It didn't surprise me that he was the one trying to save them both. He was like that. Just something in him always wanted to do good. I truly believe that boy has a spirit that's coming back. In fact, an old Indian woman told me so. She said Daniel would come back to me someday. So, I have to believe—for him. And me."

Mary looked out the window. "That night sky feels like it could wrap me up in a blanket of desert air and make me feel safe...almost. He's always part of me. I feel him. And at times I think I can actually see him."

"Maybe that's what happens to the young souls. They take their time to leave us—if at all." I was trying my level best to be compassionate while staving off the effects of the past hours, and to my credit I think I was pulling it off.

Mary said her goodbyes, we wished her the best, and promised if there was anything she needed, anything, to give us a call or knock on our door. We could feel Mary Wysocki's love for her boy and I could see her son. I wished I, too, still had my Quentin, and this thought made this desert feel even more alone—and never the place where you meet people under the best of circumstances, or really, the best of anything. There's always some tweeker still rambling around in a junker searching for a new way to exist in the desert, or maybe a grieving mother still searching for her son. This place is like that. In Needles you're living on the red planet. Ask any shaman and he'll tell you that wherever you are out here is nowhere even near your life on that other planet the astronomers call Earth.

CHAPTER 11

CUB'S

The obvious need to replenish put us smack in the cooling embrace of the most wonderful retail store in downtown Needles. This would be my favorite liquor dispensary located adjacent to the Amtrak Station, on a main street, where the big palm is. Ask anyone. I've heard that some locals call it Palm's, but the sign reads Cub's. I like Cub's. No nonsense spirits at a no nonsense price, which coincidentally, can lead to nothing but a lot of nonsense, really.

Cub's is a brilliant empire. Owning a liquor mart in Needles is like printing money. Could it be any other way? Living in this hardtack part of the country suggests that ducking solar flares of 120 degrees is reason enough to raise the daily tumbler. Cub's has it right. The armory of spirits at this liquor emporium provisions the drinking public with popular name brands, and the cheaper, but no less effective off-label gin, vodka, scotch, and whiskey. No matter the pedigree, you'll find the courteous staff at Cub's—or Palm's—busy stacking the handsome, highballing rows, flagged with bright signage trolling for my attention. Cub's knows their market. And the market is good. Everyone, and I include myself, appreciates the sleek and shiny linoleum floors dotted with polished corrals boasting mountains of half-gallon party-size spirits sporting "STAFF RECOMMENDED" stickers. Boxed and stacked, the bottle, crates, and packaging are tagged with the bright promise of incredible, everyday savings. It's comforting to know Cub's cares about my wallet.

The well-coached Cub's counter team knows their stock in trade and chats up the boozy, but fickle fraternity with easy, chirpy patter about hops and barley and lagers and the 21-year-old single malt—"*Worth the wait*"—and blending the perfect frozen party Margarita—"*Don't forget the nachos!*"

Cub's is where I met Chet. He owns the place. Chet is just over six feet, thin framed, his heavily tanned face showing 70 years of desert folded into a sketchpad of etched lines. Chet's a bad mother fuck, no doubt about it. A former Needles cop, who, like a lot of desert creatures, knows how to bite when backed into corner. But if he likes you, Chet will break out his private stash of *Herradura*, pour a shot, and push it your way. A gesture that makes you feel like family—and that's when you're totally fucked.

"Welcome to the Mojave. Just like this desert, we're all a little thirsty." Chet motions bottoms up and we are enjoying his expensive tequila.

"Straight up Needles." I toss the squat, thick glass back right along with Chet. And I, too, feel closer to Needles, at least for that moment. We smile and nod, and he sits down behind the counter in his leather high-back chair. It's hard not to love this corner of Chet's World. The worn, deep maroon leather carries noticeable cracks matching the creases that line Chet's thin face. Once this desert gets a hold on you, you wear it—a short syringe of Botox maybe for Chet's 71st? Yeah, right, I got enough going on without fucking with this guy, Chet.

Chet pours another for us and the tequila flames our love for all things Cub's. I'm feeling the warm flush of Chet's generous shots mix with the cooling chill of the store's industrial AC. This is nice, and even nicer with the friendly background chatter of people selling liquor for a living. I think I even catch the background sounds of *Kenny G* putting a bluebird on everyone's shoulder. All in all, Cub's is a very pleasant shopping experience. I especially like the smartly arranged mini-bar featuring the short travelers for the ride home.

And I can also appreciate the XL gallon plastic vessels of which, we all agree, are perfectly suited to fortify any desert weekend. When partnered with the 48-pack of spicy Slim Jims or "hand cut venison" flavored extra-bold MSG Nitrate-infused jerky, well, my friend, you are most definitely making a statement. By comparison, my eight civil-sized liters of Stoli, cartons of Menthols, and packs of Orange Nicorettes are welcomed with a smile and the shared approval of the efficient counter staff, winking that indeed, I do have it all under control. Yessir. This is Cub's, no judgments here. Except my purchase of Nicorettes did cause Chet to shoot me a look that made me feel like a pussy who can't handle some fucking, harmless nicotine and why am I even bothering with a piss poor substitute for the real deal. Chet can't comprehend that I smoke and chew the hard, gummy square for a man-sized wallop of nicotine that would deliver a severe case of angina as his blood platelets occlude, trying like hell to boot up and push through his thickened, plaque-coated, opaque arteries.

So now it's a little before noon, and I'm sitting in my car, the engine idling, top's up. The welcomed shade from that lone palm casts what passes for a shadow over the Speedster. I fiddle with the car's erratic air conditioning hoping to fend off the midday sun. The vents stutter against the high-noon radiation burning through the chocolate brown canvas top. In this part of the world, just keeping the interior cool is a miracle of modern science. I think I'm getting better at staving off the coupe's red leather from branding me like a hot poker stuck in my back.

My radio reception moves somewhere between festive Mexican and mindless Adult Contemporary. I'm pretty convinced this Mexican shit kicks the doors off Adult Contemporary, even with *Toto, Ambrosia, and Madonna* in the lineup. But I think maybe this is only the happy result of Chet's booze, my *pharma* grade, and the courteous Cub's staff. It's true what they say about terrific customer service. It does make a difference.

A knuckle raps on my passenger window, startles me, and brings me back to the parking lot.

It's Chet.

He slides into the seat trying to find a comfortable way to assemble his tired frame into this small capsule of German automotive engineering that's a bit tight for the aging patriarch.

"Fuck doctor, you trying to get out of here without talking to me about your prescription pad…'cuse me, *our* scrip pad?" Chet is referring to the kind of 'scrips' he can make a boatload of money with. Pharmaceutical Fucking A-1 Liquid Cocaine prescriptions written by yours truly. It's good to have a physician-on-call in the desert. Just ask Chet.

"Demerol, Oxy, Coke, or Dilaudid would be good."

"I can scrip for coke, and call it done, but that's as good as it gets right now; we both know what's real," I say, keeping my eyes on Chet, waiting for his reaction. I glance in my rearview mirror, and all I can see is heat. Fucking Needles. Must be 120 by now.

Chet shows no patience for anything else but business. Chet likes his money. He likes a conversation to go his way and I know he likes his *cocaina* pure.

I notice the bulge in Chet's beltline. His .38 Firestorm revolver may be super light, but Chet's made it clear that his pistola can tear a hole. The grip, a rich pebbled brown looks good with the smooth, buffed, satin nickel finish. How do I know this? Chet loves his gun and in-between tequila shots, has proudly pulled out the shooter and walked me through some of the gun's finer points. And yes, there are stories. Some of which might even be true.

"*Nada, para ustedes, mi amigos.*" My broken Spanish is an attempt at making this uncomfortable business meeting less so, and perhaps seem innocent, friendly—hell, maybe even likeable. But Chet will have none of this. He turns the vent toward him, hoping to get some of my Porsche's AC chill flowing across his light blue, worn denim shirt. I break out my vial and with a flick, I load the blade of my penknife with a little of the pure white, and raise it to Chet. He looks at me, and accepts my quick bump as an offering of sorts.

Chet delicately snorts off the end of my knife. "Sweet Jaysus, that's what I'm talking 'bout." He rubs his nose hard. "Damn, Doc, I love this thing we got going…"

"Way it's always been between us," I say, a feeble stab at being friendly.

Chet and I go back about a year ago, when we came to know each other. Chet is a retired cop who discovered some past paper on me and, along with information from an internal Needles PD source, decided that I would be a very good friend to have, because as I said, Chet does like his money. Chet also knows that he has this little town wired and can pretty much do anything he wants, just as long as everyone gets theirs. Chet had known something was up when I first walked into Cub's. He noted my large liquor order, my gold Patek, even glanced out the window and nodded toward the Speedster and made small talk about never seeing many cars like that driving through *his* town.

Never having seen me before and he being an ex-cop, Chet got to thinking about me. A lot. Chet could count on his old cop habits still getting his dick hard, so he started prying. His connection on the force dug around and uncovered other scraps of legal work. Chet and his pal started to stitch together a compelling story about a hugely successful plastic surgeon out of Los Angeles—a Dr. Dominic Martinez, who happens to have a predilection for certain lifestyle amenities, like ampules of liquid cocaine, and a bullet proof method of acquiring the purest Peruvian on the market; illegal prescriptions—and that this physician had some past issues with those fucking badass and pissed off Russian gangsters. One, in particular, who was secreted away in the witness protection program. Chet is a wise old bird who sees an employment opportunity right here in Needles. So, instead of finishing his day off with his usual shot of *Herradura* and an easy ride back to the poolside Kingdom and thick steaks with his wife, CC, well, dear old Chet starts to become a bona-fide workaholic.

God knows he has the time.

Chet's efforts pay off. It doesn't take him long to knit together a chain of events. Soon enough he has me playing the role of their personal Leprechaun skipping across fields of green and taking them to the end of the rainbow for their own pot of gold. My illicit and questionable past is their very fine future that would most definitely add buckets of money to Chet's pension. I was going to come in very handy for Chet and his family. Chet approached me with his own *quid pro quo* agreement. My scrip pads would pen his silence. That was his deal. Take it or leave it. There weren't a lot of options to his offer. I would write the scrips. Chet, CC and the boys would manage the inventory and distribution. They had contacts, guns, and should they need them, enough boys in blue lined all the way up to Scottsdale, Arizona. Nobody was going to interfere with the family. Chet bullied his way up and down the Colorado. We got busy.

We liked the cash. I was burying stacks of bills in the middle of nowhere out in the wasteland of Needles. The Mojave became my very own bank. Withdrawals were a little tough, but you couldn't beat the hours.

"Ok, when we gonna get cranking again?" Chet is polite and appears patient, but that's just the pharmaceutical coke. It's pretty mellow and shows a nice, even buzz.

"By tomorrow." I say, ready for him to go.

"You know Doc, let's not fuck this up. It's a sweet-ass little money shaker." He rubs his nose again and throws a furtive smile my way. I look at him and I see he's starting to squirm under the influence of the Speedster's pathetic AC, the rush of my *cocaina*, and the heat of his shots. He's uncomfortable, and I like that.

"You're covered…maybe sometime you can come out to our place, and grab a bite. I like company." I also mention that we can fire off a few rounds with his Firestorm, kind of a bonding thing.

Chet shakes his head. "That VistaVue hole in the ground? Never been out to that piece of paradise and never the fuck will. I like a large house, a pool, plenty of shade, and some room around me." Chet is feeling like its way past his time to exit.

He fumbles with the door's hardware. "How the fuck do I get out of this thing?"

"Same way you came in, use the door," I reach over and pop the handle.

"Miserable piece of shit," Chet grumbles, his phlegm rattling around. Must be time for a nap. He rubs his nose.

"I'll be sure to pass that on to Dr. Porsche." I wink, knowing Chet knows nothing about Ferdinand or fine German machinery.

This low profile, vintage Speedster is built for the road, not parking lots, and certainly not for a six foot, coked 70-year-old ex-cop sitting in the Needles' midday sun. Chet struggles to pull his long, gangly frame out of the compact interior. I watch him slowly ramble toward the Chet Magic Kingdom of shiny promises and manufactured pleasantries stacked amid our favorite lubricants. Like I said, a little Botox could take years off his face, but not the stories off his life.

Chet had me, and I had a few loose ends with Maxim Gorikav and the issue of a dead wife who decided that my operating table was as good as any exit ramp to leave this planet. Fuck. Fucked. Fuck it. Died on me. In my office. In my hands. Of all people, a Russian fucking bad guy's fucking wife—seriously? The in-surgery complications that caused her death, and now the mother fucking complications to my life were a shit-storm of nothing but complicated. This was not good at all. I hate the guys who can kill you. And they all wanted to kill me. *Batter up. Now playing for the DEA, wearing Number Fucked-Up-His-Life, Dr. Dominic Martinez,* and that's how scrips, the Russians, and the Needles' ex-cop, old white guy, Chet, are all playing on the same team. Wonderful. I shift the Porsche, crank up the Mexican music, light a Menthol, and leave the parking lot to a lone palm tree and the tequila-shooting-Chet and his amazingly courteous staff who are as shiny as the sleek and polished linoleum flooring. Glancing in my rearview mirror, I can see the heat waves vaporizing the Cub's Liquors sign as shimmering particles of a past mix with the day's dust. My AC burps a cold blast, the Speedster smoothly whines into 4th and I am on the road and it all feels chill. I think maybe I am starting to like the sounds of Mexico more than I thought. *Una Paloma Blanco* comes on and I crank it up. Sweet. It's about a white bird locked in a cage or something. Like I said, good Mexican can kick the doors off Adult Contemporary. *Buenos Dias, Chet. Pinche tu madre.*

CHAPTER 12

SCRIPS

The mile road out of the VistaVue lot is hardpan dirt that winds and twists down to an intersection welcoming me to a more civilized asphalt that offers me a speedy entrance to the rest of the world.

I like my dirty, dusty road out.

It's what I want from the hardscrabble outland of Needles. Nothing easy. Nothing soft. It's a tough-as-nails road that with every shift through the long, winding corners kicks up a slide under the Porsche's wheels. Maybe that's why VistaVue is working so well in my life. The road ahead is the road behind. It's a dry, pebbled, compacted dirt, uneven in spots, and even a little questionable about where it's all going, but you would like this road and the way this coupe drives it. You would like to throw this Speedster through dirty, round sweeping curves that always show a little slide under it. Going fast is fun. Smoking, shifting, working the pedals and even fucking with the car radio while making the Speedster scream around this snaky desert road is even more fun. The road down leads to the intersection. Dirt meets asphalt on this direct shot into Needles. Once I'm on it, the Speedster grips this very nice road that, indeed, shows us all the wonders of honest engineering. I am pushing the Porsche into first, winding it up and through the gears. I only wish my mind could work as smoothly as this power and torque, overriding my demons and letting me find another gear and another way to make this desert work for me. For us. My world seems forever flat. I could have had it all—fuck that, I *did* have it all. I get on the newer paved road. It is black, smoothed with only hints of the desert dirt blowing across it. Maybe someday I can find my way home. And further away from who I used to be.

The steering is tight. The Speedster hugs this stretch, and I am moving sweetly. I listen to the engine throw down and it feels good as I press the pedal, the obedient machine efficiently responding while the hot, dry air rushes by me, signaling the distant promise of whatever is down this road. I am on my way to writing scrips and getting paid handsomely. This is why I am smoking a Menthol, enjoying the flatness of the late evening sun painting the horizon with a heat that acts like a drying agent varnishing desert colors. This is also why I am carrying my Glock, which you would also like as much as driving my Speedster.

Speeding straight into the evening, I look over at the piece sitting on the passenger seat neatly holstered next to two magazines, each carrying thirteen dangerous .40 caliber bullets that can do a lot of damage to everything the round might meet. Everything. One in the clip and two back-ups gives me thirty-nine rounds. I bought this gun and had it outfitted with a superb, high-intensity light that throws a white illumination.

The brochure says "big target illumination," and the brochure is not only right, but nicely written. It cheerily carries informative diagrams highlighting each feature of blowing things up with a handgun, and the well-designed callouts show us the science behind shooting things dead.

The white and bright high-intensity light can even illuminate small targets. The reference to "small targets" is a bit disquieting. I'm not so certain the American public is buying a Glock as their weapon of choice to click off a few rounds and take care of their small varmints. Then again, it was exactly what I wanted for my own particular rat problem.

After our liquor emporium meeting, where wildly successful outlaws meet in parked cars in parking lots, Chet called and wanted me over at his place around 6:00 in the evening. He didn't make an offer to bring Helena. Fine with me. She doesn't need to be part of Chet's rodeo. Writing scrips and getting Chet and his companions to fill and sell was, so far, working out pretty well. Still, I'd seen a few moments frozen in time where the family, bags of money, piles of *pharma,* and poolside parties with ex-cops might need a little back up, which is only me and my bullets.

Chet's phone call is a mandate on how we play together and move even more product.

"Doc, we wanna step up the delivery and start having you write a little more, know what I mean, *keemosabie?*"

"Of course I know what the fuck you mean." I say, looking out the window of the Airstream. Helena looks up from her book; she knows who I'm talking to and only gives it a moment. She'll hear more later. She's used to our Chet calls.

"So what the fuck, let's all get busy." Chet says.

"I hear you, Chet, and I feel you, brother," (I think that calling Chet, 'Brother,' is a terrific device that may cue important male bonding.) "…but we have to be a little more, ah, judicious in how we—"

Chet hacks, his wheezy smoker's cough interrupts. "Don't use those fucking *fiddycent* words with me, my fine *Federales* friend. I want what I want, and I know what I know." For Chet, this exchange passes for clever.

I politely point out and respond with a gentle memo: "Let me remind you on how many scrips of pharmaceutical mother fucking cocaine we can fill before we hit Defcon Fucking Plaid and we light up the switchboard, and then we can all kiss this venture farewell, good-bye, *Adios comprades, feliz navidad—comprende?*" Chet comes back at me with a lightening round.

"Last month, we turned about $200,000 and could've easily doubled that. We got people who are hungry to turn and burn all the way up the Colorado River. This is a big stretch of desert. I got us in, through, and paid up with everybody who is anyone."

I am impressed with Chet's arithmetic. Generally, that's the domain of his better half, Cynthia.

"I like the bags of money, too. I'm just saying to dial back so nobody gets hurt…"

"Nobody's gonna get hurt 'cept maybe you, mother fucker…but you're a Doc, so maybe you got something for the pain…"

I can hear Chet light a cigarette and it sounds good, but then the visual of his esophageal cough and aging desert lungs suggest I, too, try to cut back and wait another fifteen minutes, or at least until I am on the road. This is hard because just talking to the Chet makes me want to seriously chain-smoke my Menthols. I pop an Orange Nicorette. I've heard the stories about the man, and after being in bed with him, I can tell you that all of them are true. It's been said there are bodies buried out there in the vast stretch. I think you can see the souls buried in the canyons of Chet's thin and sharp face. He's greedy, connected, and doesn't give a shit because he doesn't have to. He, too, can make people disappear, and like me, has done some identity work on his *compadres*.

His past with the Needles force gives him and his two sons, Phil and Roy, also former Needles' *policia*, the world on a string. So yeah, when I talk to Chet, I want to get in and get out. That Firestorm .38 tucked into his leather belt and faded dungarees is just a small reminder of the big shit that can get into a new strain of very wrong, very fast.

"It is what it is, and I can only do so much. I know the backend of scrips and I gotta say, the mantra here, Chet, is pretty simple: don't get greedy or you most certainly will go down, period. End of story and have a nice fucking day, if you catch my drift." I wasn't overtly glib in pointing out a few of the facts that demand attention in our line of work. Although, I am not so sure Chet liked where this was going. Putting a cap on revenue is not what senior management wants to hear.

"I got bills like any asshole out here," Chet coughed a stringy hack. "'Tween those boys, trucks, and them Mercedes, we got overhead, Doc. We're all looking for a little scratch to make the day go down just that much better. Chrissakes, don't even get me started on CC…I know she has her eye on that new Caddy."

"Jesus-Fuck-Me-Christ. Do I look like your broker?"

"Get a grip, Doc. Just saying we got bills."

I hear his tension lighten up. We agree on a meet at his house, and we agree that life is a motherfucker, but that our biz is making it rain.

We don't want to fuck it up. So, we agree, as outlaws do, to get what we want so we can get to the other side of a payday.

"Tonight, at your place, scrips with me and get you what you need—within reason."

We both know that our lives are a loose arrangement that covers each other while running hard from fear, loathing, envy, revenge, and a few other biblical points of interest that Moses—or Charlton Heston—must have covered. We both want the same thing, sort of. A goddamn revenue stream that can quietly allow us to live the American Dream right smack here in Needles and maybe even let us both give back to the community. Ok, I made that last part up, but still, Cub's does sponsor a little league team and there's always my anonymous donation to AA, a church group, or something, and it all looks good with the Chamber of Commerce. So yeah, Chet and me? We got it all going on. Except that we don't trust each other, which is pretty common in a lot of business partnerships and an equal number of marriages. But what the fuck, other than the occasional lying, guns, ammo, and drugs, it all seems to be working out pretty nicely.

"Your place?" I ask, accepting Chet's invite.

"My place." Chet reciprocates like a good host.

"Six?"

"Perfect, dinner's on me. I got a side of cow so bring your *appetito.*"

"Who else?"

"Phil and Roy."

Chet's sons are a pain in the ass. Boys who like to push their weight around. Former cops who like their pickups big and their boats bigger so they can out-throttle anyone out on the Mighty Colorado River. It's no picnic being in bed with these two, but Mother of God have you ever stacked a hundred-fucking-large into a leather bag on a hot after-noon chased with an ice cold Pabst and a smoke that's every bit as good as the one you light up after sex? One hit and you want that rush again.

Money is a great equalizer, and we like it so much. It does apparently seem to keep us all at the trough, enjoying our scotch and grilled rib eye and reading from the same playbook—for now.

"Want me to bring dessert?"

"Yeah, bring me some of them big thick stacks of green with a cherry on top." Chet thinks he is funny. His laugh triggers a harsh, rattling, coughing attack that's so severe I'm not sure he'll live. He does.

We hang up.

I take a cold shower, turn up the AC and sit down for a minute to check in with Helena. She lines up a few rails, pours a cold Pabst over ice, and lights a Menthol for me.

"Don't be stupid." She is looking out for me. "Don't do anythingk dumb." Apparently she has a list for me ranging from stupid to dumb.

"Anything else I should not be?"

"Don't be dangerous whit heem and deese boys and heese CC… promisingk me?"

"Not me, baby. I am like a ninja, in and out, top to bottom and home before the stars come out." I kiss her, inhaling her care and concern. She kisses me back, harder. "And deese?" She says coyly, dangling the Speedster keys.

Time to go. Time for the meet at the Kingdom of Chet and CC. Time to fly. I am speeding down the road listening to my inner child telling me to get the fuck as far away from the Chet Ranch as fast as I can, but for now, the responsible adult behind the wheel is happy to have a little Glockmeister as a backup plan out on this playground.

Nobody likes a shootout, but pistols do make a point. I am not going to sabotage my current life for Chet, Phil, and Roy because they are not comprehending that the FDA, and other very smart and organized federal branches of our nation's government, keep a pretty close eye for errant and egregious scripwriting—particularly for 100% pure laboratory-tested cocaine that would make the country of Peru salivate. I could tell you how better living through chemistry can transform the contents of my liquid dropper into the purest cocaine flake on the planet, but then I'd have to kill you. At least you'd go out with a smile.

I love this stretch. The fine, smooth asphalt carries the Speedster straight into the horizon as the evening light plays against every shade of brown and beige and dust. I am watching the speedometer tick up to 90, and I am sitting in red leather seats in a vintage Porsche that feels spectacularly weighted and grounded as it races on this straight edge, a black ribbon that can take you from here to somewhere. You would like the drive. Even with the Glock sitting shotgun.

93

CHAPTER 13

FIESTA

Shifting the Speedster up the circular driveway, I note that The Chet and Cynthia Kingdom serves as a cautionary tale. Doing hard time in this desert could lead one to believe that, yes, the adobe-ranchero-*con*-cactus architecture actually starts to make sense. The possibility of suffering from a mutant strain of architectural Needles Stockholm-Syndrome frightens me: "We were against the cactus garden at first, but once we saw how the fountain and desert gnomes worked, well, we just had to have it!"

Then again, after being out here for nearly two years I can believe in anything. Nothing surprises me anymore. I was told by some guy who had been moving around in a Cranberry Red 1974 Pontiac Sahara station wagon that the desert is just going to swallow up whatever you believe, and hand you something you won't ever talk about again. The guy seemed like he knew what he was talking about. I liked him driving a Sahara in the Mojave. It worked for me. I took it as a sign. I was ready to believe in anything. That happens a lot out here. The desert is good at telling you what you need to know, at least that was my take on this torched outland.

I park next to the shiny and suspect Auto Row of BMW's, custom F150's, Mercedes, and a spotty number of new American muscle cars that make my Speedster's low-slung, German profile look a little lost among the steroid, horse-powered crowd. I do a quick bump of my *pharma*, pop two Orange Nicorettes, check my Glock, and tuck it under my seat along with the extra rounds. Phil and Roy will be here along with God knows who else, and I figure that if the shit starts going down for whatever reason, I can cleverly find my way to the Speedster and work it all out. No, wait. Recalibrate. I am counting on "clever" to get me out of a Chet-style jam?

I may be giving myself too much credit. I rethink and come up with a better idea—tuck the fucking Glock securely into the back of my belt and make a note that while *clever* is admirable, in the event of a Chet, Phil, and Roy meltdown, clever may be just a tad overrated. Like I said, nobody wants a shootout. My brilliant decision of strapping the Glock leads me to believe that I am very smart, but in fact, it's just that I'm feeling slightly euphoric, which I attribute to equal parts *pura,* Nicorettes, and Glock ballistics. I fire up a Menthol just to take this moment to the next level, and I am immediately rewarded. My brain tells me it's all fucking good even if it fucking isn't. Chet and Cynthia's Kingdom overlooks a small, shallow valley. I take a minute and enjoy the way the late sun sends a brushed evening patina across the wide, endless valley, the shadows and light playing up the lines of hill and rock. I like this light. I like this time of the desert. It's lovely. I've been to a few of these poolside parties and spent some time working Chet, Cynthia, and his crew so we can all feel good about our business. I can hear the sound of a live Mariachi band, their bass guitars and romanced vocals drifting out, flying into the early evening desert. Mariachi music mixes well with the smoky, carnivorous smell of big meat seared with Chet's own BBQ sauce. Chet's proud of his thick, dark, brown brew that he's sampled to the Cub's Frequent Buyer customers, of which I am one. I can hear the buzz of poolside conversations that feel almost friendly. I know this crowd and they like their money, drugs, and sex. Not all that different from the Hollywood Hills, just hotter, flatter and with a lot less money to buy their way out of desperate.

And because a number of guests are outlaws, you never quite know who's pulling up behind you on a darkened, desert road. I take a deep drag, flick the last of the Menthol into the massive, ornate fountain, walk up to the large, double Mahogany and glass front door and press the bell. I look back at the bubbling fountain and notice an absence of birds except for a single, lone cactus wren dipping its small body into the cooling water. The music is louder now. The petite wren shakes and stutters, drying its wings and flies off to its Saguaro, or Cholla nest protected by the dense gauntlet of piercing, needle-sharp cactus. Smart.

When you meet Chet's wife, Cynthia, you are struck by how petite the woman is. Standing just shy of 5ft and entering her late fifties, Cynthia has employed a questionable regime of erratic dieting, conditioning, trainers, and food trends to help her battle the progress of an aging metabolism. So far she's managed—pretty well—although I might suggest a little eye work just to get those lids up, easily taking off an extra five. "Pert and perky" might be the lazy way to categorize Cynthia. Salon blonde, blue eyed, with a face that isn't quite as hard as the heat. It's easy enough to imagine that at one time the younger Cynthia turned heads.

She likes her jewelry, and lots of it, preferably in silver. She loves her stones turquoise, big, veined, and important. Her Cadillac, white. And her Margarita's with any party and her men, well, she likes her men just like Chet. Which of course, means she likes her money made by men like Chet.

Cynthia moved to Needles with her first husband, who was also a cop, when she was just twenty-eight. She has a drive for business, but her real skill is working men and driving them.

And like Cynthia herself, her various enterprises have fallen to fits and starts, but the girl keeps on plugging. Chet likes this about his wife and will tell you how he noticed this right away, when they first met out at the shooting range. He liked the way she could load a pistol and click off a few with the best of the boys, and she seemed to like his hand-tooled leather holster. Between the guns, money, and high life, it only made sense for the two of them to do something together. Cynthia will let you know, of course, that she is Chet's salvation and he would be lost without her and that this place on the hill is all her doing. "Honey, I insisted that all the tile come from Nogales. Poor Chet nearly choked on the price…'til I went down on him, then that boy was all mine. As you can see," CC will tell you, pointing at the tile, laughing at her candid anecdote about how sexy she can be. "I know what it takes to make my husband come 'round."

Chet usually comes back with his standard, rehearsed, "Darlin' you know that story's only half true…betcha' can figger out which half."

Chet is proud of his wife. He'll point out how much he leans on "CC's" vision and will remind you that his downtown Needles liquor mart, Cub's, just wouldn't be Cub's without "CC getting out there, kicking ass, and taking names. Hell, that little girl made me and that store, and goddamn if she couldn't franchise the fucker." While Cynthia will take credit for their "Ranchero Living" and the successful expansion of the liquor store, she will also let you know that in no way are Phil and Roy her boys.

"Chet's kids, all him, all his," she pointed out one afternoon when I was over picking up cash, counting out scrips, and lounging poolside. Little CC lives large in Needles, dealing with Chet, Cub's, and the incidentals like our scrip business. I know she prefers that you call her Cynthia, although after a few Margaritas, she often refers to herself as CC. So, Cynthia knows how to play all sides, and if you know this, you will understand, and maybe even appreciate, how much work she puts into the Kingdom.

"Doctor, glad you could join our little fiesta." Cynthia greets me with a kiss and has her hostess buzz going from the early afternoon cocktails fanned by the flirty rhythm of the Mariachis. She offers me a wink, raises her celebratory Margarita, taps it with a ringed finger, and gestures outside to the poolside gathering.

"Chet and the boys are gonna be so happy to see you." She smiles. "The year's been good for all of us."

"I could definitely use one of those." I suggest, avoiding her buzzed, cozy cheerleading. I nod to her thick, colorful fiesta glass.

"Couldn't we all honey? Chet has me a on a three-Maggie limit, but fuck it, we all know he can't count." Cynthia snickers at her own joke and hazily leans into my shoulder, recruiting me as her confidant and drinking soldier-in-arms as we walk across the massively tiled living room and out toward the patio.

Thankfully, my synapses are firing with my own pre-fiesta chemical happier hour and I'm pretty confident that with a rail of blow, chased with a double Margarita, I could even connect with Cynthia's blousy buzz. My Nicorettes are keeping my bloodstream nicotine-rich, but I do like to smoke, so I light up a Menthol, kicking it all into overdrive. I exhale, slowly.

Yeah, I'm good with how my immediate release of dopamine, serotonin, endorphin, and adrenaline pathways are all pulling in synch, like a brilliant rowing crew manned by a featherweight female Harvard coxswain who enjoys fucking the whole team after a sweaty, mile-long row.

The patio is spotted with the desert consortium of tanned people and boots and jeans, sandaled toes, shorts, bathing suits, bikinis, and lots of cleavage hanging on to the end of the day. It's as if the late 70's were found and updated into a kind of new desert makeover where the hairstyles, mustaches, and clothes, along with the obligatory desert silver and nouveau gold bling is groomed by the very newest of new money. Everyone has that early evening heat on. The lubricated mingling of the patio people is a delicious elixir of music, alcohol, dope, and an entitled sense that they have life by the *cajones,* even if most of it is lived outside the law.

That some of the patio people are former cops is ironic. Immediately, I see Chet motion for me.

He smiles and shows a lot of teeth. He is happy. Or at least I think he thinks that's what happy looks like. I grin and raise my glass.

The cactus wren is home by now, nestled deep into the hole, guarded by pointed lances. She has pulled up the gate. The desert is moving into the night.

The patio and pool is a tribute to carved Arizona Flagstone, and maybe CC's expert blow jobs. Chet's custom, industrial-grade BBQ spit easily handles an entire side of steer and is a monument to CC's high desert living. The Phil and Roy show are working the guests. I catch their nod toward me and we all know why I'm here. The Mariachi band picks up the tempo and the beautiful ranchero people dance around the pool patio trying hard to show a version of rhythm.

A hot, young, breasty blonde wearing aviator shades and metallic-gold bikini bottoms with a white, fishnet cover-up, dances up to me and asks if I have a light. Before I can answer, she puts a spoon of something up my nose. It's bad blow, but I pretend to like it, light her smoke and she smiles while dancing off before I can flirt back. I was going to give her a taste of my *pura,* so she missed the fuck out. I watch her shake to the beat as her skimpy bikini bottom slowly rides up her firm, cocoa brown ass. She seemed nice.

Welcome to the Needles high life. I feel right at home with excessive poolside soirees. I come straight from the loins of the fucking Hollywood Hills, where my patio and pool were generously sprinkled with heavy A and D-Listers either on their way up, or trying like hell to make last minute coinage that might salve the wounds of a crashing career. It's hard to watch a death spiral turbocharged by bad decisions, aging bodies, unscrupulous agents, or the fickle whim of life's wheel of fortune spinning out of control. Yes, I know this festive ecosystem very well. Nonetheless, I remind myself that I'm here strictly on business, and I try mightily to maintain the sober decorum expected of a former surgeon who carries an impressive resume of work for the Federal Government for fuck's sake. I like to remind myself that I have rubbed shoulders with Russians who would think nothing of stealing every fucking car parked in front of this party pad, torch the place to the ground, go out for some greasy Chinese, and then come back and torch it some more.

The young, paunchy waiter comes by and I discreetly slip a five into his top pocket. *Sure, I would love another, add some liquor to this ice, would you, compadre? Gracias.* Although I'm not sure how he's done it, but the evening's host appears to be have hung an entire side of beef on a huge, stainless steel rotisserie, and he's wielding a large paintbrush dripping with his very own brand of Chet's Famous BBQ sauce. "What's up, doctor? Lots of good people here…fact I used to work with some of 'em. I think I even arrested a few of the motherfuckers."

Chet winks, the cigarette dangles lightly from the corner of his thin lips. It bounces as he talks. More loosened hacking graveling into the laugh. The cigarette's gray and black ash packet finally falls lightly into the warm air, softly floating down onto the pointed toe of Chet's black, pebbled snakeskin boot. "I know Phil and Roy wanna chat some, and we can do a little damage in the back." Chet hacks as he brushes the meat with his deep brown sauce and lights up another smoke. I grin and nod at Phil and Roy as the evening patio posers bump along with some kind of white desert dance grind that must amuse the hell out of the smiling Mariachis. *Chinga tu madre mother fuckers,* they are thinking as they play for Chet's patio people.

"Phil and Roy might want to get the high sign, and retire to your office," I suggest.

"Meat?" Chet slices a thick, black slab charred piece. I look past the white Chinette plate holding the cut.

"What, you like it bloody?" Chet asks, looking slightly offended by my lack of fiesta table manners. "More of them beans?" He asks, lifting his jaw toward a simmering black kettle of the side dish.

"No, I'm good. A few cocktails and some of that business *mo-mo* and we should be good to go. I've got an early tee time," I joke, finishing my second Double Maggie Extra Salt. It stings my sunburned lips and almost makes me want to find that girl in the white fishnet with the bad blow who is lost in the sea of delightful pool people working the Ranchero Living food chain. She's out bumping and grinding with someone she'll regret.

"Like them Mariachis? Two bills for four hours, and that is original fucking Mexican, my friend. Not some half-ass DJ'd salsa La Bamba shit."

I smile at Chet's appreciation for *Musica Folklorico* and look over at the gold-toothed musicians sweating as they thump out the beat for these Tommy Bahama-wearing assholes who dig a fiesta as long as it comes with freebies courtesy of anyone. CC's playing hostess to the beautiful patio people. I notice she gets a look from Chet. She grabs another Margarita from the stocky, middle-aged waiter, and heads to the back of the house. CC is nobody's fool. She can smell money, no matter what Chet has on the grill. And she likes it charred, rare, bundled, sliced and carved. Anyway she can get it, and the getting's been pretty awesome. Always is with Chet and the boys, compliments of yours truly. Not that they were hurting to make a dollar, but with my counsel and doctoring, the desert has opened her loamy, soft, hot thighs and invited the boys over for a righteous roll in the hay. Those buckets of money have everyone lusting for more.

"Let's do this thing." And for some reason, when I say this, the thought of Gary Gilmore pops into my head. Weird. Must be the nicotine triggering a release of even more serotonin. Maybe it's just the Mariachi music that I like so much. Chet puts his paintbrush back in the aluminum pail of sauce, grabs his bottle of beer, a crumpled pack of smokes, and we leave the patio people to their free fiesta. Chet glad-hands his way through the buzzed crowd.

I am following. CC and the boys are at the far end of the pool and disappear through the floor-to-ceiling glass sliders into the house. The loose patio people have no idea where the hosts have gone and could care even less. The *musica* thumps loudly as sparklers come out, roman candles are lit, and a buzzed partier pops an emergency road flare. It's all very drunk and loose, and the party goes to another level when someone follows with a powerful M-80 explosive into the pool. The loud percussion shoots a nuclear plume of water high up into the air, showering a few of the dancers. This excites everyone.

It's quite a fiesta, especially when the Mariachi's break into a heavy brass Herb Alpert number and sends the fringe fuckers dancing and moving into each other. The warm evening on the Chet and CC patio feels like a safe place to lose yourself, so they do.

We sit in the large, leathered, tiled office that is Chet's, or Cynthia's, depending on whom you're talking to. Phil and Roy are sitting on either side of Chet, who's holding court slouched back on the expanse of the leather sofa dotted with big, brass studs, while Cynthia sits off to the side in an extra-large leather wingback. The chair seems to swallow her. It makes her look even smaller, but no less formidable. I am also sitting in a deeply cushioned leather chair facing my business partners. We are gathered to discuss how we can continue to discreetly move even more pure *cocaina* by writing even more scrips, and in doing so, keep the Brady Bunch in heavy clover.

"Doc, let's do a little math here and figure that if we could get a *hunnerd* grand of medicinal, we could cut it and make a nice living." Clearly Chet is making a vain attempt at being chairman of this confab. I see his boys give the old man plenty of room to hold court.

Cynthia is giving him the eye. Clearly, he has no clue how to run this fucking business.

"That would be a good thing, but writing a hundred grand for scrip pharmaceutical cocaine is, well, a mother fucking lot of eye surgery." My voice trails off as I begin to sense that is not what the Chet family wants to hear from their government-sponsored physician.

I mention, yet again, that pharmaceutical cocaine is used mainly as an anesthetic for eye surgeries. The group looks at me. The eye surgery reference is lost. Chet, Cynthia, Phil, and Roy all light up at the same time, and exhale, blowing smoke across the air-conditioned office that's centered around a large, oval glass coffee table. They collectively nod and show an affirmation that, indeed, eye surgeries and lots of them are the magic sauce to successfully attaining pure *pharma*. It seems they appreciate my lesson in ocular medicine. Maybe I do have their interest.

"Here's how I see this thing: last month we moved heavy medicinal blow, and if we cut our Mallinckrodt..." (My reference to the only pharmaceutical manufacturer of pharma grade cocaine impresses the family as I see Chet turn to CC and raise an eyebrow acknowledging that indeed, they do have the right physician for the job.)

"We can make enough dough and everyone home happy, but I can't, we can't, expect to write and move and fill more scrips than that."

Roy interjects, "So, what you're sayin' is that—"

"What I'm saying is, look, we got about ten people working for us moving scrips, and we pushed enough *pharma* to light up Peru. So, now we have to back off. That's what I'm not only saying, but that has to be what we're doing." I light a Menthol, break out my vial and scoop some *fina* with my penknife and take a hit. I place the vial in the middle of the table and look at Chet. Cynthia looks at me, then at Chet. Phil and Roy are looking at each other. Cynthia empties a fingertip of tobacco out of her cigarette and sprinkles a generous dose of my *cocaina* into it, twists the ends of the cigarette, lights it up, takes a big drag, holds it in then slowly exhales. Her eyes lazily drift with the onset of her toke. With every drag on her loaded smoke, I mentally time out the release of chemicals.

I visualize her neurons drafting the lead car in the Daytona 500. I am sure she is hitting around 223 mph, and although the steep bank of curves present a hint of trouble, CC seems to be in control of the straightaway. The trigger of pure hydrochloride firing in her brain is my friend. The supercharged, cocaine-toking-CC flatly announces what I greet as good news for my future at this fiesta. I'm even feeling good enough to toy with the thought of finding the especially sexy bad-blow-aviator-chick. Probably not my best idea of the night. I snap back to the attentive family still sitting in front of me. I have work to do.

"I think Doc is right," CC proclaims as dopamine central fires up the horsepower and sends it racing down the track. "He has a point. We shouldn't get greedy, just enjoy the ride, and be smart. Hell, Doc's been good to us." CC is on a roll. She very much likes her Marlboro liberally iced with the finest pharmaceutical cola. She's right, I have been good—for so many of life's incidentals that include money, drugs, and more money.

CC raises her Margarita in my direction. I like her gesture graciously charged by the heady contents of my vial. I'm looking for more backup from anyone gathered around the table, but for now, CC will serve nicely as a fine advocate for the generously scribing family physician.

"I'm with CC," I say, raising my hand seeking a vote. I look around to see if there are other any other takers. The boys just look at me. Chet just looks at me. CC is now looking at me.

Chet thinks I am too glib, and he doesn't seem to appreciate my attitude and management style. So, he decides to make a point and pulls his gun out of his waistband and places it on the table, which, you will find, should you ever have the occasion, does not come across as a particularly friendly gesture, especially at a fiesta on a warmer summer night with guests in attendance.

"I want you to move some mother fucking product for us, and let me take care of any nosey cops, agents, or whatever the fuck badge the good guys are wearing these days." He leans his skinny frame forward. For an old guy, he does a pretty good job of staring straight through me, which I am finding very fucking uncomfortable.

His .38 sits there heavily. Phil and Roy follow suit.

First Roy.

Then Phil. Brotherly love.

Their guns are on the table to back up Dad. The metal chunk of pistols placed on a glass coffee table carries an unmistakable sound that can give one pause.

Phil and Roy are staring at me.

They, too, have some very nice weaponry in the .38 range, although their pistols appear larger. I'm not sure if that's an effect of my friend Peru, or the other friend, Maggie-Extra-Salt, or the combination of all my synapses pulling together. I have allies, even if they are all in my mind. It's good to be liked. The guns are nickel-plated, chrome, or dark and black and have nubby, brown and thick handles for gripping and pointing. Chet sees me staring at the glass table and can probably guess that I am thinking how much killing those guns can do. He's pretty spot on.

At this point, with three pistols on the table and chemical imbalances out of balance, the evening could go terribly wrong, so I am hoping to lean on clever as my standard go-to. I sit there looking and smoking and offer a small smile, and wait. It would probably not be a good time to do another bump. Or another Nicorette. Hell, even a stick of Wrigley's. Although, I do like the idea of another Margarita, which I am almost certain CC would go for as well.

The momentary and awkward silence with guns on the table is broken when Chet takes charge.

"All I gotta say is you, my good doctor, have one more play and then we rest. I'm gonna take CC's advice and let it go for now. With this next round, we will quietly stand down and take a break. Once we, actually I mean *you*, get these scrips moving again, and we unload, we'll consider our deal done—for now."

Chet looks around the room. I sense a moment of proud fatherly resolve as the family patriarch. He then quietly picks up his Firestorm .38, cocks the hammer, leans forward on the edge of the leather and brass sofa, and points it straight into my face. With the long reach of his lanky frame and arms, Chet's Firestorm is uncomfortably close to my face. There wouldn't be much left of me. Even with the cooling air conditioning and the mild high running through my body, I can feel my head pounding. He purses his thin lips together and makes a faint, soft whistling sound. I think Phil and Roy are familiar with dear Dad's theatrics. I know Cynthia is. Still, Dad and his thick, pebbled-handled Firestorm can make anyone nervous, especially family.

"You hear what we're saying, doctor? Ain't' nobody messin' with the money. I got mouths to feed," Chet says looking over at CC, waiting for her sign of approval that, yes indeed, he is the man in charge. CC says enough with her sip and holds her glance at him, a tender moment between husband and wife. See, compromises. It's how the best relationships work things out. Also, CC doesn't want anyone dead in the office. Certainly not during her fiesta.

My Glock dug into my back. The metal was at body temperature by now. The pistol felt like it gave me options. I knew it was wise to avoid Chet's question and deflected it with a smile and a nod over to CC. "We're all just fucking with each other, Chet. I think CC's got a point. Nobody's going sideways. We get the deals done, then I go." Chet bore a hole in me. He was thinking. Wheels turned.

CC interrupted his busy mind. "So, one more deal and we can take a break. Makes everyone happy, right baby?" CC added as she raised her Maggie toward him.

"You always got my back, darling. Let's go make some money." Chet laughed loudly, rattling his aging lungs. He then holstered his Firestorm into the waist of his black jeans, the gun hidden by the loose, white cotton embroidered Mexican wedding shirt.

Phil and Roy kept quiet. CC took a sip of her Margarita, relieved that the Firestorm wasn't going to ruin the fiesta. The family relaxed on Chet's tidings, glad to hear that for now, everyone's going to make piles of dough and chase it all back with free ice cold Pabst because they own a successful liquor emporium in downtown Needles.

I tossed a vial of flake over to the phlegmatic patriarch. "Here you go, Chet, a little *mo-mo*."

My move was as smart as the darting side-botched lizard. I knew when to duck and cover. I know Chet is always up for free blow, especially when it is the fluffy, abalone-shell-brilliant white and works with his weary and aging physiology. The buzz from *pura* is mellow, and Chet's body has an easier time metabolizing the *producto de Mallinckrodt* cocoa leaves.

Phil, Roy, Chet and CC appreciate the relaxing gesture, and like good partners behind any business enterprise, they acknowledge my being a team player. It's almost as if we were at, say, the company cafeteria. Chet and his boys holster their shiny weapons. I pass the vial. We light our cigarettes and raise a few shots of *Herradura Anejo,* sponsored by the wonderful people at Cub's. Maybe it's more like a company picnic. We talk money, timing, and the next score. We even talk about buying bigger boats.

Chet got up off the sofa using the boys' shoulders to steady his frame. Phil and Roy passed my vial around and then tossed it over to mom. CC loaded a dose in her cigarette, fired it up, and inhaled deeply. The toke rolled her eyes. CC does a woozy, little tango step over to the office bar to pour herself another.

Chet moves to the balcony with his two boys. Phil and Roy bob their heads to the bass line of the catchy thumping of the festive Mariachi.. The boys and their Dad are a loaded, happy group overlooking the patio and pool scene.

The early sky shows the first stars appearing with random shades of blue scattering across the evening twilight. I walk over, lean against the wrought iron balcony and play out the Chet family moment.

The delicate balance of pure *cocaina*, Nicorettes, nicotine, tequila, and Margaritas mix nicely with the Mariachi's play list, bringing comfort and aid to the lost patio people. Sunglasses have come off as bigger fiesta glasses with stronger drinks come out, and the smoke and smell from the side of slathered, grilling meat flies skyward, floating out into the valley. Close your eyes and you could be deep in Mexico. I was far away from my pool and Hills of Hollywood.

Chet pushes into me, pats the small of my back, and whispers into my ear, "Hey, doctor, how much you pay for the Glock?" I pull back to look at him with a straight-up poker face, unfazed by his shit, and wonder how the fuck he knew because the only way to handle this is to fucking handle this. So I lock eyes and whisper, while reaching around and patting the small of his back.

"I didn't buy it, asshole, I took it off a dead mother fucking Russian."

Chet doesn't react. He just stares straight ahead and down at the pool. "You know, those Mariachi's are a deal, and I'd hire 'em again, except for that good looking fucker playing the trumpet. Name's Pepe. I think CC likes him." He laughs triggering his smoker's cough lining his lungs, and then he leans over and spits the phlegm off to the side. "And she don't even speak Mexican."

The patio settles into an evening dance of late arrivals and early departures as cars wind up and down the driveway. Here, high atop the Chet and Cynthia Kingdom, we can see it all so clearly. It's only when you get down deeper into the valley, and closer to Needles, does it all become a little hazy.

I say my goodbyes to my business partners and leave them with endless possibilities of running bigger quantities promising generous, tax-free paychecks. The Mariachi music bounced up through the open patio doors. I bounced down the stairs. *Adios mi familia.*

I pulled the top down on the Speedster and drove out of the Chet and CC Kingdom, leaving the fiesta patio crowd lost to the tequila, Mariachis, and Chet's bloody side of steer still hanging from the industrial-sized rotisserie.

The low-slung coupe held tight against the blacktop as the high-topped Cholla cactus whipped by my racing piece of silver. I leaned over and tried to coax the pathetic AC on high. The vents sputtered, finally clicking on cue. It was time to blow. I licked my cracked lips wishing I had that honey bee balm. I pushed on the pedal, accelerating the smooth curves of the Speedster deeper into the red planet as the evening light of the Mojave bathed the convertible in warm, gold tones. The rush of dry, desert air swirled through the compact cabin. The red leather seats and intense July heat created pools of sweat that dripped down my back. I searched the radio dial and finally landed on static-free Mariachi. Every day's a fiesta.

I imagined happy Concho-wearing musicians playing without a care, pitching their life stories in plaintive voices recalling love and death and sadness. I drove harder into the west and watched the desert sky dissolve into a gentle breath of colors. The varnished evening light turned from deeper pinks into a favorite creamy blue that tore a hole in the atmosphere. Constellations were just beyond, dotting the universe where Quentin lived. The sun was setting. The road back was the road within. I took a deep breath on the memory of Quentin and that smile. Two years, not even a thousand days and who the fuck knows? Maybe someday I'd do the math and figure out how many hours were clocked after the day we both stood on the massive, pitted concrete of the 6th Street Bridge. The pictures of him sometimes appeared on their own, out of nowhere, from everywhere. It was a rewind to the minute when my fourteen-year-old son went away. I wished the Speedster had another gear so it could kick up over a hundred, hoping the distraction would help shake the images.

The dry wind swirled, a tightly wound dust devil spun off out into the dirt like a top and then into itself, disappearing. Rows of wild yucca flew past. Out toward a rocky range a wake of turkey vultures floated, dipped, and hovered, riding thermals. They were hunting. The Speedster's pistons pumped. With the leather seats now cooler, my back drier, I was heading home, but still homeless. Quentin was gone. There was no bridge out in the desert. Why would there be? The only water running through the dry, cracked rutted, flatlands of thorny cacti was the flowing ice melt, now the welling currents of the deep Colorado River. I gripped the steering wheel.

I'm gunning down the road when my mobile rings and the caller ID reads 'Phil'—motherfucker. I don't pick up. I shift the Speedster and move down the black desert asphalt, light a smoke and do a quick bump. Looking up, I can see the first stars push through the last of the evening. I am happy to be out of the Kingdom and heading home to Helena. Considering the guns, blow, tequila, Mariachis, and Chet's bloody meat, I thought it was a very fine fiesta, really. Considering.

CHAPTER 14

LOVELY RITA

One thing I like about Phil is his twenty-year-old daughter.
I like her because she knows herself. That, and she is incredibly
gorgeous.

She is also trouble.

And she knows this, too. In fact, she likes it. Rita is a smart, clever,
and dangerously subtle schemer who is very good at moving, conning,
and playing the sides.

When you first meet her you think that she is a perfectly pleasant young woman, but you would be perfectly wrong. That's ok; you
would not be the first. Rita is tall, striking, and she is always wonderfully tanned in a sort of biscuit tone that is often reserved for tanning
sprays and booths, and what apparently could be a lot of airbrushing,
but no. Rita is twenty and she lives in the desert, and so her color is
distinctively hers, and it works nicely.

Rita likes to catch you looking at her, so she will always wear something insanely short and tight, and thankfully for the Needles heat,
that is pretty much always, everywhere, anytime.

And did I tell you Rita was a swimmer? Only thing is, the same
girl who kicked ass in the 100-yard butterfly and had more than a
few institutions of higher learning trotting out full ride scholarships
decided to get out of the pool and trip into a life that didn't involve flip
turns, chlorine, a stopwatch, or endless laps.

Yes, Rita liked the water, but she also liked swimming with sharks:
fencing stolen vehicles, distributing steroids, and moving (just for

close friends and family, of course) the occasional pound or two of high-octane weed.

Old habits die very hard for Rita, and you have to give it to the girl, she's true to her workout discipline from days in the pool. You'd think that between runs with desert rats, moving product with criminal intent, and a young life that's chalked up at least three felonies in any state, it would be tough scheduling quality gym time. I'm not sure if she's dedicated or vain, or maybe both. I should comment on how her large aquamarine eyes flash a steady brilliance, projecting a lot of confidence. Maybe arrogance? Yeah, more like that. Rita is a testament to big gym time and spotting bigger guys who also have a lot of time to hammer out a frightening number of squats with big ass iron. So, yes she does; Rita gets away with a lot. Partly because she's a pretty cool little cat with a killer body who knows how to work a room, and has the ear of her enabling stepdad, Phil, who is forever backing her play. Stepdad Phil makes Rita twice as dangerous. Nobody fucks with her. She's made that abundantly clear and on occasion has flashed me her favorite sidekick, a razor sharp 9" Finnish Puukko that she carries in her purse. This is a very good blade for working wood, gutting fish, cleaning game, and of course, calling you out. She likes that part. A lot. It's her way of messing with you. Just a nod and a glimpse of the Puukko, and you get the picture: big bad girl with a blade backed by the ex-cop stepdad asshole that likes to move pure Peruvian.

I didn't take the call on my way home from Chet's fiesta. After repeatedly watching my cell light up at now 1:00 in the morning, and with a few short tumblers highlighted by the delicate hit from the dropper, and Helena's selection *Supertramp—Breakfast in America,* is especially good when the desert sparkles at this hour, heightened by eighty degrees of dry warm taking you deep into a night that is crystal clear and wraps this desert up in the deepest black. Helena is intent on threatening Chet and the family. She is a bit unsettled, to put it mildly, at the current state of the family's accelerating demands of my talent and time. The clever girl can get a streak going that could easily take any Needles *Bratva* down to the ground.

"Chet, deese CC, and deese boys eese trouble now, more than ever, and we will have to puttingk them to pasture."

Ok, fair enough, and I agree with most of what she said, but the nuances of how to delicately extricate myself are lost on our Russian blonde baddie. Nonetheless, we've got ample Stoli, droppers, and some downtime, so I am putting this in the All Good Column. So, what the hell, I am feeling invincible; I pick up Phil's call.

"What's up Phil?"

"It's Rita."

"Caller ID says Phil," I say, my post-midnight buzz humming right along.

"Fuck him," she coolly mandates with a straight up bravado that tells me something is seriously not good.

"Fuck Phil?" I ask while cutting a crisp, thin rail of white just to clear my mind for takeoff. I glance at the mirror to check out my eyes and general condition. Other than the expected pupil dilation and a slight flush spreading across my face, I'm looking pretty good. It's amazing what a light desert tan can do to hide the sins of my late nights and extracurricular vices.

"Must be a bad night somewhere. Are we calling this important or can it wait, and why the fuck do you have me on your Dad's phone?"

"Stepdad. He's passed out, and I knew you wouldn't take my call. Some shit's really huge right now with Phil and Roy and that bigger asshole, Chet."

"Care to give me a clue?" I am crystallized in clarity as I shake my tumbler cooling the last of our Stoli.

Rita is her own best lawyer. "Like, they don't want me moving product any more. I was, like, fucking excellent at it. Fucking awesome, as a matter of fact, so I want to know if you want me in or out of this deal. Because if you tell all of these assholes, like, I'm in, well then, I am the mother fuck in."

"Rita, this isn't my call, it's Phil's."

This shit was now really starting to bother me because we don't like any hiccups in this oiled machine, and right now the Rita and Phil

Family are a fucking wrench. Phil must have a reason for asking Rita to take early retirement.

"Yeah, but they'll listen to you."

I have to take a breath and pause. I look out the window and wonder how the universe put me smack in the middle of the desert, and that maybe I should pay someone to track my family history and lineage to find out where the Martinez clan turned left and put me in a longitude and latitude of horribly wrong.

So, here I am sitting in my wonderfully appointed blond laminate and stainless steel cocoon, the cooling AC bathing my immaculately aluminum tube, listening to the Rita recital and trying to figure out this new version of a Phil fucking. Between Phil, Roy, Chet, Cynthia, the family enterprise, and my holding some of this shit together, I was starting to lean into the side of throwing up my hands and declaring a serious *fuck all* and leave everyone to deal with the fallout. That would be too easy, and way too eventful. No, this was a Rita and Phil thing with a side of Chet working the angles. Somebody saw or heard something that requested the lovely Rita sit this one out, thank you. Who knows, maybe CC, after a fourth Maggie, got the ball rolling by getting into Chet's head. It would be just like her.

"Let me talk to him, just sit tight. Or, maybe we see what Chet has to say."

"Fuck 'em," Her voice is clear and controlled.

"They told me I was out—told me that was the way it is." Rita is rock steady.

Hey, you spend ten years of your life pulling five hours a day of lap time burning a timed pulse into your brain and you know how to get centered, fast.

Rita continues her aggressive stroke. "Well, guess what? It's not the way it is, and they won't exactly like the way it isn't or will be. This is not legit."

Rita is not so lovely. The girl is on a mission. She is doing laps. Her DNA is routine, paced, directed, goal oriented and geared to just stroke, breathe, flip, and do it all over again and again.

Phil and Chet needed to handle her. Actually, after I did a rail and looked at my Patek—hell it was only 2:00 in the morning—I realized that this would be on me. I needed to get a swimmer back into the lane.

CHAPTER 15

MR. EUGENIA'S

Needles at 8:00 in the morning in July has a heat that seems to sear every particle of the desert into a dried piece of kindling firing up a new level of hot doused with kerosene.

I believe the Chamber of Commerce politely refers to it as a "dry heat."

Bearable if you happen to be from Hell and sitting neck deep in the cooling waters of the Colorado River with an ice chest of frozen beer. Yes, it is dry. It is heat. It is fucking Needles in July. I only mention this because when I pull into the parking lot, I really can't think of anything else except where to park, and how nice the AC feels powering through th small portal making me feel clean, drying the sweat off my shirt so I look like I haven't been up all night. Air conditioning is a wonderfully manufactured climate that conditions the air, which means that it's actually changing the molecular content of the air moving through my front seat, into my lungs, and across my face, pulling me through the morning. Eye drops feel good, too. So, I flood my pupils, blink a few times, check the mirror and remind myself that my terrific, new life in Needles is only temporary—at least for now. I do a spot check on my eyes, face, skin, and basic health condition, which I have to say, is a testament to good genes and my ready and daily intake of physician-approved vitamins.

I guess my use of pharmaceuticals and drink hasn't overshot the runway. Although, I toy with the idea of cutting back on my nicotine. I notice the occasional abstinence seems to work wonders—occasionally.

I had agreed to Rita's suggestion that we powwow for a breakfast to sort through her, and now "my situation," with the family. Last night, when I talked to Rita, we both agreed that, yeah, Phil had kissed her off, but the move appeared to have the hand of Chet with a hint of CC.

At this hour of the day, and with my ever expert skill at governing my substances, only charged by my morning ritual of nicotine and Orange Nicorettes, I'm rewarded with the cooling, tropical dose of mint and citrus, plus a double shot of the most fucking awesome legalized drug of the century, nicotine, which by my book is a pretty sweet deal in a parking lot on a Thursday morning. I am starting my day with eggs and Rita. God help us all. I exhale.

This is early for me to be anywhere, but particularly here at Mr. Eugenia's. The nearly empty parking lot is littered with a scattering of Ford and Chevy trucks moving Mexican laborers. Occasionally, you'll run across a wayward tourist down from the Grand Canyon who apparently is lost and looking to recalibrate because certainly nobody is coming to Needles in July. Certainly not at this time of the morning, and most certainly not to Mr. Eugenia's.

I spot Rita's car. Her beefy, metallic silver Mustang coupe with custom chrome rims and heavily tinted blacked-out windows is selfishly parked diagonally across two spaces, so nobody can park next to her cherished ride and chance a ding on opening a door. You would not want that to happen. Rita is obsessive about her machines, among other things.

Mr. Eugenia's Coffee Shop is a beacon of beige stucco topped with bright red, roof tiles. A large, plastic sign is hooked up and tethered to the side announcing in no uncertain terms, that indeed, you should *Ask About Our Kids Eat Free Buffet.* It is a sweet deal if you are trying to stretch a dollar in the family budget.

It's not unusual for the folks to bring their kids, take up a booth and have the wee ones discreetly shuttle a bounty of plates for the entire family. Everybody's working the hustle. Mr. Eugenia's does have a cap on the free food offer—up to age five. Personally, I think you're good up to about eight, especially if they're on the shorter side.

I think it was, at one time, a fast food place because they kept the drive-thru window, but now you can't drive up. Not that you would want to anyway, because inside is where Mr. Eugenia's really shines.

I heard the guy who owns it had been a Catholic priest who had left the order, got married, divorced, and had to squirrel away some of his cash because the ex-wife had an awesome attorney who wanted to take the wayward priest down. So, Bobby, the priest, went into a partnership with the guy who had the lien on this former fast food palace, but the partner dies and Bobby gets the restaurant without putting up a dime. Everybody thinks it's a gay thing. Whatever. I have it on excellent authority that Bobby cut a deal with his ex-wife and would pay her cash over a period of time so she wouldn't have to pay Mr. I'm A Fucking Awesome Attorney nearly as much as his ego insisted. Now she lives comfortably in Nevada, and Bobby sends her a nice round figure every month. I imagine she lights a votive candle to the Patron Saint of Good Deals Gone Wildly Better. Why did Bobby do this? Partly some version of love, partly guilt, sure, but mostly for the two recipes she gave him: absolutely knock-out Huevos Rancheros and a closely guarded family recipe for a chocolaty-espresso, creamy mole sauce that could out-dance anything in the state of Oaxaca. Like I said, inside is where Mr. Eugenia's really shines. There's a profitable card room in the back with regulars who like their AC on high, their highballs on ice, their non-smoking signs non-existent, and their women not here. There's a limit to the ante, but so far nobody's put a number on it.

I pull around toward the front near some of the shadier areas to shutter the Speedster under the awning of a few palms, close enough to the exterior misting that lines the eaves and casts a spray. A cooling embrace to the entrance, baptizing all of Mr. Bobby's patrons.

The gentle mist is a nice touch. Thank you, Mr. Bobby, for the cooling anointment that greets me as I push through the glass front door, and I immediately see Rita. She lazily flags me, holding up two fingers in a peace sign. The murmur of regulars and strays is left to a few booths and a counter that serves the single regulars. Everybody looks up. Heads bob back to the paper and breakfast, coffee and the shared morning of useless banter about the desert, who's fucking who, and probably some speculation on how to make a dollar doing nothing. Too hot for work in July. Too hot most months. People looking for a way to slide into an opportunity or such. It won't take much, just a little something on the side. The famous kids-eat-free buffet sits clumsily to the right, diners at the U-shaped counter are straight ahead in the middle of the coffee shop, and *Rita And The Fucked Up Party Of Two* will be sitting in a booth against a bank of windows over to the left. Rita has picked a fine and smart seating arrangement, offering plenty of window space, so we can easily check out who's coming and going in the parking lot. I think Rita would be a good person to partner with on a surveillance team. She would look especially hot in those camo-green night vision goggles, and I fantasize about running late night covert ops and flirting over the click and buzz and static of our Radio Shack walkie-talkies.

"Don't get up." I slide into the dark red, plastic upholstered booth and notice that at this ungodly hour Rita is looking pretty damn good, and I am feeling pretty damn bad. Could I get some coffee, please.

I motion to the teenage busboy.

"Good to see you, too, doctor." Rita lowers her ultra-black wraparound sunglasses and strikes a pose that plays to her strength. That would be sex. At her age, what else you going with? Rita brushes back her dirty blonde hair. The sunglasses are back on. "You look like shit." Her early morning statement shoots a few holes through my parking-lot-mirror check and I have to agree, I feel even worse than Rita's cold comment.

I was hoping the healthy glow from my tan would help hide the effects of my string of late nights. I flash on the need to dial down sometime soon. Tomorrow is nearly always the next day. It's good to have goals.

I try to establish my alpha-ness, or whatever I'm hoping passes for manly, patriarchal come-uppance. "I think the sunglasses are a bit played."

"Fuck you, too."

"Charming." I say, looking around hoping nobody thinks she's my daughter.

"I need to get back in the rotation. Like now." Rita presses the folds in her red cotton napkin.

Our waitress comes over, attempts a smile hoping she can muster enough shop charm to pimp her tip and hands me the menu, which I don't need.

I hand the menu back to the red and beige uniformed, spray-haired Missy Tip who's pushing fifty and knows how to handle a six-top of sweet little monsters with chain-smoking parents who are already thinking that ten percent on the bill is probably too much for buffet service. Especially when it's get it yourself. It's hard pimping for anything more to a gluttonous dining public intent on stiffing you the minute they come through the door. Try the older couple on the two-top with a map out and baseball caps, that's easy money.

I turn to the Missy Tip and try my best to smile, but that hurts my head so I manage a simple, "Huevos, hot sauce, tortillas, juice…Rita?"

Rita looks up at the waitress and dismisses her with a weak 'I'm-good-with-coffee-can-we-get-the-fuck-out-of-here' face. Yeah, that one.

So, here we are.

The issue is family business and how Rita is going to handle her end of things. I'm acting as the referee and counselor making sure we all stay on track. Rita launches into a speech on her conversation with Phil. Nothing new here.

I listen through my morning haze. Coffee isn't cutting through. The hot sauce might.

Rita's sexiness almost does. Wait, yes, it there it is. I watch her mouth move. I think I can feel my dick.

"Phil's an asshole. He thinks I was skimming off what I was moving.

He doesn't realize that I am fucking accountable for every dime of the load I was responsible for."

"How much?" I'm back into the negotiation and counseling part of the morning, and my lust affair with Rita, still very much the bright side to our meeting, is responsibly on hold. I give her my full attention trying not to think about what it would be like to have her sitting on top of me in the Airstream with a cold one, the AC on high, and the late evening twilight brushing against her blonde, young hair with those smooth, muscled, swimmer's loins and toned Kegals gripping me and riding what would surely be the absolute fuck of her life.

I take a sip of the black coffee and catch her doing math.

"I was in on this deal to move at least 1,000 grams. If we were in Colombia we'd be lucky to get $2 a gram, but guess what everybody, we're not in South America and I'm getting close to $450 a gram. That doesn't appear to cut it with either Phil or Chet, and don't get me started about his wife..."

Yes, we really are having this kind of a conversation at this time of the morning. And I think that this is actually the perfect place for diners like Rita and me to hash out drug deals over acceptably clean Formica tabletops. It's our morning coffee klatch of Folgers and eggs, diluted fresh juice, and bear claws melted in the microwave. My Huevos arrive. Yes, more caffeine, please. I don't think it would be wise to suggest a spot of Bailey's as a topper. Although, I'm sure our waitress would be up for it (*That shiny 20% gratuity is well within reach.*)

I cowboy up and try to show restraint, wisdom, and maturity. "Rita, if I remember correctly we agreed on the market value, a number we knew we could get—last count, exactly $900 per gram. So, you're talking nearly half the value. When you bring that back to stepdad Phil, Uncle Roy, and the Chet and CC show, of course they're going to ask questions." I believe I am quietly sincere, and in my own way, I could be considered calming.

Rita takes off her sunglasses knowing just how beautiful her aquamarine blue can look against the palette of early-morning-coffee-shop.

Leaning into me across the small and compact table, her look is determined and fierce as a flip turn on lap twenty-five.

"Doctor, let me square this up and set it right. You can do anything you want from here on out, but unfortunately for you, Chet let me *know* what he knows—and now *you* know. I'm aware of your deal with some government shit, something about Russians and a life before VistaVue."

She's now a little bitch, and I am pissed that I even have to listen to this, especially after she told me I look like shit. And especially since I just mind fucked her five minutes earlier and made her come so hard asked me if I wanted a threesome next time. I, of course, did. But it was too late for that kind of action. Now, she had entered the stone-cold-bitch category.

I suddenly feel a sharp point push against my thigh. Lovely Rita has pulled her Puukko out under the table. She's letting me know she's feeling a little pressure and I might want to share in her, uh, situation.

I wince. That is one fucking sharp blade. "Is that a threat or are you seriously making a point?" I wonder if the double entendre connects as I force my hand against hers. I push back, turning her wrist inward, feeling her hand surrender.

"You get where I am going with this," Rita whispers. "I am up against it with those boys and you have to back me."

"I get it, but I wouldn't go there if I were you." I hiss. I like my attitude. I can be a tough son of a bitch. Especially if my breakfast plans run into a snag.

Just then, Mr. Bobby walks over to our table. Unaware of Rita's blade work going on under the table, he offers me a familiar handshake and smiles at Rita who is very good at smiling and simultaneously working her knife while my Huevos sit half-eaten on my plate, and I haven't even touched my tortillas. Mr. Bobby is playing the early morning host, snapping his fingers to alert the busboy that the table needs more coffee and water, *pronto.*

"Julio, mas caffee, y agua, por favor para Rita y Dominic.." Mr. Bobby smiles and asks if everything is good. We both assure him that it is wonderful, as usual.

"Thinking it's 90 and breaking 120 by late afternoon…" Mr. Bobby's talking weather, just to make conversation, which is really fucking terrific and fucking timely because at this very moment the people he's talking to—me and Rita—are engaged in our own morning squabble. As I look at Mr. Bobby, I see that indeed he is a fairly handsome fellow who would remind you of say, Liam Neeson, but with a darker side—the padre who works the parish, baptizes the children and winds up sleeping with their mothers. That Liam.

So, Mr. Bobby is tall, and lean and frankly, dresses almost too well as the proud proprietor of a downtown Needles coffee shop whose ex-wife resides in Nevada and who has a history involving an irate attorney chasing him down. Standing 6' 3", slender, and with excellent teeth, which might well be veneers, Mr. Bobby likes his casual desert chic of wrinkled chino slacks with a green faded Lacoste polo and expensive cocoa brown leather sandals. It all works. He could be hosting a pool party. I can see the gay rumor thing. Mr. Bobby's still talking heat as he continues his hosting banter, scanning the room, doing a head count to see how many plates he is place is moving. He's keeping a careful eye out for buffet hombres who could indeed be eating into his profit margin.

Rita looks at me, hard. I stare back.

We both smile at Mr. Bobby. We also have excellent teeth.

I am still gripping her hand under the table. He notices my body leaning into the table, hard, but like so many lessons learned in the backrooms here, Mr. Bobby doesn't ask too many questions. He looks past my obvious awkward position and flashes a flirtatious smile at Rita.

Mr. Bobby is fine with whatever is going on under his table in his place at this hour of the morning. He also has a buffet to keep his eye on and a few questionable employees he's pretty sure are skimming, but who the hell isn't in this town.

"Rita was just asking," I nod over to Rita, "if it's too early to play a few hands, just to keep the morning… interesting."

"Game won't show up till lunch." He grins and flashes a really terrific smile. This dude could still seriously pull some pussy. "Money goes off at noon."

We promise to show up at that hour, although we won't, and he returns to the business of his morning customers. Mr. Bobby knows we don't know jack about cards. Mr. Bobby is as predatory as a crafty desert scorpion that can smile while stinging, and Mr. Bobby always knows where his next meal is. For today, it isn't us. His card game is chump change compared to our own Texas Hold 'Em dealt by the shark Chet, CC, and the boys.

I turn back to Rita as we continue our little Mexican standoff. I can see my reflection in her oversized LVs.

"Ok, here's my side of the deal. You turn and burn grams at $450 and finish the rest of the load. I make sure Phil and Chet leave you the fuck alone and put you back on the program. But like they say, nothing good lasts forever, and this won't."

Rita flirts easily. It's a dance. The practiced, sassy flip of her shoulder length hair. The half-smile with those thick, pouty lips. Hell, as transparent as it is, she makes it work. She appears relieved because she can now see the bright light at the end of a long, dark tunnel. Fuck it, I know what the girl is all about. We are working each other.

"And you want?" Rita asks, locking in on me with the slow melt of a half-smile. She pulls her hair up and back, slowly moves her hand around, working out whatever stress she's carrying in that gorgeous, young neck, and fuck me, those are some nice cheekbones. My professional profiling kicks in and I have to say, I honestly wouldn't touch them. I wouldn't even recommend implants. Not now anyway. Give it a few years and she might be a candidate.

"You know what I want? I want you to *not* know what you think Chet told you. See how amnesia works? One day everything's good and then, poof, for some strange reason you can't remember anything at all. Really no cure for it."

"You should know, you're a doctor." Rita said brashly.

"That's right, I'm the mother fucking doctor. I make sure you get something on the backend—without the family side—if you catch my drift, and you shut the fuck up, and I mean *for-fucking-ever*. You don't, and my next offer is going to hurt a little. Kinda like this," I turn her wrist hard inward so the Puukko puts just enough of the sharp steel against her bare thigh. "You will not like my move at all. We good?"

I dab my cold flour tortilla in hot sauce, slowly finishing the bite. Rita is thinking loudly, and we can all see the gears grinding, redlining into fifth. "Done. Now, will you please let the hell go?" Her voice surrenders. I don't trust her. I keep the pressure on her, making sure she feels it.

"Jesus Christ, ok, ok, I get it..." She grimaces. "Jesus." Rita rubs her wrist.

I shift in the booth, raise an eyebrow, and let her have the knife. The girl is steady as she massages her hand. One more lap before she kicks into her finish. My pen and scrip pads are the Holy Grail for everyone involved. She's not sure if she won, I won, or if it's a win-win. We agree that this is where we stand on a Thursday morning. She looks out for me, I look out for her.

Building our own protective ecosystem of survival out in the dry topography spiked with sharp cactus, snakeskin boots, big ass boats, and bellied ex-policia fantasizing about a sister city called Peru.

"Fucking Huevos are the best." I light up a Menthol and inhale deeply to feel the wonder of nicotine race, dilate, energize, and relax and do it all so well. And all at the same time. I pop a Nicorette to supercharge it all and make it even a thousand times more freaking awesome. It's always better with protein to start the day. I can feel the dopamine swimming in my brain. Wonderful.

"By the way, this is a coffee shop, right? Then maybe they should get some coffee that doesn't freaking suck." She says this loud enough to be overheard by Missy Tip who deadpans a look at me and glances over at my breakfast pal, lovely Rita. Our bored waitress comes over and only pours me a refill, looks at me and cracks, "Honey, you know we got an all-you-can-eat buffet for the kiddies." She tosses a look over at Rita who is now sporting her Vuittons and a painful, red wrist.

"Next time, maybe add a little hot sauce to your caffeine," I throw a $50 bill on the table, a mercy tip for our waitress trying to make it through another morning, and yeah, Julio the busboy was pretty on it with the water refills. "I'll call Phil or Chet, and see what I can do to make this all go away and put you back into the rotation."

"That would be nice…I can make bank for you." Rita tosses a showy, pouty face that's this side of flirty, but tough, always tough. Then, she smiles angelically through a practiced narcissistic flip turn. The girl keeps everyone guessing.

"Our side deal earns plenty, just shut the fuck up and do what we're told…just keep swimming." I say, doing my best to keep the clock tight on this girl.

"You know I will. Kiss bye, doctor." Rita is now over-the-top with twenty-year old giddiness, knowing she may be home free.

Her attitude ramps up. She brightens and gets up, struts out of the restaurant, looks back at me and blows me a kiss. Something tells me I'm in trouble. Hell, of course I am. The waitress catches this and with the round, bottomless red-capped coffee pot in hand, simply shakes her head at me. The busboy is still staring at the young, hot, and striking Rita. Men in the coffee shop follow her tan, muscled legs, her tight ass wrapped in denim shorts, and the way Rita can tease with a turn.

They don't know about the Puukko in her purse.

Walking out, I stand for a moment under the spritzers that throw a light, cooling mist on my face. I think that maybe if Mr. Bobby could reach back into his priestly past and toss a sacrament or two my way I could get right with the world. I think maybe if I could just stand here and grab some energy to deal with Rita and my next move I could recharge and hit the reset button.

But I know this won't happen.

Still, the misting water feels good and mixes well with the heat and the dry, warm, wind that's kicking up across the parking lot, sucking every inch of moisture from the cooling spray. My skin is dry, and I wonder if a pre-bedtime moisturizing treatment might be the ticket.

I know Cindy Crawford has a line of new, dermatologically-approved products that work wonders for her. Although, I am still not sold on her mole.

I watch Rita speed shift out of the lot. The throaty, low-end torque on her Shelby twitches the car's thick back-end as she exits with a quick, sharp right and straight through a red light. She couldn't give a fuck about traffic. Her tires chirp on the smooth, new asphalt. She is a bullet. Gone.

A troop of hungry kids and tired parents walk past me and spill loudly into the entrance to Mr. Eugenia's. Chances are pretty good they know the family buffet when they see one. There's no missing the screaming, extra-large plastic sheeting in big, bright, eye-popping yellow letters that nearly reach through your car window and throw you and the kids into a wide, Mr. Eugenia's red, plastic booth. Who knows, maybe Dad's here for the cards and the kid's buffet thing is the bait. Whatever he's got going, it works for our priestly Neeson look-alike. Like I said, Mr. Bobby is a fucking scorpion. The desert is his home.

I look out past the lightly colored concrete parking lot and see nothing but heat morays sheeting up against the horizon. I almost feel my lips chapping in real time, the blistering sun peeling back my dermis. My forehead feels stretched by the intense temperature showing no mercy. The concrete reflects the heat, and I can feel it rise up against my body as I walk to the Speedster. A dry heat, as they say, that can bake your bones if you're not careful.

I get in, hit the AC on high, gun the coupe quickly out onto the two lane blacktop, and throw the car past its gears, trying to get whatever thermals can flow through the windows on this road back to VistaVue.

I dial up Helena. She sleepily picks up and I tell her to get strapped.

We're going to take a little drive.

Everyone into the pool.

CHAPTER 16

HYDROCHLORIDE

I'm not even sure how I feel today. Or about the day. Or about my life. Or about Chet and the crew that I've fallen in step with. Fuck, I am getting irritable because I am tired. And no, I am not hitting the class CII controlled substance *du jour*. I need the break from my brain that has a mind of its own and is relentlessly running down endless scenarios between Rita and the boys.

This fucking town is exhausting—well, at least my brain is. Maybe just a small icebreaker with the tumbler? No, let's wait a bit here. This is a tough little pause for me because the beauty of my droppers is that this pure form of cocaine hydrochloride charges straight ahead into my Mesolimbic reward pathway, and really I can't say enough about that wonderful road leading to the holy grail of Serotonin-Norepinephrine-Dopamine-Reuptake Inhibitors. I can see why mice keep hitting that Ark-of-the-Covenant lever. I wonder why the lab techs don't.

And the other nice part of my particular chemistry set of choice is that cocaine hydrochloride is water soluble. So, thank you, I will have another. Later.

After my breakfast with Rita, my chat with Helena, and my interior monologue with yours truly, I ran through a few predictable scenarios that I'm surely borrowing from wildly popular action-adventure movies. I've got the blade-packing Rita, *fina* product, money, and the Phil thing. Righteous. On the other hand, there's the Chet family, big piles of dough, fat rails of *pura fina*, a distribution line, this fucking heat, personal pharmaceutical issues, and let's not forget the memorable CC and her pecking at Chet to keep that dough moving through the wilderness and right up their circular driveway. Terrific.

Naturally, I've got to sell the boys on bringing the girl back into play. Phil will need a convincing speech how his step-daughter, the lovely Rita, is still a go-to girl who's run into a minor speed bump with the load and dollar count, and why can't we all just get along (*thank you, Rodney*), so that we can get through this, get our money, and get lost (*courtesy of Chet Baker*).

My move out of my other and past life to my now and present way of living was supposed to be safe, quiet, and solitary. I was hoping for a life unencumbered by the ridiculously complicated way I used to live. And guess what? It followed me out here. Instead of my weekends with the gorgeous ones, my money-churning practice, and those mother fucking, surgeon-chasing Russians, I've got an illegal scrips business driving dollars for a nasty posse of ex-cops who have me in a non-regulation choke hold, and still I'm forced to deal with those mother fucking surgeon-chasing Russians. And another thing, my brand of medicine wasn't about saving lives, fuck no, it was about saving egos. So, don't even consider me in the same league as the good doctor who selflessly flies into Nairobi to handle a Malaria outbreak.

No, I was the licensed asshole who would wake up with a searing, head-banging, glassy-eyed hangover, sandwiched between two naked girls who somehow tripped into my place in the Hills, and now I'm just rewriting the book on a new strain of déjà vu. I've found myself playing along with guys out here who are just like the guys back there. Everyone wants to grab what they can and get a monster grip on of their version of the good life. But you know what? This desert is the Mojave, and it's going to fuck with all of us because this desert is one bad motherfucker who has been rolling with the homey's since our galaxy decided to launch this planet. It might do us good to study the earth's rotation to the sun and see why this longitude and latitude get the direct hit from the death star.

But no, we fall in love with the roaring Colorado river, and the desert flowers that blossom in the spring, and the national park and a host of lame excuses and move right into land where the top of the food chain are rattlesnakes, Gila monsters, scorpions, and cantankerous pensioners holed up in a double-wide. Read the charts people. The Mojave is a desert for a reason. You wanna strap it on and see what Mother Nature can do to you in the high sun? How about a desert kill zone of bone chilling, freezing winters that'll have you ordering Polartec Patagonia out of the REI catalogue. Be my guest; you're in for some big shit. Right now, I'm like any soul out here trying to get by, just another soul seeking another way out of the life that's becoming one long chase in a town held hostage by the vacant stare of this desert. The Mojave doesn't blink. And believe me, if we're not careful, we can all end up being that tweeker crashing around in an old junker at 2:00 in the morning. Or even a surgeon locked up in a shiny and spotless metal canister just waiting for another day to become tomorrow, marking time until it's a yesterday. Time bleeds out leaving nothing more than a carbonized fossil of what could have been a life.

That's how it is out here. Today, it's me and this desert. Let's all just take a moment to remember that I'm working as a hired hand to drop some dough on these fine former officers so they can purchase extra-large Mercury 300 HP power plants to move their bigger boats faster on that big, bad Colorado. After we do the big money count, Helena and I are going to be busy tunneling our way out of the dirt. So, let's put Rita back to work and get on with it. Now, Phil will, of course, talk about loss of big money, what the fuck Rita is doing, and how trust in the family is an issue (honor among thieves), and spout his usual litany of bullshit that we've heard from him before. So, I am counting on Chet to quickly get tired of Phil's whining and shut his son up. But Phil has a zero-tolerance temper, so yeah, that's going to work out real well with the parents.

On the other hand, today my head is clear, my mind is sharp.

My eyes are on the prize, and my hands are steady, so the pause that refreshes is good for me as I continue to work the problem. Thank you for today the first day of the rest of my life—that poster from Desiderata.

Either way, I'm armed with a book of ready platitudes that will help me just get through this moment in time so I can get on with living in the scree and make it through a July in Needles.

I shower and shave as Helena throws together some of her nearly burnt bacon and two this-side-of-sunny eggs, a bit runny, but it's the thought that counts.

"I may need a little back up."

"Vhat else is new." Her tone is playful, but I can sense she is up for an adventure.

"I'm hooking up with Chet and Phil at Butchero's."

"Vhat you needingk?" Helena's query is a little too eager, but I get it. My Russian baddie would like to get out of the house today.

Helena is my perfect wingman for a lot of reasons. Notably that Chet and Phil don't know Helena. She can be there just in case the boys get a little testy.

"Have no idea." I said. I tell her that the one thing I know is that I never really know.

"Dheese boys can be problem."

"There's always something…big money, *producto de Peru* on the table, and the wunderkind, Phil, causing a ruckus. You know it's always a bitch. Maybe I should just say fuck it and blow this who deal up?"

"Doc, deal not finished. Come clean from dheese so we cashingk out." Helena is a hard liner who's been through enough to see the big picture. The girl is fearless.

"I know. I just want to press the bright red button and nuke this place and take those assholes down with this desert."

"Vhat dheese gettingk you?"

I needed to hear her calmer voice about getting out clean and making sure we all go home happy with an extra slice of cake. Helena's a tough 26-year-old you can almost pull out of central casting if you're looking for the hardened femme fatale type with a tongue for the Czech and Slavic dialects, some Polish. Someone who also speaks French, which I happen to like a lot when she's in the mood and moves those eyebrows and I lose that moment in time.

Helena serves up her version of breakfast and takes a moment to change into her Audrey Hepburn version of Mojave covert ops, wearing a tight, black French cut t-shirt, black linen shorts, and black boots. Black doesn't seem to be the go-to color of choice in this desert in July, but the six feet of her stupendously long legs and platinum blondness can pull it off. She wants a drink, but she can't have one. She also wants a hit from my formidable medical arsenal, but that's off limits, too.

"Maybe time for quickie?" She shoots me a look, aware of her cheap entendre.

"*Nyet*, on the job." I cut to the chase. She sees that I am on point and all business. Although, I do like her hint. The suggestion of sex right now is just a bit pressing for my ability to multi-task. I explain that we need all hands on deck. She looks at me.

"Vhat is meaningk?"

"Hands on deck, it's a saying….means that everyone—"

"Vhat is deck, like on boat?"

"Yes, wait, what? No, no hands, literally…never mind."

We consider the options for tonight and discuss that we should show up early and she'll go in alone, sit at the bar and play nice. I'll be at a table when Phil and Chet show up; it'll be obvious who's who. The evening is settling in and nocturnal creatures start to stir, and if you listen you can hear the coyotes talking. They like to eat at night. Coyotes are clever survivors and predators who hunt in packs, which is not good if you are small prey and happen to be out after dark. It's best to be hidden under a warm rock, nestled deep in the safety of a burrowed hole in the high Cholla or tucked into aluminum wrapping with the AC on high.

I light a Menthol and ask Helena if she's in the mood for steak.

CHAPTER 17

HELENA WANT A GUN

"*vhants* gun." Helena is petulant. Cute. But still. I have no time for this.

"No, thank you. We do not need a Russian with a gun."

I suggest she just pack a few of my razor sharp, industrial grade, carbon-bladed scalpels. She's insistent.

"Let me touch it…vhat harm in me havingk?"

"Here," I toss her the smooth and balanced metallic firearm. "It's loaded, don't point it at anyone." She likes feeling the heft and heaviness. Of course she does.

"Oh, dheese eese strong, dangerous eese good." She says. She is feeling powerful from holding this kind of pistola. Helena likes feeling dangerous and deadly. She coyly hides the gun behind her back, trying to tease me into giving it to her, which perhaps, under other circumstances I just might. Not today. I remind her that this sidearm is mine.

"Look," I said, "My gun, my meeting. I do not want a bunch of guns going off."

She lit a smoke. "Seems shame, gun whidout using…givingk me dat." She points to a piece of hardware over in the corner.

"The nail gun?"

"Vhy fuck no? I'm no killingk anyone with dhis, vhat you calllingk it?

"Nail gun."

"Whid dheese nailingk gun…bright yellow…like being bad bee whid sting."

She picks it up, aims, points, and pretends to click off a few rounds like it's a loaded .38. The girl impresses me with her relaxed nail gunning skills. I glance at the clock and my Degas print, the one she would have reduced to thrift store status had she, in fact, pulled the trigger.

"I dig. 5/8 inch nails, 3.5 pounds, biggest compression deese portable badass boy." She says while expertly loading a magazine of galvanized nails into her new-found toy. Looks like she's dabbled in some kick-ass remodeling because the girl definitely seems to know what she's doing. One more reason I find her dancing eyebrows hot. The girl's at home with power tools.

It's now about 8:00 in the evening and the Needles' heat is still beating us up.

This is the time in July when the desert starts to shed that dry, rocky brown and re-skins itself by raking the landscape into a deep, tawny leather of bronze and gold colors you see on the postcards selling you on the wonderful vacation we're having in the middle of nowhere (*Wish you were here!*)The color moves slowly across the palette of dirt revealing a softer, more persuasive desert luster that promises lost souls the hope of a new day, someday, and we agree that the heat is not even worth talking about. It's at least 110 in the shade.

I could use some lip balm.

We are driving to downtown Needles and the meeting with Phil and Chet.

"Turn eet up." Helena reaches for the radio. "Jesus, I love fugingk dheese song." She pushes the AC portal toward her and rolls down the window. As the Speedster flies down the road, the rush of warm air moves past her face. She puts her arm out of the car window, letting the air current play with her hand, gently moving it up and down—a desert distraction on the physics of flight flying past the Speedster. Helena breaks into her own Balkan karaoke, singing along with '*El Jinete' (The Horseman)* about a man who's so in love with his woman he wanders alone, riding through the desert with a desire to die to meet his beloved again.

I like to watch the dust of the desert disappear in my small, square rearview mirror. It feels good to see it go goodbye. I think about the west coast and how I miss seeing that last remnant of sun finish off the day behind the flat earth of the heaving Pacific. I like how the last of our thermonuclear solar star sprays out a sheeting of blue and black, making it a good time to spot the first stars. In this moment, and in this sky, I can almost see atoms and particles, too.

We come up hard and fast over the smooth asphalt rise, and the small town sits there in a big, flat pan of land washed down by the wide and cooling Colorado River of water.

We're heading to a place called *Butchero's*. They do a nice bistec with whiskey.

"Helena, cómo le gustaría su filete?"

She laughs at my bad Spanish and pulls out the nail gun, then looks at me and sings the chorus—*Por eso lleva una herida. (That's why he carries a hurt.)*

The girl has pitch perfect Spanish with that cutting, hard Russian guttural accent. I'm not sure whether I'm in the desert or hidden away in the outlands of the Urals. Her smile is pretty dangerous, too, and I think that Phil better watch his back or he is fucked. *Lo siento mi amigo.*

CHAPTER 18

BUTCHERO'S

Butch is a motherfucker. And he is dead. So, he *was* a motherfucker. A liar and a thief, or so I've been told by other liars and thieves, so there must be some truth in that.

However, Butch was also a moneymaker.

His *Butchero's Grill and Bar* is popular and busy, and coughs up big coin for his wife. So, she is happy now because although Butch is gone, he left her a nice slice of Needles that prints money. How does it do that? By serving the biggest cut of porterhouse and cheap beer with nasty and cheaper shots served in a décor that is straight up leather and brass.

On occasion, Butch's wife will drop by to check on her money maker, but little is required of her other than to say hello to a few regulars, show her face, and be nice to the employees who have been here longer than anyone ever expected. Even them. You would know this place and probably have even been in steak and beer places that closely resemble *Butchero's*. It is dimly lit, and it has those red, glass hurricane table lamps with some kind of black fishnet cover on them, big oak tables and booths, and lots of oak fans and a very long bar with oak and leather stools. Last time I checked, the fashion faux pas was fishnet in a steak place, or maybe I'm thinking of fish netting in a seafood joint. The saving grace is, of course, the bar. They've done a marvelous job of backlighting the extensive, handsome and inviting selection of liquor bottles that proudly promise bright lights and great adventures to come. After a few shots, I am sure even the red hurricane lamps will look marvelous stretched tightly into their cheap, tarted up black fishnets. I make a mental note to never meet a septuagenarian coke fiend here. Again. Ever. And that means you, Chet.

The staff is uniformed in black slacks, crisp white shirts. Younger, tanned waitresses who spend their day boating or rafting on the Colorado have their hair pulled back in tight ponytails. Veteran hair sprayed waitresses carry the desert with them. They call everyone 'Honey.' They all know how to move steaks and liquor and are very good at working the table to push that tip. I am ok with throwing the extra dime down on the bill because, for God's sake, they are working a steak house in downtown Needles.

The Big Steak starts at four fingers thick with *Butchero's* special Bourbon-Haberno-Horseradish sauce that is seriously mixed and meant for red meat. You get your steak the way the cook likes it and that's ok with everyone who comes to *Butchero's*. How else would you want your steak other than red and bloody, charred black, and chased by cheap, big pours of golden whiskey that make this meat taste even better than you remember?

After a few shots you won't even notice the lightly pooling blood. Order up and dig in. Pass the Habanero.

Helena's seated at the long, mirrored bar populated by couples and hopeful singles busy gabbing with the bartender and doing shooters. Two guys are playing dice ignoring one of the single girls trying to horn in on their game. There's money on the bar and the young men are busy getting toasted. Helena watches their game intently, looking up occasionally to check on me.

I've grabbed a table near the men's room so we're pretty much out of the way. I'm only a cocktail in before Phil and Chet show up.

I can tell Phil's slightly agitated, so I order a round of beers, whiskey chasers, and of course, I immediately send Chet into the men's room with a vial of my *pura,* so he can mellow out his 70-year -old self. Then, I do the same for Phil, so everyone is seated with an early start on libations and the *mo-mo.*

I can see Helena at the bar, and she's behaving. Phil and Roy have their back to her, so I can discreetly watch her while I'm talking to the boys. I like this set up and I think I am really fucking brilliant when I put this whole thing together. Phil and Chet start talking about how they just want to make sure the money flows as sure as that big river rolling through this hot, parched piece of misery. I want that, too, so I can consider my next move. I'm pretty much done with this desert and make a mental note to call Jack and tell him it's time for me to get moving. He may have an idea or two because God knows I am fresh out. And now I have family feuding to deal with.

Phil's pissed at Rita, Chet's pissed at Phil. And the garrulous, bickering boys are so taken with their own situation neither of them notice that I'm a little nervous. Although, under the circumstances I think I am pretty swell at holding a steady line, sitting upright and not smoking too heavily. Thankfully, the warm shooters are doing what the FDA says alcohol should do. It's a depressant that calms my central nervous system even here in the midst of a *Butchero's* meet with the silverbacks arguing even before we've ordered appetizers.

Between the two of them, and yours truly sitting as the anointed table ref, I would hope that we could all just calm the fuck down. Apparently, that's not going to happen any time soon.

"I want that little bitch out of the game…she has fucked me over for the last time. I don't care that she isn't my daughter, even though, God knows, I've always treated her like one. And now I, *we,* are getting stung by her skimming," Phil says as has he leans forward and into me with his very best desert cop look. His short, cropped hair is tightly trimmed in a crew cut topped by a black and gold BassPro baseball cap.

This 'high and tight' cut is shaved so close to his head, I see a hint of a sunburn on the sides, and I can only think that this is his impression of a marine drill sergeant, or just a mother fucking hard-ass; take your pick.

Chet throws back his second shot and lights a smoke, so I'm pretty sure he's hitting on all cylinders. Between the *pura*, shooters and nicotine, this is a good night for old Chet. He's not talking. Yet. I think he wants to see where his son goes with all of this as part of the Chet mentoring program, or maybe his jaw is locked up from the big hit of my *cocaine.*

Phil continues. "Here's what I want, and you can decide which way you want to go, Doc, but I want you to cover whatever she's been light on—that's coming out of your end—and she doesn't get back in. Rita is...well, I'd like us all to agree that she's mother fucking done." Phil brings the beer to his lips and then adds, "And we all know way too much about you and Hollywood, know what I mean?"

Phil's words are neatly wrapped into the background patter of *Butchero's* patrons, the kitchen pushing out platters of sizzling steaks, the din of the bar, and the general room noise of an evening getting rowdy. Nobody is paying attention to our table of three discussing my past, their present, somebody's future...and Helena, thankfully, is still behaving nicely. This is good.

"I'm backing Rita. I'll cover her end, and she's good to deal..."

"What? Doc, are you fucking her?" Phil asks, looking at me then at Chet.

"No, Phil, but I will most certainly be fucking you if you continue down this path, asshole," I say with the warrant of a threat that I know should piss him off. And it does.

"Whoa, whoa...nobody's fucking anybody here, boys," Chet chimes in sensing the Phil vibe and makes an attempt at leading this meeting. By this time, however, I note that Helena is absent from the bar. I scan the room and she is nowhere.

"You little fuck," Phil says, "I got more people on this one hand..." He growls, holding up his hand, just so I get it. "...who can come down on you hard the minute we finish our last deal, and you will be standing there naked without us protecting your play, *capice?*"

"I didn't know you spoke Italian," I said with a smirk.

Phil looks at me quizzically. He does not like the smirk. Chet gives me the paternal nod, shrugging, signaling that Phil certainly can be one fucking idiot, but he's *his* idiot. I do a quick, surreptitious, casual scan of the bar and don't see my Russian, but I have faith that she's under control, somewhere.

"Here's what I propose, and you fellows tell me if we can get moving on finishing with Rita. I talk to her, she comes under me, and she makes up for her last "light" count. I'm responsible for the girl from here on out. Rita is a good earner, Phil gets the money owed, we all get fat and sassy, and it's on the down low, know what I mean?" I stare directly at Phil.

Phil looks at me, then lights a smoke, "Doc, what the fuck have you been smoking?"

He downs a shot and shoots Chet a look. We all see that Phil is still out of sorts. He exhales a thick stream of smoke out of his nose and fiddles with his lighter and ashtray. He continues staring hard at his dad as if Chet has an answer. It's a father-son moment that only a Hallmark could capture.

"No reason for anybody to get up in anybody's face, know what I mean," Chet says, trying to fill in for the silent Phil. Chet signals our waitress over for another round. Chet lights up his lungs with another smoke. I hear the phlegm building up in his chest with a low rumble as he coughs, wheezing hard into his beer. Jesus. Chet should get that looked at.

On a good note, I see that Chet is behind my play, and he knows how to calm the temperamental Phil Thing that's sitting at the table making life difficult for all of us.

"Phil? You good?" I say, hoping this squares it.

"Fuck you. Fuck him. Fuck all of this."

Phil is looking at me, then at Chet, and then realizes that this is not his night. Phil abruptly gets up, flips me off, and head's off to the men's room.

Chet sits back, we order a round. The welcomed whiskey arrives, and I raise a patronizing toast, "To all good things." I eye the room scanning for my Russian remodeler.

"Doctor, I think we may have a goddamn quorum," Chet says and right as we throw back our whiskies, we both hear it.

"What the fuck, Doc? Chet says to me.

"What-the-fuck exactly," I add, looking over his shoulder.

We hear another loud scream and the commotion of doors slamming and a world of hurt coming out of the far corner. Everyone in the place is nearly frozen and rattled, and just about everyone at *Butchero's* is trying to figure out what the hell is happening.

Some motherfucker is in a world of hurt and that motherfucker sounds a lot like Phil.

Phil comes limping out of the bathroom with blood pouring out of his shoe, and a nail in his right ear lobe that's dripping blood down his face and chin. Big Phil is in big pain. His eyes are wild and his BassPro cap sits awkwardly up and a little higher off his head. Pain, as served at *Butchero's,* is a tortuous bitch with a bite, so I would suggest that you stick with the steak.

Our waitress is frantic and shouts at no one in particular: "Is there a doctor in the house?" Yeah, it was a first for me, too.

Phil is grimacing hard and is letting us all know that he is a victim in great distress.

"Who was that mother fucking bitch? Goddamn, somebody get me a mother fucking ambulance right the fuck now, and a cop right fucking now, too. Jesus Mother of Christ." Phil is agonizingly loud and is holding his ear and hobbling to our table.

The galvanized nail protruding through the middle of his fleshy lobe does make a statement.

I like seeing this sweaty asshole, Phil, all 6'3' of him, limping over on one foot, holding his ear while blood fills the leather Topsider. Sperry makes a nice shoe. Apparently, it's made to hold up no matter what you throw at it. Or drip in it. Phil should have worn his boots tonight. But then maybe he would have two ears wearing metal.

Whoever fired the shot knew what they were doing and could probably frame a house, too.

"Honey, can you grab the tequila, the cheap stuff?" I calmly asked the waitress standing next to Phil. I think we can go on record and safely say this is the only time I've actually ordered booze without any intention of adding ice.

The fiery-proof tequila is an exquisite go-to astringent that only burns a helluva lot.

I like this for all the obvious reasons. It's good to be the guardian of Phil's pain levels.

Phil sits down, puts his foot up onto the table and is breathing hard. I immediately and liberally douse the 110-proof tequila on his wounds. Phil's face tightens up and he turns white, red, and then white again. There are about 8,000 nerves in the foot and Big Phil has some big feet, so I like where this is going. It hurts him like a motherfucker and this makes for a terrific supper show.

After pulling out the nails from his foot and ear, and helping Phil make it through his near-death incident, I place the metal pieces on the table and we talk about how the evidence might help us track down the assailant. I tell the boys that if we could only get forensics on this, we might be able to solve Phil's night of terror. This is much like an episode out of CSI.

Phil is dazed, maybe even dizzy, lightheaded with some after-shocks mixing with his adrenaline, the body's natural morphine. But after catching his bearings and settling into the chair, he starts to enjoy the free rounds of three-finger shots that come with his place in the sun.

In short order, he is loosely and drunkenly acknowledging the sincere wishes from the *Butchero's* attentive staff, and from the concerned and now quickly exiting patrons, all of whom will never forget their big night out at *Butchero's.* Chet agrees to drive the dazed and slurring Phil to the hospital for sutures and whatever morphine and painkillers the two of them can weasel out of the medical staff. As Phil leaves under assistance from the phlegmatic Chet, I gently remind him that it appears we agreed on bringing Rita back in. He simply waves me off, just barely able to, again, give me the finger, which is about the only body part that wasn't nailed.

"Don't mix your meds," I suggest, secretly hoping that he does. I sound professionally sincere to the relieved diners who smile widely. They are glad to see there is a doctor in the house. A pretty brunette in her mid-forties and slightly in her cups asks if I do 'house-calls,' and I politely decline saying something about not being covered. She tilted her head to the side, playfully leaned down and loudly whispered in a giggle, "Honey, I have my own plan," which she found funny enough to lose her balance, slightly weaving backward into the boozy arms of her date, or husband, or whoever the guy was that was buying her drinks.

Chet, ever the dad, and a little high himself, looks back and yells back at me, "It's all good, brother, all good."

I smile and give him a thumb's up, and wonder where the fuck Helena is, but I think I already know.

Walking out of *Butchero's* and across the parking lot toward the Speedster, I see the soft glow of a cigarette ember. I pop the door handle and slide in. Helena is coolly playing with the radio dials looking for good Mariachi.

"How did you pull that off?" I ask sliding in, releasing the top, pulling it down.

"I am at empty stall, he come. I turn out lights…pull trigger nailingk him."

"Literally," I say.

"I am pushingk him hard into sink. He doesn't know what the fuckingk…" Helena grabbed me with a kiss.

"No lights?" I was impressed.

"I like dark. He swing, missingk me. I pop nail into foot. Two in his ear…beautiful."

Helena tosses the butt, points the nail gun out the window, pulls the trigger and slams a nail into the palm tree next to the Speedster. "Right through ear. Now fuckingk guy eese easy shoppingk for…"

"Meaning?" I ask, vigilantly looking around, just to make sure there's no Roy or his crew lurking. Those boys are good at that.

"He eese needingk diamond post…"

"I think I noticed that ear shot, inventive."

We do a bump of the *mo-mo* and I wheel the Speedster out of the parking lot, turn up the radio, and hit the AC to work with the warm desert night. It feels good to have the *Butchero's* meeting behind us. '*Quorum,*' I didn't even know Chet knew Latin, impressive.

"Vhat is happeningk whid Rita, she eese back?" Helena asks. She is juiced on the flood of adrenaline.

"She is now," I say, mildly jacked on my own skilled, emergency medical response talents that once again make me feel like I'm a doctor.

Helena is ravenous for a cheeseburger, pink, and I'm still in the mood for a big thick, steak. Off in the distance we hear the yelp of a coyote that tells us the pack is back together. I believe they like their meat rare, as well.

CHAPTER 19

POOLSIDE

Three days after cocktails and nails at *Butchero's,* the call came in from the Chet and Cynthia household. Chet told me that Phil seemed to be healing nicely, thank you, and the recent unraveling of events was explained away by noting that our dear Phil and his sordid slip of a life had made more than a few enemies in the desert who wouldn't mind nailing him. Phil's years on the force and conversation with dad and brother Roy over dinner showed him how he could be a whole lot smarter and richer, if he only started seeing the opportunities. "Like your brother Roy and your goddamn old man," Chet chided. Phil took notice. Knocking down doors and knocking back beers with bikers, meth cooks, boosting cars, boats, and eighteen-wheelers, Phil and his crew heaved big sacks of money in the back of his pickup. Roy and Phil did their time on the force, said adios and shook hands with the real gift of this desert: money. I'd heard from Phil that his biggest score was about three years ago when he lucked in on a band of illegals up from the Calexico-Mexicali border working a truck stop. Phil came out of a diner near the stop and watched some girls getting in and out of trucks. Phil pulls a girl over to the side, flashes his old Needles police badge and tells the girl, who's all of about seventeen, that he's going to pop 'em for hooking. He has friends at border patrol, and if she doesn't give up her pimp, he's going to send every one of them back to Sinaloa or Juarez and let them figure out how to make a peso in Cartel country.

The young girl starts crying and lying and trying everything——even offers to suck him. He can have all the girls, just so she won't have to pin a name on her dude and where he's staying. An hour later, Roy's on the road. Then, they're both down at the rat hole motel two blocks from the truck center. The brothers walk into the motel office, come up from behind the greasy, Cheeto-licking motel owner and put the barrel of steel into the side of his head.

The owner pees himself, gives up the keys to two rooms, says he doesn't know who's in which room. Roy cocks the hammer back of the guy's head, tells him he better shut the fuck up, takes the keys and they move down to rooms #8 and #9. They quietly slide the first door open and find a four-year old Mexican boy sitting on the bed watching cartoons and eating out of a box of Lucky Charms. The brothers exit quickly. They go next door. Now, Phil's just thinking he and brother Roy are going to scam a quick buck off the booty the girls have been turning over to the pimp, but fuck no. Phil and Roy open the door, pistols aimed, and surprise the fuck out of three Mexican dudes who may be pimping lost pussy, yeah, but better than that, they've got five pounds of glassine crystal bagged up in half pounds and quarter ounces ready to go. The brothers pop a few caps into the Mexican's knees, bang a pistol butt across the older and louder Mexican who is spewing rapid fire about giving up his dealer. Roy tears up a porno mag, stuffing the pieces into the Mexican's mouth while Phil tosses the room just to make sure they got all the dope. Phil makes a quick call to his brothers on the force to come and get these assholes out the fuck of Needles. That was a righteous score. Phil and Roy still grin over that fat heist falling into their lap. Five pounds of uncut meth bagged like the motel was some kind of a dealer's drive-thru. The bagged pounds of shabu went off at the Phil and Roy fire sale price of $15,000 a pound with a ten percent cut to the favored boys on the force. Seems the only reason the meth smugglers were even dealing in chicks was that one of the guys had a sister that was bugging him for some money. He got pissed at her and told her to get the fuck out there and make some of her own. So, she did. Phil and Roy put almost $80,000 into their wallets. Righteous.

Phil was unable to positively identify the assailant who nailed his ass in the dark bathroom. He was absolutely certain this was the hand of a spiteful red-headed dancer who worked at the Route 69 Club and had fallen out of favor for Phil's attention and was probably still reeling from other acts of questionable legitimacy in which she and Phil were embroiled.

I believe Chet mentioned something about this dancer and Phil doing a drug deal that had gone about as well as their romance. Now, the particulars of just how the ex-girlfriend, weed-dealing stripper would even have known of Phil's social calendar and where he would be on any particular night, was left to wild speculation by everyone in the family.

Chet has called me up to the Kingdom to circle the wagons and regroup to make sure we're moving forward, and agree on details of distribution. Yes, we know Phil's a liability, but the boy is ready to get back in the saddle.

Chet's been the primary caregiver in nursing his son, while simultaneously soothing CC to keep the machine oiled, the family on track, and fuck, Roy is one avenging big brother who's been making everyone just a little nervous. Someone outside the family was needed up at the Kingdom to help quell frayed nerves, and evidently, that would be me.

I arrive at Chet and CC's. We're going to run through the details on scrips, distribution, cities and how this is going down. Most importantly, who and how much we have to grease so we can all benefit from a soft landing with this final deal.

I walk through the house and out onto the large expanse of patio toward the pool. The umbrellas are up, the drinks are out, music is on, and really, it's a picture right out of *Desert Living,* except for the pistols next to the chips and the plate of blow.

Phil is lounging under the shade of a rainbow-colored umbrella. His wounds are wrapped in beige gauze now spotted with dried blood. I notice his face isn't reddened just from the high desert sun, but more from his recouping on a strict diet of Vicodin, *cocaina,* beer, and nicotine. Chet politely hands me a cold one and points to a patio chair closest to him. I get to sit and watch the family at their finest, trying to figure out what went terribly wrong with the Terrible Phil Thing.

Phil is stubbornly hesitant to even thank me for my *Butchero's* medical aid, and as I bend down to check on the gaping hole in his ear, he pushes my hand away, "Forget it, Doc. Could you just mind your own fucking business."

He's a petulant bad boy. Sure, Phil, have at it, but that foot and ear are not looking like the picture of well-treated wound healing.

"You should look up the word 'fester'," I suggest.

"Fuck everyone," Phil says to no one.

The family agrees that this Phil shooting is anybody's guess.

Take your pick.

This desert is rich with predators that would enjoy seeing Phil feel the sharp sting of a little payback.

It was never easy with Phil, and the family was acutely aware of his disastrous miscues. And yes, while they were furious that one of their own was the victim of what was unanimously agreed a brazen and violent act right in their own backyard in downtown Needles—a freaking nail gun in the men's room, for fuck's sake. CC was fuming that Phil had brought this kind of attention on the rest of the family and crew.

"This is exactly the kind of crap we do not need, and maybe the little bitch could have nailed his balls. Maybe then he would start thinking with something else," CC told Chet who was growing tired of the whole deal and disliked any interruption in his life and to his money. More importantly, Chet knows that if CC even starts to sniff that the well may run dry, somebody's going to pay—and yes, that would be Chet. So, he's rapidly jumped on the Fuck-Phil-Train.

Sorry, Phil, but we gotta go grab that brass ring. Now, please shut the fuck up. And, son, tell that dancer to put some clothes on. It was also pointed out that as daring and inventive as the *Butchero's* shooting was, they were in fierce agreement that spending even an ounce of energy avenging Phil was a complete waste of time, and the consensus was drafted: fuck it, let's get on with it and leave Phil and his dancing partner behind. So, there you have it. Phil gets nailed—again.

Chet offers the first salvo, "Ain't no secret Phil's chalked up more'n his share of enemies who'd like to get even. Coulda been bartenders, dancers, dealers, or perhaps even a few of Needle's finest who could've spotted him at *Butchero's* and called in a favor…right?"

"Fuck you pop, Philly's just had a bad run." Roy defends while lying on the chaise. "I got your back brother" Roy says picking up the rubbing alcohol to wipe down his gun, sighting it he snaps the cylinder open and shut. Spins it and sights. Family poolside distractions on a fine summer day.

"I dunno know about that 'bad run' honey," CC looks over at Roy. "Turn over any rock and you'll find folks waiting to hurt your brother." CC said hoping to twist the knife a bit in her least favorite step-son.

She signals to Chet that it's time for another Maggie.

"That little bitch, Darlene, is going to pay for this," Phil says, looking down at his foot. He gingerly feels around his healing ear.

"Darlene?" I ask.

"Phil used to call her 'Oh-Darlin' when they were deep in lust. Right Phil? It was cute." Moms can be so, what's the word—annoying.

"Yeah, girlfriends can be a prickly bunch, especially when they're spending time on the pole," I say brightly, happy to make a joke that only upsets Phil even more. I light a Menthol, walk over to the bar and pour a stiff, tall vodka over ice, toss in a lemon slice for appearances, and sit down next to CC and hand her a vial of my *pura*. She winks at me. Chet catches this uneasy and absurd flirtation from his wife and glances at me, making me uncomfortable.

"Nobody should ever say her fucking name again," Phil admonishes us all, and we agree that yes, she is one fucking dead bitch. Can you believe she would even try to do something so goddamn stupid knowing who Phil is—or even worse, knowing what he could do to her? Exactly, Phil, we're behind you brother. Now, pour another, do a rail, and let's get some *pura* moving. Roy raises his beer and in an odd toast of sorts, hails to a time in the future when he, Roy, will personally take care of this Darlene chick because we're family and no bitch is going to come between him and his little brother.

Oh shit, now I'm not only feeling guilty, but very concerned that the Phil and Roy Show will go after her during their debauched down time. I make a mental note to find Darlene and give her a head's up with the suggestion that she should probably cut her dancing career short, look for a quick exit out of Needles and pursue a new life where the heat is a little less hot. Alaska could be an option. Better yet, if she could just get her ass over to the San Fernando Valley, there's enough of LA she could easily get lost in.

My sunny disposition is interrupted when I notice Roy is now up on the diving board, doing some kind of white boy dance. Watching ex-cops sunning in the midday Needles' heat with a drink and a smoke in hand while bouncing on the diving board playing King of the Pool is a ridiculous way to spend my day, but I need to get through this and move on so we can put scenes like this behind me.

Roy moves and jerks to *Guns N' Roses' Sweet Child of Mine* blasting over the speakers. Chet, CC, and Phil are lounging behind black-framed Ray-Bans, hands wrapped around cold beers with big, metal pistols next to the wooden bowl of Guacamole. I exhale and grin knowing this is the end of the world as we know it, and yes, I do feel fine.

Lucky for the Darlene chick somebody's going to pull her off the pole and make sure she's on her way out of town. Or at least that's what I'm thinking as Axl hits the high note on *"Where do we go now…"* I have to admit, Slash crushes it.

I really must be going.

CHAPTER 20

MY NEW PARTNER

Speaking of pools, cops, *pura fina*, final deals and the crew, I had a swimmer eager to get back into a lane, so naturally I did a quick bump on my way home and dialed Rita to share the love about her absolution and enrollment into the Chet and CC rank and file.

"You're back, and you're mine," I said to Rita, my mobile embedded in my sweaty hand still a bit shaky from the evening's event, or substances. Not sure which—maybe both?

"Bigger than ever," she said with a little swagger.

"Yeah, sort of, in a way. I am personally on the line for you, which means you are going to pay very close attention, so we can get through this," I explain.

"Tell me what and where, and I'm yours, Doc."

"You're on the line for $900 a gram. I can write 20 scrips, you get half and Chet gets half. That's what's on the books."

"And my side?" I knew Rita wasn't going to forget our *quid pro quo* deal arranged over Huevos, and under the table with our Puukko knife contest held at Mr. Eugenia's.

"That's covered with another half not on the books, so your take is at least $20,000. That's all you, just for being the coy, demure, and very quiet type, which I know is a stretch, but maybe when you look at a stacks of hundred dollar bills neatly lined up in a black leather bag, you can see how wonderful life can be."

There was an audible pause, and I could hear the Rita gears. Her mind was being pushy.

"And that would be non-negotiable," I pushed back.

"Done."

I could tell this was Rita feeling good, and I didn't want to be the buzz-kill, but I did have to remind her: "Rita, remember, if Chet or CC or anyone finds out about your end on this, well, that desert heat can get cold fast."

"I'm good to go, Doc; you and me have this."

"So, here's how we work it: you have your crew of ten running scrips as far up as Bullhead City in Arizona, dialed into ten pharmacies, split between the two states. On a good day we're pumping and dumping ten scrips in each state in just two days. Then into Laughlin, and burn an additional ten—just for you. Your deal, your money."

"And the other ten that are mine?"

"I keep those and can write them whenever. Better let the snowstorm blow through, and then take your final ten up to maybe someplace bigger and further away like Scottsdale."

"I'm good with that, I know where you live." Rita can threaten in a way that feels like a joke between friends, but her edge is there, hiding under a rock. Stroke, kick, turn, and strong finish, she was just getting warmed up, She could see daylight.

I was depending on my relationship with Rita and her big payday to keep her sane, keep the boys happy, do her job and get in and get out. I had to love Rita and her skill at staying on task, keeping the routine down, and just doing the laps. She's a wild card, and I needed her to be a pin-stripe professional and not get wound up with any of the Chet, Phil, or Roy bullshit. And I also pointed out that it would be in her best interest to stay the fuck out of CC's gravitational pull.

After my call with Rita, I'm still nervously working through every step. The desert is blowing by on my way back to VistaVue, and I wonder if it's the Phil and Roy brotherhood that always makes me a little edgy, or the Class II controlled substances?

I turn up the exotic Zeppelin desert anthem, *Kashmir*. The hypnotic orchestral strings transport me as I race across the flat, dirty sand. The hot wind feeds into the cabin of the Speedster. My brain is the last to let go and travel with Page and Plant. I don't like loose ends and I have more than a few right now as I consider how Phil and Roy are playing this. Because they are tapped into the matrix of Needles cops who can snap-to when handed the fat envelope, what's to prevent the crew to step all over me once this deal is done?

Like I said: loose fucking ends.

The Chet and Cynthia Kingdom has high, thick walls protecting the family against the other world. All they have to do is pull up the gates, pay off a few of their closest boys in blue and they walk with every dime. They're nowhere near the dead bodies. A false report is filed, the next of kin notified, and Helena is toast and out of the picture with the Airstream and the Speedster orphaned and up for auction. Or worse, become the property of the family. Game, set, match, and thank you for playing. Fuck, the Russians would be a little upset in being denied the killing, but they'd just have to learn to live with it. I'm sure Maxim would adapt. He'd just go kill somebody else. Jack would have to step in and deal with that crazy part of his job. And Helena? Don't even ask about that event. Maybe Jack could rope her in , set her up, and help her disappear to safety starting another new life over again.

It's not easy being me in July in Needles, and I hope the drive back helps clear my mind. I also wonder if Jimmy Page has been back to Morocco, if that place was ever as hot as here, and how much Kif did he and Plant, Bonham and Jones smoke with those North African roadies?

Rita and I are meeting tomorrow morning to fire up the afterburners and get this party started. With our shares of the *pharma grade cocaina* about to hit the streets, Ie could pocket what's fair and hide vaults of cash in the desert floor.

When I got back home and walk through the door, Helena is busy on her laptop and humming a Mariachi tune but not in a perky, obnoxious Doris Day way, but more in a dangerous, hushed way that makes her so fucking cool. She's a big fan of *Enrique Bunbury* and turned me on to his cover of *El Jinete.*

"More on the Chet and CC crew today, and what I'm about to tell you is how I'm playing this so we all get out clean."

She could see that the look on my face was all business. It was my serious side. I was drinking a virgin Fresca with a lemon wedge, and although I had my Nicorettes at the ready and a Menthol on my lips, there was going to be a 24-hour moratorium on a few of our favorite things.

Who knows? Maybe I could get a 24-hour chip and turn a corner.

Tomorrow, I know that when I kick the Speedster into fourth and we fly down the freeway to finish with Rita and the crew, the deal is done.

I walk outside scan the horizon line of a scorching July in Needles when the sun can blister the rust off a can as the evening leaches into deeper reds, oranges, and purples that paint our very own version of the Northern Lights, but without the magnets and the spectrum of the sun's radioactivity reflecting back into our atmosphere. We don't get the whole Aurora Borealis show you'll catch on the Discovery Channel, but it's just enough to make you want to cruise up to Sweden and book into the Artic Bath Hotel and Spa to catch the real deal.

Helena joins me, wraps me up in her arms, and leans her head on my shoulder. The desert red sky bounces off the flat rocks as the first star appears away in the twilight. We are on Mars looking out at our universe draped in that deepening blue-black heading into night. We are lost together, now just trying to find our way around the planets.

"I am thinkingk I can see my mother."

"I am thinking I can see Quentin."

I kiss her and nuzzle into her neck, and hear her sigh.

It's enough for me.

CHAPTER 21

RITA'S DROP

Pistols. Carry one and things start to happen. Carry two, and things start to happen to you. More than that and you have a fucking situation on your hands. This is what Helena told me this morning as we were going in to meet Rita, exchange scrips, and get the last mile moving with Chet and the crew so they could turn and churn on the big dough.

Helena is a bright girl. She is also coming with me. Due to my zero tolerance for extracurricular substances, we are beautifully matched with bright thinking, steady hands, and clear eyes. Really, I have to admit, we are looking like a pretty cool couple who know our way around cooler cars, big sunglasses, and ways to make buckets of fast money, faster.

Helena is lying next to me and I consider making the morning move, but right now it feels a bit played. We have a lot on our plate in the middle of nowhere trying to extricate our life from a few problem areas. I consider signing up for an intensive Tony Robbins weekend and find me, whoever I am, or think I am. Just walk across the freaking hot coals and call it a day, right? I could probably get that together and invite a few other VistaVue residents over for a spark of conversation, a few cold ones, and when we're feeling particularly sassy, break out the coals, take off our shoes and play some Tony Robbins CD's just to make it feel like the real deal. Barring that desert dance, Helena and I are pretty good at knowing when it's absolutely necessary to back off with our shared Peruvian friend. We know it's smart to dial it down when facing the pointed barrel of a Chet or Phil and Roy issue that's about to blow up or go off. And right now, we want to make sure that the desert boys are in-check and everyone is good with everything. I wonder about Tony and the coals. I could do that. I know I could. See, already he has me believing. That dude is good.

Nicely, I have been thinking ahead, so yes, I do have buckets of cash stashed away in this broad, brown beating of desert dirt. And while I am currently under the influence of Chet and former police officers that also happen to represent the criminal element, I like knowing I'm nearly out of the Chet and CC family life. I know they'll hate to see me go. After all, when I walk so does a freight train of money. A loss all around, but what's the worse that could happen? Chet can go back to running Cub's and CC can go back to running Chet. Phil and Roy can go back to running with demons, boats, and whatever they can pull off the pole—or off the border.

To my earlier point about fucking me over, taking all of the cash, and stepping over dead bodies, why the fuck would they let me say adios? They don't have a choice. We're feeding off each other.

These boys know that I know how to write the bad scrip using various medical identities. But I could easily bring them down just by penning a terrifically horrendous number of scrips under one license that would flag any pharmacist worth his continuing education credits. Nobody likes a nosy pharmacist who starts asking questions. No, indeed, we do not want that kind of inquiry. We do not want the suspicious jotting of paper, a phone call, or other acts of brave citizenry that would ultimately bring major heat on our distribution chain, and in turn, on this fine family of law and order. No, if you were to ask Chet and CC, they would be the first to raise a glass to a good run, a terrific business partnership that had its day And, yes, thank you, we did put a few dollars away. "Chet insisted on $50,000 in a ladder CD and vowed not to touch it for five years, didn't we, dear?"

I make sure they get theirs, they make sure what's mine is mine. Everybody's got a blue bird on their shoulder. It's how we all get along in this desert. We give a little we take a little. We live to see another day. I mean, honestly, why would you want to fuck up a future that could have you sitting high, wide, and handsome on a Sunday running your boat up the cooling Colorado with a cold beer in your hand, some *mo-mo* in your pocket, and that dry desert heat gently browning your lovely bikini-bottomed water toys to a lusty, toasted cinnamon?

It's a fact that burying big cash in the desert heat feels better than fine.

It almost makes the dirt feel cool. Almost.

We are meeting Rita at a gas station just outside of Needles.

We get there and I see that Rita is parked in the shade, and we can hear the deep, low bass driving through the interior of her car (*Whitesnake's Greatest Hits?*). I am thinking that the girl must be happy to be back in the fold. Problems with your stepdad, particularly when moving a highly illegal product have a way making those family get-togethers a little weird. So, indeed, it's best to get past the various issues of shorting the count, dealing behind dear Dad's back, and being dangerous enough to scare the shit out of everyone living in the Kingdom.

Rita wants to run and gun in her metallic silver, 650HP Shelby Mustang that can suck a black hole out of the deep Saudi oil reserves while moving her sweetly down the open road toward the bright future of working out, counting bundles of cash, carrying a sharp blade, turning heads, and buying new wheels whenever she wants.

Those probable and prosecutable felonies and bad deals gone wrong haven't had much of an effect on Rita. She'll be the first to point out with her ego-boasting attitude that she "sure-as-fuck" is working the dream without really working at all. Living outside the law is best served when your family is the law. It's nice to have friends on the force.

Rita is deadly, sharp, smart, and young, but in too much of a hurry to see that she needs a way out before this dry dirt will grind her bones into fine desert dust, leaving her breathless and broken, pierced by the sharp points of the Saguaro. Nasty business, this desert, especially when you believe you're an immortal. Rita is in for a rough ride, no matter what gear she shifts.

I pull the Speedster up next to her wheels and roll down my window.

This is a meeting of silver cars that go can go fast with big sunglasses that make us feel faster. I reach over and hand Rita a stack of scrip neatly bundled in a brown, pebbled leather notepad minus the notes. She seems a bit tense even for a catty little pro like her.

"Inventory for everyone including you with the back end later as promised." I say, happy as fuck to make sure she is on her way, or almost on her way.

"Who's she?" Rita asks, looking suspiciously over at Helena.

Helena shoots her a look, and then toys with the moment by turning up the volume on the Mariachi music hoping to tweek our young, head-banging rocker.

"Somebody I know."

"She looks like a nobody you shouldn't know."

Nice. But expected. Remember, Rita likes the attention. Helena reacts with her own swordplay by turning the volume up even louder. Helena pucks her lips and blows her a kiss.

This makes me feel warm and cozy because I have nothing better to do than find myself sitting in a gas station mini mart trying desperately to stay on the down-low, while two girls decide that right fucking now would be a very good time to break out with a battle of the bands between *Whitesnake* and Mexican. I reach over turn the radio down, lean toward Rita's car window and tell her to focus on the scrips right there in her hand, the day ahead, and to make sure she gets what's hers and that Phil gets his, so we can all get ours and get the fuck out of here.

"I think you can turn this in a few days…call me when it's over," I say, surprising myself by trying to show Rita a mature and caring side, which is extraordinarily hard for me because I am rarely any of those things at any one time. There's no easy way out of my head or into my heart. I have my moments but I need my substances. Living out here without a few vices is nearly impossible, and I'm pretty goddamn sure nobody's really tried it yet. Why would they? Giving up ice-cold beers and Menthols in the morning would leave your system with only caffeine, sugar, and the newspaper. This borders on lunacy and frankly, as physician, I'm not so sure I would even feel good about suggesting that kind of behavior modification. The desert will most certainly kill you first.

"Maybe you can buy your new *somebody* lunch," Rita nods toward Helena, "I think the dude at the counter just tossed fresh dogs on the rollers. Add a Big Gulp and you're golden. What girl doesn't love a big, thick piece of meat in the morning?" Rita shrugs, lowers her sunglasses, and turns up *Whitesnake* as she throttles her Mustang into first, pushing hard on the accelerator to smoke her tires. With an impatient flip of her hand, she waves *Adios*. I dial up Chet and give him the news that Rita is taken care of and we should meet over near the boat launch.

It's time to get wet.

CHET MEET IVAN

His left hand is interesting. Or more specifically, the palm of his left hand is interesting. It is scarred, but not in the way you would think. It does not show a cut, or suture marks, or a line of torn and healed flesh that has been sewn back together in surgical repair. No, this scar is the result of heat. It is a distinct and intriguing scarring of skin, and it makes the inside of his hand, the palm, look like tanned hide—a kind of stretched, flattened, and shiny leather without a wrinkle or a line. He told me how it got this way. It had to do with blood-red rubies and people who were intent on doing damage. People who wanted to teach him so he could teach others. Bad men who wanted him to know why they are, who they are. So, they strapped him down and buckled him down on his back with both his arms outstretched and open. And they gave him a choice. He chose his left because his right hand was the last hand he used to stroke his little boy's head when he left his house this morning. So, they took a large piece of flat metal, and they made sure this metal was ember and molten hot. Then, they opened his palm flat and then pushed the metal onto the palm and pushed it harder again, like they were ironing his flesh. The metal seared deep into his skin. Today, his palm has a memory, a shine, and is the reason why he is a fearless man and unafraid of anybody. He explained to me over my iced vodka and a late summer night that after you have had molten metal ironed into your hand and you pass out and lose all your bodily functions and plead for death, begging to die, then you are ready for anyone. He will tell you that he is lucky. At least he has one good hand that can feel the skin and love of his son.

This is that man. And he is my friend.

He is even more dangerous than the melting point of metal.

My friend is a Russian. This is the man, who, as mentioned earlier, would be one of those very bad men who would kill you, torch your house to ash and oil and then come back and burn it again just because he can.

He is here. And he is going to help me out.

After leaving the lovely Rita, I dial my friend, Ivan. I helped him get a new start in this country—and a new identity. Surgically. Together, we pieced a new way to live his life. Ivan is a former Russian who liked gems. Big rubies. Ivan always had a soft spot, a weakness for grassy-green emeralds, anything in the rough-cut carats on the black market that could travel in tight, small spaces. He is now a 100% American businessman, straight up legit. He's got a successful business with boats and yachts, and his gorgeous wife is a lovely woman with an up-market interior design business and new-moneyed clients in Laguna Beach. So, make no mistake, while I can work with Chet and make sure we all get ours, Ivan will make sure I get mine.

By the way, his name isn't even Ivan. I just call him that and he thinks it's cute. His wife thinks I am charming.

Now, here's the best part of having a friend like Ivan. Although Chet, CC, and I can walk away knowing we could definitely fuck with one another, we won't because that would be seriously stupid. However, I like to hedge my bets, especially with Phil and Roy in the mix, so I opt for an insurance policy. This would be Ivan, and he is more than happy to help me find my way through the desert. Ivan likes being out here because this feels like another America that is big, western, and is the sort of place where animals and killers live and love.

Ivan says he likes it hot. He likes the cactus, and the telling high-pitched yip of the coyote, and the roadside gift shops with snake rattlers, and reddish-brown, stripe-tailed scorpions suspended in amber, frozen in their own honey-colored limbo.

He is also poetic in his way of seeing his life and watching the way the American sun sets low in the west. Ivan talks to me about his love for the Clint Eastwood and Samurai movies. Ivan tells me that he will keep his eye out for gunslingers, and I can hear Sergio Leone playing as the background soundtrack for Ivan's time in the west and for his love of scorpions.

The day is opening up to a July blue sky, wrapping us into a desert hot that we just need to grind through. I am glad I am wearing linen today. It's a neat geographic trick that the big Colorado River water rumbles through giving predators and population a reasonable shot at life, or at the very least, the idea that we can survive here at all. Big water is big business in Needles. The river travels in big gulps and shows us how much fun you can have in the desert as long as you are on a boat in the river in July. This big water makes us all feel that we can make a run at carving out a life in this place. We bring a lot of water to this dirt just so we can call it home, but this desert could just as well give a fuck about us, and soon enough we'll realize we're facing certain death living under the Needles sun as we wait for the water to run its course. And it will.

Helena and I pull up to the Amtrak station and wait for Ivan.

He is not arriving by train. We are only meeting him here because it is a good place in what passes for downtown Needles with lots of people and a large parking lot, and I found out this morning that Helena likes trains, so that is a happy coincidence.

"This is a bad man who is a good man, if you know what I mean," I say to Helena.

"Ghut to us." Helena is a quick study and she knows I like that about her.

We are sitting in the Speedster continuing to wait for Ivan.

The air conditioning rattles just enough to make me think that it's about to go, but then the cooling machinery finds its second wind and starts pushing enough cold to make the slightly distressed red leather seats feel nice. We are having a pleasant moment looking at trains, people, and the hopeful arrivals and departures, or even those passengers just sitting in their assigned window seats, looking out at this train stop and wondering what goes on here and how can anyone live in Needles. Perhaps it's best just to stay on the Silver Meteor and count the monotony of high barrel cactus as Needles safely tumbles past you while you enjoy the trip out and beyond to another planet. There's simply no reason to get off here. Especially when you know that the rest of your journey will be everything Amtrak promises with scenic windows, comfortable seating, and a great pouring of libations and the clinking of glasses in the bar car that keeps everyone lubricated so your travel by train is exactly as expected. The motion of the train is an engineering marvel that transports you. It is mesmerizing. So, you are keen to keep ordering a few more with your newfound friends, and with every drink the possibility of getting lucky is part of the ride. You'll see. The train is that kind of a place moving away from this kind of a place. Helena and I agree that we should get on board and play with the romance of train travel where food, drink, and companionship are rolled up in one handsomely appointed sleeper that even offers turn-down service with your favorite nightcap.

This is something I would like.

I think Helena would be a lot of fun in a sleeper on a train traveling away from here. I make a mental note of this great idea.

"Vhere would go?" Helena is playing with her Hermes, opening and closing it.

"You tell me." I like the way she can light her cigarette, exhale, and snap the metal case shut in one, precise move. It's a sexy punctuation to anything she does. Snap. Click.

"Sombwhere cold, yes?" she says with just enough tease to let me know she's serious. Maybe she's thinking cold like Gdansk or cold like, say, a bad winter in LA where people would have to grab a sweater and layer up at an evening concert at the Hollywood Bowl listening to the band Chicago, which I don't like at all.

"You know I like it hot," I said, and putting my seat back as far as it could go.

"You and heat. Soon you are dryingk up to a nothingk. Maybe you like hot like dheese," Helena whispers and leans, kissing me hard. Helena's soft and warm lips are a surprising twist to the morning, and it definitely demands that I kiss her back, hard. So, I do and she likes it, a lot. I could tell. At that very moment, I want to throw the Speedster into high gear and rocket back to the Airstream. I'm sure Ivan would understand and catch up with us later. I play with the idea and look over at Helena. She is stunning in her linen shorts and fitted white cotton blouse. Her soft, shiny hair is pulled back into a ponytail peeking through the back of her baseball cap, and her big wraparound glasses make her face seem smaller in comparison. She reminds me again of her take on Audrey Hepburn who has recently arrived by train from The City of Los Angeles. Helena's high cheekbones and attitude can carry her twenty-six years a long way even when she snaps her gum. Helena takes her glasses off, hangs them on the dash, moves herself to face me, and I can see the slightest breeze of the Speedster's AC tenderly move a few strands of her hair in what must surely be slow motion. I inhale her.

"Hold thought." She says, lighting two cigarettes, putting one to my lips while rolling down the window to get a blast from the desert. The girl is smooth.

"When did that start," I ask, wondering when we decided it was a good idea to have train sex without the train, or the travel. So really, it's just Amtrak train parking lot sex. Almost.

"You know you always lovingk me," she purrs, wise beyond her years.

"Have I…you're absolutely sure of that?" I said teasing her back. I am lost to her.

"You know I never wrongk." She softly bites the lobe of my ear and grabs me for another and much deeper kiss. I feel my cock stirring, and I want to unbuckle my pants. I kiss her hard. She weighs into me, and I can feel and hear the brush of her linen and cotton that is a sexy snare drum to the background white noise of the Speedster's AC. Her breath is that deliciously carnal blend of young six-foot blonde, mint gum, and good tobacco as we kiss and start to neck. I am lost in her wet, warm, soft lips. I think that I should remember to write a personal note of thanks to Dr. Ferdinand Porsche for his remarkably visionary piece of German engineering that is everything as billed, especially when parked. The interior sparkles with a pheromone-rich mix of soft skin, moist and wet fragrant notes that mingle with what surely must be a perfect blend of warming desert air and hotter sexual tension paired with the texture of her fresh cotton. Jesus, even the AC is working right along with Helena's wet lips. My golden moment is handsomely packaged in the vintage red leather cabin of Dr. Porsche's 1965 Silver Coupe Speedster. God I love this car.

Helena is now straddling me, which is not easy to do in this two-door convertible in the parking lot at the Amtrak station, no matter how good she is at working small spaces. However, it's becoming evident that with her very long, killer legs and the confined cabin of this coupe, a few things could go very wrong.

Either I'm going to cramp up early and the whole deal is an embarrassing wash, or perhaps just as bad, we make it through my physical duress and are in mid-coitus when there is *interruptus* because one of us has knocked the car into neutral and the Speedster has slowly crept across the parking lot while we are fucking our brains out.

The Speedster will invariably end up on the tracks and local authorities will be called. Either way, and as much as I would like to fuck her, and it's quite obvious she would like the same, this is a not what Dr. Porsche had in mind when showing his investors early designs of his Speedster. No, this love fest will have to wait another day. Both Helena and I awkwardly untangle our bodies and return our trays to their upright position, as it were.

"Was that good for you?" I am my most charming when faced with disaster.

"I have better." Helena is good.

"Ever in a Porsche?" I'm no slouch at the tit for the tat.

"I vhink I vhud like somethingk, biggness…maybe somvhingk like dheese," she says, pointing out the window. I turn to follow her long fingers and gorgeous eyes.

Right now, I hate Ivan so very much because a huge black SUV, with even bigger wheels and a large, weighty steel bumper that must be used for towing, winching, or doing something other than driving is coming straight at us.

Apparently this large, black Detroit piece of metal can also double as an emergency roadside assistance vehicle, or is simply a very good and handy option in case the Apocalypse happens to ruin our day.

Ivan pulls up next to us, dwarfing our sweet and sleek little coupe.

I see his chrome metal spinners spinning. These monster spinners are popular with the new breed of nasty rappers who are instantly crazy rich and drive around with monster entourages. Ivan would most certainly wish to be part of that entourage. He would be good at handling the paparazzi and groupies, and generally kicking ass for grilled-up gold-toothed gangsters with platinum chains and mega CD downloads. No doubt Ivan would like to pose with the posse. He does like to make an entrance. Ivan is just shy of 5'5, a wiry, muscled, rough-coat terrier, friendly, but he does need a lot of room. Today, he is wearing tight Wrangler faded jeans that are too long and cascade in wrinkles over his ridiculously expensive and shiny black leather, custom-tooled cowboy boots. He likes to wear his jeans this way because that's how the brave and reckless bull riders on the PBR circuit do it. His belt is big and black, and he is wearing a white, mesh shirt that is cut to show off the hours he spends with his trainer. Ivan is ripped. His shoulder-length hair makes him look younger than his fifty years because it is still a shaggy mix of shades of brown, and he has lots of it. He has a strong face with a good chin which could make him appear stern, but he is kind. His wife has told me how much she loves the wide, Roman nose I gave him; a neat trick that nose. I loved it when I did it. I still consider it one of his better features. Ivan has deep blue eyes that can be eerily piercing if your heart is not in the right place.

I introduce Ivan and Helena. They exchange pleasantries in Russian.

"Na obed ja lublu est salat iz ovoshej?" Ivan asks what Helena likes for lunch.

"Ya nikogda ne yem pered obedom," Helena says she never eats before dinner. Which is not true because I have seen her eat a huge stack of pancakes at my place, certainly before dinner.

Their pleasantries continue, and I honestly don't know if they are still talking about favorite cities or favorite food items. She's probably talking about how nice it would be if he, a fellow Russian comrade, could give her a gun.

With the morning growing toward noon, we're collecting ourselves in the nearly empty parking lot, doing our best to coolly get our game on before heading over to meet the boys at the boat launch. Ivan has the back-story on who's who, and what the fuck, and where we are today with the Chet and CC business arrangement. Helena and I get into Ivan's big car. Ivan gives me strange look like maybe he knows we were an item in the Speedster, but I chalk that up to the paranoia of lust and love that seems to happen when you think everyone knows you are sexing it up in public places. I look up at the tall light post thinking there must be surveillance cameras out here, but then I remember this is Needles and am not sure if they budgeted for that. I think I'm in the clear, and then suddenly remember, *'Oh yeah, I don't give a fuck.'*

Other than a few travelers getting on and off the train, the Amtrak station is a transitory place. People here are on their way to somewhere else. The heat sparkles off the long, bright skin of the Silver Meteor as it readies to depart. The sound of the train's whistle is loud and powerful and makes me feel like we should be on this train.

I look at Helena, she looks at me, and we both like it. Helena is sitting in the back of Ivan's SUV, cleaning her sunglasses and asks me if I want her to clean my gun. I do not. I get the double entendre, too. She is frisky and I'd like to play, but my neural pathways demand a professional like myself be on his A-game. Sex and chemicals go on the back burner.

I can't help but notice Ivan's heavy bling of clear and speckled, honey-colored amber.

"What's with the scorpion thing? Lucky charm? You got about five of those bad boys hanging around your neck and one on a lanyard. You're like some kind of shaman hiking through the galaxy. Don't get me wrong, I like the look, just asking if you got something going on with Santeria minus the chicken blood?"

Ivan's steely blue eyes lock in on me. I can see he is seriously intent on making a point. "These are my brothers, and we're all frozen in time, Doc, just waiting to be released, just waiting for our chance at redemption. Or revenge."

Ok, I get it. I think. Ivan's a little over the top, but I'm ok with his notion of drawing the parallel of our lives lived like scorpions now locked in the amber and sold as a souvenir—what the hell, it's the desert.

"That's a pretty wide spread redemption. Then, you got revenge… both can get a little ugly."

"I am counting on it."

"Which?"

"Killing the men who put fear into my wife and son." Ivan looked up at the sky, kicked the dirt with his polished boot, and fingered his smooth, flawless, frozen prey. "This scorpion will kill again." Ivan said, talking right past me.

"Well, my friend," I said, pointing to his suspended talisman, "for starters these bad guys today are my bad guys. Second, the Russians who are after me, aren't your guys. Third, those little beasties, the ones hanging around your neck, are nasty hard cases who have made a living out of this rock, so we gotta give credit where credit's due. Those bad boys can freaking bite…well, actually more of a sting. Next thing you know we're heading to emergency and possibly last rites, if you want 'em."

"Russians or scorpions?" Ivan's sarcasm is on point. "Tell, me, Doctor Dominic, how much cooperation we want—I can be persuasive," Ivan says.

"I don't want to hear from these assholes again. I gave them the keys to the kingdom. They are getting theirs and those two big boys—Chet's sons. Well, let's just say these are problem children. So yeah, we want to make sure everyone understands that this desert is big enough for documents to get lost, paper to vanish into thin air, and that we have people who can fuck with their people."

"What about wife?" Ivan asks.

"She'll do what he does."

I'm still thinking about my parking lot tryst with Helena. I can honestly say that Dr. Porsche could have offered up maybe a few more inches in the cabin and he wouldn't have lost a dime in the dynamics of the design.

The Silver Meteor slowly pulls out. A blast on the whistle signals that Needles is on its own. The civilized Amtrak travelers are ordering cocktails and happily waving goodbye to anyone at the station, even us. Ivan's big black Escalade leaves them to their clean, scenic, viewing windows. We could be waving back, but they can't see through our tinted windows. They have no idea that we, too, are travelers, but with *our* drinks and service, we also get to carry real guns. Except for Helena.

We are now driving down the road and we are sitting up high in this black motorized condominium of a car. Helena is wrapped in the huge, black leather bench seat humming a tune while watching a DVD—*"The Mighty Colorado."* Ivan picked it up at a gift shop. Ivan is hitting ninety. The Escalade is a battleship ticking along with really awesome AC. I am sitting next to Ivan, happy he is here. I want Chet to be happy, too. But chances are excellent that he will not be.

"Vhee losingk deese Colorado," Helena says, importantly, and the way she says this almost makes me feel like I am on a tour with a ridiculously hot Conservation Corps guide.

"Only water," Ivan says. "Someday this desert will return to what supposed to be and everyone goes back where they are coming from."

"I want out. If I get past one more deal and Maxim, I'll tip my cap to this desert as I turn a page. Out of Limbo, out of Needles, out of the monster grip. Adios Chet and CC."

Helena and Ivan shoot each other a look and leave it alone. They are not sold on the Limbo thing. As for me leaving Needles? Helena has heard that one before. She knows how much I like the stacks of cash. She's not sold.

"Bummer, vhas just likingk dheese places," Helena clicks her gold Hermes open, lights, and she exhales coolly. Audrey Hepburn would like Helena.

This is a very good time for more nicotine, so I pop at least three Orange Nicorettes. Ok, now we're rolling, thank you Jesus. I was having a moment. Just going back through the past. Yes, the matters at hand did demand my immediate attention, but just for a moment I floated. I closed my eyes and went to place that was a little out of body, part memory lane, pieces of regret, and those pesky bits that seemed to come out of nowhere thanks to a massive adrenalin surge mixed with my heavier than usual dose of nicotine. Nothing unusual here, just me driving up to meet Needle's finest in a mammoth SUV driven by a bad man carrying heavy ammo, my nicotine habit mixing sweetly with a rapid adrenalin pulse, and Helena coolly snapping her gum. I open the large, center console and do a quick inventory of what Ivan is working with today, and I look at him thinking that he too, has lost his mind. Although Ivan is concentrating on the road ahead, he picks up on my vibe as I grind on my Nicorette and stare at him. He knows me well.

"What? You know I am never taking chances," he says, his hands responsibly gripping the pebbled, leather steering wheel in the Highway Patrol-approved 9 and 3 position.

"It's a fucking arsenal." I should have known. Ivan rarely goes light.

"You never know. Look, if Colorado can disappear," he says while checking Helena in the rear view mirror. "Bad things can happen to all of us. I am like boy scout being prepared so only the good will happen." Ivan raises his shiny, leathered and waxy palm reminding us of evil. "Not again like this piece of skin."

"Colorado eese long, long river," Helena informs us. "Nearly 1,500 miles…soon, what? Nothinkg? Endingk of storytime."

See what I mean? Sexy and smart. Helena would seriously look awesome in that dark green Conservation Corps uniform, but as we pull into the Big Boat Marina And Launch (*Campers welcome!*), my fantasy of Helena taking me on a guided tour of the Grand Canyon and asking me if she could look at my visitor's guidebook and pressing her breasts against me will have to wait.

I could see Chet and his boys, parked and leaning against their cars near the disappearing current of the mighty Colorado, near the big boat launch with his big boys, all of whom are about to meet my friend, Ivan, who happens to have more than two pistols.

And that means we may have a fucking situation.

The AC is blowing through Ivan's luxurious ride, and I am sitting in the plush embrace of this well-appointed and impenetrable burl walnut and leather bunker protecting me in my moment as my mind wanders back to a time when I decided to get the fuck out of LA and get the fuck into Needles. I was thinking it was nice that I still had contact with the Fed side who know how to contact me, but right now, at this moment in time, I felt very alone. And lost. And maybe I was getting to a point where I stopped giving a fuck because I'm powerless, or at least feel like that. I keep thinking I have this under control, but I don't. I have flares, guns, and Russians so it only feels like it. Nope, the jury just came back and their verdict is unanimous: Doctor Dominic Martinez doesn't have shit under control and remains guilty as charged for whatever.

"What the hell are we gonna do, Mr. Ivan?" I asked in a small breath, looking around the SUV's huge cabin. I'm sure the A-team would like a plan of action. I know I'd feel better.

"Kicking some ass, doctor." Ivan smiles and glances back at Helena. In the mother country, this marina showdown is a spring weekend in Minsk. Ivan and Helena look out the window. Helena comments on the number of boats, snaps her gum even louder and taps me on shoulder. "You are havingk second thoughts…eese good to do….but dheese men needingk to go…"

"Desert rats…Buh-Bye," Ivan adds with his personal, Russian stamp of the stereotypical flight attendant salutation.

I can see why John and Bobby were so heavily stressed during the Bay of Pigs. They had to deal with armed Russians who didn't give a shit. Tough to play chess against people who have a death wish.

Once, and I remember this all so clearly, I had it all mapped out. Down to each particle of modern living that you would expect from a d octor driving a Speedster through the canyons and hills of a city full of starlets. Every day was neatly wrapped in a privileged present, at least for a while. And most certainly during the early years of my mind numbing ingestion of party favors—today is different.

Today, I am traveling across the flatness of the boating marina's parking lot and headed straight toward Chet and God knows what. The reality of this minute at this marina comes roaring back and does a nice job of pushing my moment to the side. Time to deal.

CHAPTER 23

BOATING

There is a wonderful world of boating waiting for you here. There is big water pooling, glassing, and foaming, and rushing down from the Rocky Mountain tributaries to new places that only extreme currents would know. Rushing eddies of water for the red-spotted toad, western diamondback, or the desert pocket mouse. Deep, cooling, currents that began streaming in from the universe, powered by the very forces that tossed and shifted the behemoth plates of crusted earth and opened up new oceans. This river's march began as a patient and persistent trickle at nearly 10,000 feet up in the clean air and moved slowly downward, always down, maturing into a strong-willed channel of wild water that cut hard through the rock, and into a crack, then opening up a new vein, a fissure and finally into a wide, generous, charging flow that just kept on cutting and slicing its own path to wherever it wanted to go. The water decided that this arid and dry canyon and winding gully should receive all of it. A gesture measured by scientists in cubic meters, controlled by the weight and muscle of dams, and praised by the early Cocopah, Chemehuevi, Mojave or Quechan tribes who saw their ancestors and life in the embrace of this river. Today, the water is here at Needles and the wonderful world of boating at the Big Water Marina and Boat Launch is that current that will carry me.

You might typically see the expected boats on trailers, fueling pumps, decks, and ramps and the grocery store with a trinket and gift shop supplying everyone with everything required for a wonderful boating experience on the big water. Your boating manifest is a cheery

Styrofoam cooler of ice, beer, liquor, more ice, chips, deli, and more beer. Load up, ice up, pack up, get down to that boat and get out there, because as Helena so smartly informed us, we may be running out of runway here in the baked brown of this desert town.

This thousand-mile river of water is washing toward a final and certain end.

And then our desert will be dry, hot, and flat and not a place for boats and beer. The currents and melted ice will stop. This land will buckle back into itself. Survivors will find particles of H2O deeply ingrained in mineral deposits. Certainly, you can forget the pool. And as for the boat, it might be a good time to sell. Just ask Helena.

Weekends in July are always crowded with the swarm of recreational boaters launching and drinking and dropping big power into the river without what could be considered adult supervision. Grab a beer, take a hit, gas it up, launch a boat, crank it up, and power on. That life vest is around here somewhere. What the fuck, as long as we all know where the goddamn booze is, we are good for lift off. But today, on this mid-morning in the middle of the week, it's only dotted with a few water stragglers and a scattered litter of boats moving in and out, and owners moored to the general mix of tiresome boat duties that are far more boring than what the glossy watercraft brochure pitched as your promised slice of boating fun. (*The super sleek design, combined with extra-roomy compartments offers storage and quarters for six, beers for twenty-six and you, sir, are spending quality time with your family—Anchors aweigh!*)

So, here we are on typically sunny, clear day in July at The Big Water Marina and Boat Launch. I've worked a deal which is about to go down with a doctor who is about to get out. I was also in the company of guns and a crew that would help the meeting come to order and find the source. I've arranged this meeting with Chet, Phil, and Roy with the intention of spelling out the final details of our highly lucrative arrangement that's put enough money into the desert economy for more than a few cops and family.

It was time to lock up shop.

Chet knows that Rita and I have met and she has the scrips, and that deal will be finalized. Beyond this, it's *vamanos.* I told him that CC was not invited to this confab, which he mildly protested, because although we both agreed that she is a royal pain in the ass, Chet knows CC will not warm to the subject of the well running dry. I sold him on the manly notion that this was his *mano y mano* moment. No chicks allowed. He bit.

It was time I kissed these motherfuckers goodbye. At least that was my thinking as I remembered it as I sat in Ivan's Escalade and took a moment to collect myself. I could see the boys standing there, waiting for me.

"It's time," I said, hoping I could man up.

"Lockingk and loadingk." Helena seemed to channel a thicker than usual accent with her cinematic black-ops tone of voice. Ivan and I turned around and looked at her. We raised our eyebrows.

"We don't say that," Ivan said while loading hollow points into his shiny, nickel-plated .357 Colt Python with smooth trigger action and howitzer huge 8" barrel.

She shot him a look with a biting half smile that she hoped would bug him, tugging tightly on her baseball cap. "Doc has Glock, and I got nothinkg." Helena was acting up.

"You got this." Ivan tossed a snub-nosed flare gun onto her lap.

Helena looked at him. "Vhat no gun? Vhat hell, I am asking for gun, I am gettingk Home Depot."

"Trust me, you've got three rounds of high intensity, high heat phosphorous flares…just point and shoot." I am oddly patient considering I can still see the boys standing over there and they are hot, armed, and probably fucking high. I am feeling stressed.

Helena was not impressed with the weapon issued. "So, you are vanting to signaling dheese fuckingk coast guard?

"With that, you are trouble. Let me tell you little girl, fire into a man and you disfigure him for life. He may live…but not way he wants. It looks innocent, but so do you." Ivan had a point.

"Like we need this now?" I can see a slight shake in my professional-grade surgeon's hands—never a good sign.

We got out of the SUV and immediately felt the solar punch of a July in Needles. The searing heat toasts us like an open furnace and even with the big water of the Colorado River right here, I still feel the dry, high noon radiation wicking away whatever drop of moisture was left in my skin.

We stood in the shadow of the SUV facing the Chet squad that was lined up under the shade of trees in the far pitch of the Marina near the smaller boat launch. Chet, Phil, and Roy have their backs against their new cars. Ivan's SUV is behind us. In Chet's impressive Latin parlance, this was a *quorum*. They were surprised to see Team Doc.

"What the fuck?" Chet stumbled. The man could be eloquent.

"What the fuck, indeed," I responded, the Glock securely tucked into the back of my belt and causing its very own pool of sweat to drip down my back. I needed to hydrate.

"Fucking, hell, it's your lucky day," Ivan suggested, the big Python shouldered in his holster that was almost making him look smaller than his 5'5" frame.

"Who the fuck are you?" Roy stepped in.

"Yeah, what the fuck?" Phil said stepping next to the big brother.

"Your Dad already sayingk that, asshole," Helena stated, her hand holding the flare gun tight to her side, awkwardly palming it to hide its profile and purpose.

Che, Phil, and Roy are visibly nervous. They should be. Ivan can have that affect. He may be short, but this is a powerful man with a well-oiled, black woven leather holster and a long Python gun barrel that has a distinct way of adding shock and awe to anyone's day at any marina. But maybe the real story is Helena. At over six feet with her long legs and killer looks wrapped in those big sunglasses her dress for success summer linen ensemble could easily have put her in the Club Level at a Dodgers game. The jet-black flare gun with its fat, pug-nosed barrel did make an oddly intimidating accessory, but she can pull this look off. Helena's Coast Guard-approved fashion statement is making

Chet, Phil, and Roy even more nervous. Hell, she made me jumpy. I know she made Ivan think dirty Russian thoughts.

"Who's he and who's she?" Phil demanded, attempting to make a name for himself and show his dad and brother what a tough son of a bitch he could be.

"People I know," I said. Then, I added, "Russians."

"Well, then maybe they should be the fuck in Russia," Phil said, looking at Roy, pleased with his retort. Roy gave him a thumb's up. They're tight like that.

"You could not find Russia on map, asshole," Ivan spit through his lips.

Helena liked Ivan. So did I.

"I'm surprised there's so little trust here, Doc," Chet stammered. "I mean, what the fuck? We have you covered. Ain't nobody gonna do anything but what's right by you."

"Exactly, and today we're going to keep it that way." I surprised myself. I was almost getting pretty good at this.

Roy tried to assume the lead. "So, what the fuck else do you need from us?"

"Shut the fuck up, Roy," Chet growled, "let me do the talking. Same goes for you, Phil. Everyone just shut the fuck up and let me and the doctor figure this out."

"Good thinking, Chet. Time to close up shop...goodbyes are always tough."

"I got shit on you, doctor." Chet tried to posture and show the yearlings how their old man works.

"We got people who know people." It was Roy.

"You deal with us or you're a dead man." Phil chimed in, feeling a hormonal rush of testosterone.

The threat of someone killing me makes my mouth even drier. I can feel my heart bounce...maybe it was arrhythmia, I thought. I should schedule a yearly when this is over.

So, here we are in the heat, next to the water, armed with guns, and trying to end a business arrangement that has paid off handsomely. An arrangement that some would never like to see come to an end.

As the lead dog, Chet took it upon himself to again make a few points. He stepped forward, but stayed close to his boys for protection and family support. His eyes were hidden behind dark, wraparound sunglasses that were altogether too young for the age and shape of his face. If it were up to me, I would have waved him off the Oakleys and suggested a timeless classic, more toward the Wayfarer tradition with a beefier frame. Black, of course.

Chet then tried a more diplomatic approach.

"You and I know that this is solid gold, and nobody needs to get their knickers in a twist. We just agreed that after this little deal we would hang up the spurs for a while and let the dust settle, before starting up with a new and improved money machine."

The look on his face told me he wanted to wrap this up for god's sake, and please don't let CC in on this cry for help. Chet wanted to be the lead dog on this negotiation and bring a bone back to the wife.

"Doc, we know how to work you." It was Roy. Roy was looking bigger than ever. I wasn't sure if he had put on a few, or the plaid cargo shorts were just a bit loud for a man his size. Roy was stepping up his game, and I think Dad liked to see this side of his son. Another proud moment in the Chet family album. *Quick, someone snap a picture.*

Roy continued with his bully gavel. "Ain't none of us going anwheres…hell Doc, you've made a sweet little bundle yourself." Roy was dead on. I had indeed.

Phil snickered as he piggybacked onto Roy. "No reason to kill the golden calf, Doc. Few more deals, we all going our separate ways, and your secret's safe with us," Phil glanced over at this Dad and Roy to see if his personal twist on the deal would fly. It was a family business, apparently everyone had a say in what was going to happen next. Or, at least, do a little brainstorming under the July sun right here at the first annual company outing.

I was starting to get a nervous, queasy feeling. The one that most certainly seems to happen when you're facing bad ex-cops who have a hunger for the Peruvian and leather satchels stuffed with money. I wanted out and they wanted to stay in, deeply in. And with the sun overhead, my waning nicotine levels, and the sense that Ivan was twitching, it all made me a little faint like I was hitting a super low Glycemic Index and needed a donut, or a lemonade, or whatever the AMA suggests at a time like this.

I have no idea what prompted my next, fucking brilliant move. Only it did prove that I should do a better job of monitoring my vices and avoid future situations that would include any of the following, in no particular order: low blood sugar, high sun, crazed ex-cops, crazier Russians, various weaponry hitched into the small of my back.

"Those days are over," I said as I reached behind my back, found the metal and pulled out my 9mm Glock. I pointed it directly at Chet. I spread my feet apart and assumed a steady, by-the-book stance that I had practiced at the shooting range.

"What the fuck, Doc," Chet yelled as he jumped back, grabbing Roy, hoping that a son or two would step in and save him from a gun-wielding, former plastic surgeon.

I tightened my fingers around the Glock's thick, textured grip, still warm from the heat. The piece of metal felt good. The gun felt friendly. I felt like maybe I was getting the hang of this. Although, my palms were sweaty, which is to be expected considering the current noontime temperature, the event in progress, and the wildly fluctuating state of my charged metabolism.

"It's fucking over. This is the last of it…" I could hear my voice waver, so I set my jaw harder, clenched my teeth and was certain that now would be a very fine time for a dose of nicotine. I dug into my pocket and pulled out a Nicorette, popped it, and started mashing it like a madman. I breathed in the moment to collect myself. Yeah, that was the nicotine being my close friend and associate. I could sense an immediate leveling of my blood sugar. My brain swiftly climbs to a heightened state of alert that you would expect of anyone holding a pistol in the heat in Needles. I turn the Glock sideways, hoping that by gripping the gun with this kind of a move I might magically reduce the shakiness of my hand. I have seen this pistol grip technique popularized by gangsters and hit men in many profitable movies green-lighted by successful producers who know a thing or two about gunplay and such.

I think it makes me look like I, too, am at ease with many firearms. I was now commanding serious attention that allowed me to drive home a fucking point to these assholes: I was not going to be fucked with. Even with the tickle of sweat trickling down the side of my face, and my less-than-cool firing range stance, I was holding court with the bad boys of Needles and I would be leaving the business. My resignation was not without the concern of management. Nobody likes to leave money on the table. Least of all CC.

The Glock felt damp in my hand, but I liked where the day's turn of events was going. I also knew that my back-up crew was not only armed and dangerous, but also fucking Russian, so they could take this marina to a whole new category of bad.

"I need you fucks to understand something…I have people like Ivan," I waved my gun over at Ivan, and I think he liked my gesture and the notoriety as I continued to paint a picture of who was backing my exit. "Bad people can do good things for people like me. Ivan is just the mother fucking beginning of some dangerous people who don't like ex-cops but love ex-surgeons. Very mean people, like Ivan, who will come over to your desert home, lay it bare to the ground and make it right for anybody but you and your family. If you do not understand this, you are already in your grave, buried and killed. But if you do understand this, then you will be boating next week. It's entirely up to you, *compadres*."

I swear I thought Ivan had grown another four inches just on that intro alone.

Chet, Roy and Phil couldn't quite figure me out. On one hand, I was their very own scrip-writing physician who made them a ton of money. On the other, they could see I was totally out of my mind, and even worse, armed with a 9MM Glock backed by a posse and a big, black SUV. Chet looked a little pale in the face, which is hard to do with the high desert sun in July that can turn you red in less than five minutes, and a give you a very nice tan in about ten.

Nobody wanted a scene but everyone wanted to make a point. Nobody wanted to fuck with the next level, but then this was Needles, right? And weird shit happens out here when you're standing out in July. Things can go sideways. Fast. It's a fact. Criminals, Russians, bundles of money, lack of sleep, too much nicotine, and bullets and pistols mixed with this searing heat can fuck with anyone. And well, it was all starting to fuck heavily with us.

"Doc, don't do this. We got a righteous thing here, you and us. We could be printing fucking money." Chet was agitated because he was going to have to sell CC on this meeting. It was definitely not going his way and Chet is jonesing for another money hit. I know the signs well.

Roy wasn't going to let the old man give it all up so fast. Hell no, this was Roy's future, too. He was fanning the flames and itching to get into it. "There's more paper on you than you even know. We have you tied up till we want to let go. This is our deal, and right now, you do what we want, when we want—ain't no other way."

But it was younger brother Phil who was the first to fall to the high whine of the Needles' heat. High noon in July can push anyone over the edge, but with Phil's zero tolerance for life—and my manifesto on where this ends, *here*, and when it ends, *now*—Phil hit his wall and went ballistic.

"Fuck you, too, Doc. You don't fucking own us!" Phil yelled, pulling his gun and aiming directly at me. Ivan pulled his. Helena pointed hers, well, her flare gun anyway.

Roy pulls his, looks over at his Dad and brother, hoping for some direction on what to do. "What the fuck? Pa, whaddya want?"

Ivan looks at me seeming to ask what the next move is. I look at him. I got nothing. I feel the Nicorette drying up in my mouth, so I swallow the tiny, hard ball and for a minute I think it's stuck in my throat. I feel dizzy.

The only one without a gun is Chet.

Six people, four pistols, and one, stubby, fat, flare gun that was probably the most dangerous because Helena really wanted to fire that bad boy and has no clue about what she was doing. A burning hot phosphorous flare direct to the face would make for a bad hair day. But it was Ivan who made sure he got off the first round.

"Ivan, shoot the fuck out of Phil's truck…now." I yelled in a dry, high pitched squeal. The adrenaline constricted my throat. I accidently swallowed the Nicorette.

"Which one?" Ivan calmly responded.

"The new, big white fucker." I popped another Nicorette.

Ivan fired off a few rounds into Phil's brand new, White F-150 With The Super-Duty Tow Package And Four-Carbine Eddie Bauer Gun Rack.

Phil dove behind a small palm tree and shot at Ivan's SUV. He missed the Escalade, instead, hitting a larger 25-foot Boston Whaler sitting in the parking lot. Roy hit the deck.

"You shoot like a pussy." Roy said.

"Show me what you got big brother."

Roy fired off a shot, hitting Ivan's SUV. This was by far the worst possible thing that Roy could do. Ivan loves that monster. Ivan would rather he take the bullet than his black roller.

"Not good, mother fucker." Ivan triggered his mammoth Python, blowing a few more holes in Phil's F-150. Then, he promptly clicked off rounds into Roy's matching black Ford. *Shots fired, truck down.*

Chet grabbed his chest. I wasn't sure if he thought he was shot or he was having a heart attack. Helena reacted to marina mayhem and was able to grab Chet, pull him from behind and point the stubby flare gun directly at his head as she marched him over to our side of today's *quorum.*

"Ivan, vhat fuckingk vant me to do?" She yelled.

"Ask the doctor, it's his show."

"Doc?"

"Blow his fucking head off."

"Wid deese?" Helena held up her pug nosed flare gun. Chet's long, skinny body looked limp, as if Helena was holding him up.

My adrenaline kicked in "Fuck it…Chet do you get where I am going with this?" I liked the tone of my Glock-armed threat. Everyone knew I had a gun, a bad habit, a medical degree, and perhaps even Federal agents on my side. I commanded attention from everyone who was armed at the marina. I felt great. Although, the Nicorette felt as if it were stuck smack in the middle of my chest.

"Fuck you Doc." Chet is turning red from putting his 70-year-old body through this kind of morning exercise. Helena still has him wrapped with her flare gun pressed tightly against his head, the fat barrel kissing the aging skull. She pushes him hard over towards me.

"Phil, Roy, toss your guns…" I said, proud of my professional gun-play. The Glock no longer feels slippery in my hand. I like the control. I like the gun and how this is all going down.

I take two steps into Chet. "Where's your goddamn boat?" I hissed into his ear, my spit showering the side of his face, which is a pretty cool effect and I see why this is used in the movies, as well.

"Why?" He rasps. I could hear the mucous aspirating in his drying, fibrous lungs that could probably use a managed treatment of low dose cobalt radiation.

"I will ask you again, where…the…fuck is your boat?" More spit from me. Helena presses the pistol deeper. I can see Chet's face twisting. His business deal has gone so far sideways that he'll have to file a very bad report with CC and things could get even worse for him. Explaining all of this to CC could prove more painful than Helena pushing her flare gun harder into his scrawny, lined jowls.

By now, both Phil and Roy are staring at the wall of Ivan and his thick Python 8" nickel-plated cannon. Ivan is speaking harsh, hard, and fast in Russian and is bent on making a statement. We're pretty sure it has to do with losing a body part or dying soon, but so far nobody's asking for a translation. Ivan also makes sure the boys get a good look at his hand and the shiny, leathered patina of his seared skin that shares a moment of his dangerous past. "Take look, remember this hand and what means… says I am not afraid of shit. And Doc says you are shit."

Phil and Roy, even with their former law enforcement training, have no clue on what to do. Ivan has taken them out of whatever game they thought they had. I'm thinking that right about now Phil's metabolic rate is making his ear and foot throb with memories of the painful *Butchero's* dinner date.

Chet finally has enough. "Boat's over there at the end of the small ramp, slip 43…*Cubbie's.*"

"Good," I say, with a straight face and a hard look. "Let's all go boating, and see where a day on the Mighty Colorado takes us." I light up a smoke. I feel the sweat dripping down the middle of my back. My shirt is drenched. I can see why the SWAT guys have to pour a few just to come down after the rush of kicking in doors. I consider Jack, my agent and his boys and their life of crime fighting. I think that maybe with the right training I could do this kind of a job. I exhale. Now that is a good motherfucking cigarette.

After handling Chet's threats, various gun waving, my extremely low blood sugar, and swallowing that nasty hard ball of a Nicorette, I take a moment to admire my approach to desert desperados and gunfights. Chet and the boys walk in front of us. Between the nervous sweat, grim expressions, and Phil and Roy's insolent attitude, with Chet limping alongside, and, of course, the arsenal of pistols, we didn't quite fit the marina demographic. The one bright spot: Helena, looks like she belongs on a mahogany and teak and brass Chris Craft, but generally she can get away with anything at anytime. On the other hand, Ivan's western wear is clearly not Nautica. Neither is his Python. At best, we might pass as a pathetic group of outside sales reps at a team-building event for a Scottsdale window and shutter company with new offices opening in Phoenix.

I was feeling relieved that maybe I could see some daylight soon and leave the Kingdom for a new life on another planet.

"Nice boat, Chet." I said.

"Nice enough, I guess, Doc, sure as shit we can work something out…lemme talk to CC and figure something out?"

"Fire it up and head down river…just another family on vacation, right?" I said, showing Chet a bright smile indicating that he was very fucked.

This big 45-foot powerboat, *Cubbie's,* has plenty of room for all of us to sit on the deck and point pistols at each other. Only Chet and Phil and Roy don't have theirs. We have ours. And we have Ivan. The temperature hovers around 110 in the shade without a trace of a breeze, the river is a mirror and the current is strong. A boat flies by spraying and carving the smooth glass.

The scantily bikinied partygoers hoist and wave their beers, as if we too, were part of their brown-skinned boating fraternity. One of the young and gorgeous things smiles broadly, gracing us with her terrifically white teeth, her sweet, summer freckles look fresh and innocent. She lifts up her top, pimping us with a teasing glimpse of perfect breasts that show us what a day on the water can be. We wave back as if we, too, are on the water having fun in our big, expensive, and beautiful watercraft. Even Roy manages a weak wave, a knee jerk reaction to the bare breasted gorgeous thing. His smile is clenched. Phil just looks at his older brother. Phil is fuming about being on Dad's boat crewed by that money-churning, turncoat Doc, and his gun-toting Russian illegals.

"Let's head out for a while, have a cold one—and Jesus, Chet, did you not pack any sandwiches for us today?" I really do enjoy seeing his boys burning in the high sun.

"Phil, how's that foot healing? And the ear?" I wink at Helena.

Helena stares at Phil. "Vhat happened your ear…your foot… lookingk like bad pierce job maybe…?" Helena does have a winning smile that looks perfectly at home on a gleaming, mahogany and chrome deck.

Phil refuses to answer, trying to ignore her tone and attitude. His big size and small ego are easy prey for Helena, as she twirls her flare gun while staring down Phil the ex-cop and desert gun fighter.

He looks straight ahead trying to figure out what went wrong today. Phil is a larcenous ex-cop who is not a happy boater having fun on the water. Neither is Roy.

Roy is looking at his brother Phil like Phil has no balls and what the fuck they could take me Ivan's presence brings them both back to reality. Helena sits smoking, long legs crossed, and spinning her trusty flare gun, relaxing with her Coast Guard-approved rescue accessory.

Phil wants to show Roy how to play this game. He has decided that Helena is an easy target. "The boys keep all the big toys for themselves?" Phil asks, nodding to her flare gun.

Helena smiles at him.

"Last time I used one of those, we needed more beer…fired off a distress then fired up the BBQ waiting for reinforcements, more fucking beer…damn that was a day on the water…" Phil says.

Then idiot Phil pushes the wrong button. "Lots of naked chicks, too, right, bro, man that one nasty little bitch…"

Helena moves faster than Phil and quickly jams the gun into his mouth.

"Maybe needingk reinforcement now, like big ass brother, yes? What about big brother, time to be ridingk on white horse savingk dheese day?" Phil is breathing harder through his nose, Roy cannot believe they are taking this from some chick sticking the barrel of a flare gun into his brother's face.

"I am not thingk so," Helena pulls the gun out of Phil's bruised and bleeding mouth, while Roy stammers and sputters.

"You needingk bandaid? "Now shutting fuck up, enjoy river, assholes." Helena says flatly, sitting down and adding a Willis-inspired whisper of '*Yippe-ki-yay, motherfuckers,*' for emphasis while coolly lighting her cigarette.

Roy and Phil shrink in size. Phil uses his shirt to clean up his bloodied mouth. He glowers at Roy—*Where the fuck were you, bro? I want to kill this bitch.*

This big boat is very nice and very powerful and we have Chet at the helm and as we motor down the river, we are the perfect photo opportunity the Needles Chamber of Commerce would love, except for the guns and assholes, outlaws and rogue cops. Other than that, yes, we are members in good standing of the river's fun loving boating community.

"People thinking you are from Chicago?" Ivan says as Chet winds up the engines and we are speeding along the wide and deep Colorado.

"What the fuck you talking 'bout?" Chet asks, still thinking he is the captain of this craft.

"Baseball team, Cubs—Chicago, right? *Cubbie's*, name on boat?" Ivan says.

"Yeah, sure, you Russian prick—not even close." Ivan just looks at Chet and smiles the way you don't want Ivan to smile. Ivan's Python weighs about three pounds. Ivan handles it like it maybe weighs three ounces, and in one motion sticks the barrel up into Chet's thin, aged chin.

"I pull trigger. You fish food." Ivan has a tight grip on Chet. And with the barrel posted up against his thorax, Chet winces hard and I seriously think he is going to die from either holding his breath or a cardiac event. It certainly won't be from my *pharma*.

I see that this is probably a very good time to interrupt Ivan and the Chet dance and inquire about a few other pressing matters.

"So, Chet, here's what we're going to do, you're going to tell *me* exactly who I need to know that *knows* about me." And if you do that, Ivan puts his Python away and we can all smile, break out a few cold ones and call it good."

Chet is looking older than his seventy years. His day at the Marina has taken its toll and he's trying to put on a good face for his boys, but that moment, too, has passed. Chet just wants to go home to the *ranchero* and collect his dough. Chet wants his payday. Chet wants to lounge poolside with his wife CC and hang a side of beef on the grill with Mariachi music floating over his newly remodeled patio and pavers. Chet's tired. Chet is ready to talk.

"A guy...name of Casey.

"Shut the fuck up, Pa!" Phil swallows hard, staring even harder at his dad and then at Roy.

Chet impatiently waves off Phil, and continues like he needs to get out of this somehow and if that means looking like a pussy, well, fuck it, there could still be a payday for him and CC.

"Casey used to work vice…now has connections with Internal Affairs." Chet coughs in a spasm, his face turns red. With the events unfolding on this Mighty Colorado, his aging, narrowing, constrictive lungs are having a time of it. Chet is stressed and so far his boys haven't been much help. It's not going to be easy coming back to CC from a day on the water with bad news about my exiting the firm and the abrupt end of their money train.

"Casey is a detective. He knows who the fuck I am?" I look at all three of the Kingdom Crew. "What are you gonna do about it?"

"Not following you, Doc…" Roy is the bright bulb.

"Follow this. I stop writing scrips. Product stops arriving. Product stops selling. See? Everything works on supply and demand and I just stopped the supply. The good news is that if you ever come across another physician, that sucker can pick up where I left off and boo-yah, you are back in business with a…and I don't think I'm exaggerating here, you're back with a mother freaking huge demand just waiting for product. So see, there's a bright side to everything. You'll be the snow-kings of the desert. So much snow people will be wearing Patagonia out on this motherfucking river. You'll see. Phil and Roy might want to put snow tires on those big modern vessels… know what I mean." I flash a grin underlining my lesson on Supply Side Economics.

I pulled Chet into me and within a breath of my mouth I dictated the next move so I would be very fucking clear.

"You need to take care of Mr. Casey if you want the back end of your split which is what Rita is holding at this very moment. I got you covered and if you get me covered with the Casey's of the world, then yeah, we'll all be good. Until then, we hold your end. That's a lot of dough and I know a lot of people might be very interested in where that money is."

"Fuck, Doc, now you're blackmailing my old man?" Phil was wild eyed and takes a step towards me, but holds back. He's smartly caught the stare from the icy blue eyes from my very own White Russian watchdog, which, incidentally, I could most definitely use right now. No, make that a tall Stoli, squeeze of fresh lemon, followed by a fat rail of my *pura*.

Ivan steps into Phil's face and he fires his Python into the air just to calm everyone down and make a point, plus he loves to shoot that gun. It loudly echoes through the river, bouncing off the walls of this massive waterway. Vacationing boaters might raise an eyebrow to shots fired, but again, out here, and by this time, the beer and bong ratio has the water rats cranking it up and are deep into their heat on. No problems on the river, officer.

"The detective—Casey—wanting him out and taken care of this week," Ivan looks at me proud of his improvisation. I liked where he was going with this. The bad man had come up with a good plan on dealing with Casey.

Helena jumps right in, riffing off Ivan. "And make clean, no doingk deese dirty Needles business you are known about, you are old, miserable, man." Those sunglasses are working for her.

"One week, Casey gets quiet," I added. "And we release your end of the scrips."

Chet looked at his boys, they looked at him and we sat there for a minute until Ivan fires off another round from his very loud 357 Magnum Python armed with hollow points. The explosion ricochets across the water, traveling at the speed of sound toward the river's end somewhere deep into the canyon. The few party boats in the distance are dialing up the hard rock, shooting beers, and getting naked. It's hot out here. And everything goes. His long-barreled gunshot only registers as a kind of white noise covered by the boat speakers now blowing up Metallica across the glassy water.

We agreed that the Chet family takes on Casey and I am out. Chet will get his and we all walk away safe and sound as outlaws happy to know that loose ends are tight and the desert is our friend, again.

"I gotta say, Chet, glad we could have come to a reasonable way to finalize this deal, but now it's time to say *adios, mi amigos…*" I want these boys off the boat. And I wanted to make a point not to fuck with me, or us. These badass ex-*policia* needed a lesson in boating safety and I thought a primer on the proper use of life vests would be a good start.

Chet and his boys protest and rant about that this is their boat, and what the fuck? Why did Ivan have to shoot their new trucks? I tied the lifejackets together and tossed them into the water, pointing out that there's enough traffic on the river that it wouldn't be long before a good Samaritan would surely pick up the boys—or what the hell, better yet, maybe even a sleek, gorgeous boat with some fabulous party people would save the day.

Helena goes below, finds a six-pack of beer, scrounges around and lands on a half empty jar of peanut butter. She gives it to Roy for their dining pleasure while bobbing on the river. Roy takes the jar and throws it over to Phil throws back a spiteful stare at his big brother for relegating him to the rations detail.

I am standing on the helm. "Have a cold one on me, Chet."

The boys look up at me, seething with hurt pride and the weighty loss to their bank accounts. They really don't like me saying adios to the poolside pavers and to the life in the Kingdom. Chet stares at me. I smile at the three of them, the sun is high and I am happy to be calling them out on their hold on me.

Chet and Roy and Phil stand on the deck wearing nothing but sunglasses, t-shirts, and their shorts, and in Phil's case, just for fun, we had him strip down to his paisley boxers.

Three of them are lined up—burly, big, and out of shape boys with their wheezing old man. Roy is in charge of the beer. Phil has the jar of peanut butter. Chet clutches his pack of smokes and a lighter, which Helena, ever the consummate cruise director, has thoughtfully placed in a re-sealable plastic baggie. So, sure, in a way, it's a typical day on the river that the whole family can enjoy.

Helena also offers up that she would happily fire off a rescue flare to help everyone out.

"Everybody into the pool!" I like my enthusiasm and take-charge, management style.

"Let me see diving today." Ivan presses a heavy nudge of his cannon into their soft, ex-cop bellies.

Chet tries to save face with a warning. "Let's go boys, kiss these mother fuckers adios…but not goodbye…you ain't seen the last Doc, count on it."

His progeny jump in. Chet goes last. We're standing on the deck smiling down on our three unemployed business associates now busy treading in the cool water.

"Should I call CC and let her know you'll be a little late for cocktails and dinner?" I hold up my mobile.

Chet flips me off and the boys scream some girly epitaphs at us threatening that they got the whole fucking Needles police department on their side and we are in a world of hurt and we better watch our backs and we are going down.

"Good to know, bring them on, assholes!" Ivan yells back at the Colorado swim team.

"And you are havingk small penis envious, motherfuckers," Helena joins in on the boating festivities, pointing her flare gun at them.

Just for fun, I throw a vial of my *pura* to Chet. The glass vial makes a small blurping splash in front of him. "A little *mo-mo*, my friend, no hard feelings. Don't get it wet." Chet swoops the small parcel out of the water. He always did like my *pura*.

I gun the engine and the boat surges and lifts nicely out of the water and we are flying across the Colorado toward The Big Water Marina and Boat Launch. I looked back and spotted Chet resting on a life preserver, lighting up a smoke. Phil and Roy, the ultimate party animals, appeared to be fighting over a much-needed beer. Family fun on the water, it just never ends.

"Maybe good time sendingk swimmers bon voyage gift," Helena says dryly, checking the two cartridges. She readies the squat, fat pistol and aims directly at the trio. The flare ignites and the white-hot phosphorous trail looks like an RPG missile skimming across the top of the water, nearly hitting our three fish, kicking in the water, hoping a friendly boater might come by to help Needles' finest out of a jam; preferably the flirty girl with those All-American summer freckles.

Chet had a fine boat and the craft handled tightly and the bright, high, hot sun is beating down on our warm faces and bare shoulders as we wave to another lucky boater also out for a day of the high life. Ivan jokingly taunts Helena to lift up her top, but she's far too shy, unless she happens to be in my Speedster parked near a train in downtown Needles.

Standing tall with her long, strong legs balanced beautifully on the gleaming mahogany and teak decking, and looking rather magnificent in her linen shorts, capped by her black-framed, designer sunglasses. Helena looks as if she were on holiday on our sunny island of Capri. She lights a smoke, puts it into my lips, gives me one of her patented, sexy winks, and points her jet black flare gun skyward, firing off a shot that ignites and screams upward like a small, sun leaving a signaling trail of grayish-white against the expanse of blue sky. It is a day on the river. We're pretty sure our boys out there floating in the winding Colorado can see Helena's flare arching high in the sky offering them their own moment of hope. In the distance, we see the gorgeous bare breasted native at the bow of a speeding boat thunder by the boys, spraying their sun burned faces with the cooling, icy blue melt of big water moving to an almost certain end.

CHAPTER 24

RIO DEL LUCE

After our day of boating with Chet and family, we are doing a bit of re-grouping. I asked Ivan to stay close while I map out a plan of action to get to Darlene and talk her through the storm that's going to blow her way. We dropped Helena off in VistaVue. Ivan and I continued to his place. He had checked into one of the better hotels, the Rio Del Luce, and informed me that he requested room service to please empty his mini-bar. Ivan, God bless him, is seriously sober, so I politely keep my various and sundry vices discreetly within my reach and definitely out of his. I do not want his Russian boozy slip on my watch. And certainly if Ivan were to relapse it would be up to me to share this news with his wife. No thank you, I had enough on my plate. I was getting smarter every day. Or so I thought.

I have to hand it to Ivan, I mean, really, after a day in this desert is there anything better than walking into the cool hum of your spotless hotel room and finding your favorite adult beverage complemented by a host of shamefully over-priced salted snack foods? Ivan did agree to hang around for a few days, which is nice and useful although his sponsor might take issue with him wielding weaponry while assisting my *pura fina* business. Ivan's sobriety is a welcomed backstop to my questionable habits, and should we need him to put down the Big Book and pick up that big piece of an armory, his Python will come in handy.

Ivan was in Los Angeles when I lost my boy. Ivan was there with me when I told Jack it was time for me to go. Ivan's been a shoulder.

We sat in the small, bare lobby of his brick and clay Spanish style hotel. The two young, heavyset women in cleanly pressed white blouses and black, cotton slacks had worked their way up to desk clerks. This was July, so they busied themselves with a lack of work.

Once in a while a white reception phone would ring, triggering a happy rush of responsibility. This was a better and more important job than housekeeping. Their corner of hospitality, the reception desk, featured a phone, a computer, a service bell, and pamphlets on what to do in the Mojave, Needles, and the Grand Canyon was neatly organized and arranged for easy guest reference. One of the clerks would come out from behind the wood and marble reception desk and add a pamphlet or two on an especially popular attraction. Time moved slowly here at the Rio Del Luce. The women checked their cell phones. They laughed at each other in an easy conversation helping them both battle the boredom of a slow month. For a minute I took them for sisters, but it was only the same body type, the dark hair, and matching uniforms. I signaled one of the girls. She came over, glad to have been called on. She was pretty. She had bright, brown eyes, darker eyebrows. She had small streaks of blonde in her jet-black hair in her attempt at doing something young and cool. I wished she had not done the blonde thing. Her nail polish was red with hints of a metallic sparkle that was popular with girls her age. She stood in front of us, her pen and pad at the ready. She was on the job, efficient, and her broad smile told me she liked her job here, no matter if she was dying of boredom. It beat the sketchy alternatives, if any, of other mindless minimum wage jobs out in the desert.

"What can I get you, sir?" She looked at me, her Spanish accent thick but Americanized maybe from a few years of high school out here.

"Something cold. You have tonic water with lemon?"

"Same." Ivan said with a surprise in his voice. He tilted his head.

She jotted our orders. "Anything else?"

"Just make mine a large, or a tall or something big."

She smiled again. "*Si senors, uno momento.*"

"Tonic water?" Ivan asked, looking at me, wondering what I was up to.

"Big surprise. It's hot, I'm thirsty…I was only thinking of you. No reason to tempt fate."

"Don't worry for me. I can handle myself. Order whatever."

Ivan wanted to change subject from whatever I wasn't drinking. "Gorikav still on the prowl?"

"I kinda fucked myself on this one."

"You too hard on yourself."

"Somebody has to be. I should just let Jack handle this mess."

"He will. He gets paid to clean up after you."

"What about you?" I asked.

The young, broad-smile in the crisp white shirt returned with our drinks and placed them with coaster and napkins, on the side table between Ivan and me. "If there's anything else," she asked.

"We are good," Ivan said, and he took the bill from her, gave her a twenty. "Keep the change."

"Thank you, *gracias*, just let me know, I'll be right over there." She pointed to the reception area where her coworker was busy wiping down the reception counter again.

I raised my tonic water to Ivan. "*Nostrovia.*" I said in a salute.

"Never toast without vodka, Russian believe bad luck."

"Fuck the Russians…I mean—not you."

"Fuck it…and the Russians.…*Nostrovia..*" Ivan said clinking his glass against mine.

I swallowed. The icy bite of the tonic and lemon quenched me. I almost didn't miss the vodka.

"What are you referring to…me?" Ivan asked.

"The deal with those rubies…that over?"

"Rubies, emeralds, a lot of gems disappear…I took care of guys trying to take care of me."

"Seems like that thing was only yesterday…before…" Ivan could see where I was going.

"Never forget your son." Ivan said, his voice only a low whisper. "Look at me, doctor. What happened was not fault of you. Remember him with joy. Yes, it is sad…tragic but you have to have life now, and have to live for that boy. Time to get out of yourself."

"You don't even know." The glass felt cold in my hand.

"You telling me you only father with pain? You only man who has this kind of pain down here." Ivan pointed to his chest. "Time for you to get home, get this Maxim out of your life and find home somewhere out there."

I don't like preachy, it makes me uncomfortable, agitated. . "Fuck it…what's the point…" I said sharply. Ivan saw my anxiety surface. He jangled the icy glass, swallowed.

"Get off pity pot. Maybe you do need vodka." He was upset with me and he turned to flag the receptionist for another or the bill. "Pay attention to what I say and let's take care of your business.'

"I have to call Jack."

"See already good plan."

"Jack will take care of this."

"His job to clean up after your mess." Ivan was being a friend. I could see that.

"He always does." I said, looking down at my empty glass. Three fingers of vodka could revive the slice of spent, yellow, citrus that now looked pathetic trapped under the melting, misshapen ice cubes.

"Here, take this." Ivan reached into his pocket. "Open your hand."

My open palm met his thick fingers as he dropped a sizeable stone into it. The emerald looked like a piece of green, jagged glass. I rolled it around my palm. It caught the lobby light.

"For him, your son." Ivan said, closing my palm. He squeezed my fist tight. "And for you."

"Let's go." I said.

"Home?" Ivan asked.

"If that's what you want to call it, yeah, home."

We drove back to VistaVue. Ivan turned up the soundtrack to *A Fistful of Dollars* and sharply whistled through the theme. Ivan hit all the high points before the chorus.

The desert was starting to make sense to me now. All I had to do was look at it through Ivan's eyes. I rolled the raw, sharp emerald over and over in my hand. We were living Ivan's western. And I realized Ivan is a damn good whistler.

CHAPTER 25

DARLENE

Helena and I are putting a plan together on how to deal with the Darlene situation.

I light a Menthol, lean back with a tumbler and consider just how busy my life has become with the Chet crew, burying bundles of cash, assuaging the many moods of Rita, calling in Russian terriers, packing pistols, making sure Helena gets whatever Helena needs, and generally checking off a daily to-do list that makes my head hurt.

But I have it all under control.

Just sit tight, let me think about it, and yes, that tumbler is icy cold and is a nice drink, isn't it?

It's just another day trying our hand at problem solving.

Helena and I talk about Darlene and how bad we feel for the girl, after all we're responsible for her new life on the run. Although Helena pulled the trigger that sent those galvanized pieces of shrapnel into Phil's fleshy ear and foot, I'm the card carrying adult here, so it's on me, really. As I understand it, Darlene's got a hard, dancer's body and while she's fit enough to work a solid six hour shift on the pole, the petite paramour is no contest for the Roys of the world and forget it with Phil, he wants what's his—and right now that would very much be Darlene.

By now, Darlene would be smart to be driving to Vegas. By now, Darlene would be stitching together a new life. By now Darlene would have put large miles between her past and her present so she can have a future. By now, the girl would be whip-smart to be somewhere else.

But none of that is happening because right now Darlene has no idea she is pegged for Phil's *Butchero's* piercing.

Our red-haired dancer doesn't know she's the target of Phil and Roy's divine retribution, so I'm thinking this could get ugly and we better get to Darlene before Roy starts to prove how much he loves his dear brother. I didn't consider the *Butchero*'s Restroom Hit going sideways—at least like this. *Mea culpa.*

When the loveable Phil concluded that his injuries were the dark work of his past dalliance with Darlene, and his bloodied nailing the result of a heady desert tonic consisting of two parts drug deal, one part pole romance, and one part Fucking-Up-With-Phil, well it was time to get the girl out. Phil and Roy were not going to let this one go. No doubt about it, these boys had revenge on their sun stoked, coked out brains, and with the Needles brethren looking the other way, the Chet sons could do some serious damage. I had no idea what their next move was going to be, but I knew they were hitting piles of blow, downing shots, and calling around town.

Chet and CC wanted to move on, but well, boys will be boys.

I called Rita to check in and find out what she knows about Darlene. I got more than expected, but then what was I expecting?

"Phil is fucking over the top pissed at you, your boy, and that chick," Rita said, stating the obvious about her stepdad and my posse, while proceeding to recount the fallout from the Big Marina highlights. "I hear the shit went down and Phil loves that fucking truck… don't even ask about Roy…they're off the charts. You don't even want to know what CC is saying. Seriously. They are rocking…Chet's little concerned about their cash flow. I told them I have the scrips and shit, but then Phil brought up some dude in vice or something."

"Yes, indeed, we went over that while boating." I wasn't going to offer up anything more to Rita. I like having control over those boys and admittedly I am pretty cool under the circumstances and it feels good to be a step ahead and pushing a few of the Chet buttons. Oh, and Rita is a handful. I like to keep a tight grip on what she needs to know.

"Chet and the family get theirs after incidentals are ironed out," I say, keeping the details to myself.

Rita wants to know why my sudden interest in Darlene, and I explain that I'm simply being a good neighbor. "I think she's in a little bit of trouble with her former boyfriend, Phil...at least that's the way I heard it up at Chet and CC's. Looks like Phil's pointing her out as somebody he needs to get medieval on...and no surprise, Roy's backing him."

Rita continues to school me on girls who dance and the stepdads who get into bed with them. I believe I saw the same episode on Jerry Springer. Maybe it was Montel.

"Yeah, heard she nailed him at *Butchero's*..." Rita is trying to play know-it-all.

"Dancer at Route 69, right?" I say, and note that Helena's antenna is up.

"Yeah, she's a featured dancer or whatever—lap dances, she makes bank and acts like a fucking movie star, but guess what girlfriend—you live in *fucking Needles*...yeah, right, shake your booty while it all goes up your nose." Rita is on a rant about drug use, which would make a terrific public service commercial running at 3:00 a.m. when most druggies are snorting the last of their grams or hitting the last of a pipe. At least she knows her target market.

"She's got red hair, she's young, and she likes guys like my stepdad. He only hooked up with her for a little while...I think she drives a red Camry or a Honda or some other piece of Asia."

Some people wear their heart on their sleeve. Lovely Rita carries her point of view right next to her honed and razor sharp Puukko.

After hanging up with Rita, I tried calling Darlene's cell. No luck, her mailbox was full. Helena and I decide we should take a field trip to visit the Route 69 Center For Wayward Pole Dancers to see what we can dig out of the desert, notably a red-haired star-fucker and headliner who charges big for small favors and drives something Japanese that gets a million miles to the gallon, which undoubtedly our dancer will appreciate should she decide to step on the accelerator and travel across the desert to anyplace but here.

The evening could hold the promise of salvation for sinners seeking redemption. And like the clever, resourceful *Coyote* who is leading his tired and frightened group of illegals across the border to their promised land, I silently recite my request for absolution, offer Helena a bump, and reach for a Menthol. Helena fires up my phone. We want to put a call into Phil and see where he is on the Darlene payback. Helena dials Phil and hands me my mobile.

"Fuck you, Doc…" Caller ID is a terrific piece of technology.

"Well, thanks Phil, wanted to call and see what's up with– what's her name, Darlene?"

"Me and Roy are taking care of it." I can hear that Phil is obviously in his truck. I hear him do a bump.

"It?" I want to play with him. I can hear him mumbling a side conversation with Roy.

"Maybe I can talk you out of doing bad things to innocent people?" I give Helena my *'What the fuck look.'* as I try to multi-task with the road, Phil, and the job at hand.

"Innocent? I know that chick, I know where she is and I know that me and my brother are taking care of business, tonight…no way is that little bitch going to get away this shit…"

I hear Roy shouting something in the background. Phil laughs.

"Not if I get to her first." I said, surprised at how tough I sound.

"Fuckingk you asshole." Helena tosses out a thought for the boys.

"Hey Phil, remember, no texting and driving."

Phil hangs up on me. Evidently we're all traveling into the same town looking for animals that go bump in the night. *Perdóname, Padre, Porque He Pecado.*

CHAPTER 26

PHIL AND ROY GO FOR A DRIVE

Let's be clear about Phil and Roy. These are the kind of guys who can find trouble in their sleep. Fortunately for these two, the Phil and Roy brand of behavior is backed by some brothers in blue who like the fat envelope of cash sealed with a wink and a nod. This is a very good arrangement for Phil and Roy. Everyone wins. They can steal, deal, run the river, and slyly stay a step ahead, leaving law and order codes flying behind their big trucks. Our Chet family princes are groomed to rule, but if things don't fall in, according to their world, they find safe harbor at The Chet and CC Kingdom, which always welcomes them with pool and views and music and housekeeping and that wonderfully stocked bar. Chet likes it when the boys drop by. CC not so sure, but what the fuck, fellows, come on in and let's break off a piece of the Peruvian and kick back out on the patio. Phil is thirty-three and his older brother Roy is thirty-eight, or as Roy will beerily announce, "We're in our thirstys" while flirting with the waitress tasked with keeping his table happy. And it is a monster of a table. Phil is 6'3" 250 pounds, Roy is 6'5" and at just north of 300, it's been suggested that Roy might want to take a break from the all-you-can-eat trough. In their world, everything is big. Except their women, like Darlene, for example.

These two former high school footballers lead a charmed and boundless life in this desert place where a summer in July paints everything with a sharpened dryness, a flatness, and sameness that invites the lawlessness of predator and prey. The desert is a good place to be for Phil and Roy. The boys like it out here. The desert is wide open, but hidden. A secret stash of rutted back roads and misdirected, forgotten trails that lead desert prey to nowhere, except where our boys want to take them. It's easy to get lost in this piece of our planet, it's easy to disappear and quietly become another piece of rock. Another soul covered by a layer of scree.

Phil and Roy have made their deal with the dirt. Get up in that big truck, and if you squint hard enough you can see straight down that long, skinny asphalt road that narrows and disappears deep into the horizon and into the end of their world. These boys will take you down a road and lose you in a dry land that will wear you like a scrap of leather. They own Needles. Want a truck? Take one. Looking for that extra pound of weed? Done. Like that sleek and teak powerboat, no problem, we've got a new registration number. Steal it, drive it, grab it, sell it, deal it, or hell, fucking torch it—whatever you want, it can be arranged. Being a cop from a family of cops is fun, but being big ex-cops with the run of Needles, well, now, my friend, you're talking, because it's all yours for the taking. Spend time with Phil and Roy and you can see they've got years of pursuing larcenous hobbies that pad their wallets, fuel their boats, lease their new trucks, and keep their high life very high. The boys like their richly oiled, pebbled alligator Tex Robin cowboy boots, weighty and bright sterling silver belt buckles studded with expensive, old pawn turquoise, and they'll be the first to tell you how comfortable a mother-of-pearl snap-button cotton shirt can feel when it's Needles hot. These are big boys with big appetites hard at work in a small town in a big piece of desert. Phil and Roy have made Needles theirs.

It gets quiet at night. It gets black at night. And when the desert gets dark, you almost forget there even was a day. Day is for burrowing deeply underground. Night is for feeding, killing, hunting, and maybe just surviving. Night is also a time to go clubbing. For our nocturnal boys Phil and Roy, the July heat crackles under the wide tread of fat wheels rolling custom trucks fitted with big spots—huge diameter desert lights illuminating deep desert roads leading to places where coyotes prowl, and where the thick and long and deadly fast Mojave rattlesnake warns you, beware, this piece of dirt is home. I live here.

My call into Phil told me enough about tonight. I could see it was business as usual. The boys downing *cervezas con Herradura* and warmly buzzed. It was easy to picture the pair sitting high behind the thickly padded, leather steering wheel. They are speeding toward Route 69 hoping to find Phil's romantic interest, Darlene, and see why Mick and Keith's *Start Me Up* reigns as the pole dancer's wet dream. In the middle of a summer night when you can feel the brilliance of the stars load the infinite sky, and you stand there in the very middle of what appears to be nowhere, you feel how this place can swallow you and then cover your life with the next day's dirt. It gets dark in the desert for little girls, but darker still for big boys who don't know that the light at the end of the tunnel, well boys, that light just might be a train heading your way.

Two weeks ago Phil had found himself on the wrong end of a nail gun and the brothers made it clear that they hold Darlene responsible for Phil's physical and emotional stress. The family is upset because Phil is such a fuck up. But Roy likes to be the big boy. If I recall, Roy's shared expression of brotherly love was something like, "That bitch is so fucking done."

This means I need to get an audience with Darlene and draw a very real picture of what's about to go down, and offer a reasonable perspective on why it's in Darlene's best interest to look into other opportunities for employ outside of the immediate area. Helena and I will point out the merits of moving to another city or perhaps even another country. And should I need to be more persuasive, I will lean on a colorful, medical discourse about what the human body can't endure. Failing that piece of brilliance, I will simply remind our darling dancer that Phil and Roy don't do well when agitated. And yeah, probably offer her a large sum of money to disappear.

Then again, maybe Darlene's charms of working a crowd can be convincing enough to sell Phil on looking elsewhere, making it ok for her to stay in Needles—Darlene can continue her dancing career, enjoy that spotlight a little longer, buy a new Hyundai, moves in with the UPS guy, and pretty soon she's looking for a sitter. It could happen. But then we're dealing with the wild card—Roy. He'll want to wade in and start schooling everyone on how the big, older brother can make it right for the family and espouse familial righteousness. Roy will talk story and crank up Phil. Together, the boys will relive past lives on the force and with enough blow and beer, Roy will ramble about the unspoken code of the brotherhood and why the fuck don't we get on our horses and ride the fuck into town? Phil will like this. Chet and CC will not be too thrilled with the notion. Personally, I'd just like to see the brothers simply sniff out other grifters who have dotted Phil's life. Our boys spin out on distractions, deals, steals, and their own interpretation of the pursuit of happiness. It all leads to nowhere, and then they're back running the final load of scrips, relaxing poolside and the dancing Darlene is home free. *Ranchero Living* could be very good to them. The boys just have to let go a little.

CHAPTER 27

NIGHT

You would like this drive at night. Well, perhaps not this particular drive on this particular night when you can hear the distant yelp of the coyote cry and the meter of a chirping male mole cricket pimping his bad self and looking for a little love. You are driving a Speedster with the top down and a lovely, tough Russian girl who knows how to sing Mariachi is sitting next to you and you are driving down the road on your well-deserved vacation with your soft, black leather Tumi bags neatly tucked into the back of the Speedster and the dry desert air is blowing by you making the moment incandescent. You can hear music float past, and you note that yes, indeed, clear and dry and warm is a wonderful way to travel. You might ask your traveling companion to crack a cold beer and light a Menthol for you. You would take in the desert night sky and I'm sure you would smile. The shift of the gears, the low slung and tight ride sits you down smoothly on the newly paved asphalt and the easy mechanics of machine and motion against a warming, desert wind will make you believe that you are due for goodness. It's true. Take the wheel. And remember, if the mantis-like mole cricket can find love out here, chances are, so can you.

Helena and I like our options—sort of. I've got to get Darlene out of harm's way, and keep the Chet and CC family busy with the next run of scrips and then maybe everyone can take a breath, but fuck, then there's the small problem of one Detective Casey and that door has to be sealed. It never stops.

Helena looks at me as we come through the elevated sweep of the road. She gives me a wink, places her hand on the gearshift, I work the clutch and her delicate touch throws the Speedster from 4th to 3rd and the engine growls in the downshift. I like how Helena can light a cigarette while doing this. It's a pretty sexy move other Porsche drivers would appreciate.

Roy is driving his big truck fast and hard down the frontage road, smartly staying clear of the Interstate. His little brother Phil is sitting next to him. As you know, Roy and Phil like their vehicles. Currently, the automobiles show a bit of wear, bullet holes being what they are.

Phil's truck is a brilliant white. Roy opted for the deeper, meaner cobalt blue that's almost a midnight black with silvered custom wheels and proudly displays a *Needles Police Association* sticker on his back window. This a good sticker to have on your truck and is a beacon to all the brothers letting them know you're a member in good standing with the Fraternal Brotherhood of the Big Fat Envelope. It's more of a club than an association and everyone pays heavy dues.

Roy's truck has bigger desert lights that sit up on his roofline, racked on the top. With the easy flick of a switch he can turn night into day, throwing wide beacons of extreme light into a desert night that's darker than his truck. On occasion, Roy is known to turn to his passenger and boastfully perform a countdown like he's launching a rocket and then hit the switch and the white-hot, high-density halogen illumination blinds the oncoming car. But for real fun Roy likes his "halos" to freeze an animal in its tracks. The squeeze of the trigger and the exploding rifle report sends a sharp signal informing the desert that a polished, metal jacket has pierced deep into the skull or hip or heart, exploding through the skin and flesh, and a desert brother will now leave the planet confused about why their nocturnal instincts could have been so goddamn wrong. *Salud mi hermano.* The finger of God in this desert is Roy. He and his deep cobalt blue truck roam the flat, desert unchallenged, feeding at the top of the food chain, looking down on Needles, and running the desert with his suspect crew. Phil opens another beer, does a bump from his vial, passes it to Roy and the two brothers are speeding toward downtown on a July night in this summer of revenge.

The truck is cool, plush, and features a gun rack as part of the interior. No rifle in the rack tonight. Phil and Roy are hunting with roofies, a Taser, and some rope.

"Fuck man, what do you want to do with her?" Roy is pitching his brother Phil.

"Show her she can't fuck with me."

"She already did, *asshole*." Roy has always enjoyed working Phil.

"Well, that was her fuckup." Phil is a big, fleshy, mass of high.

"Tell you what I want—payback on your favorite mistake. We find her, we take her out, and drive out deep into the dirt…"

"Maybe to the reservation, dude," Phil suggests trying to sound like he has a clear agenda.

"The girl gets a message," Roy says, emphasizing his allegiance to Phil's wounded ego, ear, and foot.

"Yeah it's called shut-the-motherfucking-up…" Phil laughs at his own cleverness, and cracks another beer.

"How you like us now, *bitch?*" Roy says, firing up Phil's buzzed state.

Phil turns and grins at Roy and raises his beer, and in one long drink, drains it, and tosses the bottle out the window, lights a cigarette, and squints at the lights of Needles that look like bright, shiny objects fallen from the night sky. Phil is seriously high on blow and is edgy and sweats a little. He splits a half a roofie to take the edge off, and calm those big ex-cop nerves. Phil opens his window so he can feel the desert, too, but he can't.

That same night sky follows us as we head to the same place for different reasons on roads that share constellations hanging above the desert air. Like I said, you would like this drive, but maybe not so much on this particular night.

We pull into the crowded parking lot at Route 69, walk in, and we're immediately hit by the rush of fragrances favored by dancers. The wall of musk and the mix of Drakkar Noir saturates the scene with the sweat filtering through the heavyweight AC power plant flooding and hypnotizing the Needles thrill seeker with their very own dose of lost. The music is dialed into lighting and dancers and groups of the partying glitterati and the club is rich with the flow of excess and testosterone and money. Helena and I stand toward the back discreetly mapping this modern topography of lust, greed, and booze. Route 69 is the smartly dressed thrill center, a young man's tribal ground zero where cash is piped through a handy bank of ATM machines conveniently located nearly everywhere in the cavernous layout featuring five bars that efficiently dispense pricey, watered-down drinks ordered by boys eager to get fucked up and the women who promise to do the fucking. The mirage is real. And center stage truly is in the center, flanked by two side stages featuring the minor leaguers warming up and hoping to someday unseat the MVP's and get into the big money. As we walk through and around the pulsing crowd, we note the discreet warren of private rooms where the girls make as much as a very good dentist on a very good day. And they're not using nitrous for those whiter, brighter smiles.

We think we catch a glimpse of Darlene in the far corner, but no, we are very wrong. The spotlight suddenly comes on center stage and can now we see our girl confidently prancing out wearing a transparent, full length, black body stocking showcasing Darlene's young and lean body stacked in 4" gold pumps. Darlene's long red hair and black, silk number is the perfect fashion accessory to some very nasty power pole moves.

She is a rare combination of classic Rita Hayworth meets naughty, erotic pole slumming. Helena is less than impressed with Darlene's stage production. "Big fuckingk deal" is how she eloquently sums up her thoughts on the matter. I pretend to agree. Darlene struts to the center of the stage and starts grinding to *Welcome to the Jungle*, expertly undulating and thrusting her hips against the pole, moving her ass and pussy in a teasing rhythm that tingles every lad dipped in Drakkar.

Darlene is a tribal ritual of sex that sends the sweaty boys looking for the easy climax of a ready, back room lap dance. I can't take my eyes off her and see why she is, indeed "making bank."

Helena grabs my attention, and also digs into my arm even harder. We start looking around for Phil and Roy. I can feel them far off in the distance. There is a truck coming this way with big lights and big boys who are on a mission as dark as the sky, and they want to turn on big, bright lights that have nothing to do with dancing.

Immediately after *Jungle* and as Darlene finishes scooping up dollar bills tossed across the stage, Helena connects with her. Darlene ushers us past the young, pony-tailed "dressing manager" sprouting massive arms attached to his short, bullish, and ripped body that's stretched into a cliché—the Lycra-tight black tee that I think is not only smart club attire, but it makes his jugular pop so it looks like another muscle. (Getting his steroids from Rita?) His clean-shaven baby face doesn't quite seem to match up with his chiseled-ness, but I think it works. Our guardian of the gate can intimidate while courteously steering the drunks away from the dressing room and back to the club. The dude is definitely in charge and he's very aware that the girls' dressing area is the Holy Grail for buzzed legions seeking to connect with their new, favorite fantasy. Not to worry, our boy at the door has this portal to happiness on general lockdown.

In keeping with current lap-dancing-nightclub-stripper etiquette, I press a mini-bindle of my *pura* into his hand and he discreetly pockets the gift, flashes a grin, and then, like a good scout looking out for the franchise, he heavily checks out Helena as she presses by him. This is not a good move. This is not what you want to do with a six-foot Russian platinum blond who's survived the mother country.

Helena grabs him by his balls and is into his face: "Don't vhu havingk enough pussy to keep trackingk of?"

Oh-oh. This is not what, *Mo-Mo*, the juiced boy is expecting and he's not sure of what just happened. Our boy looks at me searching for some helpful male backup. I simply shrug, *Dude, I just hooked you up with some of the finest Peruvian, do yourself a big favor, do not fuck with the Russian chick.*

We're sitting in front of Darlene and she is expertly counting her dollars with the practiced speed and efficiency of a cartel accountant, has two cigarettes going in the ashtray, and a short rum and coke. The dressing room is swarming with a flurry of shift changes, money counting, cigarettes, dressing, undressing, music thumping, and it all gets washed back with a cocktail or two and a few necessary lines of meth or coke, anything that helps the club girls chase their dreams so it all can feel less than it does.

"All apologies for breaking up the evening, but we really do need to walk you through what's about to come down." I try my absolute best to be on point and straight with the girl.

"Seriously, vhee do, darlkingk girl." Helena says. Darlene just looks at her. Helena's accent and her long legged Balkan and platinum blondness can be stunning. I watch Darlene get wide-eyed just trying to follow Helena, a creature from another planet. Like I said, Helena's dancing eyebrows can mesmerize. Considering our time, and the uncertainty of when Phil and Roy might show, I do my best to keep Darlene focused and instill a sense of urgency, so I give her a quick recount of her past lust with Phil and do a pretty good job of weaving in that whole weed-deal-gone-bad thing and talk her through the *Butchero's* incident and how Phil is absolutely certain that she, Darlene, his former main squeeze and drug deal partner is the one responsible for the bloody deed. I also mention Roy, too. And Chet and CC. They all think she did it. Although the parents have washed their hands of yet another of Phil's terrific fuck ups, Roy and his little brother want someone to pay. That would be her, Darlene, our dancer.

Darlene doesn't say a thing. Darlene is nervous. Darlene is not happy. She is sitting here looking straight at me and then at Helena, then swallows her rum and coke, plucks a smoke out of the ashtray, lights another cigarette, inhales deeply, and looks at us like we have lost our fucking minds. I assure her that we have not. Helena also nods, confirming this fact.

"You're telling me that that fucking family thinks I grabbed a what?"

"A nail gun," I reply.

"Nail gun? Whatever the fuck that is…" Darlene looks in the mirror and primps. A habit.

"He thinks you shot him– in the men's room…."

"And why the fuck would I do that again, please?" she asks, putting her cash into a leather clutch.

"According to Phil it has to do with that bad weed deal, past sins and the jealousy thing…"

"He fucking wishes. I dumped *his* ass."

"I can see that, but the boys are thinking…" I say, looking at Helena. We want to move this conversation along.

"And guess what—he still owes *me* from that deal…" Darlene's fiery bravado is a neat piece of stage work, but not where we want this to go.

"Darlene, honey, those boys are heading this way and we really need you to look at what you might want to do next…" I am a fucking diplomat.

"He expects *me* to walk away from *this*?" she says, pointing out the world of Route 69 and its roomful of chaos as if she were looking out on the Lanai of her timeshare on sunny Maui.

"I know, I know, there's a lot at stake here and you've got a life but…" I shift from diplomat to evangelist to life coach.

"I am not going anywhere—and as for that fat fuck Phil and his brother, they can kiss my ass." Darlene breaks out the last of her rum and splashes it into the remains of her glass. (I think I could use one of those, too, but maybe taller and definitely with better rum.) This is not the way we were all expecting or hoping things would go, and Helena and I look at each other.

"Darlene, what if I paid you to get out of town?" I suggest, going straight to the point. Cash generally carries the day.

"How much?"

"$10,000."

"Cash? Upfront?

"Now. No strings."

"You give me ten large and all I have to do is walk?" Darlene isn't so sure that's all there is to it.

I can understand her questioning the two people currently sitting in front of her. We don't come across as annuity and investment advisors. Darlene knows what it takes to put $10,000 into her pocket and it generally doesn't include walking away from something. Or somebody.

"Where's the money? I wanna see it…all of it." Darlene is young, but not dumb.

"Trust me, you'll have it tonight, once we're outta here, but seriously we gotta go," I tap my Patek, "or there may be no money to get…"

Still, Darlene requires more information. "How do I know they won't come after me?"

"Short term memory loss. Once the boys get busy with the distraction of their dough and deals, you're a fucking footnote." I'm thinking that's about all I got right now. I'm almost ready to have Helena knock her out and carry the girl to her Hyundai.

"And you're giving me money to split—because why?" There's no quit in her game of 20 questions. Ok, we'll all play.

I go with something more philanthropic, something about a higher calling. "Chalk it up to me being generous or a Good Samaritan or maybe I just want to make a few things right—past sins and stuff—you walk, you cash in—everybody wins."

Darlene settles into a moment, pauses, looks around, and lowers her voice, "Bullhead City has some clubs…dancers are making big money in Scottsdale…could be good for me…"

"Smart girl," Helena taps her watch, "Timingk to go."

Darlene gets it and gets busy throwing odds and ends, clothes, personal effects, and a bunch of makeup into a large, overnight bag carrying an identity tag in the shape of a butterfly. Cute.

The erotic, exotic Darlene has a softer side. Put her in a day job working as a temp or admin assistant, watch her commute to work in her little Japanese auto with a butterfly sticker on the bumper and you're looking at just another cute young thing trying to make her way through life. Darlene picked the wrong lane during her formative years and decided that making bank was more important than making a life. Ok, we get that, but the girl has a spirit and a force that could have been, or maybe still can land on this side of normal. Maybe. Hell, given the circumstances, Darlene could have even been my receptionist. I quickly tap out a few rails from my personal *pura fina* for Darlene and Helena and it's time to get Darlene away from here and into the safety of another zip code.

We could be out of here, she could be history, and the boys could be out of luck, but then that's not going to happen.

"Well, hello, motherfucking party people!" Roy loudly announces as he and Phil bust into the dressing room. Phil and Roy are high, loud, and their bigness barges into the room. Fuck. We were almost out of here. How the fuck did they get past *Mo-Mo* my personal concierge and dressing room manager? I see a metal star tucked into Phil's belt— badges, fucking badges. That Brotherhood of the Big Fat Envelope does pay off.

"Phil, Roy…you guys cops all over again…outta be a law against that…"

"Shut the fuck up doctor!" Phil shouts, sweeping his arm across a small table, noisily scattering ashtrays and empty glasses across the floor. Girls move fast and vanish into the pumping club.

"You first…" I'm the glib, smart ass with too much *pura* in my system. Phil makes a move toward me, but Roy steps in.

Roy is not happy to see me in Darlene's dressing room. "He said shut the fuck up, doctor." Roy's face is red. He's in a hurry and would like to hurt somebody, and now would be good. I would be the logical choice.

Phil pushes forward, offering his opinion of things as they are. "You know Doc," Phil adds to Roy's understated eloquence, "I don't like your shit: that move down at the marina and now, what? This?" He points to Helena and Darlene, the petite dancer cowers hoping that

Helena's size and presence will protect her from the gathering storm. "Yeah boating can be a water hazard," I say, desperately trying to regain some leverage here, but failing miserably.

"What part of shut-the fuck-up do you not understand my friend?" Roy is trying to be all business. His high, vacant stare is more sinister than Phil's boisterous temper.

"He understandingk all of it, asshole," Helena says, bravely stepping in.

We soon find Roy's boiling point. Roy glares at her and pulls his Taser, threatening and moves toward Helena. Roy points the Taser at her, then at me then at Darlene then back to Helena. We get a good look at what an armed Taser looks like stuck in your face.

"Not gonna happen," I say, sweeping my arm in front of Helena, offering a kind of pathetic barrier between them. I mean fucking Roy is a big ass boy and I must be out of my mind. Or have another gear in me.

"Let's go Darlene—now!" Roy is seething.

The sweating, glassy-eyed brothers are already a menacing duo, but when they're this high, nothing is going to stand in their way. Especially when they have a furry, cute little rabbit trapped. And especially when they're standing next to each other holding a large, black Taser loaded with body-dropping electrical currents ready to go at the twitch of a chemically-induced trigger finger.

Darlene, already terrified just to face Phil, but with Roy on the warpath, is frozen, a deer in the headlights as she leans up against the makeup counter, facing the two avenging siblings. Helena and I are standing next to her. A few of the girls who came into the dressing room after Phil's heated blow up have discreetly slipped away, demonstrating an uncanny expertise at exiting when large, bad guys playing *policia* show up high, armed, and pulling one of their own out for questioning.

What we have here is a situation. Pretty sure this is the typical stripper and lap dancer dressing room mix of chicks, drugs, and threatening guys who are high and armed and in the middle of the desert in

July. Terrific. My mind races with one thought: *Way to go doctor, you've really played this one well.*

The interesting thing about life is that the more you plan, the less you can plan for. Case in point: the Phil and Roy boys and their plan that includes ropes, roofies and a Taser. Their plan says that they have this night wired and are going to squirrel the girl out to some desolate part of the desert and teach her a lesson. We're not sure what they have in mind. But it's not good. I believe the universe generally trumps ex-cops who are high and have dark intentions and big trucks with bright lights and a host of other past lives that have caused great harm.

I believe in the universe.

Tonight, the rules of our universe have recruited other forces, notably *Mo-Mo,* my well-muscled bouncer strapped into the body hugging, tight tee. Evidently, he's had his eye on a closed circuit screen and he's been observing the spin cycle happening in the dressing room and decides to flex some of that workout and step up for yours truly. His short, stocky, massive and muscular frame is good to have as backup because we don't have a lot of options here—blush and eyelash curlers make lousy weapons. Could be the bindle I generously palmed him, could be his infatuation with Helena, maybe he even has a crush on Darlene. What we do know is that he sees the way events are unfolding and steps in to join our back stage meeting with Phil and Roy.

Mo-Mo must have fucked with the club house lights as we see the dressing start to flicker and pulse, and we can see the rest of the club break out in a frenzied fit of shouting and commotion as the boozy, dancing crowd is hit by a sense of panic. We quickly react to the opportunity. Helena and I move Darlene past Roy and into the arms of *Mo-Mo* who grabs her, and pushes Darlene from behind the curtain and out the stage and she does what comes naturally—the girl starts to dance. There's another girl already up there and she's not sure what and why Darlene is up on her shift but thinks, *Whatever, dudes like the girl-on-girl thing, so if it helps with the tips, I'm cool with you, sister.* This is good. The boys can't touch her as she shares the stage and we quickly exit to meet up with our boy wonder and he informs us that he's pulled his car around the back door.

Phil and Roy give chase trying to get their hands on Darlene. Their hefty, weighty beefiness is working against them as they try to move against the tight, crowded dressing room and stage area, and are having a time of it just pushing through, raising their voices and elbowing hard into the crowd, jostling bodies to the side.

"Move, move, move asshole!"

"Thank you mother fucker now take this drink and shove it… outta the way dickhead!"

The ex-cops can't get through fast enough. The entire club is moving, swarming through tables, chairs and the bar area filling the floor and wedging Phil and Roy who are trying like hell to muscle past anyone and anything that stands in their way of their dancer, me, and Helena. The boozy audience is a stampede of bodies, a sweaty, fucked up, wildly raucous crowd that does a mindlessly good job of keeping Phil and Roy from getting close to Darlene as she nervously dances toward the back of the stage, ready to bolt with our bouncer. Helena and I are moving toward the exit and we're keeping an eye on Phil and Roy who seem to be losing some of their early buzz. It's a race to the door and Darlene is out and into her new best friend's car and she is off to another life in another club.

We make it through the back as Phil and Roy come running up fast and back us up against the exterior exit door and in the shadows of the back of the club. They are not happy at all. I can smell their sweat and booze and bad ideas tumbling through their pores and breath. They both could use a mint.

Helena makes a move on the sizable but high Roy, grabs his Taser, pulls the trigger and tags the fleshy pecs sending the searing voltage that locks up his muscles. Roy stiffens like a board—"Aaaaaaagh!"— and the big boy is down. You get one shot with a Taser before having to recharge, and Helena made it count, although I'm sure she wishes she had tagged his balls.

"Motherfucker, you bitch!" Phil shouts as he tries to aid to his fallen brother.

Helena stands back and paces like a boxer who's scored a KO and is waiting for the official call. She tosses the stun gun toward Roy's rigid body.

Two high-heeled dancers quickly skirt by in skin-tight short-shorts barely covering their moneymakers. The girls demonstrate proper pole etiquette by pretending hard not to see the dark scene with the panting Phil, the squirming Roy and the six-foot, platinum Russian who is standing over him. The surprised girls wisely skate on past the road kill. Not something they see everyday in a workday where they've seen everything.

"Nicola Tesla sends you his love, asshole," Helena whispers, and I like her ironic and random reference to the brilliant and inventive Serb. She steps back and lights a smoke. I light a smoke. We stand there watching the brothers coming to the realization that Darlene is gone, Roy's been whacked, and Phil is fucked. They know that for now, we've put the issue of revenge and payback out of reach, and that sure, we'll finish our deal with scrips and the rest of the *pharma*.

"I would suggest you keep busy with some other areas of interest, like your end of that other bargain," I say, referring to Detective Casey.

Route 69 continues to pulse with a rhythmic, muffled, percussive beat that pushes hard against the walls of the club. Each time a customer walks in and out, the acoustics can't contain the heavy music and it loudly ripples across the desert and into the heat and through the night. The club pounds out the promise of girls, sex, and the high life right here in one spot in one place at one time.

"Hey, Phil, make sure you get home safely now," I say, hoping he can hear the smirk slide across my face. Phil knows he cannot fuck with me or Helena or even Darlene. The girl will get her $10,000 tonight. The fat envelope will carry her to safety and make sure the dancer stays tucked away in another desert somewhere out in the wasteland.

Out of the parking lot light a buzzed middle-aged man wanders by and looks at me, stares at Helena, and then tries to focus hard on making out just what the hell happened to Roy, his big body laid out on the asphalt in the back lot of a Needles' strip club. He catches his balance, steadying himself and says to me, "Dude, you for hire? 'Cause my kids can be a pain in the ass."

As we walk toward the car, Helena runs over to Roy's truck, leans in and hits the light switch blazing the big halos onto the brothers up against the wall. It's how you find and freeze animals that prey under the cover of night. Just ask Phil and Roy.

We slide into the Speedster, relieved to have this night behind us, and like any couple in the desert in July, we like the heat and the moment where everything seems possible as we travel through this flat expanse of geography that's really just another vacation spot on a postcard welcoming us to the rush of the Mighty Colorado River. Helena bites the tender of my ear. I smell her sweat and the dark smoke of tobacco. She bites harder and I turn to kiss her mouth, deeply. Her soft lips make me feel safe. She smiles. I feel careless and excited that she sees something in me, something I wasn't sure I had. Goodness? Not certain about that, but we were able to put it out there for Darlene. We pull out of the club's parking lot and I shift into 2nd and Helena calls Darlene to set up a drop for her payday so she can feel the cozy goodness of Ten Large tucked between her legs. Helena begins to play with the radio dial searching for Mariachi. I touch her hand, softly, turning it off. I want to listen to the music from the club fading across the dirt and I want to watch the endless night sky dance over a road so smooth and so warm, we are weightless.

CHAPTER 28

AND SO IT GOES

It was just after dark when the three young climbers found Casey's body.

They said they would've walked right past the hole, but a brilliant gleam of what they thought was quartz caught their attention. Instead, their flashlight beam found the top of Casey's polished, nickel-plated .38 revolver still holstered in his belt. Their shiny, gruesome discovery introduced the rock hounds to Detective Casey, his six-foot and weighty frame twisted and wedged into the black divot gouged out of the steep, metamorphic quarry.

At the time of his death, Casey was forty years of age and had over fifteen years on the force, the last ten with the loyal Needles brethren. Casey liked this desert. He liked to be alone in it. He liked to dig it, sift through it, pick at it, and spend days chipping his way through the geological strata of quartz, limestone, ore, and the sediment of magma left behind when other sands and creatures roamed the dirt. Bigger creatures who would not play well with the Needles brethren. Casey liked the rock that could only come from the shifting plates chaptering geologic stories about this place. *Geologic time events*, he called them, and he loved the striated recordings captured and released through the chronological layers manufactured by heat and pressure—the simple and studied beauty of the geologic time scale preserved in this landscape. Rock and dirt and the geology of this desert had a finite order to it. It was all so evident. Linear. He liked how the dirt talked to him. It had tales to tell. Casey himself had nearly become a part of it, a particle in the deep dirt he loved so much. Casey would have been lost forever in the shale if the climbers hadn't randomly pointed a light in his direction. But maybe that's how it is sometimes out here in the universe. The smallest reflection back invites discovery within. Casey knew that. And he knew a lot about me.

We're at home and my mobile rings, it's Chet. I can hear Chet breathing into the phone, "Nobody is going to stand in the way of the money. Nobody. It's taken care of. Casey's gone." Chet's voice sends a flush of blood racing into my brain and my world vibrates, feels lost, desperate, and cloudy, and wants to be forgotten. I am watching time squeeze into a new measure of slow. There's a hum and a buzz to the adrenaline sucking into every one of my cells.

I don't like the voice on the phone. I don't like knowing a man slipped into the universe and that his soul is tethered to mine, and the connection is pulling me down into the abyss. I thought I was better than that. Maybe I'm only just like that and I need to wake the fuck up and come clean with who I am.

Casey woke up that morning and then he went away forever. And maybe, so did I. Chet told me about Casey. He said some boys on the force called Phil and Roy and gave them the news. The coroner reported that Casey was the victim of a perfect storm of Neurotoxic venom, exposure, dehydration, and internal bleeding. Casey suffered more than his share of the shit. At night, this desert can take your temperature down fast, and if you're battling a Diamondback, a broken arm, and your body is tightly wedged into a hole, well, you are in a world of hurt. Word on the street with the nosey, gossiping locals was that it seemed odd for an experienced law enforcement professional like Casey, that he wasn't able to get a shot off hoping that somebody, somewhere, would hear something. People shrugged and chalked it up to how this desert can kill you in so many ways. And it seems that Detective Casey had dug up a few of his very own. Casey was a regular guy who got caught in the middle of what can only be considered a difficult situation. He knew about my past and about the Russians and had uncovered documents that Chet not only found very interesting, but obviously, very rewarding.

Yes, Casey had unearthed some stories in the middle of the desert, and this time his discovery had nothing to do with geology.

Rita called and we agreed that the scrips she had were ready to go. The business was heading back to a new normal and like a support group fresh out of rehab, we're all moving forward. It's amazing what a payday can do to assuage personal issues. Ok, perhaps some of the family is harboring a grudge for the Big Boat Marina and Route 69 incidents, but I like to think that those are just bumps in the road. I could use the injection of capital. I had given Chet and CC and their wonderful boys about a week to deal with the Casey portion of this little bed of thorns. Terrible, I know, and certainly not where I would have gone, but again, I was forced to have them deal with the loose ends. I didn't want it to go this way, but with Russians bent on making my life come to an end in surely what would be a fucking lot of pain, Casey had to go. Survival of the fittest? Yeah, sure, that works. I thought about bringing in Federal help, but knew that they would just fuck up everything, and really what were they going to do, suggest a move? Recommend another venue for ex-surgeons? Perhaps hijack another identity and another life in another country? What's the point? I'm in the shit now. No, I opted to let Chet deal with it. And it got ugly. I pour a tough, three-ounce shot of iced Stoli, chilled to the mother-fucking point and it is a righteous hymn. I pour another. A few more and the bite of the bright, sharp vodka and heat and AC gives my conscience a safe place against knowing that Casey would still be alive if he didn't know fuck all. According to the way Chet tells it, the pit viper's fangs pierced the back of his knee.

The bite went hard and deep. The Mojave rattlesnake did what comes naturally and the quick, muscled strike put Casey in a seizure. His breathing became labored and then Casey would convulse in his own vomit, his rapid pulse pounding out toxin-rich blood. His body steeped in the poison blood, flooding fluid into his lungs and then he would start to wheeze, metering out a slow, erratic death rattle of his own. If Casey had regained any kind of consciousness, he'd be aware that it's now pitch black and he would face the worst of it, finding himself stuck and trapped in a deep hole allowing him only to look up and watch the eternity of the night, witnessing the universe waiting for him. Soon, it would all fade to black and the memories of days in the dirt, a life of silent discoveries, and the small championships wrought out of desert duels would glide over him as he fell into shock, extreme exposure, and deadly dehydration.

It wouldn't be long now.

The black sky invited Detective Casey to join the endless constellations that dotted his desert sky a billion years ago.

Casey closed his eyes and left.

CHAPTER 29

JULY AND JACK

This is a quiet morning and I am feeling wasted from the fallout of my life that put me in some rather delicate scenarios—the last being that deadly, dirty conclusion of the late Detective Casey, rock hound.

Like any captain of industry, I need to regroup, settle accounts, and take stock of a day in July. And as I watch my morning play across this dry, flat of desert scrub, my moment is interrupted by a phone call. It's Rita and she's on her way over with the cash count so we can all say adios to Chet and CC and their posse of bad—*vamanos mis amigos*.

This is my life and my morning and my July boxed up and neatly arranged to fit perfectly into my riveted fortress shielding me from the relentless desert solar flares bent on piercing my July morning. I feel like a sardine tinned into my aluminum package. I dial into the day, pouring a tumbler of very black, very iced coffee, and light a refreshing, cooling nicotine-loaded Menthol—my morning smoke offers me a deep inhale that delivers that first and satisfyingly rich dose of Heaven. Madison Avenue had it right. I could taste the fine, toasted tobacco sweetly saturated in a heady chemical mix that's brilliantly engineered to deliver dose after dose of minty flavor. I exhale and watch my steady stream of smoke gently expand and tap against the glass window before vanishing into the filtered air, the smoke cleansed and churned through the AC and blasted out and into the land of Needles.. I pour another iced coffee and take a long, easy swallow setting up the perfect caffeine and nicotine punch that dilates my day. I feel like I'm ready to punch over my weight class.

This shiny metal home keeps my life in a good place—even when faced with young misfits like the dangerous Rita who can be heard gunning up in her muscled Mustang. She comes up the dirt road fast and hard and then slams the wheel to the right sending her screaming hemi into a quick slide, skidding to a stop, snapping out a big dusting of sand and light scree that floats high into the air, and wraps Rita's Shelby in a dry, blanket of fine desert. The beast is panting. The girl does like to make an entrance. I think Rita has a bad case of swimmer's ear because for fuck's sake, her stereo is dialed into a new volume of Judas Priest that makes her darkly tinted windows tremble. There's something just plain dirty about Detroit metal wrapped in thick black and fat tires, darkened windows, and a body dusted with a fine sheeting of desert. And this is how Rita and her Carroll Shelby Mustang arrive at my doorstep in the middle of a morning in this part of Needles with that kind of girl commanding the roadway.

I watch her check herself out in her car window, bobbing to the inner percussion of a beat still inside her head and as she skips toward my Cloud, the dirt she's stirred floating off in the morning heat. Her cutoff shorts and cowboys boots and Panama fedora are set off by the silver mustang, and she is carrying a large, leather bag which I know holds our dough and most likely her slightly curved, cutting Puukko, along with her attitude just waiting for anyone who wants a piece of Rita.

This is my life. Where it goes from here is anybody's guess. I pour another coffee and give the fridge a glance knowing there's a little hit of iced salvation stored neatly into a quart that's perfectly cold and frozen and too, could be a refreshingly nice option to help me settle my day, but I opt to let that go. For now. Rita is here.

Helena is tucked into the bedroom and is told to just sit tight. I see my phone light up as Rita comes up to the door. Fuck, and now Jack is calling. I have to take the call but can't afford Rita to be part of this conversation. I quietly tell Jack to hold for a second and then smile and ask Rita to leave the bag and get me a carton of smokes and if she wouldn't mind, pick up some Stoli reserves.

"Lemme take the Porsche just so I can see what it's like to be you."

I throw her the keys to the Speedster. She offers me a flirty smile and leaves, spinning the Porsche through the gears as I watch her wind down the dirty, dusty road out. Fuck, she drives my German like her beefy Detroit wheels.

Over the years Jack and I have become close. He's my federal advisor and mentor and counselor and keeps information moving so I can keep on living. His 8x11 beige and tabbed official job jacket says he has to call me once a month to check in and make sure I'm still alive—if I'm not, well, Jack has some explaining to do—could mean he fucked up or somebody's smarter than him. I've been an honorary member of the Witness Protection Program for more than two years. A god-awful long time to be out in this piece of playa trying to keep it together until I get the news from somebody up the food chain informing me that it's time to move. The mere, yet very nasty, fact of dealing with the threat of Russians trying to track me down has been, well, let's just say it's a bit rough around the edges. Looking over my shoulder isn't a holiday. Some days, a fast bullet by any of Maxim's guns seems downright welcomed, particularly if he could take me out in the July and August months when the sun is busy igniting our longitude and latitude with a flamethrower and we're all feeling like death. They got a valley down the road that says exactly that.

It's nice to know that Jack knows where the Russian bad guys are and keeps me posted on anything heading my way. I'm actually not in the Fed protection program I only worked for them until a major fuckup when I lost Darya on my operating table in the middle of Bel Air. I found out that Russians don't like other dead Russians, especially a family member and especially mothers of their children and especially if they didn't kill them. Go figure.

When it was time for me to *vamos* out of LA, Agent Jack Murphey wanted to send me the occasional postcard so he could keep tabs. Part of the department's policy, but not part of mine. I got out and wanted to stay out. As much as I liked my own personal Fed, I had to measure just how much information Jack deserved. He wanted to know where I landed, but so do the mad Russians. It was nice to feel loved. I said thank you very much, but it was time for me to get a life in anywhere but Los Angeles and Needles seemed like the perfect place at a time when 'perfect' meant hiding out in the middle of nowhere.

"You ready?" Jack asks.

"The other place," I say.

"Heard you've been busy."

"Somebody in this house has to make a living."

"Yeah, that's what they said about Casey." Jack is deadly serious.

"That was fucked up," I said, sounding sincere because I am.

"I'm sure Casey thought so, too." I could hear Jack's voice laying low waiting for the sarcasm to cut.

"We both know my scrips business was green-lighted by you guys. Like the bumper sticker says, 'Shit happens'."

"Don't fucking talk to me about that asshole Chet and his entire family of assholes. You have to keep a lid on the bad boys."

"I thought that was your job." Booyah.

"I could do my job if I knew a few details." Jack is good.

"What? I'm supposed to send out the bat signal every time I get rubbed the wrong way by jerks like the Chet clan?"

"When it comes to dead detectives, that answer would be affirmative motherfucker." Jack is now less than professional.

"It was either gonna be him or me, and I figured that if you wanted me to continue working with some of your turned Russians, then you want me standing upright. And breathing."

"Casey had shit on you, so what? He wasn't doing anything with it." Jack is a skilled debate captain and a tough federal government-issue agent of the first order.

"And I know that how? Fuck, Jack, all Casey had to do was make a call to some Balkan Bads and he is set for life. Russians would have loved to give our departed Detective some extra large front money.

Remember, Casey wasn't exactly a Boy Scout," I said, feeling righteous and vindicated.

"You know the scrips shit has to end."

"Headed there," I say.

"See you there tomorrow, two o'clock sharp. Pay attention to Rita. Our file on her tells me she's a fucking liability, but you already knew that."

"And thank you for stating the obvious," I say, looking out the window. I see Rita pressing the Speedster fast on the road and back into my morning.

I hung up and tossed my phone over on the couch. Rita walks in and puts the bag on the counter. Immediately, I see her glance around the tiny footprint of living space.

Those fierce aquamarine eyes want to see if that fine, leather cash bag is still here. She asks me if I want a morning opener. She doesn't wait for me. She pours two.

"Let's call this an early brunch, why not?" Rita poses with a sly grin. She is terribly sexy in her creamy-grey snakeskin cowboy boots wrapped around her defined and tanned legs. I think I would like to fuck her, but this would be a very poor choice in desert living. She catches my thought and flashes an even nastier, teasingly tempting and coy smile that says exactly what she knows about men, and me.

Rita interrupts my lost daydream of having sex with her, "Here's to you and here's to me," and holds up her glass, tips her fedora back and leans against the kitchen counter showing me just how tan, fit, young, and sexy the girl truly is. She knows how to work a room. No matter who or what's in it. She wants to command attention. So she does.

I salute back with a raised glass and toss back the drink. The coffee was nice but this brace of a morning Stoli hits me in the sweet spot and I remind myself to rethink the iced coffee thing. True to my physician-approved program of better living through supplements, I grab a handful of my mega-vitamins and down those to help ease the ingestion of Russian Vodka and Peruvian marching powder. Small, tidy spaces, and the sweeping, cleansing chill of the AC make the morning appear civil. Even with Rita standing with a drink in hand, waiting for the count, and finally ending our business and moving on, it all feels like she was just coming by for a coffee and a chat. But here we are. Rita's strong swimmer's body looks killer in her faded-blue denim cutoffs and boots. Her white tee sets off her tanning booth time.

Rita looks good standing with the black leather bag of cash from a pad of scrips sold and distributed from Arizona and into California, following a line up the Mighty Colorado and back again. That river of water cuts a ribbon through the canyons and if you follow it, you too, will understand how it feeds the Mojave and how we fed the Mojave, too. From Needles up to Bullhead City and into Scottsdale our pharmacies and dealers served the desert ecosystem—and it all finally arrives in a leather bag delivered by a twenty-year-old girl who can swim faster and longer than most and is more dangerous than all of them. It's been said that the Mojave rattlesnake when forced by hunger and desperation, will swim. The snake finds an inner drive, a re-wired compulsion that eliminates the fear of water and over-rides the biological warning signs to stay the fuck out of the water. Instead the desire to eat is too powerful and the water, now, just an element to overcome so the snake can survive. It swims and it eats. And it's been said by Indians, that the snake will teach others to do the same.

I look at the bag and smile. Relieved that I made it work. This is my life. This is far from Hollywood and the operating table. I accept this new normal of surviving in the desert. Like the brochure says, it's a lifestyle.

We stand next to the blond laminate dining table, Rita tosses me the bag, I unzip it, reach in, and start pulling out small, worn bundles of cash and I neatly place each bundle onto the Cloud's well-crafted laminate top and then simply turn the bag upside down and shake it, watching the cash pour out and spread across the top of the table. $300,000 in small bills spilling across a table can do wonders for your morning.

"I blew through those scrips in record time…we moved more product in three weeks …no fuck ups…you're welcome."

"Always good to hear…no fucking of the ups," I say with a hint of my tired sarcasm that flies over Rita as she is zeroed in on the stacks of cash and I'm sure she has a heavy metal tune rocking in her head.

"Good crew with a heavy connection in Phoenix…rock n' roll my man…rock n' roll," Rita is bobbing. She is anxious to feel the money. I think she would like to smell it, too.

We smile, and then sit back and have another drink. We light our cigarettes and stare at the mountain of cash that sits in front of us and I am almost certain I can hear the roar of the Mighty Colorado. Then, I started thinking of her Puukko and how this girl could be so wrong we would never find level again.. I went to the cupboard and pulled out an ampule and hurriedly make another Stoli and imbibe in something tried and true. And something I could control.

This is July and Jack called, and he knows some things about some Russians that I should know about. Other than that, Rita is a cluster-fuck.

CHAPTER 30

MINCES

Just when I think the dog-eared chapters of my beautiful Hollywood life are history, my ugly Russians are back. I hate these Russians because they make me nervous. They are very good at finding people alive and then making them found dead. These Russians have deep pockets and like to throw buckets of money at anyone and anything and so yeah, I'm feeling a little edgy. Money is a powerful drug. It buys a lot of favors and even more information.

I told that Slavic asshole, Maxim, I wasn't comfortable with operating on a heavy smoker and that his fucking, insistent, significant other had a very good chance of significant risks complicated by her nasty Russian habit of smoking since she was about five. Sure enough, Mrs. Slavic pulls a Code Blue when her body decided it was time to start pushing a massive blood clot deep into her collapsing lungs, and the thick and gooey clot decided to kill her right on my table, in my office, in Bel Air. Perfect.

Perfect because I helped her along. I was under orders to let her slip into the eternal abyss. The Feds wanted her gone—she wanted a little work done. The timing was impeccable. I set up Maxim and gave him a backstory on the risk involved, he bought it, and off we all went into the OR. Only this time, the patient was a footnote to the afternoon's appointment. I explained that anything can happen under the knife, and we always do our best and we always try like hell to reduce the risk, but things being what they are can never be 100%. I further explained that mother fucking stringy and nasty piece of biology settled in and did what a clot is supposed to do. Maxim didn't buy it. Neither did the rest of his gunslingers. So now I'm living the dream right the fuck here, in Needles, looking over my shoulder, packing a Glock and hitting my own Menthol habit hard. And now, as Jack has revealed, there have been small slips along the federal highway that just may have tipped somebody to something we don't feel good about. Little things like that. Always a comforting thought. So, sure, my day is already looking fabulous.

I checked to make sure the alarm system is set, pour a quick, short shot of the arctic Stoli, and dial Helena.

"At Boot Barn," she says, and I sense she is mindlessly walking and talking.

"Good place to be in Needles," I add mindlessly talking and drinking.

"I am likingg legacy black Nocona's with deese sharp, pointed, needle nose. Vhud you want me to buy you?"

"I'll take the Tex Robin Kangaroos, five row stitch. Size 11."

"Puttink eight grand in my hand and they are havingk your name on dem."

"I have to meet with Jack. You know where the dropper is—go easy." I sounded oddly paternal about my *pharma*.

"I am beingk regular Girl Scout," Helena teased.

"Time for me to see what various Russian people have been up to these days."

"Read Pasternak…you are doctor," she laughs on the reference to Zhivago. "Get gun, grab Russian girl, work a fed, find desert, livingk in Cloud, seems you havingk under control."

"I would prefer not to be dealing with Jack and Russians but what's a surgeon from Hollywood gonna do with his spare time in a desert that has nothing but spare time?"

"Whatever you vantingk…even me." She is a good flirt.

"I have you in Noconas, black." I say, happy to flirt back.

"And nothingk else?" Her voice sounds even sexier on my mobile.

"Great minds think alike." I finish my drink, and on that teasing note, we hang up.

I look at my watch, eye the Stoli seeking a short second, but I reconsider. It's time to go.

I catch myself thinking that shopping for boots seems so normal, while I am on my way to meet Jack and talk about my life that is not so normal. I would very much like to be with Helena trying on those new 5-row stitched Tex Robin's at the Boot Barn in downtown Needles. But I am not. I am on my to meet up with my own personal federal agent who is a fine example of your tax dollars at work, thank you.

I could feel the dry, brittle, mid-day sun baking the pavement, the scald, shimmering off the sidewalk, and bouncing up through me. Walking into the diner, I find relief in the cooling current of the AC dialed on high to battle the burn of the Needles heat and it offers me a welcoming chill that wicks the sweat off my shirt. The few patrons sprinkled along the counter and in booths seem to appreciate the wonder of our manufactured microclimate protecting them from the red planet outside. An older woman with sparkling, electric blue eyes, and a deeply lined and tanned face, smiles at me, creating even deeper rivers of rugged terrain on a face shaped by a life in this desert.

I look around for Jack. He is here, and I slide into the booth, and across from him. We're sitting in *Minces*, a stamp of a diner that seats only about twenty people. Small, friendly, and decorated in the desert tradition of wagon wheels, cactus, amateur desert taxidermy, and scorpions encased in liquid amber, frozen in time, now harmless, but a warning of what can go very wrong in the dirt. Which is why Jack is a welcomed sight. He's a calming influence over my influences. Jack is a sincere and pointed agent who has seen his share of bad guys, agents, policies, and the protection program. Jack, I think, likes me, or at least leads me to believe that he cares. Jack is good at making me a believer.

He's a straight up fed who likes order, rules, regulations, and ok, maybe the occasional "sensual masseuse," and sometimes a few too many cocktails, but in general he is a machine gun kind of a guy. More importantly, Jack does not take shit from anyone. He is a little over six-feet, 200 pounds, a fit and physical sort who likes his moustache trimmed, and his shortly cropped blonde and grey hair in an even neater crew cut. Typically, he wears aviator shades, khakis, and a basic short sleeve shirt, blue, and tries to stay way from patterns. He looks federal in every sense of the word—straight as an arrow and exactly the kind of guy you would want on your side in a knife fight. Right now he's just the kind of guy who can have a bite at the local diner and chat about Russians who want to kill me like he's chatting up the deeper implications on a Racing Form at Santa Anita. He talks to me in terms of long-shots and odds and generally tries to help my anxieties out with a best-case scenario that has me living and getting a nice tan just for a bit longer. I can see that Jack is very good at lying.

The sea-foam green walls at Minces carry black and white photographs of an America discovering the automobile along Route 66, charmed by the new romance of motels with TV, free ice, swimming pool, and a hamburger joint. Large, flaxen, water-bags hang on the front of the cars, cooling the engine so travelers can beat the high sun and make it safely across the endlessly flat stretches of road introducing the family motorcade to the hospitality of the southwest. (*Real, live Indian dancing! Watch a war party come to life!*)

"See that little bit of poison right there?" Jack points to a small, glass bottle of amber that encases an even smaller creature, floating in limbo. His world at an end, his body and killer instincts, harmless, the scorpion floats. I wonder what he was thinking when he was stopped in his tracks on his way to feeding on his next desert meal.

"Nasty bit, no thank you," I said, bristling at the thought of reaching into a shoe and the evil cousin biting into the fleshy part of my hand. I believe that would cause a lot of swelling and equal parts of throbbing pain and a hurried trip to the ER. I am a goddamn physician so I don't believe that I am far off.

"It's a bark scorpion."

"Bark worse than its bite?" I reply, looking around for some service.

Jack continues to examine the bottle of amber and holds it up to the light.

"This little guy wants to kill you, flat out. No hesitation, no questions. You come close to him and he will try to get very close to you."

"Reminds me of why we're here."

"But this little bitty bark scorpion is kind of an oddity—you see, he likes it hot, but not too hot, and he doesn't like it super dry, he likes moisture, so why does the little bugger live in the hottest, driest mother fucking town in the country? Simple, it's where the food is. And where he ended up. He's also very blind which makes him easy prey for other not-so-nice predators looking around for their dinner." Jack slides the amber tomb over to me.

"I can feel an analogy coming on," I say.

"Bark scorpion only gets to be about three inches—one sting and it's strongly suggested you head straight to the antivenin. Infants, toddlers and elderly are toast, the rest of us, have a better chance of survival."

"Pass the antivenin, and make mine a double." I light a Menthol.

"Yeah, this little guy, all two inches of him, only has one job, and that's to kill you with a sharp, intense, and painful sting that you will not forget—ever—or five minutes, whichever comes first."

"Kind of like you, my dear friend, Jack," I say, "Intense, but without the stinger and painful part." I'm now impatient for at least a cold beer. Jack catches my nervous energy.

Just then, a tall, skinny Korean guy with square-framed Tortoise-shell glasses, and a wispy mustache is at our table. This tall Korean is holding a nervous, small, smooth-coated, brown dog in the cup of his right hand and interrupts our pleasantries about antitoxins, death, and desert assassins.

"What are you fellows having?" He says, mustering up something beyond a flat and bored and into a query bordering slightly irritated and impatient. Obviously, the wait-staff of one is not in it for the tip.

"Well, for starters, we're definitely not having dog." I look at the Korean and then at Jack.

Jack interrupts. "I'm with him, no dog, either, watching my weight."

"My Minces is a service dog," the tall Korean guy says blankly. "I named him after this place."

"The owner must be thrilled," I say, raising my glass of water.

"That would be me," our Korean dog lover quickly snaps, not quite a bark.

So here we are in a diner, in Needles, with a Korean guy who is taking our order with a small dog in his hand, while I spin a bottle of solid amber encasing a killer scorpion and waiting for the download on bad Russians who want me dead for a bad case of biology that happened a few years ago in Hollywood.

Like I said, the days here in lovely Needles just get better and better. Jack stares at our Korean waiter. "The service part has me intrigued."

"Minces is a comfort dog that helps with my anxiety." Our Waiter-Owner-Service-Dog-Lover is trying desperately to work the problem of us sitting in his booth.

"Small comfort," I say.

"He means because of the size of the dog…small…" Jack points out the obvious, and continues to charm our waiter.

"So when you bring our food, does the dog, that's a Chihuahua, right? Does the dog come with the order? And how do you write the order if you have a dog in one hand? Just asking." Jack has a point.

"Minces is a Teacup Chihuahua, fits into my pocket," our Korean guy-waiter-diner-owner proudly states, and swiftly places the dainty, nervously vibrating canine into his apron pocket. Jack and I watch the small dog turn and twist, the little body moving as the Korean smiles, and whips out a pen and pad. Ok, now I am seriously pissed that I did not have that other shot back at home. I light another Menthol, and pop a Nicorette, waiting for my rush to help deal with whatever the fuck is going on here at Minces, the Diner, and with Minces, the Anxiety-Relieving-Service-Teacup-Chihuahua.

"Whatever the fuck you do, don't order the tea," I say, the joke glides over the head of our nervous waiter.

"May I ask, what did you do before you owned this place?" Jack asks, now trying to be polite, his expression is straight faced.

"Technology. Silicon Valley. I was in IT: you know codes and applications, data in data out." The Korean is warming to Jack. "I sued my boss for sexual harassment and won, so yeah, kind of like my own personal IPO. Minces and me found a home here, even though Minces can't handle the heat. When he gets too hot, I just dip him in a cup of water, right here in the kitchen and cool him off. So, what are we having?" The Korean likes Jack, but I can tell he still has reservations about me, no surprise.

"Lets go with four ice-cold Pabst beers, extra-large plate of fries, and a clean ashtray. And please, the beer needs to be artic ice cold, not just frothy cold."

"Or just cold." Jack underscores the emphasis on cold.

"It's a thousand degrees out there, so yeah, bionic cryo cold."

As our Korean friend heads back to the kitchen, Minces continues to squirm. We're not sure if we're going to get our beers or Minces is getting a bath, but we're pretty sure we see the Korean gently patting his pockets assuring man's best friend that it's all good here in downtown Needles.

"You seem to know a lot about scorpions…talk to me about some Russians," I say.

"You know Maxim, but you don't know Anton."

"Should I know Anton?"

"Anton is part of the Russian block of about twenty heavies currently residing in Los Angeles. So yeah, you should."

"But I got you Agent Jack Murphey to keep me safe and sound."

Jack continued on his Anton profile. "And, Anton is Maxim's right hand—he's doing the legwork. Anton has Maxim's extra-large cash backing him to buy whoever's selling."

"Are you trying to make my day even worse or just excellent at being an asshole."

"Look Doc, we have plans for Anton…and Maxim."

"Terrific, now that I know this Anton I just slot him in the murderously worse than Maxim category and continue on with whatever the rest of my life looks like."

My phone goes off and it's Rita. (Jesus can this day get any better?) "I'm taking cash over to Chet's," Rita sounds rushed.

"Check in when you get there, just so we're all good." I look at Jack.

"Want me to give Chet his split?" She is being professionally courteous and matter of fact which always leads me to believe she is working the room, so to speak.

"Do that, and tell the old man I say adios and give my regards to Phil, and your wonderful Uncle Roy…"

"You got it, later…" Rita says, over the heavy metal playing in her Detroit.

"Call me when you get there, por favor," I say.

We hang up and I tell Jack about Rita's deal and nobody had to get their hands dirty.

"Rita is going to fuck this up," Jack tells me.

"She knows better."

"That doesn't mean anything to her…it means shit," Jack says.

"The girl will be fine; she delivers the cash today. I even covered her with an extra $25,000. Rita knows she's taken care of."

"Look, Doc, just be careful with her, we both know she can go to the dark side."

I glance around the room searching for our wait-staff-person-dog-lover. "Ok, ok, let's just see how she handles this and let me get back to the Russians. Where the fuck is our beer?" Upon receipt of Jack's fabulous Anton review, I am even more than thirsty.

"The dude's multi-tasking. Whenever you're waiting on tables with a dog in your pocket, slows the kitchen down," Jack says.

"Isn't there a federal agency that handles this kind of thing?"

"It's a toss up between the FDA, child labor laws and the humane society."

Jack changes our rant on Minces lack of efficient and courteous food and table service.

"Anton apparently knows something is happening out here."

I look at the scorpion. Then, I look for the waiter, or the dog, or both. Anyone with our beers would be fine.

"What the fuck, you call yourself a Witness Protection federal agent and now we have the Maxim and Antons of the world headed into fucking Needles?" Ok, now I am literally dying of thirst.

"Doc let's be clear, you're not in the program you are only *protected by agents* in the program."

"How's that working for me? Not real good, I would say."

"Take it easy, Doc, we're on it."

"See this scorpion," I say, holding up our amber bottle. "Remind you of anyone?"

"No, you're much better looking," Jack says.

The Korean waiter arrives. Jack and I immediately eye his pocket.

"Four beers, ice cold, extra-large plate of fries, and I threw in some roasted jalapeno peppers, on the house. The peppers are little *muy caliente*, but what isn't in this town?"

We smile at the Korean who decided that Needles would be a great place to start a new life for him and his Chihuahua. Minces has a pocket to live in and a diner he can call home. The place has everything a dog could want. Food, water, and industrial grade AC keeping his world chilled. I would suggest to Minces to be careful and not get too close to the garbage disposal—strange, stupid shit seems to be happening in Needles.

We crack our frosty Pabst, look outside the window, I light up a Menthol, and Jack bums one off me, still not buying his own smokes. Like our tall Korean waiter said, it's always hot in this fucking little town, and it feels even hotter when you never know what's around the corner. I hold up the small, acrylic amber bottle and blow a smoke ring around it.

I think this little bark scorpion just might agree.

CHAPTER 31

DECEIT

I am sitting in the booth with Jack. He looks at me and I look back. We are quiet. It's late and although the light has shifted, the sun is still on a slow burn making any form of shade offering any kind of respite only a foolish desert mirage. Self-preservation is here, on the inside, tricking me again to think that I can actually live in this desert.

The diner has a friendly, soft hum to it and we can hear the clink of pots and pans and dishes and flatware. The stainless steel Hobart Automatic Dishwasher is a busy backdrop to the happy rhythm and lively patter of the two-man Mexican crew. The Beach Boys' *God Only Knows* is playing through the small speakers tucked into the upper corners of the sea foam walls. I think of the Charles Manson and Dennis Wilson connection and the Topanga Canyon scene. I think of how the universe works and rocks our worlds and why Dennis is dead and that Charles Manson is only alive today because he's been placed in a maximum security facility for all of his X-inked life, protected by the law and cell and walls and guards, and who knows, maybe Dennis could have used that kind of armor, too. Why didn't Dennis get a protector just for a little while until he could see his life and feel that he had a chance at being safe, too? Just to have a chance. Jack's eloquent detailing of death from tiny predators who live under bark, and bricks and houses has sufficiently jarred me and I vow to be hyper vigilant about checking my socks, shoes, and pants and more importantly, looking over my shoulder, yes, of course, we couldn't agree more, that large boots are perhaps the most tantalizing welcome mat of all, and for

God's sake if I ever get a pair of those Tex Robin Kangaroos, I will be sure to shake them out each morning. Now, for the assholes currently living and dying in Los Angeles, those guys are another story. If only their sting could be dipped in liquid amber and hosted in used Tabasco bottles; that would be the trick. We would be smiling broadly in a cooling desert. Helena could rest easy. I could be a hero.

I would get the Russians enshrined in amber and maybe Ivan has a new keychain, so to speak. Russian Scorpions would be extinct, at least on my desert planet. For now.

I excuse myself to the men's room and do a big, fat motherfucking rail of *Peruvian pura* that kicks every synapse of dopamine into a new level of Diner Appreciation Week and it feels wonderfully sublime because nothing touches *pharma grade*. Suddenly my world, the present, in this diner, Minces, and with my agent, Jack, has a new meaning and I can see salvation and redemption along with blowing the shit out of Anton and Maxim and the rest of those Balkan bads. Fuck, I even have a desire to make Chet more money and marry Helena and adopt Rita. Walking out of the men's room and back into the clear cold of the Minces Diner makes me feel warm and I realize I have hit the mother lode—between my Pabst, my Menthols, my orange Nicorettes, my big ass rail of *pharma,* and the Korean dude's complimentary *muy caliente* roasted jalapenos, my metabolic rate is supercharged, hitting on all sixteen cylinders.

I love *Pet Sounds* and wish Dennis could be here. Fuck Charles Manson. He should be paroled just so he can die and meet The Beach Boy in the other world. After all, Dennis was the only Boy who even surfed.

Jack sips his beer throws some cash on the tab and I smoke and we both have agreed at where we go from here and how we plan on dealing with very bad men whom we need to take care of, and with the strong arm of the law, Jack is pretty sure he can make some of this go away. I will also call Ivan.

"Don't look out the window," Jack says flatly so I immediately look out the window.

"Holy fuck," I whisper, reaching for the last of his Pabst because I now have a serious case of dry mouth.

"Isn't that Rita's fucking car?" Jack observes.

"That's Rita's fucking car," I answer.

"Isn't she supposed to be at Chet's?" Jack says what we both already know.

"She is, but obviously she isn't…" I need another beer. Now would be good.

Rita's muscle car sits at the corner stoplight, and the low engine idle of Detroit muscle makes the chassis slightly shimmer, bouncing heat morays off the pricey, reflective metallic silver paint. The light turns green and Rita pulls away slowly, smartly observing all traffic laws.

I immediately call her number and it immediately goes to voicemail.

I call Chet and no answer.

I call Phil and no answer.

Jack and I stitch together various scenarios. We're pretty bright boys. He's government issue. I have a medical degree. So, we can come up with a few ideas that rationalize why the lovely Rita, carrier of large sums of illegal funds and driver of that silver Mustang, is nowhere near the Chet and CC Kingdom.

"She fucked you, brother." Jack smiles only because he likes to be right.

"I think the plural is 'us'."

"The Classic Rita Cluster, " Jack says.

"I don't like this, never mind where she is, where she *isn't* is not fucking good, period," I smartly say, and I think I can hear the roar of the mighty Colorado River rushing between my ears. Adrenaline synched with a big rail of the *pura* will do that to you.

"Maybe you should call CC and Roy," Jack suggests.

"Maybe you can get somebody on Rita," I suggest back.

"Maybe a Russian?" Jack says as quickly head over to the Speedster.

Wouldn't It Be Nice starts to play in my head as we head up to the see how Needles' finest is hanging without the expected money drop from our spray-tanned-twenty-year-old-fucking-with-nothing-but-attitude girl. The big question I ask myself is why Chet didn't call when the bag didn't come through. I shift the Speedster, Jack lights me a calming Menthol and we are burning up to the Kingdom. I call Helena and tell her there's a good shot that Jack and I will be delayed for dinner.

I'm betting somebody's in the pool—and it isn't my swimmer.

CHAPTER 32

POOL SWEEP

This is not going to be good.

I can feel a new version of bad moving fast across this desert. I roll down the window and soak up the wave of heat rushing into the Porsche and the blast of desert feels good at this moment when I can barely feel anything. Right now, the only substance holding me together is my Menthol. My hands are a little shaky from the afternoon events so I tighten my grip on the steering wheel and the Speedster is jetting us toward whatever version of hell happens to be partying on the poolside Mexican pavers tiling the Chet and CC Kingdom of bad deals gone worse.

The Speedster is sitting low and tight and sharp on the warm, and freshly paved asphalt, the bright yellow striping collides with my waning *pura* and adrenaline levels and I can appreciate the steady presence of Jack as he works his mobile trying to get somebody on Rita to track her Mustang that she believes will magically transport her somewhere out of here and to a new and wonderful world. I imagine Rita is hitting about a hundred miles an hour with a close eye on her rearview mirror while dialing up the heavy metal that will deafen and drown out her very bad decision. Rita's desert is expanding, but her world is shrinking as she throttles up and shifts into overdrive. Rita has pocketed the tidy sum of $200,000 that will only last a girl like her, about well, fuck it, she's never even going to find out what two hundred grand can do with a life. This dry desert will swallow Rita and her new bookkeeper, Phil. The Mojave is thirsty.

I shift the Speedster up the road and we pull up to the *Hacienda de Chet y CC.* Fuck, I thought that the last time I was out here would be the last time I would be out here, but our lovely Rita has pulled a flip turn and has me back into a lane.

We see Phil and Roy's monster trucks, CC's white El Dorado, and Chet's black Mercedes.

"Everyone's here," Jack says.

"Yeah, paydays are like that."

I look around. The sky is a brilliant, endless, vapor blue that wraps around our dot on the map. The desert seems to float out to the horizon line and far past the endless sand and dirt and maybe if we look hard enough we can see a Mustang kicking up dust on a straight line leading somebody out of Needles.

"Nice view," Jack says to no one. I think Jack could be really good at selling bad real estate.

"Cheap hacienda leftovers from Chet's construction scams." I check my Glock.

Jack looks at me.

"Let's try not to go there," he says.

"Let's just try to get outta here," I say, feeling a pit in my stomach.

"Doc, you're with a real, honest to goodness *Federale.* I do this for a living." Jack is being cavalier, and his attitude seems to make me a little shakier. I check the chamber, there's a full round, and the weighty heft and feel of the Glock calms my central nervous system. (How many times can you say that about a gun in your hand in the Mojave at a place owned by a guy like Chet and decorated by someone named CC.)

A pale yellow sliver with pinked stripes catches my eye and I watch the desert-banded gecko dart past me, happily finding solace under a rock. I admire his striped camouflage, perfect for hiding out and waiting for the high sun to set, prepping for his dinner in the dirt. I think the gecko picks up my vibe that this is a place we don't want to be with people we don't want to be with. He shape shifts becoming invisible.

Jack and I slip through the huge carved doublewide Mahogany front doors studded with a sea of chunky black iron clavos accented by even larger hand-forged sculpted bronze hardware (I think it works.) Chet must have hit the roof when CC handed him the bill. At first, the Hacienda appears quiet, as if the family had somehow vanished. But then we hear faint music floating out in the back patio. The music is caught on a wayward Pandora algorithm playing Barry Manilow, *Can't Smile Without You.* Jack starts humming the chorus and he is a stealthy agent who reminds me of Cary Grant in To Catch a Thief. I pay close attention to his sharp hand signals. I follow his every direction. Agent Jack Murphey is in charge. He is out of the Hacienda and staying close to the cover of the house. I'm right behind him. Manilow is louder now. Jack tries to move as smoothly as he can with his bad leg that got in the way of a big bullet that one day. He crouches and scans the patio. The crouch causes him to wince in pain from the metal shrapnel and he mouths "Fuck". I remind myself that next time we do any official bad guy stuff, to bring some physician-approved painkillers for my agent and his leg. Maybe I should toss him my vial, but rethink that gesture at this moment. He's already poaching enough of my smokes. I do a bump for him. My legs feel fine. The high-pitched Manilow vocals echo over the patio pavers, accompanying the routine dance of the round, automatic pool sweep that is busy doing laps. Shallow end to deep end and back again. Constantly cleaning. However, this pool carries a pinkish wash of blood so the efficient pool sweep has to work even harder to filter the chlorinated water.

"Doesn't blood void the warranty on those things?" Jack whispers, pointing to the blue and white disk skimming the surface, then submerging and following a pre-programmed cleaning route.

"New ones clean everything…I think." I reply, louder than a whisper.

Jack presses a finger to his lips, signaling me to be the fuck quiet. I see his eyes scan the second story balconies. I am watching a trained, certified agent in action. He is as quick as that banded little desert gecko and, like our lizard friend, seems to shape shift as I catch his form moving from left to right, gun drawn, silent as an Indian.

Jack is the first to spot Chet and CC at the far end of the pool, slouched in the patio lounge chairs, like they were hanging out, working on their hacienda tans. Then, Jack sees Roy, who is also catching particles of the desert sun, and it all starts to come full circle.

"Jack, see what I see? My rhetorical question is an empty attempt at backing Jack. I wave my pistol over toward the family picnic for emphasis.

"Chet," Jack shouts hoping to command attention.

"CC," I shout following Jack's expert federal action and hoping to do the very same.

Not a sound from any of the family, not a peep, so we move swiftly across the pavers toward the patio scene. Chet and CC are expelling slight gasping groans. Roy is completely dead.

"What the fuck?" I say. I light my 23rd Menthol and it tastes awesome.

"What the fuck? You're the fucking doctor, doctor. Looks like a motherfucking shooting gallery," Jack says, looking at me as if I am supposed to have the answers to this family gathering.

"Take a pulse or maybe just do something medical," Jack urges, and snags a smoke from me (#42), lights up and looks around, and then again looks at me thinking that I am carrying a handsome, leather medical bag. But I only have my blow, my handgun, my Menthols and a box of Orange Nicorettes with only three left in their hard-to-open plastic jackets.

Standing over Chet and CC and their quiet, tanned repose, Mariachi music playing over the poolside, this is a moment in the desert when Jack and I immediately notice something is wrong, not the obvious groaning and gasping and bloodied shot people laying in lounge chairs, but the obvious lack of one—Mr. Phil.

I doctor up and feel for a pulse. Chet and CC still have a heartbeat so it would appear the family lineage just may carry on.

"Chet and CC could use a hospital…if they want to live…think I should I ask them?" My gallows humor is lost on Jack who is into his trained triage agent-in-action mode.

"Calling it in." Jack punches in the number for an ambulance.

"I suggest they get here, uh, like now."

"On their way…check that shit over there." Jack points over at the white envelope on the table next to the now very handicapped and dead big brother, Roy.

I pick it up and show it to Jack. Jack reads it, methodically, in true federal form. His response, however, is less than standard issue.

"Mother of God, a genuine murder-suicide. At least according to this neatly worded proclamation from the eldest, Roy, a son who has penned a heartfelt tome that paints a sorry picture of son and father and mother—a family in drug-fueled distress. No way out except the only way out. Roy pulling the trigger on Mom and Dad, then doing himself." Jack smirks at the foolishly transparent attempt of a killing cover-up orchestrated by sibling Phil.

"Phil is a clever boy. He gets all of it, and they got all of this," I say to Jack.

"And apparently has a clever stepdaughter, who knows what she wants," Jack says.

"Rita and Phil?"

"Hey, think Woody and his Asian chick, Sun Lee…"

"Yi…Soon Yi," I correct Jack.

"Whatever…they seem happy," Jack says.

"Not so sure Mia feels the same way," I add.

"Hey in other countries, not a big deal," Jack says.

"This isn't other countries; this is Needles," I say.

"My point exactly." Jack holsters his gun.

I follow his lead and the Glock fits tightly into my wheat-colored, linen pants that always make me feel like I only own resort wear. I do a quick bump of my *mo mo* to help control my emotional state of being around a pool with the bodies and blood. The pool sweep continues its quest of cleaning every inch of this pool. I stand there for a moment, lost, mesmerized by the sweep's cadence and the motion. It is strangely hypnotic. Looking around, apparently, I'm not the only one in a trance. The pool water is now a faint pink and blue and white color.

"Jeezus, Phil and Rita…looks like they were outta here at the first drop of blood; what a freaking mess." Jack is a master of the understatement. It is quite a mess.

"And with this desert heat, the biology is not going to last long," I note, looking skyward, shielding my eyes from the Needles' sun like I have seen medical examiners do on popular television shows. In a few hours the bodies will swell and balloon like pool floats from the release of internal gases, which will not be a pleasant picture of pretty poolside Hacienda living.

"Phil must have been higher than shit," Jack says, inspecting the angry bullet entry points into Roy and Chet and CC.

"So Phil puts a few in mom and dad, then uses the gun on Roy, that .38 right there in his hand, and the note and enough substances ingested to warrant an argument gone horribly wrong."

"Or according to Phil, horribly right," I say, proud of my medical examiner tone and prescient observation.

"I didn't know Rita had the balls, so to speak."

"What did I tell you?" Jack points to Roy's hefty body that appears even bigger. The red paint of blood in the bullet hole is starting to dry. Everything does out here.

"You're lucky that chick never pulled this on your ass," Jack says.

And I can see that he is right. I am lucky.

"I never did like her fascination with that Puukko," Jack says eyeing the sun-dried bowl of guacamole now turning brown, and flecked with either nasty jalapenos or somebody's DNA. Circling turkey vultures appear in the sky hooked by the unmistakable *olor apestoso* of rotting bodies. The squadron has reported that a carcass or two has been spotted. The diner is open.

Jack and I quickly move through the crime scene and agree that we should go through Chet's office looking for the family ledger of accounts receivables. In short order we are rewarded with a cache over-looked by the high and hasty Phil and Rita.

"Eureka." I exclaim softly stunned by my find.

"You honestly didn't actually say that...Lemme see that shit." Jack says.

Chet was a wise little fucker who was also greedy and also didn't trust his sons. Smart Chet. We find a hefty stash of cocaine, pharma-ceutical opiates, and enough cash to shower the local *policia* with more than a few reasons to let this scene slide, and wrap up the Chet family with a tragic story of loss. Dear Phil was nowhere in the vicinity. Phil had left his truck at the Hacienda and was gone. And I have to hand it to Phil, he saw a future and how to pull it together, family be damned. I don't think he really liked them anyway. People asked about him, and several inquiries were made at his former place of employ, the Needles PD, but his absence was barely noticed or noted. It seems that Phil had covered his tracks with the oldest play in the book—money, lots of money. And true to form his fellow officers had fallen right in line and grabbed that payday of their very own. Packages of Peru and cash don't fall out of the sky on just any squad, so when Phil's finest were offered a substantial score, well, like I said, there were lots of fans of the big, fat envelope. And apparently Rita's main squeeze knew all of them. Phil is a shrewd desert killer. He knows his boys in blue can get very quiet and leave Phil alive and alone, hidden under a rock in the desert waiting to eat. A lot of the brethren went out and purchased big boats.

Jack and I agree to get the hell out of here, and leave this poolside scene to Needles questionable detectives who can pop this piñata and fund a fiesta of their very own. Jack surveys the scene, puts the envelope back into its rightful place next to the very big and very dead Roy. I check on Chet and CC. They still have a pulse and should make it if the ambulance can get here in the next five minutes. I angle the umbrella to provide Chet and CC shade, my purely professional instincts kick-ing in to assist the helpless or infirmed. Jack will follow up and give the Needles squad a call, and they'll enjoy picking over the bodies and pool and do a dance on the very pavers that CC was so happy to get when she and Chet made the Kingdom their own slice of the hacienda life. But today, well, today there would be no chips and guacamole and Mariachi and cold beers chasing big rails of *pura fina*, no, not today. And now perhaps not ever. *Ranchero Living* in the Kingdom is gone.

Phil and Rita are gunning out of wherever they are, and into a life with $200,000 large that we would very much like. This money is ours. Jack seems to be picking up a bad habit and starting to smoke as much as me. And then there's the Maxim and Anton deal. *Madre de Dios.* This fucking town is more trouble than it's worth. Jack makes a call to his crew. We shift down the road and into the last of the late afternoon sky that is pink and blue and red and perfect for my hungry desert-banded gecko waiting patiently for a flightless and nocturnal cricket. Somebody has to eat.

CHAPTER 33

LIGHT AIRCRAFT

Right now Jack is dialed into calling his boys. He is busy alerting agents close to him, his "need-to-knows" who will understand that a call from Jack on nasty deals in the desert, dead bodies, and the shimmer of a Shelby wheeled by our swimmer, Rita, is a priority.

He will call agents who know that Jack is a trusted source who has access to discretionary monies that some Federal agents seem to appreciate. Agents who are thinking of their future pensions, and, of course, the increasing cost of tuition at chosen private schools.

"Guess what, *mi amigo,* our lovebirds are up in Bullhead City, right on the big water," Jack announces, snapping his phone shut.

"And in the middle of the nearest casino action," I say.

"Nothing like a good game of craps when you're on the run," Jack says.

"I took Phil as more of a Blackjack kinda guy," I respond, my sarcasm dripping.

"Jesus, you'd think they'd be halfway to Vegas." Jack looks out the window, and lights another one of my Menthols. "Seriously? Can you ever buy your own smokes?"

"Trying to quit," Jack says blowing nicotine-rich smoke my way.

"You overestimate Phil, with him it can be anywhere you find a boat and a beer," I say getting to the matter at hand of Phil trying to walk with our dough.

"$200 hundred thou gets you a lot of action in that part of town," Jack says.

"Put a casino on the water, serve up complimentary cocktails, throw in the free buffet and that July Arizona sun—no telling how high those two can get," I say.

Jack picks up his mobile. His agents are good. "Spotted her car at a valet lot at the Riverbed Casino." Jack turns up the Speedster's AC. "Jesus, Doc, can you spend a little coin for an upgrade on your climate control?"

"Maybe you should invest in linen, Jack," I suggest. "It breathes."

We're on Arizona 95, a straight shot to the land of milk and honey known as the Laughlin Bullhead City area, which passes for big city adventure and fun for the lost and nomadic desert tribes. I call Helena to check in and make sure she's good. Jack is back on the phone, and we are tracking that $200,000 before Phil and Rita have a chance to blow it all.

I call Helena and quickly bring her up to speed on the recent Hacienda find, and the cash-rich, black, leather bag, lost. It's a nice touch, just like a calling the wife, telling her I have a few reports to finish up and I'll be home late. Yeah, just like that except for my nervous system and the Speedster are not in synch and although I'm pretty used to blood and the operating room, I tell her that from now on, no more chips and guacamole. Not ever. Helena tells me she is ready to join us, but this time, seriously, she wants a fucking gun, no more power tools.

"Honey, not the right time, I gotta head up to Bullhead city with Jack, talk to you later. Be brave…and next week we'll go to the shooting range, promise."

Jack interrupts my call. "I've got two lined up and checking out the Riverbed."

"Who are they?" I ask

"No names. To you, they're just The Twins. Trust me on this." Jack says.

"Ok…and their split?" I ask more interested now with Jack's unnamed agents.

"$50,000 for both of them and they walk, no harm, no foul."

"Fucking expensive," I remark, trying to sound surprised and cheated, wanting to bait him on disclosing more on his secret agents of intrigue, 'The Twins.'

"They're Federal, so they know how to play nice. Leaves you and me with $150,000 for the day," Jack says smugly. "I'll take that in a heartbeat." He grabs another of my Menthols and smiles. See, I know he likes me.

"Yeah and then maybe you can start buying your own nicotine…I had close to $300,000 in Rita's leather bag, I kept $100,000 for myself, and our swimmer didn't know about the other half."

"The other half?" Jack seems surprised at my entrepreneurial skills.

"I cut a deal with Roy, and he dropped off a small stipend to me for his end of scrips that we had worked out on the side, netting me another $50,000 in small bills."

Jack turns to me and then looks out the window as the flat burns by. "And I guess brother Roy won't be talking."

The plan is simple, really. We want the money. Once we get the cash, Phil and Rita are just like any star-crossed lovers who can live somewhere out there, and we're pretty sure it won't be anywhere near Needles. I don't like them dead. There's been a little too much carnage on the flat pan of desert sand and it's not even close of business day. So Jack and I agree that we let them fucking burn at the hands of our hired guns, keep the dough, wash off the dirty side of getting into bed with chicks who are young, dangerous, and ride shotgun with ex-cops who think that fucking their stepdaughter is part of the American dream. We have eager agents on our side of the law.

Phil and Rita will soon reside as a footnote to the desert scrub and deep canyons that are photographed and chronicled in digital scrapbooks. Phil and Rita are a part of the landscape that endlessly marches by in long and measured miles that stretch to a horizon point in the desert, converging into a single dimension of flat. But you wouldn't know about Phil and Rita when you travel along the blacktop on your way from one place to another place. You would never even notice their love story dried into the sediment of sand, gravel, and decaying barrel cactus.

Young love scribed into a tale of predator and prey. You know, the one with dead parents, big money, drugs, and equal parts and particles of desert creatures killing to eat. I wonder how long Phil and Rita had their special thing going. Why didn't I see it? Helena didn't even catch it. I mean, we know Rita could be a major problem, she and that razor sharp Puukko. Rita sold me well, and I bought it all. She worked her camouflage and it worked me. Very well, young Rita, believe me, you are going to hurt, but I won't be there to tell you how. Just keep that Detroit engine running and an eye on that rearview mirror. Heavy metal is going to get heavier. Phil and Rita will be ghosts to us.

The two runways sit on a strip of dirt a little less than five miles from downtown Needles and it's been this way since the early 1940's when the desert was home to an Army airfield. You fly in and you fly out. You can keep your private, single engine airplane here, but mostly the airport is home to what the aviation folks call "transient aircraft." You would start your descent and look down on the desert knowing that these two flat, straight, and parallel strips are here, waiting in the heat for you and your business. You land, taxi toward the few planes near the hangar, lock down your craft, and go on your merry way. The Needles Airport is that kind of a place where lots of parcels and packages are loaded and unloaded and nobody is paid to pay attention. You might want to smile and wave and make small talk about thermals and the heat, and ask about getting an ice-cold soda as you and your crew conduct business as usual. Even though things can get a little weird in the air around here.

Like the time a single passenger, Titan Tornado took off from here, and then sensing engine trouble, the pilot expertly landed on Highway 40, tried to take off again using the freeway as his airstrip, but unfortunately was less than expert when it mattered most and taxied straight into an oncoming Ford Fusion carrying a car salesman and a young married couple out on a test drive. In an odd twist of desert irony, the 68-year old pilot was killed in his plane on the freeway. The Ford customers survived, and according to locals, were ceremoniously given keys to the car, free of charge, by the dealership. This is exactly the kind of thing that will happen to you in this heat. Killed in a Tornado on the freeway in the desert town of Needles.

But if you are a courier for the Cartel, a cowboy bringing in a few bales of the *mota*, or, say, a Russian heavy by the name of Anton working for the even heavier Russian, Maxim Garikov, this is your kind of airport. I was paying very close attention to Jack's every word when he told me that his people said Maxim would be flying into the desert, and the Needles Airport is now classified as ground zero for heavies in a light aircraft.

We pulled into the Riverbed. This is the flagship hotel out here, the neon siren in the sand, welcoming all to this place of air conditioned microclimates and ice cold beverages, power boating, and endless buffet, and sundries, booze, cheap rooms, and enough stupid to make your head hurt as much as your wallet. The palm trees stand still. The big moon hangs over the big Colorado. The clear and clean night sky is eclipsed by the brilliance of casinos and hotels and people. The air is dry. Buzzed couples wearing new and cheap desert wear find their way to the next table, or car or room or cocktail. I would like a very, very cold beer and a brace of arctic Stoli. I would like to be a buzzed couple. Jack looks at his phone. Our helpful agents are calling. He looks at me and we sit in the Speedster looking out on the water. Jack smiles and tells me that we are winners.

I put the top down on the Speedster, lean back, and look up at the night and see a small aircraft with blinking running lights headed into the desert and it is low on the horizon. The descent is in the distance.

Jack tugs on my shoulder and we leave to collect our winnings.

Maybe it's time to buy a plane.

Maybe it's time to learn how to fly.

CHAPTER 34

LA VIDA LOCA

We're sitting in the coupe with the top down, parked at the far end of the Riverbed Hotel and Casino, smoking my Menthols, waiting to meet up with Jack's Twins. I do a short bump that works nicely with the evening skylight, and Jack heads over to the open-air bar and purchases two tall vodka tonics, courteously making mine a double. I almost feel I could be on holiday here, too. Jack is a good date. I like him and how his connections are helping out. Paid, of course, but still, assisting nonetheless. He says they are very good and I believe that they are, having seen how quickly they tracked our scofflaws, so they are most certainly worth every penny.

My personal money management netted me $100,000 after kicking $25,000 to Rita and the Chet family was ready to divvy up the $175,000 that will account for their operational assistance in getting those scrips distributed and collected by persons like the lovely Rita. That bag of cash presently residing with our lovebirds represents some hard earned cash—bottom line revenue that goes straight to my profit and lost statements that help subsidize my life in the sun. Living on the run is pricey. I'm not playing shuffleboard and waiting for happy hour with the complimentary *pu-pu* platter, fuck no. Speaking of overhead, I'm now strapped with the added expense of dipping into the bag and counting out $50,000 to Jack's Twins just to close the deal on our lovebirds.

Jack sips his drink and crunches on his ice cubes, and that starts to bug the shit out me. I also remind him that he needs to start buying his own smokes. Thankfully, he is not one for my *pura*. I slip in a CD with *Los Hermanos* playing a cover of Stevie Wonder's *Superstition*, and the *pharma* kicks in as I lean back and look up, listening to the *Hermanos* mix with the distant beat of the casino's soundtrack. There's not much I can say about holding a black, leather bag with $200,000 stacked in it. Weighty? Yes, there's a feel to it, and the feeling is good. Maybe it's more like a magnetic pull letting me know that for today, I've got a future. A large count of cash in one place at one time is a reassuring thing that lets me breathe, and a good way to end the day in this desert.

The Needles force will cover up any of the bad that went down in the Kingdom, and Phil and Rita will think they are clean. Again, they will be wrong. Phil and Rita will be left slugging it out minus their pools, their cars, their endless supply of Peru, bags of weed, and the opiates that fuel their fight to balance lives on the edge, while the Mighty Colorado River cuts deep through a flat piece of desert. Big water that can lose people to currents and cold, to the rapids and pools of snowmelt that has found its way down, down, down, straight through Needles. Phil and Rita are easy prey for the pit vipers that awaken when the bright sun has decided this piece of sky should be black. This desert lives and breathes for its killers.

Personally, if I were the Phil and Rita love fest, I would have pushed that Mustang harder and looked for somewhere way outside of this expanse of the Mojave. I would not pull over and agree that for tonight we'll just lay low at a watering hole and roll the dice. It would be my recommendation to keep moving until you hit a place on the map where you can manufacture another life. But she's twenty and he's thirty-three, and they foolishly call it a day and buy into the mirage and check into the Riverbed, falling for the attraction of roadside goodies that are as magnetic as the pull from that black leather bag.

The rush of this polished hotel and casino, the fawning and courteous attendants and valet service is candy for a young girl with a sweet tooth. She thrives on the attention. I am quite sure Rita played Phil on this one. He is a big man who is now stung by that bark scorpion we looked at in the diner, the one floating in a yellow amber liquid, the one lost in limbo. Phil has no chance with Rita, and I am happy for that. She is waiting under a rock.

Riding in a metallic silver 650hp Shelby Mustang, strapped with cash, vials of *cocaina,* a few hard lemonades, and a split of Ecstasy with the promise of endless money falling out of a bag and into your lap can make you feel invincible, until you aren't. Like I said, this is a fucking desert, so be prepared to tough it out and drive on past your drug of choice, even when it's wrapped in neon and palm trees and mojitos. Keep moving, lovers, just keep moving.

The swimsuit and thong crowd is pressing flesh and moving with the rhythm of the deep base house music. Drunken and buzzed cheers go up each time this pool scene is splashed on the jumbo flat screens showing everyone that yes indeed, you are having a fucking good time. Seriously, you are, just keep drinking. The young, shirtless DJ is spinning a mix of techno and this crowd is his. "C'mon y'all…let me know if you bitches are having a badass time!"

The Riverbed's management team did an excellent job of neatly arranging the poolside cabanas to offer privacy and a sense of privilege to their guests. Each cabana is carefully lined up along the sides of the pool, and tented in a white twill cotton, with an ingenious zippered mesh on all four sides of the tented cabana. You can see out to the pool, but the pool people can't see in. Sexy and deliciously private with large lounge chairs cushioned in a deep blue canvas, accented by a small bank of thick white towels proudly monogrammed with the large RC flourish. This private perch offers our two outlaws a secreted sense of isolation while they drink and watch the careless and carefree vacationing young things swim up to the bar and drink, dance, and order their next shot of *la vida loca* while trying to remember where the fuck they put their room key. Our sunbaked revelers are oblivious to the black, leather bag holding more money than they will ever know. It is sitting right here at poolside, stashed underneath Phil's lounge chair.

A lounge chair that looks like the one that held a father and mother's last breath at another poolside fiesta in another Kingdom in another part of this desert.

Jack told me a little about these handpicked boys. He said these are the kind of guys who make black-ops look straight-up vanilla. He said these are the real deal guys. Guys who can swallow cyanide and sleep on rusty nails. I think he was a little over the top with that description, but it did scare the hell out of me. He had me believing theses guys were responsible for the overthrow of Papa Doc and the resurgence of the wild-eyed religious Santeria cult that so many of the young people find adorable, at least in Haiti. These guys could make the desert feel cool.

Whatever Jack was selling I was buying. I wanted that bag and I wanted Phil and Rita to feel a hotter Needles piercing them to the depths of their soul. Which means hitting them right in their black, leather bag. Jack's agent's come out of nowhere, and lean into the open Speedster. Jack's right, they are ninja twins and they look fresh out of Quantico, dressed in smart, desert resort wear Khakis, fitted, short-sleeve, checkered Hilfiger shirts and trendy, snow white Adidas court shoes—the classic Rod Laver ones. It's an All-American look that frames their identically tan skin. Their tight muscle grouping, and thickly built necks could bench press my weight. The boys are so classically clean cut and so pin-neat that at first blush you might even think Fire Island gay on holiday, but these agents roll with an agenda of their own. Jack's identicals don't fuck with messy. These boys are masters of the take down. They can swiftly neutralize bad people who are much more dangerous than the higher-than-shit Phil and Rita who make the mistake of thinking that this is their world. Jack's colleagues are spot on, stone cold experts—agents who are as high and tight as Jack's cropped crew cut. Our meet and greet is short and to the point. Jack's All American Agents In Action are ready to go, and with their money worked out, they say hello, shake hands, say goodbye and they're vapor.

"Dudes were lacrosse players at Duke. I personally recruited them straight out of the academy. Found out one of them likes the ponies, the other one has a passion for Asian food…Thai hookers, and they both juice with the HGH and anabolic shit. Between injecting DHEA, synthetic testosterone and their shrinking nuts, these boys are the fucking real deal and get shit done. For a price, of course."

"Of course…Jesus…" I eloquently stammer, not sure what to think.

"I know…clean cut Midwestern types. Some things aren't what they seem, but you would know that better than anyone, right Doc?" Jack swirls his plastic cup.

It didn't take long for The Twins to find our lad and lass downing quart-sized Margaritas near the main pool of the popular and packed Riverbed Hotel and Casino, the perfect watering hole for *cocaina* killers who are crazy for each other and are trying to blend in with the tanned and oiled ones. The first indication of what a fucking mess Phil and Rita have made with their terrible high-risk-to-reward ratio decisions, is the cool way Jack's All-American Action Agents discreetly move through the poolside crowd. The pulsing, let's-get-higher-than shit pool scene is a marvelous distraction to hunting down targets. Nobody's paying attention to anything, except their smart phones, drink orders, and hooking up at the after-party, party. Our identical agents slip into silent mode, moving quietly along the perimeter of the cabanas and pool. They've zeroed in on the Phil and Rita Cabana. Coming in from behind, gently unzipping the back of the mesh tenting, The Twins announce, in unison, a sly, cheery, and disquieting, "Cabana service?" The introduction to their covert entry says, that as of right now, Phil and Rita are very fucked.

The Twins stun Phil and Rita. One Federal Agent would be a scene, but identical twin agents swiftly sliding into your private cabana can kill you. The first jet black 9mm pistol with a silencer is placed right the fuck to Phil's head. It is explained in detail what's going on so our couple can wrap their brains around this bag-of-money-conundrum that seems to be going around.

"Not an inch, motherfucker," Jack #1 rasps into Phil's ear.

"You either, Mrs. Mother Fucker," adds Jack #2, pressing his 9mm barrel into her forehead.

Phil and Rita are statues. Neither moves a muscle. The Twin Action Agents are so tight and hard that the love birds can sense that this is whole new level of shit-storm.

"That bag right there, dibs," says Jack #1.

"Fuck, you always get the money," Jack #2 pretends to whine. He is good.

"That's cuz I'm prettier…he's the smart one," Jack #1 cracks, playing along.

Jack #1 presses his metal barrel harder into Phil's temple just because he can, and Phil winces, which Jack #1 likes a lot. Wincing means he has Phil's attention.

"I ordered you two honeymooners another round of Maggies…girl said she'd be right over," Jack #2 says, while grabbing the leather bag containing the future of a life almost lived.

"Which means, *mis amigos*, we have to *vamanos*, but I'm sure you understand…" Jack #1 says while he scans the buzzed pool scene through the mesh cabana opening.

"Cuz, if you don't we'd have to fucking kill you, which I am most certain you *comprende…comprende*?" Jack #2 speaks even worse Spanish.

"*Sayanora*, asshole," Jack #1 says, downing Phil's Margarita and then adds, "Fuck, dude, $14 bucks for this watered down piece of Mexico?"

"I bet the guacamole sucks, too," Jack #2 says flatly.

"*Lo siento*," Jack #1 makes a frown on his face. "And hey kids, don't steal the towels."

Jack's All-American Ninja Twins disappear into the shadows while the Riverbed Hotel and Casino pool scene rages. Phil and Rita sit on their deeply cushioned lounge chairs staring at each other. The curvy pool server in a RC-branded bikini and sarong dips in and has to shout over the frenzied techno house music the DJ has dialed up to new level of happy.

"Two extra large Margaritas, rocks, both with salt. Cash, charge or room?"

"Room," Phil says tightly, gripping the edge of his lounge chair.

Rita looks at the server and asks, "Are you hiring?"

"Four extra shots, tequila, next time around," Phil says, staring blankly.

"Fuck you, Phil," Rita says quietly.

"Fuck yourself." Phil swallows his Margarita and digs out an ice cube and throws it hard against the very nice canvas twill cabana tenting. Phil does not like being lost in a tent in the desert without a bag of cash or a Plan B.

The Jack #1 and #2 pull up alongside the Speedster and interrupt our moment in the night watching the big water and listening to *Los Hermanos*. They toss the black, leather bag onto Jack's lap.

"Minus the fifty large," says Jack #1.

"They glad to see you?" My Jack jokes.

"Always...what's not to like? Jack #2.

"We're sweethearts." Jack #1.

"Don't bet it all in one place...or spend it at the Asian buffet," Jack chides.

Lose a black leather bag with $200,000 and the desert night can get a little heated. Lose it at the Riverbed Hotel and Casino to federal agents pushing the hard metal of a 9mm pistol into your head and this big desert shrinks to just a room in the sand that waits for the bright, morning sun to rise and begin baking every move you think you want to make.

I put the top up, turn on the air conditioning, and we leave the casino with money in our pocket, and thieves and killers lost in a poolside cabana waiting for the sun to rise. The Speedster growls low on the road back to the land of Needles. Jack has his seat pushed all the way back, his eyes are closed, and he is clutching our bag of goodies. I roll down my window to feel the hot air rising up from the asphalt, waving off the day's heat and wonder how much Rita can get for that sweet, metallic silver Mustang. *Conducir de forma segura asesino de poca.*

CHAPTER 35

HEAT WAVE

How long has it been now with the Federal boys and my current state of living in the lovely Needles zip code? The DEA had me and then I had them, and then the Russians had me and then, well, you can start to see where all of this is going. And I would understand completely if you leaned over and lowered your voice, tilted your glasses down on the bridge of your nose, and paternally reprimanded me with a "Doc, you're a big boy. You know you had this coming." And, of course, you would be right and I would have to suffer the failures for my practice and life and then look back at you and suggest that perhaps that the Mad Russians coming after my ass is not what I had expected. Yeah, yeah, I got Jack, but now I'm contending with my life in the desert finding its way into the big meaty paws of the Los Angeles Slavs who are descending into my part of the flatness to show me exactly how they deal with dead family people. Their style of a fuck-you is definitely more intimidating than anything the Chet and CC family hour could toss out with their hacienda style of revenge and retribution. Hell, the Chet Show can't compare to the heavy skill set of these heat-seeking Russians. I'm well aware of how these guys work. I operated on a few of them, I gave them new faces, and names and identities so they could live out the American dream and get on with their lives, and what? I lose one on the table, and the next thing you know, I'm suddenly the bad guy. Jesus, it never ends. Now I have Maxim, Anton, and Chekov, or whomever the fuck is flying in with the Gorikav, party bent on making my life vanish.

Maybe I can pay them off? That would be sweet. Jack doesn't think so. They don't need the money. Jack is pretty sure these guys want to make me hurt. The Russians want the feds to feel my pain. You know, another case of "I'll hit you so hard, I'll kill your whole family, Comrade."

Understandably, this sort of threat should have an immediate impact on my daily habits and admittedly I need to dial into my vices and maintain a highly improved state of clarity. Sure, that *mo-mo* followed me from Hollywood, but like I say, living out here in the dirt and watching heat morays bounce off your forehead isn't for the weak. Ask anyone in Needles and they'll tell you that to survive the grind it's strongly suggested that you go ahead and fortify yourself with whatever keeps you sane. I'll take the bet that if you do a stretch out here you will surely start scratching around for a way to fill in those blanks. Mine happens to be available in a handy dropper and that dropper happens to be pharmaceutical. And those droppers happen to be a shared contraband with the very lovely Helena who is a good soldier and can charmingly rationalize our mid-morning tumbler with a side of toast and eggs, quickly followed by a dose of the *pharma* just to smooth out the edges as we look out across the flat, trying to measure the heat.

I've discovered that Helena can expertly monitor our bad habits so we can manage the hours of living here on the red planet, which, by the way, is just about as perfect a place to bury stainless steel lockboxes of cash—metal strongholds that stand ready should events require immediate access to bricks of currency. Having money deep in the ground makes me feel that this part of my world is under control. I can hear that cash breathing and somehow I feel smarter than the rest of the desert for having dug deep into it and placed a ready reserve of cash in there, waiting. You could not argue otherwise.

Between meetings and phone calls with the feds and the constant paranoia that comes with the rest of just about everything, well, you can see why my days have a stress fracture running through them. In a way, this desert, on occasion, might pass for awesome if you're a surgeon on hiatus with a steady and legal inventory of the *pharma*. The dry and hot expanse of this place is big enough to carry a river and small enough to see your predators. The Airstream is tucked into the dirt and where, as was my original intent, Helena and I would mind our own business and safely hang out here, cooled and fueled. But yes, things got a little out of hand with our extracurricular activities and questionable companions, and really, looking back, maybe I should have just taken a pottery class and joined the local artisans, perhaps even trying my hand at working with silver. I've always liked the Southwest and the native handiwork. It's amazing what the people out here can do with a little free time on their hands. The idea of a small curio shop out here crosses my mind and then vanishes with the incoming traffic from the hit of the endorphin-rich dropper followed by my Mentholated nicotine. I'm a surgeon from Hollywood, now at home in Needles. Here we sit on the border of California and Arizona and on the big water of the Mighty Colorado. It was reported in yesterday's paper that a new residential development of affordable, single-family town homes is nearing completion, and that the local citizenry might want to be on the watch for pit vipers and scorpions that enjoy the comforts of the newly paved suburban cul-de-sac. The water, the walls, and the cool foundation of a home are a tantalizing offering to these nocturnal ones. The story went on to say that folks should remind children to look twice before picking up rocks and toys.

Every neighborhood has a story of a frantic trip to the emergency room, demonstrating that once again, out here, you can never be too careful in your backyard or at school. And, for heaven's sake, always, always check your boots, and of course, your local airport.

REDEMPTION

Jack uses the blunt end of his toothbrush to stab through the tight, clear wrapping that hygienically seals our set of four complimentary plastic cups, and pours two. Not exactly my iced Stoli, but the generic, off-brand vodka miniatures have enough bite to settle me into a moment. I light a Menthol, Jack adds Orange Fanta to his beverage.

"You know I didn't want him dead," I say.

"Nobody did, and we're all sorry as hell, but remember Doc, the man knew enough to fuck with you, big time," Jack replies, sitting down in the large, swivel armchair and propping his stocking feet on the glass coffee table. Jack had charmed the hotel receptionist for an upgrade to the executive suite that offered us a small sitting room, fully stocked mini bar, and a balcony view of the hotel parking lot, plus complimentary breakfast bar buffet where you can make your own waffles. It's the little things that make it all feel like home.

"Fucking Chet," I said, swallowing my vodka hard, ready for another.

"Casey was playing both sides with his new-found Russian friends who paid him big dough for your bio…" Jack leans back into the deeply cushioned chair, swiveling back and forth as he continues to school me on how this was shaking out. "You were sold to the Russians, Casey had a 401K plan and you were part of it." Jack waves his empty plastic cup seeking an immediate refill.

"I figured the Phil and Roy boys would shake him down, but who the fuck knew they'd kill the poor bastard?" I say, tossing Jack a mini.

"What'd you expect? C'mon you had to know it was gonna go south, with those guys… and large bills on the line? They're willing to go the extra mile to protect the franchise…Casey did his job, dug around, got the 411 on you and figured there was easy money on the table…he didn't want to be a fucking cop forever."

"Yeah, well now the dearly departed Casey is a detective—eternally. Didn't he have some federal help in his discovery?" I ask.

"We think so. We're pretty sure someone had to point out a few things. He was smart but you, Doc, are pretty well hidden inside the fed system."

"So, Casey died *por nada.* He had already committed yours truly to Maxim?"

"The proverbial cat was out of the bag," Jack says tossing me a bag of BBQ chips, a nice touch.

"And I've still got shit to deal with it after all these years, fuck Jack, can a brother catch a break here?"

"Doc, you were the one writing scrips and getting into bed with the Chet crew. Nobody put a gun to your head," Jack says, stirring the ice in his cup.

"At least not yet," I say, finishing the last of my plastic vodka. I walk over to the mini bar and sadly, only two soldiers remain standing. Unless we move to beer or the house liquor passing as bourbon, we'll be out of booze in twenty minutes.

"Pick your poison. He was either gonna get the Russians to pay his tab or work a deal with the Chet posse and take a cut," Jack says.

"Casey gave me up, and still paid."

"It's a fucked up world, Doc." Jack crunches his ice and swivels around looking out at the balcony view parking lot vista.

The desert stretches out in front of Jack's fine executive suite upgrade. Jack continues to school me on the events as he sees it. "Casey had already given you up to the Russians so I think Phil and Roy, once they started in on the job, well, those boys just wanted him off the planet, period." Jack says.

"This desert looks more dangerous than the polish of the Hills… but those A-Listers can stick that knife in you and still talk a three picture deal—cleaner than Phil and Roy—just as deadly. Out here bodies might get wedged into rocks or bleed out, poolside, but at least you know where you stand…Phil better have his boys on the force paid up and cashed out…" I add, trying to sound like I have a reasonable handle on rogue cop protocol.

"Phil's greased more than a few fellow brothers in blue to keep everyone spinning on other cases and away from the obvious." Jack

"Otherwise his fall is going to hurt. And with his swimmer along for the ride, nobody will get out of that without some serious head trauma." I say, checking my Patek and seeing that the day is getting behind us.

"Do we care?" Jack says, happy to be opening the black, leather bag. "They got played and now the two of them will have to figure out their next bad deal."

"You know I worked on Maxim two years ago," I say, bringing Jack back to the Russians.

"Tell me something new," Jack is bored.

"He was part of that arms and heroin play."

"You gave him a new, um, *him*, and so sure, Maxim was good for our purposes, the federal kind, he opened his book for us."

"Glad to be of service…I think."

"And it saved his ass from brutal gang retribution that would have hurt a lot more than losing his wife. So there you go, Doc Martinez for the win."

"Not so fast, now I get his ass coming after me, terrific." I shake my plastic cup seeking fumes. I'm still thirsty. I walk into the bathroom to get a cold facecloth and put it on the back of my neck, turn up the air conditioning and lay down on the executive suite sofa. Jack is my analyst.

"Two short years ago, you were living large and working with me and the program. You had a life that could have gone a few places, but instead—"

"Jack, for chrissakes, let's not revisit my fucked up misadventures," I bite back. I'm ready for food. Steak would be good.

The gold and hot sun is heading into evening and the desert light throws gray shadows across the parking lot and through the balcony window. I like this light. I like this time of day. The room is quieted with the background of the television letting us know that the planet is still spinning, and we're just two guys with a big leather bag of big cash, enjoying a drink or three and reminiscing about unfortunate detectives who are dead and miscreant family members killed poolside by their worse and hardened relatives, and did I mention we still have the rest of the Needles players arriving by private aircraft and yeah, we're pretty sure these guys have big guns that hurt a lot.

Like a shaman bearing peyote, I think I can see the future and if I focus on the shapes shift and move through my life out here with the ghosts of Casey, Chet, CC, Phil, Roy, and Rita, I see the desert clinging to me and I hope that someday the big water of the Mighty Colorado washes away the dry dirt of my life in July in Needles.

Jack and I are sheltered from the evening radiation. I tell Jack I see the Russians wandering across the desert coming into my world. I tell Jack I have a vision. Jack is dialed into my life. He assures me that this is not going to happen on his watch and he is sitting next to me looking out maybe trying to have my vision, too. We watch the desert from his executive suite looking for a new breed of bad scrambling hard across the landscape waiting for night. The first star in the evening appears faintly and will only get brighter once the sun finds its way south and all the other galaxies show up. You can hear the dry heat releasing from the flat, cooling earth. I open up the hotel room's complimentary and colorful Visitor's Travel Guide Book extolling the wonders of Needles and how it sits—remarkably!—on the border of two states. Jack is ordering room service while I continue to look for salvation—wherever I can find it.

CHAPTER 37

SHAMAN

"**I** like the pool at night," I say, leaning on the balcony rail and surveying the liquid scene below.

Jack points to his watch. "Two hours till dark. Personally, I like a parking lot." Jack deadpans.

"Reminds me of when I was a boy. Pools were hypnotic, the way the lights moved with the water. Just wasn't the same during the day."

"It's the fucking desert, Doc, and we're at the top floor of $165 a night motel trying to sell itself as a hotel. Talk about a fucking mirage." Jack can get like this, even with his suite upgrade. The lights, the hushed and mixed voices, and cheerful clink of cocktail glasses float up from the lounge below offering a quiet track to this scene. I'm ready for another, but I check myself, which surprises the fuck out of me. Jack sees a paved and lined parking lot. I see a pool reflecting back. Maybe that's what makes it work with us.

The knock on the door announces Jacinta, our efficient front desk clerk who also doubles for some version of room service. She politely smiles at Jack's Spanish, "*Uno momento por favor,*" as she enters with her tray. I think Jacinta catches a whiff of government on Jack—immigration? The girl is smart enough to play to his awkward and clumsy charm that he mistakenly believes is a wonderfully personal way to ingratiate himself with everyone in the hospitality industry. Jack discreetly palms Jacinta a $20, complements her bright smile and, of course, with money heading south to her family in Jalisco, Jacinta let's

Jack play it out. She's twenty, streetwise, and has ambitions on advancing to a shift supervisor.

I can see Jacinta takes pride in her earnest hotel employment. Her beige, cotton pants are smartly pressed, her dark hair is pulled back into smooth, tight bun, and Jacinta's starched, white cotton short sleeve shirt carries her name and title embossed on a square matt bronze badge pinned just above her large, round, and young left bosom. Jacinta fusses with the plates on the tray, tidies the flatware, and talks about how beautiful the view from the room is and how you can see the small range of cragged, jagged, and pointed rock formations that give Needles its name. Jack, Jacinta, and I all nod that yes, this stretch of endless dry, and flat dirt is *muy bonita y calor.* Jacinta dutifully exits, happily pocketing the generous $20, and I pour two and we walk out to the balcony.

"I think Jacinta likes you," I joke, patting my top pocket for my Menthols, lighting the cigarette and exhaling the mentholated nicotine out into the furnace of desert air. I like teasing Jack, the dude's so easy.

"She liked my $20."

"Yeah, that and your straight up *Federale* haircut."

"Being mistaken for the INS works miracles out here, Doc."

"I wish you were immigration," I say, looking into my empty glass.

"Yeah, well, with a last name like Martinez, that may not be far behind."

"Very funny. But I guess if you're not working the fields and from fucking Siberia everyone's got a shot at the American dream."

"That's how it's played here in the *estados unidos*: we can all rail against the plight of our neighbors south of the border. What else is new? Jesus, Doc."

"I know, *'how it's played'* Jack, but being a Martinez, sometimes I just get a little fed up with who the INS is deporting. I can guarantee you, it's all about being brown, and being from right the fuck over there." I nodded toward the southland.

"And you happen to be a doctor from Hollywood, so don't get your knickers in a bunch," Jack says and points to my glass. I reluctantly agree that a shorty might be the ticket for toasting the evening heat and dealing with our guests from the eastern block here on a work visa, of sorts.

So, here we are in Suite 811 at the appropriately named, Desert Mirage. Ivan shows up with Helena, followed by a new guy, a freshly minted agent-in-training. This young gun, Kenny the agent, looks a lot like Jack when he was twenty-four with the same stocky build and tight haircut, but blonder and yeah sure, slimmer but brimming with that by-the-book federal agent swagger. Agent Kenny also has more guns. Kenny is an arsenal. Like any new agent given the green light to carry the heavy metal of his choice for chasing the bad guys, kicking in doors, or generally opening a can of whoop ass, Kenny carries his new agent issue nylon duffel bag packed with the mean metal of Smith & Wesson, Colt, and the baddest boy of all, the Heckler & Koch machine pistol that's ridiculously powerful and will seriously stop anything, including whatever shape Anton or Maxim or the Gorikav party is taking. Kenny is built like a hammer and has enough firepower in his black, nylon zippered bag of goodies to take Needles hostage. Jack has let me know that Kenny's wound a little tight.

So upon introduction and greeting, and like any good host, I crack a beer for him, point to a sandwich platter with fries and a fruit bowl that seems to cover all the major food groups.

"Welcome to Needles," I hold up a cold one.

"Fuck yeah." Agent Kenny is trying to fit in and is eager to start looking for bad guys somewhere deep in the Cottontop cactus.

"Looks like you got a bag of bad." I nod to his luggage.

"You never know…Jack told me to pack and prep for anything going sideways." He squints hard, and sips his beer while trying to figure out what the fuck has landed his ass in the middle of a desert mod squad complete with a hot young Russian girl, a short wiry fucking Russian with a long-barreled Python, and a licensed, medical physician with a suspect past and a history of sharing his inventory of cocaine hydrochloride with the Hollywood glitterati and we might add, worked a day job performing facial reconstructs on certain Russian gangsters.

Agent Kenny is also taking special interest in his federal agent boss busily pouring a stiff and icy glass of vodka. He is more acquainted to the other Jack—the high and tight, government-issue Jack responsible for filling out young Kenny's fitness report.

"Fucking hot." Kenny goes to the weather. Understandable. Everyone always does.

"This is the shit, as they say," I add, trying to sound like a bad motherfucker.

Kenny is primed and pumped. I notice he notices Helena who is trying to play all of this down and I know Helena likes being surrounded by high-octane male bonding and so she postures a bit knowing she has big street cred simply because she's Russian, has fucked with some people, knows her way around power tools, and is six-feet of platinum blonde armed with dangerously long legs wrapped in her tight and faded jeans tucked into those hand-tooled, legacy black Noconas she picked up at the Boot Barn.

If we could we get a room here the Desert Mirage and kiss these fucks goodnight, we would, but as of right now, that's not going to work. I still like the train idea. Helena picks up on my lusty thoughts and shoots me a quick look that's tender and sexy and hopeful all at the same time. Hell, I don't know how she does it either. Must be the way she can make those eyebrows dance.

Kenny is constantly bringing out his metal, clicking firing pins, sighting, and checking rounds. He wants to pull a trigger. The newbie agent is seriously strapped with a monster case of ADD that's starting to get on my nerves. In fact, it's bugging the fuck out of me. Jack notices, offers me a drink and gestures to Kenny.

"Kenny, seriously, we know what you got, you know what you got. That shit is not going anywhere. Grab a cold one, and chill."

"Just making sure, boss…just making sure." Kenny keeps his eyes locked on his firing pin, magazines and ammo.

"Trust me, we're good. Take five." Kenny buys a clue. He grabs a beer and joins me out on the balcony. I remark on the light fading into the distance, wrapping the flat earth in a collision of dust and dirt and heat particles of science that rearrange themselves into a matte finish that feels like a varnished painting. It is golden. And it drenches us and fools us into thinking we can do another day out here. So we do. The desert waits patiently for this end of day because it means the cooling and dark night will be here.

"See that?" I point out the evening colors. "The payoff for sticking around and surviving another day in Needles…" Kenny picks up on my moment.

"Hanging in until the close of business day? I get it…" Kenny continues, "Hey Doc, Jack filled me in on the LA thing."

"Good for Jack," I say flatly. "What part of my sordid little tale? The first part about Maxim and his heroin and arms business or me working identities then killing a Russian wife and mother, or the other and most important part about the agency not sure they could step in and do their job and keep me safe and sound?"

"Yeah, uh, that last part…I think." Kenny leans on the rail.

"This desert…Jesus…on a good day it's fucking hot. On a bad day, it's even fucking hotter."

"And today?"

"Today, my friend, this is scorched earth." I could use a bump right about now. I light a Menthol.

"I hear you. I read the report on Maxim and his crew…"

"For the past few years my life was safely tucked away deep into this dirt and away from the shit with Gorikav."

"The good news, Doc, is you have us. And I'm proud to be part of this detail. Jack likes you and knows you got a raw deal and all…"

"But?" I pop an Orange Nicorette.

"But, well, he also explained that you got into it deep with those ex-cops and maybe if you hadn't, well…"

I interrupt. "Well, what? And did your boss and Federal Agent Jack tell you I was fucking forced into dealing with those assholes?"

"He did, yessir. And believe me, I got your back." Kenny drains his beer, with a bit of posturing, and I can see he's trying to be straight up, but maybe he's reading from some hackneyed script archived in his newly minted agent brain. Then again, what the fuck do I know. Between my lack of sleep, dosing and intake, and with this heat and guns, and messed up Russians coming from the sky, I feel a little lost. Again. I look at Agent Kenny and think, *Ok, Doc, he's a polite son of a bitch, cut him some slack.*

"Kenny, any ideas on where Maxim is spending his vacation dollars?" I'm trying to sound in control, as if I have a plan or am just another nice guy, a doctor on parade out here in the middle of fuck all who wants to bring a young agent in on his side.

I see Jack and Helena and Ivan talking. I finish my Menthol and look toward the rocky outcropping of Needles. A warm, evening breeze picks up and makes me want to love this desert, just for a minute.

"Have no clue, sir…" Kenny is sounding measured, and tries to be official, his voice is tempered by being young, minted, and ready to rock, but still government issue.

"And if you knew, how would you get rid of him?" I say, jumping straight to the point.

"I don't really need to know where he is, I just need to know which plane is his, and then we trigger it." Kenny brightens at his idea. He notices my expression of favor.

"Maxim's plane?" I say, interested, and acting again, like I know what the fuck I am doing.

"I got a little extra C4 in the bag and we pack a small, two-ounce brick in the engine, detonate at 4,500 feet." Kenny looks at me, square-jawed, and is selling me hard on just how capable he is and maybe he's done this before although I am quite certain he hasn't.

My new friend Kenny and I are on a roll, and we kind of go with the flow and start to blue-sky on how we can expertly pull this thing off. Yeah, we blow the plane out of the sky and any investigation into the explosion would invariably point to faulty electrical. Is that C-4 traceable? It would be nearly impossible to even find enough pieces of the rigged Cessna or anything bigger than a few fucking strands of Gorikav DNA.

Kenny likes where we are going with this and we agree that whatever small, bloodied fleshy scraps of Russian *corpus delicti* that falls from the sky would disappear, quickly feasted upon by vipers or the swoop of a hungry barn owl. The desert predators know a good kill when they smell it. I like it. Kenny's plan has *cajones*. Blowing up a light aircraft over the flat Mojave. The desert is our friend. Flat, rocky, dry, dirty, and empty. Boom. End of story. And afterwards we can all go back to pouring a tumbler or two with the occasional—and I do mean occasional dropper of the *pura*. Life is good, fuck yes, Kenny, my new best friend, you go boy. Just when my endorphins and logic seem to meet in a heady confluence of racing brain synapses that introduce a warm and golden moment of my future with Helena, the Airstream, the Speedster, and those buried stainless steel vaults of cash, Jack walks out onto the balcony. Buzz kill.

Jack has a plan. It's different. And it's brilliant and not just because my cerebral cortex has welcomed the introduction of the iced-cold vodka Jack handed me. No, Jack's plan is even better than a loud, satisfying thundering, fiery air crash. Jack's plan will introduce Maxim and his boys to an alternative dimension of sight and sound *(Thank you, Rod)* where these bad mother fucking Balkan assholes will end up walking the earth like that dude in the television show, Kung Fu. Jack's plan is wrapped in pharmacokinetics. Yeah, Jack has a motherfucking plan like that.

My federal agent and advisor begins to fill me in on a way of handling our Russians without the duffel bag of heavy ammo and guns which I can see is not where Kenny would like to go with all of this. And it most certainly is ruling out blowing the Cessna to kingdom come, which Kenny and I were getting excited about. I'm pretty sure Ivan and Helena would think blowing up a private aircraft is a cool plan, too. Out here on the balcony of the Desert Mirage great thinking and wonderful opportunities are being planned and offered to deny the Russians their kill. I now like this hotel and I like my assembled think tank. Terrific ideas abound and Jack offers the ingenious.

"We have a way of sending Maxim out on a little walkabout, an inner journey, so to speak, that puts him out into the hands of this heat and desert. We let Needles and the Mojave Desert take care of him."

"We do?" I ask.

"We will," Jack answers.

"No guns?" Kenny leans in.

"DMT," Helena says.

"Dimethyltrpytamine." Ivan's thick Russian accent adds even greater import and mouthful.

"Seriously, no guns, no C4, nothing?" Agent Kenny would like an explanation.

"Keep the bag prepped, but we detonate Maxim…we blow his mind…" Jack pulls out a vial of white crystals and looks at Helena.

"Kaboom…but widout noisy C4 bang. Out near deese reservation a shaman will tell you about deese Great Spirit who contacts through dreams," Helena explains. "Mystical and spiritual and a world of humans and animals—trance you out and take you places through deep and strong currents that, if you are vhit shaman or guided, you get lost. Very lost."

"And he's got this shit? I ask.

"No, the shaman won't touch this…he knows vhat he eese talkingk—he's saying deese eese too powerful and doesn't trust it… his ancestors traveled with deese peyote and always came back with visions that served deese tribe." Helena appears to enjoy tutoring us on the ways of the desert people. I wonder if there will be a quiz in the morning.

"So what the fuck, how do we get this into Maxim?" Kenny questions the obvious.

Jack continues. "DMT has been on the government watch list for years, since the late 50's as part of pharmacology and psychedelic testing that proved what a real mind fuck this thing could be. And apparently a lot of university testing just up the street in New Mexico."

"Convenient," I add.

"Indian calls it 'The spirit drug'…and deese people tripping out here. Serious recreation but vhite soul and past lives searching thing that the desert can do so well," Helena says.

"What do you think, Jack?" I ask.

"I think we trip the fuck out of Maxim and let him find himself deep in Disneyland."

"Ok, and just so I'm clear, how are we getting this into our Russians?" Kenny appears to have a point.

"I will put right into middle of fucking forehead." Ivan pulls out his Python—"And ask him to swallow. Enjoy with some Russian wodka." Ivan can be persuasive even without the cannon.

"So bottom line, I'm hearing absolutely zero, nada on the C4 anywhere at anytime?" Kenny looks around at all of us.

"There really is no Santa Claus." I tell Agent Kenny, and make a mental note that we will have to find something out in the dirt for the razor sharp newbie to blow up.

The phone rings. Jack answers. It's Jacinta. And she has a cousin who works the desk at the Needles River Inn. Jacinta is letting us know that her cousin told her about three men who all checked in yesterday. Her cousin told Jacinta that these are men who look dangerous. Jacinta also asked Jack to make a note of her cousin's name, Adoria. This is all very good, but how the fuck does Jacinta know we want this kind of intel? Jack looks at me. "Because I asked her. See how that works when you're immigration?"

With two solid agents leading the way and a hot hand who wants to blow some shit up, I was nervous that more than a few incidentals could go wrong, beginning with an eager trigger finger, automatic weapons, and Russians. And did I mention shit that blows shit up? Jack and Agent Kenny assured me that the percentages are in their favor, but still, there are no guarantees. Jack strongly suggested that I stay the fuck behind them and because I'm also a physician and surgeon, I know when to heed the advice of trained professionals. Having never been part of a federal operation where inside information, armor piercing bullets, Kevlar vests, and smoke grenades are all part of room service, I'm pretty happy with how the deal went down.

Adoria, Jacinta's helpful cousin, had set us up nicely. Once we got the keycard, it was Agent Kenny in first, followed by Jack, and then Ivan with his Python. I was more like a war correspondent or front line observer, calling my story in and staying clear of the fire-fight. I have to say, and I believe both Jack and Kenny will back me up, if you're going to take down bad, dangerous guys holed up in a hotel room somewhere in the desert, it's to your advantage to have a key to the room. Slip it in quiet as a church mouse and the element of a surprise 2:00 a.m. wake-up call is yours. This greatly reduces a lot of gunplay that can get you hurt. In fact, there's nothing quite like a red laser beam tagging your head to let you know how special your day is going to be. Our Russians were still reeking of vodka and robed in Balkan undies when Team Doc went in. Then, lined up, side-by-side, and kneeling, Agent Kenny kicks each of our Russians to the floor. Jack holds a gun tight to their necks, three red faces squeezed into the burgundy swirl carpet while Agent Kenny expertly tugs their hands together with heavy-duty, plastic cable ties. Life's a bitch, boys. Especially when federal agents are digging a knee straight into your back, sticking a gun in your neck, and cuffing you with sharp plastic 'till your hands go numb. Agent Kenny works swiftly and tightly to get our Russians lined up and out in single file. Jack is right behind him. We were in. We were out. We were as invincible as a Russian diplomat with immunity, an eight ball of blow and three girls fresh off the pole. Adoria would get a fat, cash envelope. Jacinta would be pleased. So would a family in Jalisco. As we left, Ivan hung the room sign on the door handle: *Por favor no molesten.*

Now, we're the proud owners of bona fide Russian bad guys and we're on our way out to the flat, hard-pack of the nasty Mojave that stretches beautifully out in front of us with wide open arms embracing the Mighty Colorado that says sure, big river, roll on through. Ivan is driving hard and fast, and I notice the Escalade's AC is on maximum which is exactly what I need. I pop an Orange Nicorette and breathe deeply. Ivan and Jack hold down the front seats, Agent Kenny sits on the jump seat facing our Russian cargo sitting shoulder to shoulder on the passenger bench seat and Helen and I are behind Maxim, Anton and Mikel in the rear seat. It's a party bus.

"Hello, Maxim," I whisper from behind him.

"Fuck you," Maxim grunts. "Who the fuck do you think you are?"

I slide the 14-round magazine into my Glock, pulling on the side metal release so it clicks hard and loud in his ear.

"I'm your fucking shaman, Maxim, welcome to Needles."

CHAPTER 38

SCORCHED EARTH

"**M**axim, go right ahead…tell me to fuck you one more time and I just might…I'll be glad to invite a hot Austrian friend," I pushed the barrel of my Deutsh-Wagram Glock into the back of his neck. "And make it a threesome."

I like being a bad motherfucker riding in Ivan's big, black, Escalade ESV full of bad motherfuckers. Jack is sitting shotgun next to Ivan and he turns to look back at our three assholes. Ivan glances at his rear view mirror. Helena is sitting next to me and lights a Menthol, puts it to my lips, then digs into the black, nylon duffel bag and pulls out one of Agent Kenny's guns. She likes the Smith & Wesson .357 Magnum with a titanium alloy cylinder embedded into the freakishly light scandium frame.

"Now dhis eese mother-fuckingk pistola," she says, twirling the ultra-lightweight cannon on one finger. Helena is happy to finally get her gun.

Agent Kenny shoots her a look, alarmed at Helena's cavalier rummaging of his arsenal of tight, well-maintained machinery. These are his toys. She plays to him, snapping the revolver's chamber open and shut, sighting down the barrel. Agent Kenny puts on his game face, hoping to conceal just how much he likes Helena's action. He likes that lightweight Wesson, too, but he really loves a tall, gorgeous girl who isn't afraid to play with firearms. Agent Kenny wants to pimp his government-issue persona and take it all up another notch. This is his moment to shine a light on his freshly-schooled ballistics know-how.

"There's a box of rounds in the side pocket. Takes seven hollow points. Those jackets can open a righteous blowhole upon exit. Right Mikel? You got a gun like that in Rusky?"

Mikel looks stoned face dead ahead.

"Yeah, didn't think so. That's fucking American metal, my friend." Kenny looks at Helena seeking an approving look.

Agent Kenny is dressed out in his federal swat gear and is perched on the jump seat facing his Russian cargo, his lightweight, metallic black H+K automatic sitting across his lap. He is chewing gum, his square jaw, tensed and ratcheting. I see a young hardliner who would like any of these Russians to make a move. Any reason at all. He unwraps the foil on another stick of Wrigley's and now has a wad that muscles up the vein in his temple. He winks at me, releasing the 40-round magazine and slamming it back into the automatic. I know Young Agent Kenny would still like to settle some of this nonsense with his H+K. I wink back, letting him know we're all good. I pop an Orange Nicorette and chew hard, too, hoping that the veins in my temple aren't showing. That rewarding release of nicotine is a fine addition to the drive. I sit back and think that perhaps a bump of my *pura* could work nicely, too.

"You have no idea who you are fucking," Maxim threatens, staring straight ahead.

"I think I do," I say, sounding confidently and sarcastically in control, but I am a bit distracted by the thought of a little hit of *pharma*.

"Maybe vhantingk to fuckingk vhid me?" Helena is dangerously coy when armed.

"I don't think you're in a position to say a whole lot about fucking with anybody, Maxim, you fuck," Jack now seems to say 'fuck' a lot.

"We're about an hour outside of the reservation," Ivan informs.

"You're going to need a fucking tribe to save you," Maxim grunts.

"Really? Because from where we sit, we all look pretty well fucking saved," I say.

"Hey, little Mikel, vhu likingk desert?" Helena coos softly into his ear.

Ivan piles on. "You going to love it. You and Maxim and Anton have to yourselves—except maybe for friendly Mojave Sidewinder or three or maybe fucking hundred, who knows? Who cares?"

"Dhis desert lovingk deese bad boys thinkgk they are all dhat..." Helena can't help herself.

"You boys should think about retiring out here," I add.

Maxim kicks back. "You could use a drink or maybe some of your *cocaina*, Doc. Last time I checked, that powder and your favorite Russian vodka were all that kept you operating." Maxim is not long for the desert here, and his jab is a shot to my soul. I block the punch.

"Sounds like I could use a meeting or two, you fat fuck...I didn't know you cared." I see Kenny sweating hard. I think he is about to go off with just one push from any of these guys.

"He knows how to use a scalpel." Ivan says, looking in the rearview mirror. "Maybe you want operation from him, yes? Or maybe we take different route and maybe we find a fucking hot piece of metal and let our friends grab it while grabbing dick with other hand...maybe they see what a past life feels like."

Ivan raises his leathered, smoothly ironed left hand, turning it so Maxim gets a good look. Ivan is on a roll. I didn't quite get the 'past life' part, but it did add a poetic touch to his rant, and I know the man would like to watch them pass out from holding their balls along with a searing, white-hot piece of metal radiating deep into the doughy dermis and branding their hand into a sickening charcoal stench, reeking like an industrial smokehouse choking on a fatty, piece of gristle. Yeah, that's what Ivan wanted. I could almost go along with his vision, but I liked where we were headed with the Jack Plan Of Action of letting the baked dirt show Maxim and his crew how this beat-up, brown piece of clay can lose you. Just ask Detective Casey.

He would talk you through the true panic of a sharp, tight, viper strike. You might ask the detective what it's like to go into the death spiral. No help for you, my friend, Detective Casey would say, reminding you that in just minutes you will start to sweat and gasp for breath while the desert quietly opens its arms, inviting you into the abyss. You fall to the ground and twist, convulsing, beaten by the red planet and a cold-blooded killer looking for a scrap of meat. You see nothing but a clear and brilliantly starred night sky stretching out into the deep black. This is your final breath. The viper will eat what it can, slide away, and leave you to that last sky. You are offered to the cooling dirt.

Ivan has his big, black vehicle rolling fast on the empty asphalt as we head east of Needles to hook up with our Brujo, a Helena connection. It's 3:00 in the morning and my adrenaline mixes with the dimmed interior lights casting a faint and surreal glow through the cabin—we are silent and listen to our breathing pressed into the white noise of the AC that's in sync with the steady hum of the tires on this stretch. Ivan buttons the panoramic sunroof and it smoothly slides open, revealing the rush of dry desert air and a sky that floats high above. Anton and Mikel look skyward while Maxim bores a hole into the blue-eyed Agent Kenny who would just like any reason at all.

The three Russians sit shoulder-to-shoulder on the bench seat. I want them to see the sky open to them, a last portrait of a July night sky in Needles. I want them to see how this galaxy looks when it is the last time you will ever see it from the planet. So this is how it is in the deep Mojave in the early hours strapped into Ivan's Cadillac.

Eight people brought together through circumstance, greed, privilege, and the sheer and unyielding force of a universe that has in a way, cuffed us all together. This modern day cocktail of drugs, money, and murder is a nasty piece of business and I think back at how it could have been, but this is a foolish exercise of trying to relive a past that never existed. I listen to the air and my breathing, and I have an out of body experience, floating up and out of the sunroof and I see our vehicle with its illuminated dashboard and cabin lights sailing rapidly away from me and off into the black, and then I am returned abruptly, leaving my other life of teleportation to another incarnation.

Ivan spots the turn-off and wheels the Escalade hard to the right, off the asphalt and into a narrow, tire-rutted, dirt road hedged on each side by the high cactus. The brittle brush noisily scrapes the sides of the SUV as dust pours through the open sunroof, invading the cabin, choking off clean air and we are lost trying hard to breathe through our coughing jag. Ivan hits his high beams, lighting up the road and then abruptly stomps hard on his brakes, our big wheels trying to grip the loose dirt, forcing the big Escalade into a sliding, dirt skid. We come to a hard stop, sending up a huge plume of dirt. Ivan's black SUV is a monster wrapped in a settling cloud of desert dirt, the high beams knifing through the night, lighting up the road straight ahead.

"What the fuck?" Ivan says to everyone.

"Holy fuck," Jack says to himself.

"Are you fucking kidding me?" I say to Helena.

"It is fuckingk heem," Helena announces factually, as if she's already been introduced.

He has appeared out of nowhere. He is standing in the middle of the road, the last of our dust cloud descends over and around him, the light and particles making his skin and bony frame appear as if an apparition.

"Ivan, Doc, Helena, follow me." Jack is in command, clicking on his compact military tactical flashlight that throws out a tight, brilliant LED white-bright beam.

"Kenny, sit tight and keep an eye out."

Agent Kenny nods dutifully and pulls on the barrel of his H+K, loudly locking in the metal sound suppressor and offers a half-smile to our Russians. He, too, clicks on his tactical torch, going to his infrared beam mounted on his vest casting a soft glow across the SUV interior.

The flashlight bathes our Russians in illuminated, special-ops red.

The old man is wearing a black, long sleeved cotton t-shirt emblazoned with the logo of Needles Water + Wells, baggy and worn khakis, and he is barefoot. His long gray hair is pulled back into a braided ponytail that reaches down to the small of his back and his face shows deep ravines and sharp angles. He is carrying a large and weighty stick, smoothly honed and grained. A large, dented, aluminum canteen is tied to a looped rope and hangs from his shoulder. The last heat of the desert rises up and offers his shoeless feet nothing but the dirt of this earth. He is at home. He can smell this land.

We are visitors who traveled through time and space, arriving on his planet. The Mojave is silent except for the metallic pinging from our cooling engine. The mechanical sound is eerily out of place here. I can hear the murmur of our Russians speaking in low tones. I think I can hear the snap of Agent Kenny working his gum but maybe it's just me chewing hard. We walk toward our Brujo and I can hear our breathing as our footsteps land on the dirt road. This is the man who has what's needed to transport our Russians. Our Brujo will give them back to the desert and they will be lost forever in this place where the Mighty Colorado roars. This is our Brujo and he is now *their* universe. He moves lightly and smoothly, his bony body shrouded in a canopy of black and stars.

He silently motions the four of us to follow him, and he leads us to about ten yards from the vehicle. We can see the dimmed interior lights outlining Ivan's SUV through the thick brush and we arrive at a clearing of softer desert sand, ringed by cactus, sage, and desert shrub. There is a wood and mud dwelling dug into the slope of a desert berm. The small front opening is framed by hand-cut pieces of desert wood scraps, ingeniously woven together in a strong waddling that supports the cramped entrance.

Our Brujo calls out in the native tongue of his Nuwu people as a younger man emerges from the dwelling and is holding a dirty, patched burlap bag and hands it to our Brujo who then places it at his bare feet. I notice the bag moves and I think that now would be a good time for a Menthol and maybe a drink, but I pop three Orange Nicorettes and look at Helena and Ivan and Jack. I am absorbed into the night and dirt. My adrenaline has slowed, but I notice how dry my mouth is and how thirsty I am. The silence of the dark desert and Russians and Brujos with burlap bags and waddled mud huts can do this to a man.

"Daniel, eldest son of deese Brujo," explains Helena sweeping her hand in some facsimile of an introductory grand gesture, but it only feels awkward considering the circumstance of being in the middle of the fucking Mojave with only our quiver of flashlight beams bouncing off each other and that damn burlap bag that I swear is moving. I hear the name Daniel and a chill races through my bones. My brain crackles with an electric current that comes out of nowhere, but makes my skin feel like its on fire. My memory roars back in a rewind of my time with Mary Wysocki and her tale of tragedy with her son. I remember his death at the hand of the dry reservation well. Mary's words ring in my ears about the Indian women and her vision of Danny and his soul returning someday. The desert feels like it's collapsing around me and time stands still, the vibrating buzz behind my ears is getting louder as I demand every ounce of strength to help me stand steady, trying like fuck to remain present, yet trying hard to believe that this isn't happening. Danny's consciousness and universe has reached into mine. Mary needs to know this, if she doesn't already.

"My father, the tribal Brujo," Daniel says, stepping closer to all of us standing in a semi-circle. I think I can hear Agent Kenny talking, punctuated by the continuous catch and release of a loading magazine. I am sure the Russians are wondering what the fuck is going on out here. I fire up a Menthol, inhaling deeply. The Brujo signals he would like one, too, if he may. I hand him the pack. He only takes one, but I motion that he keep the mangled, crush-proof box, and he delicately stashes the cigarettes into the waistband of his loose fitting khakis.

"And the bag?" I hesitantly ask.

"Souls of the ancestors." Daniel nods to his father and his father says nothing and I am nervous just looking at his bony face puffing on the Menthol.

"Moves like maybe a snake or rat," Ivan chimes in, and Jack seems to agree with Ivan's observation.

"Four Mojave rattlesnakes, three represent the soul of your guests who will travel," says Daniel. "These are the ancestors who will guide the chosen ones."

"So why four?" I ask. "We only have three, uh, 'guests' who are traveling."

"The fourth is their Brujo, the one responsible for their souls," Daniel educates. His father stares at me.

"And the Ayahuasca?" Jack keeps his flashlight steady on the bag of vipers. Patched and loose burlap does not inspire confidence that these vipers are under any semblance of reasonable control.

"Here in the canteen." Daniel points it over to his father.

"Ayahuasca eeese necessary makingk DMT work." Helena is apparently in charge of how this is all going down and she and Daniel seemed to have our desert séance under control.

"But our Brujo has added a little kick to it." Jack adds.

Daniel explains that the Mojave rattlesnakes are blessed with the most toxic and dangerous venom of any viper in the country. "They carry the true poison," Daniel says, but then adds that the real venom is in the old, dented aluminum canteen containing Ayahuasca, Wormwood, Chacruna, Sinicuichi, Jurema Root, Yopo Seeds, and Syrian Rue.

"Plant-based psychoactive hallucinogens powerful enough on their own, but together, well, let's just say this will kick the living shit out of the brain—I dare you to come back from this. You would probably be the first," Jack can be persuasive.

Everything is going along pretty well right up until it isn't. We hear a series of muffled shots coming from the SUV.

"Mikel on the run!" Agent Kenny shouts out. We hear the rapid fire of muzzled shots from his automatic weapon.

"Fucking Kenny," Jack says, pointing his flashlight in the general direction of Kenny and the Russians, the high beam zeroed in on the SUV. Jack takes off on a dead run.

Daniel is calmly looking over at the Brujo who has now closed his eyes and is mouthing an incantation. Daniel looks straight at me and I become quiet and calm, understanding that this is a moment in time where his father leaves us and goes into another place.

"Kenny, get Maxim and Anton over here!" Ivan shouts.

Jack is on the chase. Kenny brings Maxim and Anton over to the Brujo's circle, and presses his H+K into the backs of his Russians as he pushes them hard into the dirt

"Yours…" Agent Kenny tells Helena who quickly moves and guards them with her .357 magnum.

Agent Kenny clicks his flashlight on high, lighting up the brush, and he takes off deep into the brush in the direction of Jack, they are both running fast, tracking Mikel.

Daniel lights the fire ring and the scene is ablaze, crackling under the heated ignition of dried sagebrush. Our Brujo kneels and stares out in the dark and crouches down, laying his stick in front of him. His angular and skinny, bone thin face is captured by the flames in our morning night.

Daniel's father utters in his language, murmuring to Daniel.

"My father says the mountain lion will take care of the other one," Daniel says softly, "He is sure of that. You must call the other man back."

Now, The Brujo is down on all fours, in a menacing stance. His clear and grey-blue eyes make his face appear younger. He rocks back and forth slowly, slowly, his thin body is catlike.

Maxim and Anton are kneeling with their back to the berm, they are looking out into the black desert and into their future. We look over at our Russians who are now starting to get a clearer picture that their morning in the Mojave will not include pancakes.

"Mikel is foolish," Maxim says. "Where the fuck would he go anyway?"

"Only to his death," Daniel says looking over at his father who is now still as a statue, still down on all fours, a wet spittle of saliva glistening on his lips.

Jack and Agent Kenny thrash back through the brush.

"Fucking lost him." Jack is breathing hard trying to regain his wind.

"Fucking had him." Kenny swings the H+K strap onto his shoulder, and holsters his Smith and Wesson.

"The man is a ghost, he just flat out disappeared," Jack says.

Agent Kenny steps out toward the perimeter of our clearing and sprays more gun power out into the middle of nothing. Helena steps up and pops off a few just to try her hand with her new magnum.

She jumps back seeing the burlap bag move and twist, recoiling at the sound of her gunshots.

"I am hatingk snakes!" Helena shouts with a ferocity announcing her dislike of reptiles. She points her gun toward the bag.

"Don't shoot bag." Ivan yells.

Helena is armed what appears to be the entire ballistics division of the Smith & Wesson Company.

"Fuckingk snakes!" She fires off two shots into the air just to be heard and looks at us. The bag moves again, then nothing. We are now silent, look out into the darkened desert, we listen, but we can only hear each other. Helena continues to eye the burlap sack. The bag moves slowly.

"Now he is with the desert, waiting for his two brothers, " Daniel says, referring to the escaped Mikel.

The old man is motionless, still crouched, and staring at the fire. Then, he begins to move, standing to his feet, chanting softly and slowly. He is in his world, waiting to show Maxim and Anton theirs. He drinks from the canteen and spits the liquid across the fire; the flames hiss. He spits the drink into the faces of our Russians, as he motions his hands upwards coaxing the flames higher, and up to the sky, asking the spirits to travel into the night, and away from this ground. Daniel feeds the fire, lighting up the blackness with flames licking our faces as we watch the skinny-framed Brujo slowly move in place to his chanting. Picking up one foot and then the other, his hands still, and quiet by his sides. His voice a whispered rhythm of metered tongues speaking to his ancestors.

Jack and I leave for the mud hut; Helena brings the vial of crystal DMT. Our plan is pretty simple. We figure the fastest way to get the mega dose of DMT into their bloodstream is to mainline it. Helena lights candles and holds them up so I can mix the crystals and super-charge and fill the two syringes.

"You know that others will come looking for me—and they will find you. There's no hiding from us, you will see. I don't give a fuck what you do with me," Maxim says, spitting into the ground. He grins at me.

"Good, because I do give a fuck what you want to do with me," I say.

"You murdered my wife."

"Guess what, Maxim, I was told to kill her—news to you?"

"What the fuck you talking about?" Maxim's voice is dry and angry and he knows he will soon die.

Jack interrupts. "Doc, no need to go there. Let's just take them both out…"

"Don't worry, asshole, she went under, and she went out, and she didn't feel a thing. Not a bad way to go, considering."

"Your wife was selling information on you and we had to protect the source, we wanted you and your crew to keep feeding us…" Jack explains.

"Sorry, dude, losing her on my table was a perfect out, the beautiful exit for her." I enjoy telling Maxim that his wife betrayed him. "She was a bitch, too."

"That's not how that other cop, Phil, told it…" Maxim is playing us.

"Phil? The stupid little drugged up fuck, he doesn't know shit," Jack says.

"He got hold of me after that Detective. Ask your Fed."

"Was everyone making a buck off me?" I say turning to Jack.

"We had heard something about Phil, but Casey was the one on our radar."

"I'm not even gonna go there, Jack, but what the fuck? Phil?"

"Don't worry, Doc, he's toast, we know where he and Rita are. They're not your problem, trust me."

"Let's do this fucker." Ivan draws his long-barreled Python, a distant cousin to the four in the bag. Ivan puts it to Maxim's head for effect. "Man, this is big fucking gun." Ivan says, pushing the gun harder into Maxim.

"I am thinkingk Brujo wants doingk somethingk with deese snakes," Helena says, aiming her pistol at the squirming bag.

Maxim Gorikav doesn't look like such a bad guy. At least now he doesn't.

My sleight of hand has worked well for Mr. Gorikav. Oddly, I slip into a memory of the operating room and moving his nose, and face, and his flesh around, adding some cheekbones, taking out ugly pockets of fatty tissue around his neck. I did some fine work on this asshole, and for what? I may have changed the profile of his face, but his nasty Russian gangland bones are all his.

Jack pushes Anton face first into the dirt so he gets a mouthful of the desert. I find a vein.

"Enjoy your time in the Mojave." I send the dose of DMT, and he is on his way like any tourist or rockhound awed by the beauty of this red planet.

Jack quickly grabs Maxim, stuffs a cloth into t he Russian's mouth, and pulls his head back so Maxim is looking straight up to the night sky. Helena has the other syringe ready.

"See you later Maxim, say hello to your wife." My needle finds a sweet spot and I plunge the syringe deep.

"*Nostrovia,*" Helena says as she pushes him into the ground.

"*Adios puta madre,*" Ivan says in very bad Spanish.

"Later, boys, safe travels," Agent Kenny says, tossing a few sticks of gum into the dirt. "You might get hungry."

As I watch him under the influence of the DMT, Maxim looks like anything but the belly of the beast. Maxim and Anton are traveling on the DMT. They will find the trip to the inner soul and sanctum an enlightened road and pathway to love and the embrace the feeling that the universe is one. But with the other added psychokinetic ingredients, the confluence and interaction of drugs will only take them deeper and further away to a place of confusing visions, deafening sounds, and bad sensory overload, eventually leading to disorientation and the abnormal biology of men who cannot think or feel for themselves. If the ingredients were ingested in a safe, and guided environment, you might survive—out here, not a chance. You are given to the desert while your mind is lost.

Our Brujo walks over to Daniel and hands him his canteen and the burlap bag. Daniel ties the burlap to Maxim's ankle and places the canteen next to him. Agent Kenny cuts the plastic cuffs. Our two Russian travelers slide into the sandy dirt, next to the fire ring. The dented, aluminum canteen will be the first thing our Russians will drink and they will be lost in the desert, haunted by visions in the heat of this dirt. With the blessing of the Brujo, Daniel opens a small slit at the top of the burlap bag, letting the thick, massive vipers decide that tonight is good for a meat-filled piroshky. They will travel with souls, and they will stay or leave or eat. These are the guides that will show the Russians a way into the darkness and release them. And then the Russians will be dead from whatever the desert decides. Mikel, we are sure, is already gone.

Daniel's father has gone back into his tiny, dirt berm, a weary star traveler who has visited his tribe. He has told his son, Daniel, that he would like to teach him the way of the Yaje and the Ayahuasca. Teach him how to time travel to visit his ancestors and bring back their wisdom of living in the world on the outer reaches of this planet. Daniel and I speak about his father and I asked about his father's shirt.

"That old Needles Water + Wells shirt is something I found in an old trunk, when I was only a teenager. For some reason my father kept it. He likes it and told me it gave him a memory of son, a boy who visited him in a dream. My father says he can find water anywhere out in this desert. Anywhere. "

Leaving that part of the desert and gathered safely back in the leathered cabin of the SUV, we light up Menthols and are on the road to Needles. I sit in the back, Helena next to me, and she takes my hand as I stare out the window watching that first light come across the dead brush and cactus. As we roll on this stretch the cooling AC is friendly and familiar against the already warming early light of the day.

"I'm glad to see these fucking Russians go."

"They take what they want from anyone, anywhere," Ivan says.

"Maybe I'm not so far from these men," I say.

"What do you mean, Doc? For fuck's sake, you're not even close—yet." Jack likes his touch of irony.

"I could argue otherwise." Jack offers his philosophy and continues. "Look Doc, you're living a life operated by the feds…so yeah, sorry to say, you're working with your quota of lies and deceits…"

"I had handed over who I was to who I thought I should be."

"Fuck, Doc, we all have our vices." Jack seems to have acquired a new found morality that apparently accepts the darker side of who I am.

"Yeah, then there's Chet Kingdom, not so pretty," I say.

"You are lucky to beeingk alive, Helena says wisely. ""Doc, tinkingk about us and new life." She then leans in and kisses my neck.

Jack turns to me. "Maybe you live a different life from here on out. Maybe there will be a new you…yeah, probably not…Kenny gimme a piece of gum."

I stare out the window at the desert and it already looks deadly for anybody out there. "Maybe I do …" I hear my voice waver and I am feeling tired and resigned to this place.

"What the fuck, Doc, either you or them." Ivan can be supportive.

"And we still like you," Jack says, adding, "Phil and Rita are still out there…."

"Phil was part of the sale on me?"

"We used him, Doc, he was harmless, Casey had already done the damage."

"I want to shoot fucking Phil," Ivan says.

"I got hollow points," Agent Kenny adds.

"I have gun," Helena says smiling.

This is a morning in July in Needles and we are moving fast in Ivan's Detroit. I could use a bump and a tall tumbler on this day when we say goodbye to three Russians.

"Think they're still alive?" I glance at my Patek to check the hour. "It won't be long now, either a viper bite or the canteen, and with this heat, well, that's the thing about the desert. What you don't know, can kill you."

"It will not be good," Ivan says. "They die by their own hand."

"Maybe we have breakfast?" Agent Kenny is hungry.

"I am in mood for steak." Helena is a voracious meat eater.

"Ivan, head over to Mr. Eugenia's, they have some mean Huevos and a game of poker." I reach for an Orange Nicorette and come up empty. Maybe it's time to cut back. Helen snaps her Hermes and exhales, not a chance. She smells like tobacco and a warm desert wind and rich, red lipstick. I inhale.

Ivan cranks up the radio and we catch some commercial-free Mariachi that makes this desert feel bearable. So, we dial up the AC in a morning in July in Needles and go for steak and huevos. Maybe Ivan will even play a hand. Fuck it. This is a planet that will never let you go.

EPILOGUE

Maxim died. So did Anton. In a dark, twisted way, I could appreciate Maxim. He was a self-made man who cut his teeth working the gangs of Moscow and found his way to the front of the Afghani fighting. Maxim was a fast learner and figured out what's important to the Afghan tribal leaders and how to slyly siphon off pallets of AK-47's and RPG's in return for easy access to the bounty of the famed Afghani poppy fields. Maxim Gorikav worked the insurgents and rebels and after five years of enlisting entire platoons of Russian soldiers, Maxim Gorikav was not only at the top of his own empire, but one of the richest retired lieutenants in the Russian command. He paid everyone well so the world would have the Maxim brand of smack.

Now he is dead. He was found not too far from Anton. The two of them had made some kind of crazy headway toward a well-traveled dirt road used by guides leading tourists on night forays deep into the cactus to look for nocturnal wildlife. The open-air, four-wheel drive vehicle flashed its high beams on our Russians lying in the dirt with their swollen tongues and mouths, soon to be eaten and picked over by the desert predators. A few more days and they, too, would vanish. Their bodies cremated and folded back into the brush.

Maxim and Anton lasted almost three days. Every thirst-quenching sip from the hallucinogenic-laden canteen would trigger a mind-bending vision leaving them confused and stumbling around in circles. Those precious drops of liquid would only accelerate their trip into the abyss.

The unrelenting heat penetrating their bodies, dehydrating and making their blood thicken, forcing their heart into overdrive, desperately trying to pump more blood through their coagulating veins. There's nowhere for the blood to go so it engorges every capillary and vein and ripens Maxim and Anton for the next wave of chilling night air while their minds continue to hallucinate. The vipers had turned these souls over to a July in the Mojave.

Mikel was never found.

We're sitting in the Speedster watching the morning. The sloping divot of the tightly clipped, manicured lawn is canopied by a grove of large palm trees throwing out slices of shade guarding the pod of mourners gathered around the deep hole in the ground waiting to receive the shiny, solid hardwood box that's part of the Dignity Series, a reasonably priced, quality product that lives up to its nameplate.

The sun's radiation sears and picks at the back of your neck, and the freshly watered lawn mixes with the rising heat, creating its own weather system, slowly releasing a steam of humidity that ripens the morning, making it even more unpleasant and uncomfortable.

Grieving family members and friends stand quietly with open umbrellas protecting the poor souls from the penetrating solar rain. Two restless preteen brothers in borrowed and slightly oversized blazers shift uncomfortably, distracted, and bored. Black really is a slimming color, but, still, not what you want to wear in the sun in Needles in July. Heat is a bad time to die in this town and you would think the funeral directors would make easy money pushing the *Tent 'n Mist* package, but like everywhere, and especially here, dollars are tight and if you can quickly run through a few words for the departed and rush back into the air-chilled interior of the mourning motorcade, well, you're a few hundred bucks ahead, and everyone's happy. Personally, I would insist on the welcomed cover of modern tenting with the refreshing misting tubes that gently cool so all those attending can offer a proper send-off to the dearly departed. I might also suggest dying in the cooler, more temperate autumn or winter months. I had no choice. It was my only move, really. How many people would like to pull this off and live to tell about it? This is the first piece in my ultimate identity protection program and it opened the last window of freedom from a past life.

Of course, I had the helpful hand of Jack. He's very good at things like this. And with my steel vaults of cash buried in the desert, there is a substantial incentive for my government-issue agent who is now very comfortable with his black, leather bag stacked with bricks of small bills. I stopped by the fine Needles establishment of dignified death and dying, the Flynn & Flynn Mortuary, located, for whatever reason, near the train tracks, a lovely spot of ground, really, if you're going that way.

I should tell you that I pulled this off with the help of Jack, as mentioned, and the aid of an Irishman, John Flynn. Mr. Flynn, as it turns out, likes bricks of money, too. And more importantly, Mr. Flynn has bodies. With enough cash and enough access you get an idea of how this starts to play out. With my surgical skills and the right body type, well, Mr. Flynn, Jack and I can get down to business. Flynn assures me that I will have access to the prepping room complete with operating table and everything a surgeon would need to handle facial reconstructs. Perfect really. A clean, well-lighted place for my goodbye arranged by the professionals at Flynn + Flynn. Jack takes care of the details that help me disappear with a death and new life yet to be found. A few other minor details to be sorted out with paperwork and the Cloud, small things, really, that Jack will handle. He's a qualified Federal Agent and my mentor and advisor so we'll take the occasional meeting just to make sure that we're moving to higher ground should my past surface and present issues that Jack sees as, well, troublesome. Watching a paid crowd get together and send me off was worth the hundred grand. Those gathered seemed genuinely touched by my departure.

I see a woman in the distance, she turns to look in my direction and briefly catch a glance and a knowing recognition of a mother who was once whole—a mother who had a son who held me and mine in the safety of the tribe. Mary nodded over toward me and we knew.

Sometimes your worlds collide, other times they simply brush by each other, and gently, swiftly dance off into another direction like spinning tops that go around and around and around. Yeah, the universe can be like that.

Helena sees me staring at Mary.

"Dhat is her…hse lookingk the same."

"Better."

"Vhu wantingk to say somethingk?"

"Already have."

As we watch the last of the mourners leave, I light a Menthol and place it in Helena's lips. She inhales and then exhales smoothly. She knows that I like the smell of fresh Helena cigarette smoke.

"Vhat was touchingk for you?"

"I had a nice life, I think."

"You did. Apparently, everyone lovingk you."

"It's been a July, hotter than most."

"Dats vhat is happens when havingk Russians in desert."

"True enough…I bet you didn't know it can snow here," I say with a voice of authority who has studied the subject at length.

"Not in deese Mexico, right" Helena raises a long, gorgeous eyebrow. It dances.

I pop a Mint Nicorette, turn up the AC. It burps a bit, and I vow to get that fixed. Helena shifts the Speedster into second. I push the pedal down. She expertly tosses the gear into third and the sweet German machine gets low and sits gently into the road. Then into fourth. I love this fucking car. Helena dials into Mariachi music and starts to hum along. She looks over at me and teases to get me to sing along, too. This was my life in the desert, my time, safely tucked out in the hardscape where I can see anybody coming from anywhere, including light aircraft and people floating in. You, too, if you spend some time out here, will notice that you can pick up the signs granted by this flat, bright, hot, and dusty place where absolutely nothing can move without kicking up the dry, telling scree. And if you pay close attention to this trick of dirty, desert charm, you'll always know when company's coming. My mobile rang. It was Jack.

"Hey, Doc."

"Hey, Jack….you do know I'm dead, right?"

"Everyone knows you've passed, and we're all still pretty upset about it."

"So, you're calling a dead man."

"Maybe, depends on who you talk to."

"Like who?"

"Like guys who know where Maxim and his *Bratva* hid big black leather bags of cash."

"Seriously?"

"And I haven't even mentioned our favorite couple—Chet and CC. So, yeah, seriously." Jack hung up.

I quickly threw the Speedster into a wide arcing U-turn. Helena downshifted to third and then into second as I mashed the petal. Tires grabbed the shoulder, and the Speedster shuddered across the dirt and asphalt. Helena threw the gears into play, turned up the volume and slipped me a Menthol. The girl should be driving at LeMans. We were headed back to Needles.

— FINISH —